THE RIGHT
CALL

SOPHIE TRACE TRILOGY

THE RIGHT
CALL

A NOVEL

KATHY HERMAN

David C Cook®

transforming lives together

THE RIGHT CALL
Published by David C. Cook
4050 Lee Vance View
Colorado Springs, CO 80918 U.S.A.

David C. Cook Distribution Canada
55 Woodslee Avenue, Paris, Ontario, Canada N3L 3E5

David C. Cook U.K., Kingsway Communications
Eastbourne, East Sussex BN23 6NT, England

David C. Cook and the graphic circle C logo
are registered trademarks of Cook Communications Ministries.

The Web site addresses recommended throughout this book are offered as a
resource to you. These Web sites are not intended in any way to be or imply an
endorsement on the part of David C. Cook, nor do we vouch for their content.

This story is a work of fiction. All characters and events are the product of the author's
imagination. Any resemblance to any person, living or dead, is coincidental.

All Scripture quotations, unless otherwise noted, are taken from the *Holy Bible,
New International Version*®. *NIV*®. Copyright © 1973, 1978, 1984 by International
Bible Society. Used by permission of Zondervan. All rights reserved.

ISBN-13: 978-1-61793-740-8

Published in association with the literary agency of Alive
Communications, Inc., 7680 Goddard Street, Suite 200, Colorado
Springs, CO 80920. www.alivecommunications.com

The Team: Don Pape, Diane Noble, Amy Kiechlin, Caitlyn York, Karen Athen
Cover Design: DogEared Design, Kirk DouPonce
Cover Images: iStockphoto, royalty-free

Printed in the United States of America

To Him who is both the Giver and the Gift

ACKNOWLEDGMENTS

The Great Smoky Mountains and rolling hills of East Tennessee provide the stunning backdrop for this story, though the town of Sophie Trace exists only in my imagination. The characters I created to populate this unforgettable place will forever walk the pages of my heart.

I drew from several resource people, each of whom shared generously from his or her storehouse of knowledge and experience. I did my best to integrate the facts as I understood them. If accuracy was compromised in any way, it was unintentional and strictly of my own doing.

I owe a debt of gratitude to Commander Carl H. Deeley of the Los Angeles County Sheriff's Department for his thorough response to my many questions and for reading selected scenes and offering valuable input, as well as putting me in touch with specialists who provided detailed answers to my ballistics questions. Thanks, Carl. You are a well-connected guy and always so willing to help.

I want to extend a heartfelt thank-you to my friend Paul David Houston, former assistant district attorney, for helping me understand criminal charges and how they typically play out in the courts. Paul, we've got a good rhythm going. Thanks for your quick responses and concise answers. Seems we're always on the same wavelength.

A special word of thanks to those whose prayers kept me going, especially through a seemingly endless bout with unavoidable distractions, including my husband's back surgery: my tenacious prayer warrior and sister Pat Phillips; my online prayer team—Chuck Allenbrand, Pearl and Don Anderson, Judith Depontes, Jackie Jeffries, Joanne Lambert, Adrienne McCabe, Susan Mouser, Nora Phillips, Deidre Pool, Kim Prothro, Mark and Donna Skorheim, Kelly Smith, Leslie Strader, Carolyn Walker, Sondra Watson, and Judi Wieghat; my friends at LifeWay Christian Store in Tyler, Texas, and LifeWay Christian Resources in Nashville, Tennessee; and my church family at Bethel Bible Church. I cannot possibly express to you how much I value your prayers.

I'd like to say thank you to my sister Caroline Berry for receiving these chapters via email and saving them so I'd have a copy "off premises." I appreciated the effort and the peace of mind it gave me.

To the retailers who sell my books and the many readers who have encouraged me with personal testimonies about how God has used my words to challenge and inspire you. He uses *you* to fuel the passion that keeps me writing.

To my novelist friends in ChiLibris, who allow me to tap into your collective storehouse of knowledge and experience—what a compassionate, charitable, prayerful group you are! It's an honor to be counted among you.

To my agent, Joel Kneedler, and the diligent staff at Alive Communications. Your standard of excellence challenges me to keep growing as a writer. I only hope that I represent you as well as you represent me.

To Cris Doornbos, Dan Rich, and Don Pape at David C. Cook for believing in me and investing in the words I write; and to your hardworking staff for getting this book to the shelves. What could be more exciting than being colaborers "on the same page" for Him?

To my editor and friend, Diane Noble, for extending such amazing grace as I struggled to meet the extended deadline on this book. In spite of your mother's passing and the mountain of grief you must feel—not to mention your own pressing deadlines—you gave me valuable insights that have greatly strengthened the story line. I love working with you! You're a marvel.

To my husband, Paul, who never gives up on me even in those moments when I'm just sure that I've exhausted every ounce of creativity in my soul. What a patient, objective, persevering partner you are! Were it not for you I would've listened to the lies of the Enemy and believed that I had nothing else to contribute—and this trilogy would never have been written.

And to my Father in heaven, who knew the outcome of this story before my fingers typed the first word: I'm amazed by Your faithfulness. Though my writing schedule did not go according to plan, *Your* plan was never thwarted and the message never compromised.

PROLOGUE

Stedman Reeves leaned against a massive oak tree on the hazy hillside and looked out across Stanton Valley, painfully aware that if he went through with Grant Wolski's deal, he would end up in hell. And if he didn't, his life would seem like hell. What kind of choice was *that*?

He heard a twig crack behind him and let out a sigh of self-loathing.

Grant came and stood next to him. "Not having second thoughts, are you?"

"Look, if you'd just be patient, I could get the money—"

"I need it now."

"I can't just scrape up that kind of cash overnight."

"Then you shouldn't play poker with the big boys." Grant locked gazes with him. "I'm offering you a gift, man. If I were you I'd take it."

Some gift.

Grant held a gun in each of his gloved hands. "Pick one. You said you know how to shoot."

"Yeah, targets and wild game." Stedman studied the pistols, both Smith & Wessons, but couldn't bring himself to take either. "I've never shot a person before."

"Pretend you're playing one of your video games. If you can hit a bull's-eye, you can put a bullet through a guy's head. Here, hold these."

Grant handed him the guns, then reached into his back pocket and took out a photograph. "There's your target."

Stedman looked into the eyes of a husky young man with sandy blond hair. "Who is he?"

"Name and address is on the back. Make it quick and clean."

"What'd he do, stiff you for money?" His legs suddenly felt shaky. Did it matter what the guy did? How could he justify taking his life?

"It's none of your business."

"It might make it easier if I knew what he did."

Grant flicked the picture with his finger. "Never mind what *he* did. You're the one who owes me. Just make sure he's dead before you walk away. Which gun do you want to use? They're both stolen. The cops can never link either of them to you *or* me."

"Then I guess it doesn't matter." *A murder weapon's a murder weapon.* He handed the bulkier pistol back to Grant.

"When you're done, wipe it clean and throw it in the pond at the park. Make sure no one sees you."

"That's all there is to it?"

"That's it."

"If I do this, how can I be sure we're even?"

"I'll give you a notarized receipt for the sixty grand. Look, you owe me big-time. Either pay me the money or do me the favor."

Some favor. He rolled his head to one side and then the other, his heart racing like a runaway train. How could he refuse? Sixty thousand dollars might as well be a million.

"Unless you make this right," Grant said, "I'll make sure you never get a seat at a high-stakes poker table again. You're finished."

"Can't you cut me some slack—just this once? You know I'm good for the money. I need a little time, that's all."

Grant shoved him with both hands. "You're on a losing streak, and I don't have forever. I told you what you could do to satisfy the debt. Take it or leave it."

Stedman exhaled the words, "I'll take it." The voice was his but seemed to come from someone else. Was he really willing to murder a man in cold blood, just so he could keep on gambling?

An image of his grandmother's scowling countenance was branded into his conscience. No way could he go to her and beg for another loan. Not after he stole from her. Not after he promised to stop gambling. He had to handle this on his own. Once his luck returned, he would never get into this kind of trouble again. He'd make sure of that.

"Are you just going to stand there?" Grant said.

"No, I'm going." Stedman clutched the gun tightly, and it shook in his hand.

"Good. You've got till midnight. If you involve me in any way, I *will* come after you."

"Don't threaten me, Grant. I'm not the enemy."

"Let's make sure we keep it that way. Call me when it's done. Just say 'I ordered the pizza' and hang up. Don't say anything else, and we're never to speak of this to anyone under any circumstances. Walk away and forget it."

So that was it? Just kill the guy, pitch the gun, and get back to playing cards?

He studied Grant's cold gray eyes and stony expression. How many times had he sat across the poker table from this guy, searching his face for any hint of the cards he held, yet missing the evil motives crouching in his heart?

"What're you staring at?" Grant said.

"Nothing."

He turned to go, and Grant grabbed his shirt. "Listen to me. If it makes any difference, there's a greater good at stake here."

"Like what?"

"Like the person who'll be hurt the most deserves it—and more. You'll be doing a lot of people a huge favor."

"What about the poor sucker I'm about to put a bullet in?"

"Do it right, and he won't know what hit him. For once, his old man will be powerless. Be sure to follow the story on the news. It's going to be sweet."

I'm going to kill somebody's kid?

Stedman turned his back on Grant and trudged down the hill toward his pickup, his boots feeling as if they were made of lead. Had he actually agreed to do the unthinkable—just so he could stay in the game?

Father David's words came rushing back to him. *Your gambling's an addiction, son. Get help before they own you.*

He kicked a rock and sent it sailing. Too late for that.

CHAPTER 1

Drew Langley jumped at the loud thud upstairs and resisted the temptation to bang on the wall and dispel the roaring laughter that followed. Was he the only student in the apartment building still studying for finals?

A warm breeze rattled the blinds, and he closed his eyes, inhaling the intoxicating fragrance of magnolia blossoms wafting from the south campus of Stanton College. It took every ounce of discipline he could muster not to close his books and give in to the lure of spring.

He heard rubber soles on the hardwood floor and lifted his gaze as his roommate came to a quick stop in front of the mirror over the worn living-room sofa.

Tal Davison wet his fingers and smoothed his hair. "I see you're still studying. I guess that means you're not coming."

"To what? I thought you had a date."

"Why do you make me tell you everything *twice?* You're worse than my grandmother."

Drew put down his pencil. "Sorry, I've been focused on other things. Tell me again. I'm listening."

Tal came and stood in the doorway of Drew's bedroom, his arms folded across his chest. "I'm going over to Henry's for a junk-food buffet and beer. You're invited."

"Thanks. But I really need to study for my English lit final. It's next week, and I've got chapters of catching up to do."

"Suit yourself. I'm brain-dead. I couldn't learn another thing if you paid me." Tal started to go and then stopped. "Listen, thanks again for letting me move in here for the last few weeks. It's nice sharing an apartment that doesn't reek of marijuana. I hope I haven't been as big a pain as your other roommate." He shot Drew a half smile.

Drew leaned back and folded his arms. "Hey, not at all, man. I hope you don't think I've been ignoring you. It's just that I have to keep up the grades. No four-oh, no scholarship. There's no way I can afford to attend Stanton without it." *I don't have a rich father footing the bill.*

"Doesn't it cramp your style to go to college in Sophie Trace? Your parents are pretty close by, aren't they?"

"Thanks to the scholarship I can live off campus. That's all the independence I need. It's nice going home whenever I want. My parents really help me stay on track." Drew studied Tal's expression. "I take it you wish your dad wasn't so close?"

Tal got quiet for a moment and seemed to be somewhere else. "He's much too busy to breathe down my neck. And he doesn't care about my grades as long as I pass and he can tell his cronies that his namesake's attending his alma mater and is going to work for him after graduation."

"Is that so bad?"

"I just wish he cared more about me and less about his image. I'm not sure I can ever measure up to his expectations."

"Come on, man. You've got it made in the shade. All you have to do is get through one more year, and he'll hand you the job of a lifetime. I thought you were pumped about it."

Tal flashed a crooked smile. "I'm trying to be. It's my big chance to make Dad proud of me. It's all he's talked about for years. But there's a lot of pressure, learning to run a big corporation. The closer I get, the more intimidated I feel."

"He must think you can do it, Tal. There's a lot at stake for him, too." *Even if he is handing it to you on a silver platter.*

"Maybe I'll buy a little time after I graduate—tell Dad I'm burned-out and need to backpack across Europe for a while before I jump into the corporate world."

A grin tugged at Drew's cheeks. "Then you'd need someone to babysit your Hummer. Can I apply for the job? Man, I wish I'd been there when your dad had it delivered to your birthday party."

"It was an awesome way to turn twenty-one, all right. But I'd trade it in a heartbeat for a relationship with my dad like you have with yours."

"I guess I take it for granted."

"Well, don't," Tal said. "I can't remember the last time I sat down and had a real conversation with mine. He's either working himself to death or hiding out at the lake house with wife number four—the fashion model who's got silicone for brains."

"I didn't realize she was his *fourth* wife."

"And she's pregnant with daughter number seven. Maybe he's going for the record."

"Yeah, but you're still his only son. And you and your mother are close."

"Not in proximity. She's spending a lot of time in New York with her boyfriend. He deals in fine art, and she likes to go to the auctions with him. I doubt I'll see her anytime soon."

Drew shifted his weight. Why hadn't Tal mentioned before that his mother was seeing someone?

"Actually, I'm happy for her," Tal said. "And I don't mind sharing her Nashville house with the maid, the cook, and the butler. I'll lie around the pool and read sci-fi novels and give my brain a rest. I'm so burned-out I can't stand to think about another year of studying."

"You'll be ready to hit it again in the fall. Just think how good you'll feel when you get your degree."

Tal smiled wryly. "Would you believe my dad's executive bonus last year was ten million? I must be nuts not to be more excited about the job."

No kidding. "So why aren't you?"

"I don't know … my dad's ruthless. And the company takes precedence over everyone and everything. I want more out of life than that."

"I hear you. But if it were me, I'd at least try it long enough to earn a couple million and then go do whatever I wanted."

"I've thought of that." Tal stood up straight, the result of his beer drinking and bingeing hanging over his belt. "But I have a feeling that once Dad has me under his thumb, I'll never get out from under. What I really want to do is go to the police academy."

"Have you told him how you feel?"

"I tried. But Dad doesn't really care how I feel. It's my duty as his only son to keep the family business going. If I turn my back on that, he'll basically disown me. Not that we're close now, but it's hard to think of having *no* dad. Hey, enough serious talk. It's party time. Sure you don't want to come?"

"Yeah, I've got to hit the books. Who's your designated driver?"

"Don't need one. I'm walking."

"You think that's smart? Henry's neighborhood isn't exactly the safest part of town."

"I'll be fine. But I'll tell you what"—Tal laughed and tossed his keys to Drew—"if I don't make it back alive, the Hummer's all yours."

CHAPTER 2

Ethan Langley entered the city limits of Sophie Trace and glided across town in his old Toyota Camry almost as if he were riding on air. He turned onto Azalea Lane, the radiator spewing hot water, steam rising from the hood, and parked in front of the cottage-style two-story house at 418.

He let out a loud whoop and hit the steering wheel with his palms. "I made it!"

He rolled down the window and eyed the rolling green foothills of the Great Smoky Mountains, lush with spring growth and draped with a fine veil of white haze. It was a stark and welcome contrast to the flat Mississippi River basin of Memphis.

His cell phone rang, and he smiled and put it to his ear.

"Hi, Dad."

"Where are you?" Tom Langley's voice registered his pleasure.

"I just this second pulled up in front of the Jessups'. Can I call you back?"

Tom laughed. "Are you kidding? Go! Your mother and I just wanted to see if you made it in. We'll drive over this weekend."

"Okay. Love you, Dad."

"I love you, too, son. Give that sweet Vanessa a hug for us."

"I will."

Ethan hit the End button, and the phone rang again. He saw Drew Langley's name on the screen. "Hey, Cuz. Are we still on for golf tomorrow?"

"Wouldn't miss it," Drew said. "Are you in Sophie Trace yet?"

"Yeah, didn't you hear me honk when I passed by Stanton?" Ethan looked up at the front door. "Actually, I'm so excited to see Vanessa I don't even remember driving by the college. I just pulled up at the Jessups'. Let me call you later when I get settled in at Aunt Gwen and Uncle Ralph's."

"I'll be here studying. It's great to have you here for the summer. I've missed you. "

"Same here. Can't wait to see you."

Ethan got out of the car, his pulse galloping. Would Vanessa be as eager to see him as she had been during spring break? Would he be able to hold back his affection and not overwhelm her? Would Carter recognize him this time?

He heard a door slam and saw Vanessa come out on the stoop, holding Carter on her hip.

She moved the baby's arm up and down. "There he is. There's Ethan. Show him how you can wave."

"Hey, buddy!" Ethan walked toward the house at a slow but steady pace, not wanting to appear ominous to a ten-month-old. "Remember me? Did Mommy show you my picture?"

"Of course I did." Vanessa's smile was enticing. "About fifty times a day."

Ethan resisted the urge to take her in his arms and focused his attention on the reddish-haired, blue-eyed baby dressed in denim overalls and a yellow polo shirt.

"I can't believe how much he looks like you."

"Yes, but I think he's going to have Mom's red hair."

Ethan stopped just short of the stoop and held out his arms, the cadence of his voice slow and coaxing. "Hey, Carter … want to ride the airplane?"

"I doubt he remembers doing that," Vanessa said.

Carter giggled gleefully and reached out his arms to Ethan.

"Is that so?" In the next second, Carter was in his arms, the baby's drooling smile revealing several new teeth. "You recognize your ol' buddy Ethan, don't you?"

"Maybe he does, as many times as I've shown him your picture. I've been telling him for a week that you're coming."

Ethan, his lips vibrating and making motor sounds, lifted the baby high in the air and turned three hundred sixty degrees.

The front door slammed, and two seconds later, Emily Jessup stood next to him. "Hey, when did you get here?"

"Just this minute. Good to see you. "He tugged Emily's ponytail. "So how's it going, Auntie Em?"

"Great. Can you believe how big Carter's gotten?"

"No, and he's solid as a rock."

Emily's eyes narrowed. "You look different. Your hair's shorter."

"That's because I'm not getting it cut again until I go back to school."

"I'm glad you're here for the summer, and I'm not the *only* one who is." Emily clamped her lips together, a smile stretching her cheeks.

Suddenly everyone was quiet. Ethan turned his gaze to Vanessa. She looked as if she'd stepped off a magazine cover in her pink sundress, her dark hair draping her shoulders, her clear blue eyes the color of the ocean.

"Why don't you two kiss and get it over with?"

"Emily!" Vanessa's face turned scarlet. "You can be a real pain, you know that?"

Ethan covered his smile with his hand. Judging from the heat scalding his cheeks, his face was as flushed as Vanessa's. Leave it to Emily to cut to the chase.

"Why don't you go tell Mom and Dad that Ethan's here?" Vanessa said.

"You want me to take Carter?"

"No, let Ethan have him while he's content."

"Okay." Emily turned, her ponytail swaying, and hopped up on the stoop. "I hope you like steak because that's what we're having. French fries, too. And strawberry shortcake."

Ethan waited until Emily went inside and closed the door, then stepped up next to Vanessa, the pervasive fragrance of her perfume replacing the scent of baby lotion.

"You look radiant," he said softly. "You have no idea how much I've missed you."

"Oh, I think I do." Vanessa smiled, her eyes twinkling.

Ethan slid his free arm around her, Carter resting on his hip, and moved his face slowly toward hers. When she responded, he closed his eyes, his knees turning weak the instant her soft, warm lips touched his.

A few seconds later, he backed away from Vanessa, breathless, his heart pounding, vaguely aware of something pulling at his glasses.

Carter. He reached up and gently peeled the baby's tiny fingers off the earpiece of his glasses. "You've got quite a grip there, Tiger." He folded his glasses and slid them into his shirt pocket, then handed Carter back to Vanessa.

She laughed. "I forgot to warn you: Nothing's safe from his clutches unless it's nailed down. You'll notice I'm not wearing earrings."

The front door opened and Kurt and Brill Jessup came outside, Brill still dressed in her police uniform.

"How was the drive from Memphis?" Brill hugged him with one arm.

"Pleasantly uneventful, thanks. It's great to be in Sophie Trace with the whole summer to look forward to."

"Do your aunt and uncle know you've arrived?"

"No ma'am. I'll give them a call."

Kurt reached out and shook Ethan's hand. "I hope you're hungry. I picked up a couple man-size T-bone steaks for you and me. The girls opted for filets."

"T-bone sounds terrific. Need me to go to the store for anything?"

"No, we're set," Brill said. "But come out to the kitchen. Emily can entertain Carter, and you and Vanessa can peel potatoes for the french fries."

Ethan looked from face to face, thrilled to be home for the summer and with the people he had grown so fond of. If he still felt this way about Vanessa when it was time to go back to school, they would have to start talking seriously about the future.

CHAPTER 3

Nick Phillips locked the front door of Nick's Grill and unplugged the neon sign in the window. He walked back to the counter, where Gus Williams sat on a barstool, crunching the ice in his glass.

"You ever gonna let my sweetheart out of here?" Gus said.

"Maggie's done. She went to get her purse." Nick sat on the stool next to Gus. "I can't believe this was her last day. That gal's practically a fixture around here."

"We'll still come in every day and have lunch with the Masinos." Gus smiled and stroked his white mustache. "Maggie just won't be waitin' on us, that's all."

"So what's it like being married again?"

"Great." Gus took his straw and poked at the ice in his glass. "It's been six years since Reba died. Took me three to get over it. But the last three have been downright miserable. Maggie's a good woman. If I work hard at makin' her happy, she'll do the same for me."

"Remind me how long you were married the first time?"

"Just shy of forty-four years. It was hard lettin' go after all that time, but I'm nuts about Maggie. Of course at our age, it's about a whole lot more than romance. We've got nothin' but time to just enjoy each other's company."

Nick nudged Gus with his elbow. "Good for you. But I'm never going to forgive you for robbing me of the best waitress I've ever had." He glanced up at the flat-screen TV and saw "Breaking News" flash across the screen. "Gus, look. Something's happening." Nick got to his feet and turned up the volume.

"Emergency vehicles are en route to an apartment complex in the five hundred block of Stoneleigh, near the campus of Alastair Stanton College. A male caller told the 9-1-1 dispatcher that his roommate had been shot and killed, but WSTN News has no other details at this time. We will bring you up-to-the-minute news as it becomes available to us. We now resume normal programming …"

Nick heard a siren and glanced out the window just as an ambulance went by. "Good grief. Here we go again."

Ethan poured the last of the water into the radiator of his old Toyota Camry and screwed on the cap, chuckling to himself that it was nothing short of a miracle he'd made it all the way to the Jessups' house before it boiled over.

"That ought to do it." He handed Vanessa the plastic bottle, then slammed the hood and brushed his hands together. "I doubt it'll go Vesuvius on me between here and my aunt and uncle's house."

Vanessa laughed. "It's really not funny. What's it going to cost to get it fixed?"

"I'm afraid to find out, but it can't die on me until after I graduate. Speaking of that, I enjoyed seeing the pictures of Ryan's graduation festivities. Looks like you all had a great time. Your parents are sure proud of him."

"We all are. Summa cum laude from Vanderbilt is an awesome achievement."

"Guess I'll have to wait till he gets back from Costa Rica to congratulate him. Nothing like a month in the rain forest to clear your head for law school."

"Ryan planned it that way. Every dime of his schooling was paid for by the scholarship, so he's been working part-time and saving for this trip for four years."

The front door opened, and Brill came outside and waved as she walked briskly toward her squad car.

"What's up, Mom?" Vanessa asked.

"There's been a shooting on Stoneleigh involving a student. I need to get down there." She opened the door of the squad car and looked over at Ethan. "I hope we see a lot more of you. You're welcome any time."

"Thanks, Mrs. Jessup." Should he call her Chief Jessup? Both titles seemed awkward now that he was dating her daughter.

She backed out of the driveway and headed toward downtown, sirens audible in the distance.

"I wonder what that's all about—" Ethan's cell phone rang, and he read the name on the screen. "It's Drew. Would you mind if I take it? He probably thinks I forgot to call him back."

"No, go ahead."

Ethan put the phone to his ear. "I didn't forget you. I'm still at Vanessa's."

"Tal's dead! I think he's been shot. There's blood on everything. I called 9-1-1. The police are coming. They'll want answers. What do I tell them? I can't think."

"Slow down, Drew. Did you see who shot him? Where'd it happen? Was it a drive-by?" Ethan glanced over at Vanessa and mouthed the words *his roommate was shot.*

"I don't know. He was out with friends. I-I heard him come in and there was this loud thud—like he'd passed out. I went out to the living room ..." Drew whimpered. "He was half on the couch and half on the floor, holding his chest. I've never seen so much blood."

"Did he say anything?"

"No. He was gasping for air. He looked right at me like he wanted me to help him. I didn't know what to do!"

"It's okay, Drew. Calm down. I'll call your parents."

"No, they're on a cruise to the Greek Isles for their twenty-fifth anniversary. I'm not going to spoil it for them. They can't do anything."

"Where's Tal now?"

"I lifted him up on the couch." Drew let out a sob. "He's dead. I gave him mouth-to-mouth. But it didn't work. I've got blood all over me. What if the police think I did it?"

"They won't. Just tell them what happened. Look, I'm coming over there. I'm at Vanessa's, and her mom left a second ago and is headed that way."

"The paramedics just pulled up. What if it's my fault he died? What if I should've done something else? What if I could've saved him?"

"Drew, listen to me ... it's not your fault. Just tell them what you know. I'll be right there."

Brill pulled up behind Detective Captain Trent Norris's plain-wrap car and turned off the motor. The street was a kaleidoscope of flashing lights. Paramedics had arrived, and the front door of the apartment was wide open. She spotted two of her patrol officers roping off an area with crime scene tape and a deputy sheriff standing with Trent near the door.

She got out of the car and walked toward the apartment, and Trent hurried to meet her.

"Sorry to wreck your evening, Chief."

"Don't worry about *my* evening. Do we know what happened?"

"Victim is a twenty-one-year-old male college student, dead from what appears to be a gunshot wound to the chest. Name's Tal Davison. He was just finishing his junior year at Stanton. Lives here with his roommate, Drew Langley, the 9-1-1 caller."

Brill felt a twinge in her stomach.

"Something wrong, Chief?"

"I wonder if Drew could be Ethan Langley's cousin."

"*Vanessa's* Ethan?"

She nodded. "He mentioned that his cousin has an apartment near the campus. Does Drew Langley know what happened?"

"Not really, ma'am. He says Davison was out drinking with friends. He heard him come in and thought he passed out. Found him slumped halfway on the couch." Trent turned and pointed at the sidewalk. "Blood trail shows that Davison was shot over there, and that's consistent with Langley's story."

"Does Langley know why anyone would want to kill his roommate?"

"No. But we can't rule out Langley as a suspect. He's got blood all over the front of him. Says he did mouth-to-mouth on Davison but couldn't revive him. He agreed to let Rousseaux test him for gunshot residue."

Brill sighed. "All right, I want to talk to him."

"By the way, you'll never guess who the victim's father is: Winfield Talbot Davison III, better known as Win Davison."

"I know that name," Brill said. "Didn't he just announce another big layoff at the plant?"

"That's the one. CEO of Davison Technologies. Our victim is Winfield Talbot Davison IV. Goes by Tal."

"Makes me sick. He's about the same age as my son, Ryan. Any chance this is drug related?"

Trent took the wrapper off an orange Tootsie Pop and stuck it in his mouth. "Sure. But Langley doesn't think so. He said the victim was into booze, not drugs."

"What makes him so sure?"

"Apparently that's how they came to be roommates. Davison got tired of the stench of marijuana in his apartment and walked out on his roommate. And Langley asked his roommate to leave because he was always fighting with his girlfriend."

"So they haven't known each other long?"

"Just a few weeks."

"Has the boy's next of kin been notified?"

"We're working on it, ma'am. He lived in Nashville with his mother when he wasn't in school. She's in New York, and we've left word at the hotel where she's staying. We left a message on his father's home *and* cell phone and also sent two officers out to his lake house."

Brill felt a little nauseated, remembering all too well what it felt like to deliver heartbreaking news to a victim's loved ones.

"Where's the Davison boy?" she said.

"In here."

She followed Trent up the steps and into the living room, where detectives Beau Jack Rousseaux and Spence Marcum were taking pictures and bagging evidence.

She walked over to the corpse on the couch and studied the pallid face and the vacant brown eyes. Blood from the chest wound had dripped down the sides of his torso and pooled under his body. A trail of blood was clearly visible from the sidewalk to the couch.

"You hardly look old enough to shave," she mumbled to herself.

Trent came and stood next to her. "The coroner's here."

"Thanks. Where's Drew Langley?"

"Out in the kitchen." He motioned to an open door. "Sergeant Chavez just finished getting his statement."

Brill went out to the kitchen and stood at the table. The young man at the table didn't look like Ethan.

"Drew, I'm Chief Jessup. I'm very sorry about your roommate. I know how upset you must be, but I need to ask you a few questions."

"Ethan said you were coming."

"So you *are* Ethan's cousin?"

"Yes ma'am. Is he here yet? He said he was coming right over. It's been twenty minutes."

"I'm sure he'll be here soon," she said. "Where were you when Tal was shot?"

"In my bed. I was listening to music on my iPod. I didn't hear shots. But after I took off my earphones, I heard a loud thud. I thought Tal had come in drunk and passed out. So I went to check on him. That's when I found him …"

Drew paused to gather his composure, then told her what he had told Trent Norris.

"How much time," Brill said, "do you think passed from the moment you found Tal until you realized you couldn't revive him?"

Drew rubbed the back of his neck. "I don't know … one minute. Maybe two. It was like this bad dream. I still can't believe it."

"What do you know about Tal's friends? Would any of them want to hurt him?"

"I don't think so. Henry's this cool guy who's into jazz. Plays the sax. Casper, Jamie, and Martin are friends from Stanton. They hang out together and get along great. They watch sports. Eat junk food. Drink beer. Watch shoot-'em-ups. It's their way of letting off steam."

"Do you know their last names?"

Drew stared at her blankly. "I think so. But my mind's scrambled right now, and I can't remember."

"Did you hang out with them?"

"Not really. We didn't have much in common since I don't drink and the only sport I'm interested in is golf. But they met down at The Pub sometimes. Maybe the bartender knows. Are we about finished? I need to get my things out of here and move into my parents' house."

Beau Jack walked in the kitchen. "Excuse me, ma'am. There's a young man out here—Ethan Langley. Says he's Drew's cousin and would like to see him."

"Tell him to hold on a few minutes, okay?"

Beau Jack gave a nod and left.

"You're not letting me leave?" Drew's eyes were wide and questioning.

"I can't force you to answer more questions," Brill said. "But I would really appreciate it if you'd come down to the station and help us sort this out. Everything you may have seen or heard is fresh in your mind, even if you can't recall it yet. We can help you remember facts you may not even know are important—facts that could help us find whoever killed your roommate."

"Can I talk to Ethan first and tell him what my plans are?"

"Sure. I'll wait. You can ride with me."

CHAPTER 4

Brill glanced up at the black-and-white clock in the interview room at the Sophie Trace police station, where she and Detective Captain Trent Norris sat at an oblong table across from Drew Langley.

"It's late, and I know you're tired, Drew," she said. "I just have a few more questions."

"I've told you everything I can remember." Drew combed his hands through his hair and planted his elbows on the table. "My mind is fried."

"I need you to think back to the moment you discovered Tal was shot. You said he made gurgling sounds while you pulled him up on the couch. Is it possible he was struggling to communicate something?"

Drew looked up, his eyelids heavy. "I couldn't make out any words, ma'am. It just seemed like he was struggling to breathe."

"Think," Trent said. "It could be important."

Drew's eyes brimmed with tears. "He was dying. Have you ever listened to someone drowning in his own blood? It was horrible."

"I know what you mean." Trent softened his tone. "One of our detectives was stabbed a while back and almost died while I was standing there. It isn't pretty."

"But if Tal *was* trying to say something"—Brill leaned forward—"he'd want you to figure out what it was, right?"

"I guess so. But I don't think that's what was happening."

"Did Tal have a cell phone?" Trent asked.

"Yes, an iPhone."

"We didn't find it on his body or in the apartment or his car."

"Really? He never went anywhere without it."

"Do you know his number?"

Drew rubbed his eyes with his palms. "Not by heart. It's in my contact list. Why is that important?"

"It's possible the person who shot Tal picked up his phone. The GPS could help us locate him."

Drew took his cell phone off the belt clip, pulled up Tal in the contact list, and handed the phone to Trent.

"Thanks." Trent stood. "I'll be back in a few minutes."

In the quiet that followed, Brill could almost feel the anguish oozing from Drew's pores. Finally she said, "Thanks for talking to us. You've been very helpful."

"I hope so." Drew blew the hair off his forehead. "I'm really wiped out."

"It'll take time to assimilate what's happened. Are you sure you don't want to call your parents?"

"I really don't, ma'am. They're on a cruise to the Greek Isles for their twenty-fifth anniversary. Why spoil it for them when they can't do anything?"

"You're very thoughtful," Brill said. "Is there any other family?"

"Ethan. We're really close."

"Are you planning to stay with him at your aunt and uncle's?"

"No, I'll be fine at my parents' house."

"This might not be a good time for you to be alone. People who go through trauma like this often experience post-traumatic stress. I think you should expect the memory of what happened to stay with you for a while."

Drew traced the rim of his water glass with his finger. "You sound like Ethan. You know he's studying to be a psychologist?"

"Yes, I did know that."

Trent walked back into the room and strolled over to the table. "We located Tal's cell phone on the grassy easement about a block from the apartment. He must've dropped it when he was walking home."

"Good," Brill said. "Dust it for prints and access his phone records. Maybe we'll get a break."

Ethan Langley pushed open the glass door at the police station and walked down the steps, his arm around Drew.

"You all right?"

"I will be." Drew let out a long, anguished sigh. "I still can't believe Tal's dead."

"Me either."

"I'd never watched anyone die before …" Drew's voice failed.

"Must've been awful." Ethan waited half a minute, then continued. "Were you able to give the police what they needed?"

"I guess. I really don't know much."

Ethan listened as his cousin volunteered the information he had told the police during the repetitious questioning that had seemed to drag on and on.

"After all that, they tested *me* for gunshot residue. Can you believe it?"

"For what it's worth, Drew, I think it's standard procedure to rule out the person who discovered the body."

"Well, they did. I just want to go to my folks' house and take a shower and get Tal's blood off me."

"I'd give anything for you to come to Uncle Ralph and Aunt Gwen's with me."

Drew shot him a puzzled look. "Why would I want to do *that?*"

"Because they're family."

"To you. Not to me. I don't even know them."

"Drew, maybe this is the opportune time to put your dad's feud behind you and take the first step forward. He couldn't blame you for reaching out to Uncle Ralph under these circumstances."

"The last place I want to be is between Dad and Uncle Ralph." Drew walked faster and broke free of Ethan's arm. "I just want to go home."

"I wish you'd reconsider."

"I can't. Come on, Ethan. You *know* how it is. I'm not going to cross that line. I can't believe you'd even ask me to."

"All right"—Ethan took Drew by the arm and slowed his pace—"but I don't think you should stay by yourself until you've had time to absorb all this."

"I'll be fine."

"How about if I camp out at your folks' place—just until I'm sure you're okay?"

"You don't have to do that."

"I *want* to."

Drew glanced over at him, his eyes pooling, his nose red. "Okay. I really don't want to be by myself."

"I should probably swing by Uncle Ralph's and get some clothes."

"You can wear something of mine. Please, can we just go?" A tear trickled down Drew's face, and he whisked it away.

"Sure. My car's parked right over there." Ethan tried not to react to his cousin's show of emotion but figured he was about to lose it.

Ethan sat at the kitchen table at Drew's house and waited until he heard the shower go on upstairs, then picked up his cell phone and dialed his parents' number.

"Ethan!" Tom Langley said. "Your mother and I have been beside ourselves waiting for you to call back. I've got you on speakerphone. How's Drew?"

"He's pretty shaken up. I'm with him now at his house. I've decided to stay over here instead of Uncle Ralph's—until I'm sure he's okay."

"Why don't you come stay with us?"

"We're too tired to drive to Maryville tonight. And Drew's not going to want to leave here."

"Has he talked to his parents?" Lisa Langley asked.

Ethan sighed. "No. He's adamant that he's not going to spoil their anniversary cruise since there's really nothing they can do."

"Then your mother and I will come stay with him."

"Dad, *I'm* with him. Let's see how he is tomorrow."

"You sure you're all right?" Lisa asked.

"We need to let the dust settle. But I think we're okay."

A long moment of dead air passed, and Ethan could hear his parents whispering on the other end of the line.

Finally Tom said, "How did Ralph and Gwen react?"

"They're sick about what happened, but Ralph's not going to reach out—not that Drew wants him to."

"All right, son. Get some rest. Tell Drew we're praying for him. We'll see you this weekend."

Ethan caught the scent of deodorant soap and looked up just as Drew walked into the kitchen barefoot, dressed in a pair of denim cutoffs and white T-shirt, his hair still wet.

Drew did a double take when he saw Vanessa standing at the stove.

"I'm going to make you some herbal tea." She took the teapot off the burner. "It'll relax you."

"I didn't know you were coming over." Drew pulled back a chair and sat at the table. "I'm not very good company right now."

"I don't expect you to be. I just wanted to do something to help while Carter's asleep. I brought you cold fried chicken, macaroni salad, rolls, and chocolate-chip cookies—just in case you get hungry."

"Thanks." Drew tapped his fingers on the table and seemed to stare at nothing.

"I'm so sorry about Tal," Vanessa said finally. "I can't imagine how hard it must've been finding him that way."

Ethan waited for Drew to respond, but he didn't say anything. Had he heard her? Was he too bleary-eyed to respond? Or was he just not in the mood to talk?

Vanessa set a mug of hot water and a tea bag of front of Drew and another in front of Ethan. She poured a mug for herself and sat at the table next to Ethan.

"I was telling Vanessa that I'm going to hang out here with you for a few days." Ethan put the tea bag in the hot water, then wrapped his hands around the mug and relished the warmth, remembering that he and Drew had very different ideas about where to set the thermostat. "I've already told Uncle Ralph and Aunt Gwen what I'm doing."

"Are they mad?"

"Of course not. They're worried about you, Drew. In spite of everything, you *are* their nephew."

"Try telling that to Dad."

Ethan lifted his gaze. "Maybe *you* should. God uses bad things for good. Maybe He wants you to take this opportunity to help build a bridge."

"Not tonight He doesn't. You have no idea what I've been through."

"I know I don't. It had to have been horrific." Ethan poked the tea bag with his spoon and watched the hot water turn a deeper shade of green. The last thing he wanted to do was say the wrong thing and add to Drew's trauma. "When you hurt, I hurt. That's just the way it is."

Drew's expression softened. He fished the tea bag out of the mug and set it on a napkin. "I don't know why anyone would want to kill Tal. He was the life of the party. Everyone liked him."

"Maybe it was just random," Vanessa said. "It was late, and he was walking by himself. Maybe some punks were out looking for trouble."

"Exactly," Ethan chimed in. "He could've just been in the wrong place at the wrong time. You said yourself there're a lot of unsavory-looking characters in Henry's neighborhood. Maybe one of them followed Tal."

Drew blew on his tea. "Then why didn't they steal his wallet or his iPhone? The police said his wallet had almost two hundred dollars in it."

"Maybe someone killed him for kicks," Ethan said. "It was dangerous to be out walking alone in that part of town." *Shut up. You're just making it worse.*

Drew sighed and looked out the window. "I told him that. The last thing he said to me was that if anything happened to him, I could have his Hummer. How's that for ironic?"

Ethan leaned forward on his elbows. "You think he knew someone was after him?"

"Nah. He was just clowning around when he threw me the keys."

"Did you tell my mom that?" Vanessa said.

"Yes, I told your mom everything."

Ethan took a sip of tea. "So is the Hummer yours?"

"Doesn't matter. I wouldn't drive it now if you paid me."

"Did the police impound it?"

Drew shrugged. "I assume they did. Tal's dad will probably take it. I sure don't want it."

❖   ❖   ❖

"Mr. Davison, please try to calm down," Brill said. "I understand how upset you must be about your son, but raising your voice won't make things happen faster."

Win Davison glared at her. "Why aren't you out looking for Tal's killer instead of asking me all these questions?"

"Sir, we're gathering facts," Brill said. "And I do have police officers knocking on doors in the four- and five-hundred blocks of Stoneleigh between your son's apartment and where his cell phone was found. We also questioned his roommate at length."

Davison rolled his eyes. "According to Tal, his roommate always had his head in a book. I doubt a geek like that would notice a murderer if he stood in the doorway with a gun in his hand."

"Are you aware that Drew Langley heard your son collapse—and tried to save his life?"

"Tried, yes—and failed."

Brill bit her lip. *That was cold.* "Drew's attempt was heroic, Mr. Davison. I'm sure the trauma of giving mouth-to-mouth to a dying friend is a memory he'll never shake."

"Excuse me if I don't start weeping. His life's going to go on, and he'll hardly skip a beat. Mine won't. Tal was my only son—my namesake. I'll never get that back."

Brill studied Davison. Was she misreading him, or did he regard Tal more as a possession than a child? "I'm very sorry for your loss."

"That's two of us. I want the scum who did this."

"So do we." Trent Norris picked up a pencil and bounced the eraser on the table. "Do you have any idea who would want to hurt Tal?"

"No. That's *your* job."

"Can you give us a list of his friends?"

Davison paused, his face blank. "He was an adult. I don't keep track of his friends. Ask his roommate."

"We did, sir." Trent wrote something on his yellow ruled pad. "We were hoping to compare lists. We're exploring every angle."

"While you're exploring every *angle*, my son's killer is on the loose."

"An important part of every investigation is the process of elimination." Trent put his pencil down. "So let me start with you, Mr. Davison. Where were you tonight?"

"Me? How dare you even suggest that I—"

"It's just a question, sir. No one is suggesting anything."

"Home with my pregnant wife. Ask her."

"Do you own a gun?"

"Yes, and I have a license for it. A Smith and Wesson nine-millimeter compact. I bought it for protection out at the lake house. We keep it locked in the nightstand. The key is under the lamp."

"Does your wife know how to use it?" Trent said.

"Yes. We both took lessons at the shooting range. I find the implication insulting."

"We're not implying anything," Brill said. "Captain Norris is just following protocol."

Trent made a notation on his pad. "When was the gun fired last?"

Davison sighed. "Months ago. I don't remember the exact date of our last lesson, but I can check my calendar."

"Let's wait until we hear back from ballistics," Brill said. "Tell me about your relationship with Tal."

"What do you want to know?"

"Were you close?"

Davison shrugged. "Not as close as we should've been. His mother and I divorced when he was little. I remarried and didn't see much of him growing up."

"Was there tension between you?"

"Just the usual father-son power struggles."

"Can you give some examples?" Brill asked.

"Tal didn't see the point of going to college. I disagreed. He thought he should be able to stay with me for the summer and not have a curfew. He was wrong. He thought it was none of my business that he drank too much. I told him as long as he was my son it was my business. Stuff like that. What does any of this have to do with you finding the killer?"

"The more we know about Tal and the people in his life, the easier it will be to put pieces of the puzzle together. Like Captain Norris said, solving a crime involves a process of elimination."

"Let me tell *you* something." Davison's eyes turned to slits. "I have six daughters. Number seven is on the way. Tal was probably the only son I'll ever have, my namesake—Winfield Talbot Davison the *fourth*. He came from a long line of business tycoons. Thanks to that scum you should be out looking for, there's no male heir to carry on the family name and business." He brought his fist down on the table. "I want justice."

Brill studied Davison's stern expression. He wore the face of a demanding CEO, not a grieving father.

"We all want justice," she said. "Let's go back to my question. So you and Tal weren't close?"

"Close enough. Frankly, I don't see what that has to do with anything. You people are crossing the line here. Maybe it's time I called my attorney."

Trent leaned forward on his elbows. "That's certainly your right. But unless you have something to hide, you have nothing to fear from us."

Davison paused for a moment, then looked from Trent to Brill. "All right, let me be clear about my relationship with my son … Tal and I were on the same page. He understood who he was and the responsibilities he would inherit. I paid every dime of his college expenses and had a nice position waiting for him at Davison Technologies once he got his business degree. I bought him that Hummer when he turned twenty-one. Gave him credit cards to the best clothing stores. I bought him the best computer, best smartphone, best iPod, and whatever else he wanted. Good, bad, or indifferent, that's the relationship I had with him."

"Thank you," Brill said. "That answered my question. I think that about does it, unless Captain Norris has more questions."

Trent shook his head and finished writing something. "We appreciate your cooperation, sir."

"Don't patronize me." Davison pushed back his chair and stood, his Rolex reflecting the overhead lights. "I don't appreciate being grilled like a common criminal. I'm going to report you both to Mayor Roswell."

"I assure you, we were just doing our job," Brill said.

"Yeah, well, I've heard how you do your *job,* Chief Jessup."

CHAPTER 5

Brill shut the door to her squad car and strolled toward the beautiful, quaint two-story house she and Kurt bought the day it went on the market. She looked up at the twinkling night sky through the tree branches that hung over Azalea Lane and listened to a choir of crickets serenading anyone who would listen.

The kitchen light was on at the Masinos'. She wondered if Tessa and Antonio had heard about the shooting and stayed up to watch the news.

Brill pushed open the front door and was hit with the delicate scent of roses, a gentle reminder that she would never again have to doubt Kurt's faithfulness.

She opened the closet door and hung up her sweater.

"I figured you'd be late." Kurt came up behind her and put his arms around her, his cheek next to hers. "Vanessa hasn't come home yet."

"Where'd she go?"

"She took some food over to Drew Langley at his parents' house. She called earlier and said he was really shaken up. Should she even be over there? Is the guy a suspect?"

"The parent in me wishes Vanessa wasn't so close to it. But the facts we have now don't point to Drew being a suspect. Let's go sit."

Brill went into the living room, flopped on the couch, and kicked off her shoes. "Ahhh … that's better."

Kurt sat forward in the overstuffed chair, his elbows on his knees, his hands laced together. "So tell me what happened."

Brill recounted everything she knew about the shooting based on Drew Langley's statement and the condition of the crime scene. "Drew claims he discovered his roommate wounded in the apartment, and we can tell from the blood spatter that the victim was shot on the sidewalk outside. There's a very clear blood trail from that point to the couch. Drew's story makes perfect sense, and he tested negative for gunshot residue."

Kurt arched his eyebrows. "Anyone hear the shot?"

"Several neighbors reported hearing a popping noise around ten forty-five. No one will admit to seeing anything. But shots were reported a few blocks away shortly after the victim was shot. Our killer could be some thug who went on a shooting spree."

"Sounds like you've got your work cut out for you."

"In more ways than one. The victim's father is Win Davison."

Kurt held her gaze. "As in Davison Technologies?"

"That's the one."

"I heard he's a real control freak."

"Who told you that?"

Kurt smiled sheepishly. "Okay, so guys *do* gossip at the barbershop. What's he like?"

"I'm not sure it's fair to assess the man under these shocking circumstances, but he was intimidating—or tried to be. He's obviously a man who's used to getting his way."

"Is he a suspect?"

"Not really. His wife says he was with her all evening. But since he owns a nine-millimeter Smith and Wesson, we can't rule him out until the ballistics report comes back. So what else did Vanessa have to say?"

Kurt stifled a yawn. "Just that she and Ethan were hanging out with Drew for a while to make sure he was okay."

"She has a final next week. She's supposed to be studying."

"Actually, she did a fair amount of studying earlier today, and Emily took charge of Carter the minute she got home from school."

"Well, that's good. Who would've ever guessed that Vanessa would finish her junior year without missing a step?"

Kurt smiled. "We make a good team—the four of us. It helps that Carter's been such a good baby."

"He's a joy. Sometimes I wonder what we did before we had him. I thought I'd be eager for Vanessa to get her own place, but now I'm almost dreading it. I can't imagine how Emily will react."

Kurt rose to his feet. "Well, that's not going to happen for at least another year."

"It's hard to say what could happen between now and then, what with the way Ethan and Vanessa can hardly take their eyes off each other." Brill chuckled. "Listen to me. I sound like Tessa Masino."

Kurt held out his arms and pulled her to her feet. "Come on, Chief. Let's go to bed and leave the matchmaking for another day. You need to focus all your attention on this case."

Tessa Masino stood at the window in her bedroom and saw the lights go out at the Jessups'. There hadn't been a murder in Sophie Trace in almost a year, and this was bound to dredge up memories of Brill's encounter with the ex-con she had helped put in prison.

"Come to bed, love," Antonio said. "It's late."

"Tell that to my brain." Tessa let go of the curtain. She climbed into bed and nestled next to Antonio. "I'm wide awake. I don't know why I come to life just about the time everyone else goes to sleep."

"Probably so you can pray about all that meddling you do. I'm sorry—*intercession.*" Antonio smiled and kissed her cheek.

"It's certainly intercession when the Lord nudges me to get involved."

"I know. I just like giving you a hard time." Antonio brushed the curls out of her eyes. "It *is* the ideal ministry for a night owl."

"I suppose you're right. I probably won't be tired for hours. I might as well get up and do something useful."

Antonio looked at her knowingly. "It won't do any good to worry about Brill."

"I'm not exactly worried. But tonight's shooting probably stirred up some unpleasant memories for the Jessups. They seem to be doing so well. I just don't want to see anything change that." Tessa studied the shadows on the ceiling. "It's been a privilege watching what God has done in that family. And I've never seen Emily so happy. She adores that little baby."

"She sure does. But the one I've had my eye on is Vanessa. She was downright depressed when she came home from college pregnant, knowing the baby's father wasn't going to help her raise him. Just look at her now."

"Some of that sparkle has to do with a certain someone. I wonder if she and Ethan are getting serious."

"Is this meddling now, or intercession?" The corners of Antonio's mouth twitched.

"I'm not sure." Tessa smiled in spite of herself. "Maybe a little of both."

❖   ❖   ❖

Ethan sat on the front porch swing at Drew's parents' house, his arm around Vanessa.

"Thanks for being so nice to Drew. He's really on the edge."

"I'm not surprised, after such an earth-shattering experience," Vanessa said. "At least he was able to fall asleep."

"It was thoughtful of you to bring food."

"There's enough for lunch tomorrow—for both of you. I thought it might be nice not to have to worry about fixing something."

"You're reading my mind. It's late. You really should go home and get some rest. Carter will be up bright and early, and you've only got tomorrow and the weekend to study for your last final."

Vanessa put her head on his shoulder and nestled closer. "We've hardly had a moment together. I just want to enjoy a few more minutes. After all the weeks of waiting, it doesn't seem real that you're actually here—and for the entire summer."

"I know. It's all I could think about all the way home. I've missed you so much." He pressed his lips to her cheek. "I'm sorry our first evening together ended with a tragedy. I'm glad I can be here for Drew, but it's too bad his mom and dad are out of the country."

"You were so good with him." Vanessa looked up, her clear blue eyes heavy with fatigue. "I don't know how you do it, but you never seem weighed down by other people's problems. That's why you're going to make a wonderful psychologist."

"Give yourself some credit. You were great in there."

"Thanks, but I feel like I've been run over by a Mack truck *and* the bus behind it. You're the one who's cool and collected."

"I've always been able to look at situations objectively. Maybe that's why people talk to me."

"I did." Vanessa held his gaze. "I so appreciated that you didn't judge me for getting involved with Professor Nicholson."

"Judging you was a sure way to put up a wall. What you needed was a friend—and grace to figure it out for yourself."

"It took a while. But I realize now that my relationship with Ty was doomed to fail. I should never have gotten involved with an unbeliever and compromised my values. I regret getting involved with Ty, but I wouldn't trade Carter for the world. And he deserves to grow up without his parents disagreeing over what values to teach him. I think it's best all the way around that Ty's not involved in Carter's life."

"I've never heard you say that before."

Vanessa gently stroked his bicep. "I've worked through it. I'm completely over him."

"*Completely* is a strong word."

"Yes, it is."

Ethan's pulse quickened. Did she mean that? Did she know herself well enough to be sure?

Vanessa's perfume wafted under his nose. He pulled her closer, aware of every inch of her. Was it too soon to declare the full extent of his feelings? This relationship wasn't about just the two of them.

Timing was everything. The last thing he wanted was to scare her off.

He pressed his lips to her cheek, then again, and again, moving his mouth ever so slowly to her ear.

"I've missed you," he whispered.

"Same here. I—"

In the next instant, their lips met and he drew her in, relishing her essence, restraint giving way to eager, prolonged kisses until their beings seemed to meld and he thought his heart would pound out of his chest. How long had he waited for this? Allowed the thought of it to sustain him through the months of separation—the seconds, minutes, and hours of loneliness? At last Vanessa was in his arms, free of her attachment to Ty Nicholson, ready to see if they might have a future together.

Stop! The voice in his head seemed audible—urgent. He forced himself to back away, his pulse still racing wildly.

Vanessa's eyes flew open. What was she thinking?

Ethan hid in the silence until his passion subsided. Finally he said, "Maybe we should ease into this. I just missed you so much. I can't tell you how many times I almost jumped in the car and drove across the state to see you."

"Really?" She smiled with her eyes. "I was tempted to do the same thing, but the idea of packing the car with all that baby gear forced me to be realistic. I knew I *had* to stay focused on my studies."

"I'm proud of you. It can't be easy juggling motherhood and school. In some ways, taking college courses online requires more self-discipline."

"I couldn't do it without Emily—well, without Dad and Mom either."

"Your hard work paid off. You've almost got another year of college under your belt."

"I do, don't I?"

Ethan picked up her hand and kissed it. "We've got all summer to see where this is going. Let's take it slow and do it right, okay?"

She nodded sleepily.

"You need to go home and get some sleep."

"Are you sure you're okay here with Drew?"

"Of course. Why wouldn't I be?"

Vanessa shrugged. "Maybe I've been a cop's daughter too long, but what if whoever killed Tal thinks Drew saw him?"

"If your mother was worried about it, she would have told us. Go home, honey. I'll take care of Drew."

Brill awoke to the sound of her cell phone vibrating. She groped the nightstand and picked it up.

"Chief Jessup."

"Brill, I'm sorry if I woke you. It's Lewis Roswell."

"What's wrong?"

"Win Davison just stormed out of my living room, threatening to go to the media and reveal your *intimidation tactics*. He's demanding that the city council reprimand you publicly for mishandling him."

"What? No way was Mr. Davison mishandled."

"What happened?"

"We questioned him the same way we would any other victim's father. We needed to establish what kind of relationship he had with his son. Where he was at the time of the shooting. And that the bullet that killed his son didn't come from the nine-millimeter handgun that's registered to him. That's just standard operating procedure. For heaven's sake, Davison isn't even a suspect. What he *is,* Lewis, is arrogant and controlling, not to mention rude and uncooperative. I doubt the man is half as upset about losing the only male heir to the family business as he is that we treated him like John Q. Public. He resents being treated like everyone else. The questions we asked him were relevant to the case. I'm not apologizing."

"The city council is going to side with him. Davison Technologies' board of directors is in the process of deciding whether to keep the Sophie Trace plant open or close it and move the operation to Chattanooga. We're talking about nine hundred workers. I don't have to tell you the impact that kind of layoff would have in this community."

Brill combed her hands through her hair. "Look, I'll make some kind of statement and explain police procedure. But I refuse to say we did anything wrong."

"We need those jobs, Brill."

"Then let the city council smooth it over! What I say reflects on my entire force. I'm not going to leave the community with the impression their police officers are bullies."

"I've known Win a long time. He's not going to let this go."

Brill looked over at Kurt and raised her eyebrows. "I'm not trying to be difficult, Lewis. It's a matter of principle. It's unfair and unreasonable that the city council should lay the fate of nine hundred workers on a lie they expect me to tell—to satisfy Davison's precious ego."

"Would it kill you?"

"That's not the point. It would cast aspersions on my officers. I won't do it. I'm perfectly willing to talk to the media and explain police procedure. I can word it so it reinforces our having followed protocol and makes Davison feel respected. That's the best I can do."

Lewis exhaled into the receiver. "All right. Let's hope it's enough. Losing Davison Technologies would be a huge economic hit."

Brill realized the phone was dead. *And good-bye to you, too, Mr. Mayor.*

"I heard the whole conversation," Kurt said. "It's wrong of the mayor to put you in this position."

"I agree. On the other hand, we know people who work at the plant. Everyone does. I'd hate to see them lose their jobs because my pride got in the way."

"Honey, there's no guarantee that Davison will choose to keep the plant here if you apologize. It's about money. It always is."

"Probably." She lay down on the bed, the back of her hand on her forehead. "But I resent looking like the bad guy in this."

CHAPTER 6

Brill stood at her office window and looked out through the towering trees that shaded the grounds around city hall. In the distance, beyond the ridge of rolling foothills, the silhouette of the Great Smoky Mountains seemed to fade in and out of the ghostly haze.

She looked down at the cars parked at the meters. Fridays were always busy. Maybe people just wanted to get their business done before the weekend.

She heard a knock at the door and turned around. Trent Norris filled the doorway.

"Ballistics report came," he said. "The nine-millimeter bullet that killed Tal Davison didn't come from his father's gun."

"Gee, what a surprise." Brill hated the sarcasm in her voice.

"Are you still stewing about Davison's visit to the mayor last night?"

"Yes. I don't like being misrepresented or put in the middle."

"Are you going to apologize?"

"And let Davison get away with insinuating that we bully people? No way. I told the mayor what I'm willing to do. I'll issue a statement to the press and explain police procedures. I'll make sure Davison doesn't come off looking bad."

"How are you going to do that, Chief? He was totally obnoxious."

"Yes, but he was stressed. It was hard to think clearly under the circumstances, what with his grief over losing his only son and all." There was that sarcasm again.

Trent flashed a phony smile. "Yeah, right. I could tell how deeply troubled the guy was."

"Let's give him the benefit of the doubt and assume that he just doesn't know how to show it. It's not uncommon for people to misdirect their anger when someone they love dies tragically."

"You're being way too generous."

"I don't want Davison Technologies to close the Sophie Trace plant."

"So what are you going to tell the media?"

"I'm not sure yet. But I refuse to apologize for good police work. Now that we've eliminated Win Davison's gun in the shooting, maybe he'll realize we're not out to get him."

"I don't know, Chief. He strikes me as the type of guy that enjoys a good fight."

Ethan sat at the kitchen table at Drew's house, the newspaper spread out in front of him. He heard the shuffling of bare feet on the wood floor and looked up just as Drew walked in, unkempt and unshaven, dressed in the same denim cutoffs and white T-shirt he wore the night before.

"Hey, Cuz." Drew stumbled over to the coffeepot. "I smelled coffee all the way upstairs."

"Help yourself. How'd you sleep?"

"So-so. I couldn't get the image of Tal out of my mind."

"The shooting made the headlines," Ethan said. "I'm surprised, since it happened so late. They must've bumped another story and printed this one. According to the article, shots were reported a few blocks away right after Tal was shot."

Drew carried his cup of coffee over to the table and sat across from Ethan. "Did they mention my name?"

"Several times. Here, you want to read it?"

"So I can relive it? No thanks."

"The article told how you tried to resuscitate him."

"And yet … he's dead, isn't he?"

Ethan folded the newspaper and drank the last of his coffee. "It took a lot of courage to attempt mouth-to-mouth on someone in that condition."

"Not really. I had to do something, and I couldn't do CPR with his chest oozing blood."

Ethan reached across the table and gently gripped his cousin's wrist. "No one could've saved him. You have to know that."

Drew stared at his cup. "Have you ever watched someone die?"

"Not like that. I was there when my grandma Tremont died, but she was sleeping peacefully."

"Tal choked on his own blood. It was hard to watch." Drew seemed withdrawn for a minute and then began tracing the rim of his cup with his finger. "He didn't believe in God or a life after this one."

"Did he tell you that?"

"Yeah. I invited him to a MercyMe concert shortly after he moved in. He left at intermission. We talked later, and he said that belief in a higher power was a crutch. Some people needed it but not him. I just let it go. I should've tried harder."

"Drew, this kind of thinking is just going to make you depressed. Tal had the same choices you and I did. He chose differently. Just like you couldn't save his life, you couldn't save his eternal life either. Some things aren't in our power."

"Seems like *nothing* was in my power."

"It's no fun feeling powerless, but you did everything you could."

"Then why do I feel so bad?"

"Good grief, man. You saw your friend shot and killed. I'd be worried if you *didn't* feel bad."

Drew's eyes turned to dark pools. He buried his face in his hands and started to sob quietly, almost as if Ethan's comment had given him permission to acknowledge his emotions.

Ethan got up, walked around the table, and sat next to the cousin who seemed more like a brother, placing his hand on his back. "Let it out, Drew. All the sadness and fear and anger and guilt. Let it go."

Ethan stayed where he was, hoping his presence was comforting to Drew. What a horrible trauma his cousin had been through. He tried to imagine it and then erased the scene from his mind. Minutes passed with neither of them saying a word.

Finally Drew wiped his eyes on his T-shirt. "Sorry."

"Don't apologize. Every man needs to cry once in a while. It's like taking the cap off the pressure valve."

"I guess." Drew took a sip of coffee that had to be cold by now. "When's the funeral?"

"Don't know yet. The article indicated there would be an

autopsy. I doubt the family can make arrangements until Tal's body is released."

"Why would they do an autopsy when it's obvious he died of a gunshot wound?"

"Probably to determine whether there was foul play *prior* to his being shot, or whether he was under the influence of drugs or alcohol or something else that might've caused him to provoke the attack."

"Drunk or sober, impaired or not, he was shot in cold blood in the middle of the sidewalk. There's no escaping it."

"No one saw what happened, Drew. There might be more to it."

Tessa Masino shuffled into Nick's Grill, Antonio holding the door, and savored the aroma of something spicy wafting under her nose.

Nick Phillips waved from the counter and hurried over to them, his thick, sandy blond hair salted with gray, a roll of excess pounds hanging over his belt. He shook Antonio's hand and put his other hand on Tessa's shoulder. "Welcome, friends. I've got a zesty tortellini salad loaded with grilled chicken and veggies that'll knock your socks off. Low in fat. High in flavor. Comes with sourdough rolls fresh from the oven."

"Oh my"—Tessa put her hand on her heart—"that's what I'm having. I've had a craving for something Italian. You're the only one we know who makes pasta that tastes as good as Antonio's grandmother's."

"That's why I love serving you two." Nick winked. "Gus and Maggie saved your places at the counter. I'll be right there."

Tessa walked over to the counter and hugged Maggie Williams. "Does it feel strange being a customer?"

"I think it'll hit when Jo Beth takes my order."

"We'll all just move down one seat, dear. You fit right in."

Antonio slid onto the stool between Tessa and Gus and slapped Gus on the back. "How's it going, friend?"

"Really can't complain, but I always do." Gus chuckled, linking arms with Maggie. "Not so much anymore."

"Well, to celebrate Maggie's first lunch with us on *this* side of the counter," Antonio said, "Tessa and I are treating today."

"That's mighty nice of you."

"So what do you know?"

Gus waved his hand. "Aw, it's a cryin' shame about Win Davison's kid bein' shot in front of his apartment."

"I just can't imagine why no one saw what happened," Tessa said. "And, Gus, I do not believe the spirits of the departed Cherokee are responsible for it, so don't even go there."

Gus arched his eyebrows. "Did I say anything about the legend?"

"No, but you were thinking it," Tessa said. "Ever since Billy Dan went on *Larry King Live,* you've been more superstitious than ever."

"Well, I believe him." Gus's eyes narrowed. "You weren't the one that got caught up by red shadows and was left for dead on an Indian burial ground. Billy Dan saw what he saw. You can't take that from him."

"Fine," Tessa said. "Just don't try to turn this boy's killing into a paranormal experience. It was more than likely a random shooting."

"That's the spin the cops will put on it."

"Guess we'll see."

"Guess we will."

"I'm ready to order," Maggie said, louder than she needed to.

Antonio smiled knowingly. "Good idea."

Jo Beth McCauley seemed to come out of nowhere, green pad in hand. She reached back and moved her long braid so it fell neatly down the center of her back. "I'll take your orders when y'all are ready."

"Specials for Maggie and me," Gus said.

Antonio nodded. "Ditto."

"Coffee all around and a Coke for Gus?" she said.

Four heads bobbed in affirmation.

"I'll be right back with your drinks."

Nick came over to the counter. "What'd I miss?"

"Oh, we're just talkin' about the Davison kid," Gus said.

"Who isn't? That's all my customers have been talking about all day."

"Well, the shooting became personal for Antonio and me," Tessa said. "We just found out this morning that the victim was Vanessa Jessup's boyfriend's cousin's roommate."

Gus chuckled. "You call that *personal?*"

Maggie nudged him with her elbow. "Gus, she's saying that Ethan's cousin shared an apartment with the boy that was killed."

"Oh."

"The cousin's name is Drew Langley," Tessa said. "He and Ethan are very close."

Maggie looked down the counter at her. "According to the news, Drew tried to resuscitate the victim."

"Yes, and was really shaken by his death. Vanessa and Ethan spent the evening with him."

Gus rubbed his white mustache. "I also heard that Chief Jessup and her officers questioned Win Davison like he's the one who did the shootin'. He's demanded an apology."

"I'm sure there's more to the story," Tessa said.

Clint Ames slid onto the stool next to her and set his sunglasses on the counter. "Hi, all. Hope you didn't wait on me to order."

"No, we went ahead." Gus turned and seemed to study Clint. "Somethin' wrong?"

"Yeah." Clint let out a long sigh and slowly shook his head. "The body of a young woman was just found on a balcony at the Essex Apartments. Shot in the head."

❖   ❖   ❖

Brill pulled the sheet over the face of the female victim sprawled on the balcony floor of apartment 206, then slowly rose to her feet, hoping she could keep down her lunch.

"The victim's name is Skyler Roberts," Trent said. "She was a sophomore at Stanton. Parents have been notified. They're flying in from Atlanta. Dad's a CPA. Mom's a schoolteacher."

"Who found her?"

"Her roommate, Olivia Jones. She returned to the apartment around eleven this morning after spending the night with her sister in Knoxville. Her story is airtight. She placed the 9-1-1 call."

"How long has the victim been dead?"

"Judging from the condition of the body, she's been dead at least twelve hours. If the bullet's trajectory proves to be a straight line from the middle of the street to the balcony, we *could* be looking at a drive-by. And since gunshots were reported in this neighborhood shortly after Davison was hit, and the bullet that killed Ms. Roberts is a nine-millimeter, it wouldn't surprise me if she was shot with the same gun. Ballistics will tell us soon."

"If a gang's responsible, I won't let up until every last one of them is behind bars!"

"We've already got our snitch at the high school nosing around, Chief. If a gang's marking its territory, you can bet someone's bragging about it. Plus we should start seeing graffiti again."

"That's all we need. I will *not* give them one inch of this town."

Trent unwrapped a Tootsie Pop and stuck it in his mouth. "We're talking to other tenants in the building and neighbors in the area. So far, at least a dozen people said they heard the shots last night, in addition to the eight that called us. But no one heard a scream or had any idea that Ms. Roberts had been hit. The roommate was beside herself when she called 9-1-1. Paramedics sedated her."

"I doubt the victim had a chance to scream," Brill said. "Probably died instantly."

"I saw a picture of her. She was beautiful."

"Does she have a boyfriend?"

Trent shook his head. "No one serious. The roommate said she was friendly, well liked. Couldn't think of anyone who didn't like her."

"Have you checked her computer?"

"Not in great detail, but her emails seemed to be mostly girl talk. She had a couple hundred friends listed on her Facebook page. Nothing stood out to me at first glance, but we'll dig a little deeper."

CHAPTER 7

Brill got out of her squad car, the night air thick with humidity, the cricket choir she'd enjoyed the night before grating on her like the sound of a novice practicing the violin.

She trudged toward the front door, her purse strapped over her shoulder. The only thing hurting worse than her feet was her heart.

She pushed open the door and let the scent of flowers draw her into the comfort of home.

Kurt came out of the kitchen and wrapped his arms around her. "You must be glad to get this day behind you."

"I'd hardly call it *behind* me, but at least I'm home. Nothing gets under my skin like someone's child being murdered on my watch. And now I've got two."

He didn't say anything and just held her. She tried to imagine the weight she carried being lifted from her. It didn't work.

"Hi, Mom." Emily came down the stairs, holding Carter on her hip. She moved his hand up and down. "Wave hello to Grandma."

"Hi there, big boy." Brill took the smiling baby into her arms and gave him a tender hug, reveling in his obvious delight to see her.

"Dinner won't be ready for thirty minutes." Vanessa stood in the kitchen doorway, wiping her hands with a towel. "Why don't you go put your feet up?"

"Thanks, honey. That sounds wonderful. How's Drew Langley holding up?"

"He's still pretty fragile."

"Come on, little man," Emily coaxed Carter, "let's go outside and swing."

Brill handed the baby back to Emily. She seemed so mature for eleven, more like a little mother than his aunt.

"Let's get you off your feet." Kurt took Brill by the hand and led her to the couch. He had her stretch out, took off her shoes, and then began to gently massage her feet.

"How's that?" he said.

"Feels soooo good." She yielded herself completely to the arms of the couch, almost as if she were floating on water. "Did you drive over to the Pigeon Forge store?"

"Yes, everything's fine. Business is up. We got the sign man to come out and change the wording on the marquis. Truthfully, I'm much more interested in how you're doing."

Brill closed her eyes. "Kurt, we put a beautiful young coed with part of her face missing into a body bag and notified her parents. How do you *think* I'm doing?" She paused for several seconds, then softened her tone. "Sorry. I keep wondering how I'd feel if it were Vanessa."

"Did this girl go to Stanton?"

"Yes. Her name is Skyler Roberts. The medical examiner said she had been dead at least twelve hours when her roommate found her. Ballistics confirmed that the nine-millimeter bullet that killed her came from the same gun that killed Tal Davison. We've now recovered a matching bullet lodged in the wall at Woodall's Grocery. And a second matching bullet in the door at Milligan's Realty

Company. Our best guess right now—and it's only a guess—is that the shooter fired randomly along a specific route to send some kind of message, and Davison and Roberts were collateral damage."

"You think it's gang activity?"

"We have to consider it. A gang could have been marking its territory, or it could have been part of an initiation. But it doesn't feel right to me."

"Have you found graffiti?"

"Yes, but it's different from anything we've seen before. We sent pictures of it up to the FBI field office in Knoxville. Maybe their gang unit can identify the gang for us."

"Well, for what it's worth, every town in the region has had gang problems."

"I'm not *responsible* for every town, Kurt. If our zero tolerance policy failed, we need to regroup quickly and find out which gang it is and get those guilty of these killings behind bars. I will not have this town terrorized by thugs."

"Mom?"

Brill opened her eyes and saw Vanessa standing next to Kurt.

"The evening news is on and they released the name of the female student who got shot. I knew Skyler."

"You did?"

"Yes, her roommate, Olivia Jones, is in my singles' group at church. She invited Skyler to come play volleyball with us a few weeks ago. Several of us went over to Beanie's afterward for coffee."

"What can you tell me about her?" Brill said.

"Not that much. She was from Atlanta. We both were majoring in elementary ed."

"Did she date anyone from the singles' group?"

"I don't know, but Olivia might. She was such a sweet girl. I can't imagine why anyone would want to kill her."

"Did Skyler know Tal Davison?"

"I don't know. You want me to ask Olivia?"

"No, honey. We'll talk to her, thanks. It's better if you stay removed from this."

"Do you think the two shootings are related?"

"We certainly haven't ruled it out. We're gathering facts right now."

Vanessa locked gazes with her. "In other words, you can't talk about it?"

"Not yet."

"I'm going back over to Drew's after dinner. Ethan said he's still pretty shaken. Are you any closer to knowing who shot his roommate?"

"We're fact-finding, honey. That's all I can say right now."

"Okay. I'm going to check the roast."

Brill waited until Vanessa went back in the kitchen and then looked over at Kurt. "We haven't told the media yet that the same gun was used to kill both victims. Don't say anything."

"Honey, we've been doing this for twenty years. I know the drill by now."

A smile toyed with the corners of her mouth. "I didn't mean to insult your intelligence. By the way, did you hear what I told the media this morning about our questioning of Win Davison?"

"Yes, and I'm sure Mayor Roswell and the entire viewing audience could tell he hit a nerve when he asked you to apologize for following procedure."

"Why, did I come across as defensive?"

"More like protective. It was obvious you weren't going to let your officers take the heat for doing their jobs."

"I did say that I understood why Mr. Davison might misinterpret our line of questioning. I also said we have no reason to believe that he was involved in any way."

"You did. I think everyone got the message. Was Mayor Roswell okay with it?"

"I guess. I've been so busy with the investigation that I haven't had time to coddle the city council. Let him do it."

Ethan sat in the porch swing at Drew's, listening to the cicadas and thinking of happy times.

"It's déjà vu sitting here," Ethan said. "I've got so many memories of hanging out here as a kid."

Drew pushed the swing a little harder with his feet and flashed a toothy grin. "Remember the time you were pulling me in the wagon, and I stood up and fell out—and got the wind knocked out of me?"

"How could I forget?" Ethan said. "I thought you were dying and it was my fault."

"Your fault?" Drew poked him with his elbow. "Why would you think that? I was the one clowning around."

"I don't know. I always felt responsible to protect you after the baby died. I didn't want to see your parents cry like that again."

"I hardly remember it," Drew said. "Mom and Dad never talk

about her. Most of my memories of being a kid are good ones, especially of the two of us."

"Yeah, too bad we couldn't bottle our spirit of adventure. We could've made a fortune."

"Our poor mothers. Between the cuts and the sprains and the trips to the emergency room, it was never dull." Drew laughed. "Do you remember the time I got an ice cube stuck to my tongue? You were cool as a cucumber and I about freaked. I was sure it would never come off."

"Well, I wasn't that calm when I got a pair of scissors stuck in my wrist. I nearly passed out from the sight of all that blood. I couldn't believe you had the guts to pull them out."

"Only because I was too young and stupid to know that if they'd been stuck in an artery, you *could've* bled to death. Our guardian angels were definitely working overtime."

Ethan looked over at Drew. "Do you remember taking money out of our piggy banks and buying bread and cheese for that sweet old lady who lived on the corner?"

"Oh yeah, Mrs. Dawson … we overheard our parents say she didn't have money for groceries and was eating dog food. The thought of it made me gag. I remember how good it felt to help her."

"You want to bet our folks slipped her money but didn't want to diminish our act of kindness by telling us?"

"Probably. You know, Ethan, when I think back, it seems like the two of us have been joined at the hip for as long as I can remember."

"Yeah"—Ethan nudged Drew's shoulder with his own—"I never felt like an only child. Still don't."

"Me, either."

A comfortable silence wrapped itself around them.

Finally Ethan said, "How are you feeling tonight—about the shooting?"

"Numb mostly. Studying helps. The most difficult part is closing my eyes. I still see Tal's face."

"I imagine you will for a while. Maybe we should take my mom and dad up on their offer and go stay with them for a few days."

Drew shook his head. "I appreciate their concern, but I want to stay home."

"You sure?"

"I'm sure."

"Well, before this happened, they'd already planned to come see me this weekend. They're driving in tomorrow morning and staying at Uncle Ralph's."

The expression left Drew's face. "You know I think the world of Uncle T and Aunt Lisa, and I wouldn't hurt them for the world. But I don't think I can handle talking about this again."

"All right. I'll explain it to them, but they're going to insist on coming by to check on you. Are you sure you don't want to call your parents?"

"Positive," Drew said. "They've planned this anniversary cruise for an entire year. Why ruin it for them? Would you call if it were your mom and dad?"

"Probably not. You hungry? Maybe we should order a pizza or something."

"Sounds good," Drew said. "But why don't we wait for Vanessa? She ought to be here soon."

Ethan got up and stretched, the western sky now fiery orange. He could hardly wait to see her.

❊   ❊   ❊

Vanessa went up the back steps at Drew Langley's house and knocked on the door. Through the screen she saw Ethan get up from the kitchen table and walk over to her.

"Come in." He held open the door. "I talked Drew into turning off the air conditioner for a while and letting in some fresh air. What've you got in the Tupperware?"

"Leftover roast beef, potatoes and carrots, rolls, and a salad. And vanilla pudding—compliments of Emily."

"Wow, does that sound good. We were just going to order a pizza, but a home-cooked meal is so much better. Hey, Drew," he hollered, "come see what Vanessa brought us."

She set the containers on the countertop. "I can reheat this right now, if you guys are hungry."

"We're starved." Drew came in the kitchen and hugged her. "You didn't have to do this."

"I deliberately made more than my family could eat so we could share."

Drew raised his eyebrows up and down. "I can use the protein. If I don't ace my English lit final on Tuesday, my scholarship's going to be in jeopardy."

"Can't you postpone taking it?" Vanessa said. "I mean, surely your professor would understand that you've been through a terrible trauma."

"I'm sure he would." Drew sighed. "But the truth is, I'm so numb at the moment that studying is a welcome escape. I might be messed up a few weeks from now. As long as my mind is still sharp, I think I'd better take the test."

"And I think I'd better set the table." Ethan held Vanessa's face in his hands and kissed her tenderly.

"Careful, Vanessa. He'll steam up his glasses."

She giggled and pushed away from Ethan. "It'll just take a few minutes to get this food on the table."

She took the lids off the leftovers, aware of the heat scalding her cheeks. Was it insensitive of her to delight in Ethan's kisses in front of Drew? Would it be more appropriate to keep the mood somber rather than lighthearted?

"Ethan said you knew the gal who was shot. She went to Stanton, but neither of us had met her."

Vanessa glanced up and realized he was looking at her. "I knew her, but not well. Her roommate, Olivia, is in the young singles' group at my church. She invited Skyler to play volleyball with us a few weeks ago. We all went out for coffee afterward. That's not what I consider really *knowing* someone."

"I didn't really know Tal either, but I knew a lot about him." Drew stared out the window. "His parents divorced when he was a kid. His dad's been married four times and has six daughters. Tal was the only son. His dad expected him to take over the family business someday and was going to give him a position there right out of college. Tal probably would've become a millionaire. But you know what he really wanted to do?" Drew looked at Vanessa. "Go to the police academy."

"He might have changed his mind if he'd ever lived with a cop. It's not an easy life. They're exposed to the worst of the worst, and it can make them cynical. But I think my mom's a saint. She says law enforcement is her calling. It must be, because after all she's been through, she still loves what she's doing."

"I just hope she can get the shooter," Ethan said.

"Knowing Mom, she won't stop until she does."

Stedman Reeves keyed in Grant Wolski's number on his prepaid cell phone and held the phone to his ear.

"Hello."

"It's Stedman. We need to talk."

"I told you we're never to talk about it," Grant said. "What is it about *never* you don't understand?"

"I know what you said. I need you to listen to me. I lied. I didn't kill Tal Davison."

"Sure you did. He's in the morgue."

"I didn't do it! I followed him to a house on Mobley and waited for hours for him to come out. When he did, he stumbled around like he was drunk and then started walking. I followed him home, trying to get up my nerve. That's when a red truck zoomed past me and pulled up beside him. The passenger shot him and sped off. Man, I beat it out of there. I called and told you 'the pizza had been delivered' because I wanted my gambling debt out of the way. I figured you got what you wanted. Why not take advantage of it?"

There was a moment of steely silence. "So why are you telling me this?" Grant said.

"Because I just watched the news, and that coed was shot with the same gun that killed Davison. I don't want you thinking *I* did it. I didn't have the guts to kill him, and I sure didn't kill that girl."

"You really think I'm going to tip off the cops?"

"I don't know what to think. But I didn't kill *anybody*."

"What did you do with the gun I gave you?"

"Nothing. It hasn't even been fired. Why would I make this up?"

"To cover your tail. Maybe you tried to make Davison's death look like a drive-by, and the girl's death was an accident. Now you're panicked."

"I'm telling you, I didn't kill either of them. You've got to believe me."

"Fine. You didn't do it. Then you still owe me sixty grand." Grant laughed. "You should've kept your mouth shut."

"Come on, man, this isn't funny. What if they know I saw them?"

"*Did* you?"

"Yeah, two guys. I couldn't really see their faces. I'm sure the truck had Tennessee plates with the letter *S.*"

"What kind of truck was it?"

"Red. Fairly new. I didn't get the make and model. It happened so fast, and I was focused on Davison."

"Do you think they saw *you?*"

"Of course they saw me; they passed me. For all I know, they think I saw everything and got their license number."

"I doubt that. You'd have told the cops by now."

"Maybe they think I'm holding out! Maybe they'll come looking for me! What do I do?"

"Calm down. If you're worried about it, keep the gun and use it for protection. It's stolen and can't be traced to you. But don't think I'm letting you off the hook. For every day you don't pay me, the debt goes up a thousand bucks."

"I'll get it, man."

"Not laying concrete for Ralph Langley, you won't."

"I need that job to pay the rent. I don't gamble with my paycheck. I've always used my winnings."

"Then you better hope your luck changes—and soon. I'll be in touch. Don't call me again."

Stedman sat in the dead air that followed, his heart hammering, his stomach churning. What were the odds he could win that much money? What choice did he have? He had to try. His credit cards were maxed out, and he couldn't afford to skip town.

CHAPTER 8

The next morning Ethan Langley opened the front door of his uncle Ralph and aunt Gwen's two-story frame house and was hit with the unmistakable aroma of his aunt's county-fair blue-ribbon peanut-butter cookies.

"Hello, anybody home?"

"We're back here," said a muffled male voice.

Ethan headed for the kitchen, his mouth watering for a cookie—or even a spoonful of cookie dough.

He breezed into the kitchen and right into the arms of Aunt Gwen.

"You timed that perfectly," she said. "The first batch is still warm. Ralph actually took a Saturday morning off, if you can believe it."

Ethan grabbed two cookies off the cooling rack just as his uncle put him in a playful headlock.

"How're you doing, kid?"

"Good."

"How's Drew?" Gwen said.

"*Not* so good."

Ralph let go of Ethan and grabbed a cookie. "Did he know the girl they found shot?"

"No. But Drew tried to revive his roommate after he was shot. It's going to take some time to get over it."

"I wish I could be there to support him," Ralph said. "But that stubborn twin brother of mine would make him feel guilty for talking to me."

"People change. Don't you think Uncle Richard would want you to help Drew through this while he and Aunt Becca are halfway around the world?"

"No. I think he'd be counting on his *other* brother to do it. And since Tom and Lisa will be here any minute, I'm sure I'll get this same guilt trip in stereo."

Try listening for a change.

"Don't try to shrink my head, Ethan. Or at least wait until you get your degree." The corners of Ralph's mouth turned up. "I miss having you around here. How long are you going to stay with Drew?"

"Just depends on how he's doing. His folks will be back in two weeks. Before I forget to ask, what time do I report for work on Monday?"

"Seven. We're going to start laying the foundations for the tract homes in Misty Meadows. You going to be able to handle twelve-hour days?"

"Sure. Any chance I could come to work an hour earlier and leave at six p.m.?" He locked gazes with Uncle Ralph and tried not to smile first.

A broad grin appeared between Ralph's salted red mustache and beard. "Something tells me we wouldn't be seeing much of you even if you were staying here."

"I want to spend as much time as I can with Vanessa and Carter over the summer. All I've got are evenings and Sundays."

"You two getting serious?"

"It's difficult being away from her, that's for sure." Ethan grabbed two more cookies. "These are to die for, Aunt Gwen."

"Take as many as you want. I quadrupled the recipe so I'll have enough to freeze. Want milk?"

"Sure, but I can get it."

"No, sit. I'll get it. Give us the inside scoop on the shooting investigation."

"I don't know any more than the media's reported. Chief Jessup doesn't discuss police business with me."

Gwen's eyebrows came together. "Doesn't Vanessa?"

"Her mom doesn't tell her either. There are some things the police aren't free to talk about, not even with family."

Ralph laughed. "Nice try, honey. Looks like your mahjong ladies are going to have to follow the story on TV like the rest of us."

❖ ❖ ❖

Brill sat at the conference table in her office, the Roberts and Davison case files open in front of her, and tried to sum up what they had determined so far.

The same nine-millimeter gun was used in both shootings, and matching bullets were recovered in the wall at Woodall's Grocery and the door at Milligan's Realty Company.

Taking into account the statements of eyewitnesses and the trajectory of the bullets recovered, the shooter was the passenger in a red late-model truck going west on Stoneleigh. He fired several shots and hit Tal Davison, then turned south on First Street and fired more shots and hit Woodall's Grocery. He continued driving south five blocks, then turned east on Essex, still firing, and hit Skyler Roberts. He continued on to Fifth Street, then turned north and fired more shots, hitting Milligan's Realty before arriving back at his starting point on Stoneleigh. Five square blocks. That could easily have been done in a few minutes.

What kind of message was this shooting supposed to send? Neither victim had any obvious connection to a gang or drug dealer. Were they just some random shooter's collateral damage?

She heard a knock on the door and looked up just in time to see Trent come through the doorway.

He walked over and stood at the conference table, reeking of cigarette smoke. "We have a witness who said the shooter's truck was a Ford F-150."

"Good. One more piece of the puzzle."

Trent smiled. "There's more. We know that the bullets we recovered all came from the same gun. And ballistics has now determined that the rifling profile of those nine-millimeter Luger-type bullets is unique to Smith and Wesson's second- and third- generation semiautomatic pistols, which includes all four-digit model numbers. They're the *only* known manufacturer to use that rifling profile."

"Well, that narrows it down. And we already eliminated Win Davison's gun. Now we're getting somewhere."

"I see you're looking through the files. Did you come up with something new?"

"No. Your detectives did a thorough job. Have we heard back from the FBI's gang unit about the graffiti?

"Not conclusively. They want to take another look at it. But they've never seen this graffiti before and aren't convinced it's authentic."

"Then we're on the same page. This looks to me like someone trying too hard to make it look like gang involvement. The question is who—and why?"

"We have no motive in the death of either victim."

"Yet. We're obviously missing something." She paused for a moment and considered what she was about to do. "Trent, close the door and sit down for a minute. I want to talk to you about something."

Trent pulled the door closed and sat across from her, his hands folded on the table.

She locked gazes with him. "When did you start smoking again?"

He got that I-don't-know-what-you-are-talking-about look on his face and then stared at his hands. "How'd you know?"

"You reek of cigarettes."

He sighed. "You going to lecture me too? Because Trish is already on my back."

"She'd like to keep you around a long time. Whatever happened to giving up smoking for her and the kids?"

Trent shrugged. "It's too hard. I find myself sneaking around to have a smoke—like a schoolboy behind the barn. I'm a grown-up, for cryin' out loud. I should be able to smoke without being made to feel guilty by the reformed smokers of the world."

"I never smoked, Trent. I have no idea what you're going through. But I have some idea what Trish is feeling. They practically had to pry the cigarettes out of my grandfather's hand, even when he had emphysema and then was diagnosed with lung cancer. I saw what it did to my grandmother—and my mom. He said he couldn't help it."

"Maybe he couldn't."

"Or didn't want to badly enough."

"Easy for you to say. You've never been addicted."

"Fair enough. But there's so much available now to help people who want to quit that there's no excuse to stay addicted."

"I'm not looking for excuses. But not everyone can stick a Tootsie Pop in his mouth and kick the habit like Beau Jack did."

"So find a support group."

"Not my style."

"Try the patch."

"I did. It made me nauseated and made my skin itch."

She sighed. "Look, your doctor even has medication you can try."

"The truth is, I like smoking. I only tried to quit for everyone else."

Brill studied his face—the spittin' image of Denzel Washington. "You're forty-one and fit as a fiddle. Why do you want to jeopardize your future by turning your lungs black?"

"Hey, just trying to keep all my body parts color coordinated."

"I didn't laugh the first time you pulled that line on me, and I'm not laughing now. I can't tell you what to do, and I won't bring it up again. But as a friend, not as the chief, I'm imploring you to do everything you can to kick the habit. God gave you a healthy body. Don't deliberately mess it up."

"And if I don't quit?"

"I'm praying you will."

"Hey, no fair." Trent half smiled, lacing his fingers together. "I guess it couldn't hurt. Trish already has her Bible-study group praying."

"Prayer's not a magic wand for a habit you *don't want* to break."

"I tried. Nothing worked."

"Trent, you're one of the most disciplined cops I know. You dot every *i* and cross every *t*. Be honest with yourself. You're a slave to cigarettes because you're *choosing* to be. Okay, enough said." Brill stood. "I thought you should know how I feel."

"Anything else?"

"No, you're free to go."

Trent lifted his eyebrows. "I wouldn't exactly call this *free.*"

Ethan stood at the curb on the south end of Cherokee Valley Park and opened the passenger door for Vanessa, then reached in the backseat, unbuckled Carter, and lifted him out of the car seat.

"Hey, big guy. You ready for a picnic?"

Vanessa laughed. "I brought everything but the kitchen sink. All he really needs are his toys and he'll be happy as a lark."

"Here, I'll get that." Ethan took the picnic basket from Vanessa. "Where do you want to go?"

"Why don't we sit under that beautiful shade tree over there? Then if Carter gets fussy we can come back and get his Pack 'n Play and put him down for a nap."

Ethan headed for the towering oak, Carter on his hip and Vanessa next to him, an old patchwork quilt under her arm and the toy toolbox in her hand. Was this what it felt like to be married?

"The weather's gorgeous." Vanessa looked up at the bluebird sky, her shiny dark hair falling down to the middle of her back. "I'm so glad I've got you for the summer."

"You've got me, all right." He smiled. "Will you look at that view?"

Beyond the rolling green terrain of the park, the spring foothills were cloaked in blue-white haze, the Great Smoky Mountains barely visible in the distance.

He drank in the beauty for a moment, then walked over and stood under the tree. He handed Carter to Vanessa and took the quilt and spread it on the ground.

Vanessa set Carter on the blanket and sat next to him. How did she get her figure back to almost perfect after gaining thirty pounds when she was pregnant?

Ethan sat cross-legged facing Vanessa and watched Carter dump the contents of his toolbox on the blanket.

"Did you ask your uncle if you could get off at six?" Vanessa's clear blue eyes were provocative.

"I did. No problem. I just need to go in every morning at six."

"You're really going to work twelve-hour days?"

He took her hand. "Sure, I need the money. You know what it's costing me to go to college. I'll be paying for it the rest of my life."

"I'm saving a fortune by taking online classes," Vanessa said. "I'm just glad I didn't have to quit. I need my teaching degree so I can take care of this little scamp."

Ethan looked at the beautiful baby on the blanket. Reddish hair. Bright blue eyes. Angelic smile. He looked like his mother and not at all like Professor Nicholson. He shuddered to think how different each of their lives would be had Vanessa allowed Nicholson to pressure her into getting an abortion.

"So you start working Monday?"

"Yes, we're going to lay the foundations for Misty Meadows."

"Will you be working with the same crew?"

Ethan stroked her hair. "Just Stedman Reeves. Everyone else is new."

"He's the guy you worked with last summer, right?"

"Uh-huh. Uncle Ralph asked him to take me under his wing, and we really hit it off. I'm looking forward to finding out what he's been up to."

CHAPTER 9

Early Saturday evening, Brill and Trent sat across from a frazzled Cynthia Davison at the oblong table in the second interview room. Her flight had been grounded overnight in Dallas due to bad weather. And it had taken her until noon to book another flight, which just added to her fragility.

Brill glanced at her watch and hoped no one heard her stomach rumbling. "Ms. Davison, would you like something to drink? We're not quite finished, but we'll wrap this up as quickly as we can."

"I don't want anything to drink. I want to know why my son was gunned down on the sidewalk." Cynthia dabbed her eyes. "What kind of community *is* this?"

"A very nervous one," Brill said. "No one will rest until your son's killer is caught. We just have a few more questions. The gentleman you were in New York with, Chance Brouchard. What kind of relationship did he have with Tal?"

"None. Chance hadn't met Tal yet. That was supposed to happen this summer." Cynthia pushed her wilted hair out of her face. "They were so much alike. I was hoping Chance would be the father figure Tal deserved. Win was such a bully."

"Have you spoken to your ex-husband?"

"I spoke. It's hard to say if Win heard a word I said. He's too busy feeling sorry for himself. That's just like him, though. He'll be consumed with losing his namesake and he won't even realize that he isn't the only person who's lost something precious."

Brill folded her hands on the table. "Tell me about *your* relationship with Tal."

"We were close. I raised him by myself." Cynthia put her fist to her mouth and choked back the emotion. "I thought I would die when he went off to college. I felt so alone. So unneeded. I struggled with depression and saw a counselor. He said I needed to fill the void with something enjoyable. Nothing helped until my sister introduced me to Chance. I do believe he's my soul mate."

Trent picked up a pencil and bounced the eraser on the table. "You must've trusted Tal to have left him on his own while you were attending art shows in New York."

"He's twenty-one. For all practical purposes, he was on his own at Stanton. But his father lives here." Cynthia's cheeks turned bright pink. "I have a life, detective. If Tal needed to reach me, all he had to do was call my cell phone or leave word at my hotel."

"Did you know Tal's friends?" Brill said.

"Yes. His closest ones, anyway. Henry's a musician, plays the saxophone in a jazz band. Martin, Jamie, and Casper are students at Stanton."

"Have you met them?"

"A few times. They all came to Nashville the Saturday after Thanksgiving to go to a concert. They stayed with me."

Trent leaned forward on his elbows. "Can you think of any reason why one of them would want to hurt Tal?"

"Not at all. They seemed to get along famously. I could've done without the beer drinking, but the boys were enjoyable company."

"Your ex-husband seems to think that Tal had a drinking problem."

Cynthia wiped the mascara out from under her eyes. "I had some concerns about it too. What difference does it make now?"

"We're just trying to establish where he spent his time and with whom. We're looking for a motive. We've questioned each of the friends you mentioned. They seemed fond of Tal and devastated by what happened. There's nothing that would lead us to think any of them were involved."

"Everyone who knew Tal liked him," Cynthia said. "He wasn't the kind of kid who made enemies. I got the impression the shooting was random."

"It's possible, ma'am." Trent wrote on his ruled pad. "We're looking at all angles. So you haven't met Tal's roommate, Drew Langley?"

Cynthia shook her head, plucking another tissue from the box. "But I feel for what he's been through. What a brave young man."

Brill's phone vibrated. She took it off her belt clip and checked to see who was calling. "Excuse me a moment." She got up and walked outside in the hallway. "What is it, Beau Jack?"

"We've got another body, ma'am—a real heartbreaker."

❖　❖　❖

Brill turned on to Fifth Street and spotted flashing lights. A small crowd of people stood behind a police barricade on the sidewalk, and the WSTN-TV camera crew was set up across the street.

She pulled next to Detective Beau Jack Rousseaux's plain-wrap car and looked over at the freshly painted tan bungalow and the For Sale sign in the front yard. Beau Jack was standing in the driveway near the detached garage.

She got out of her squad car and walked toward him, and he met her halfway.

"Where's the victim?"

"Over there." Beau Jack pointed to the side yard.

"Who found her?"

"Next-door neighbor. He came around here to mow and spotted her on the ground."

"Have you ID'd her?"

"Not yet. She's Caucasian. Twelve years old, give or take. She sustained a gunshot wound to the neck and probably bled out. The house is vacant. The owners moved out a few months ago. The Realtor said she hasn't shown the house in a couple of weeks."

Brill walked over and knelt next to the body. She held her breath and slowly pulled back the sheet. The girl's skin was too badly discolored to tell what she looked like, but she was blonde.

"This child's been dead awhile."

"Yes, ma'am. The medical examiner will have to tell us for sure, but I'm guessing thirty-six to forty-eight hours."

"Have you checked with missing children?"

"We're doing that now."

Brill covered the girl's face with the sheet and stood, her throat tight with emotion. "If I ever get used to this, detective, it'll be time to get out of police work. Show me where she was shot."

Beau Jack led her to the front steps. "Blood spatter indicates she was sitting on the bottom step at the time of impact. The bloody handprints suggest she struggled to get up, and the blood trail leads to the place we found her. She probably tried to run after she got shot and collapsed. She would've bled out quickly."

"Why was a child her age sitting on the steps at a vacant house?"

"We found a pink backpack in the corner of the front porch. There's no name on it. All we found inside was candy and potato chips. But we also collected wrappers and empty Coke cans on the porch. If her parents registered her prints and DNA, we should be able to identify her."

"The body decomp puts her death in the same time frame as the other shootings." Brill looked over at the street. "We know the shooter came this way. I want to know who this child is and what she was doing here."

"I'm thinking maybe she's a runaway and was using the porch as a place to hang out and sleep. She would've been hidden from view."

Brill sighed. "Too bad she wasn't sleeping when our shooter drove by."

Tessa Masino peeked out through the curtains and watched Ethan and Vanessa, hand in hand, amble down Azalea Lane, pushing Carter in the stroller.

"What's got your attention, love?" Antonio's voice was rascally. "Let me guess: Vanessa and Ethan?"

Tessa let go of the curtain and sat at the table. "I think their relationship is growing into something."

"And this is your business because …?"

"Vanessa is a prayer concern, Antonio. You know that." The corners of her mouth twitched. "They do seem suited, don't you think?"

"Hey, don't get me in the middle of this. You're the *intercessor*, which I hope doesn't become a synonym for nosy neighbor."

"If caring about someone's future equates to nosy neighbor, then I plead guilty."

"I care." Antonio took a bite of black cherry ice cream. "Vanessa's a sweetheart, and I want her to find a good husband who'll also be a dad to her little boy. But those two kids have another year of college to get behind them. And then graduate school for Ethan. They're better off not falling in love right now."

Tessa patted Antonio's hand. "Oh, come on. It's fun to watch a budding romance. After all the Jessups have been through, it's wonderful to see a little sweetness and light over there."

Antonio wiped his mouth with a napkin. "Can't argue with that. They've been through the mill since they moved here." He picked up the TV remote and released the Mute button. "Let's check this out. Looks like breaking news."

"WSTN News has just learned that the police have identified the girl whose body was discovered earlier this evening in the side yard of a vacant house on Fifth Street but won't release her name because she's a minor. According to a source inside the medical examiner's office, the girl had been dead between forty and forty-eight hours when she was discovered.

"Police believe the girl was shot in the neck while sitting on the front steps of a vacant house and then walked about forty feet into the side yard, where she collapsed and died. Her body was discovered by the next-door neighbor who was out mowing his lawn.

"Detective Beau Jack Rousseaux told reporters that the bullet that killed the girl came from the same gun that killed Tal Davison and Skyler Roberts during Thursday night's deadly shooting spree.

"Rousseaux would not elaborate, but he told reporters that an accumulation of Coke cans and junk-food wrappers found on the porch of the vacant house led police to believe that the victim had spent some time there. It is unknown at this hour whether the girl had even been reported missing.

"People here in Sophie Trace are both stunned and outraged that three young people have been shot and killed by an unidentified shooter who is still at large.

"We will keep you updated with the latest details of this story. This is field reporter Liza Edmonds reporting live from Sophie Trace …"

Tessa put her hands to her ears. "I can't listen anymore, Antonio. It's bad enough that three people have died—but a child?"

Ethan nestled next to Vanessa on the living room couch at Drew's. How much longer before Drew went to bed and he could spend some time alone with her?

"The news isn't very promising." Drew turned off the TV. "Three victims, and the police still don't have leads."

"At least they know what kind of truck the shooter was driving." Vanessa linked her arm in Ethan's. "Maybe someone will put two and two together and call the police."

"Vanessa's right," Ethan said. "Whoever did this must be nervous that he killed three people."

"Or proud of it." Drew chewed his lip. "I'd like to get my hands on him for making Tal suffer like that ..." His voice cracked. "I'm going to knock myself out and get some sleep. Thanks for bringing me dinner."

"You're welcome," Vanessa said. "Good night."

Ethan got up and put his arm around Drew. "You're coming to church with us in the morning, aren't you?"

"I'm not in the mood for praise and worship *or* a bunch of questions."

"I can shield you from the questions," Ethan said.

"Well, you can't hide me from God! And I really don't want to talk to Him right now, *okay?*"

"Okay. But He can handle your anger. It's one of the stages of grief."

"Ethan, stop it! I really don't care what *stage* I'm in. I just don't want to go to church or be around people."

Vanessa shot him a look. Was she telling him to back off?

"Fair enough." Ethan squeezed Drew's shoulder and then put his hands to his side. "Get some rest."

"I will. Good night."

Ethan waited until Drew went upstairs and then turned to Vanessa. "Come on, let's go out on the porch."

"I can't stay much longer. I need to get home. Carter almost always wakes up at least once. Emily's an angel to watch him, but I don't want to take advantage of her."

Ethan took Vanessa by the hand and went out on the porch.

He pulled her into his arms and let his lips melt into hers, and then slowly, reluctantly, longingly he pulled back and just held her.

"I've had such a great time today," he said.

"Me, too. The picnic was fun, wasn't it? And Carter sure loved it."

"He's a beautiful kid. Takes after you."

"Hopefully that will make him less curious about his father," Vanessa said.

"You ever going to tell Carter why his father didn't stick around?"

"Not until he's old enough to understand how dangerous it would be to go looking for him." Vanessa was quiet for a few moments. "But I'm not going to lie to him either. I think it's enough for him to know that his father disappeared and the authorities couldn't find him."

"Are you going to tell him that his father wanted you to get an abortion?"

"No. He doesn't need that rejection on top of everything else."

Brill sat with Trent on one side of an oblong table; Lonnie Benchfield, the father of the latest victim, sat on the other. Two of Brill's detectives were questioning his wife in the other interview room.

"Mr. Benchfield, I know this is tedious and you're tired," Brill said. "But I want to go over a few things again."

"You should be out looking for the killer." Lonnie raked his hands through his hair. "You know *I'm* not the one who shot Natalie."

Brill folded her hands and held his gaze. "Tell me again why you didn't report your daughter missing."

"She threw one of her teenybopper tantrums and said she was going to her grandmother Sewell's house."

"That was Thursday night after dinner?"

"Right."

"And it didn't occur to you to check and see if Natalie got there okay?"

"No, we assumed she was fine. She only had to walk eight blocks." Lonnie's lip quivered, his gaze fixed on his hands. "Look, you need to understand something. Natalie constantly pitted us against each other. We were grateful for the peace and quiet. We had no reason to think she wouldn't go to her grandmother's. She'd done it plenty of times before."

"Weren't you concerned the next day when the school called and reported her absent?"

Lonnie's cheeks flushed. "No, we figured Natalie talked her grandmother into letting her skip school. My wife covered for her, told the nurse she was home with the stomach flu."

"Are you in the habit of letting Natalie's grandmother make those decisions?"

"No, but school's out next week and Natalie wasn't going to miss anything. We thought it was more important for her to get a grip."

Trent picked up a pencil and wrote something on his ruled pad, then bounced the eraser on the table. "If this hadn't happened, when *would* you have checked on your daughter? What kind of father lets a thirteen-year-old girl leave home and doesn't even check on her for two days?"

"Look, I'm not proud of the way her mother and I handled this, but we thought she was at her grandmother's. I told you Natalie's a troublemaker. We just wanted some peace in the house."

"Do you have other children?" Brill said.

"We have a son, Garrison. He's two."

"How did Natalie treat him?"

"A lot better than she treated her mother and me."

"You said you don't know why Natalie didn't go to her grandmother's house. I'm not buying that."

"What do you want from me?"

"I want to know what you aren't telling us."

Lonnie cracked his knuckles and glanced up at the two-way mirror. "All right ... she might've been trying to punish us."

"For what?"

"For taking away her cell phone. She's on that thing day and night and went way over on her minutes *again*. I locked it up."

Trent threw his hand up. "That explains why we didn't find a cell phone in her backpack. Why didn't you mention this before?"

"I didn't think it was relevant."

"*Everything's* relevant," Trent said. "When did you take her phone away?"

"The day she left. Right after she got home from school. She didn't blink an eye when she handed it over. She knew what she did."

Brill leaned forward on her elbows. "I can understand why you didn't expect to hear from Natalie. But wouldn't you have expected her grandmother to call and tell you she had arrived safely?"

"Not really." Lonnie's eyebrows came together. "My mother-in-law doesn't like me. She sides with Natalie on almost everything. I figured her silence was just her way of rubbing my nose in it."

"Why didn't your wife call her?" Trent said.

"Ask *her.*"

"I'm asking *you.*" Trent put his face in front of Lonnie's. "You left your vulnerable young daughter to fend for herself and didn't even check on her. At the very least, that's gross negligence!" Trent brought his fist down on the table. "You could be looking at jail time. So I suggest you wipe that indignant look off your face and answer the question."

"Jail time? But I … I mean, all we wanted was …" Lonnie hesitated a moment, then lowered his voice. "All right, all right, I'll tell you. We didn't call because it always ends with my mother-in-law's lecture on how we wouldn't have these problems if we took our kids to church. Like that's going to solve everything."

Well, it's certainly a good starting place, Brill thought. "We'll need to examine Natalie's phone records and see who she'd been talking to before she left. You said she had a computer?"

"A laptop. I'll give you her phone, her computer, whatever you want. But I'm done talking. I want a lawyer."

CHAPTER 10

Brill inhaled the aroma of fresh-brewed coffee and smiled when she remembered it was Sunday. She turned on her side, pulled the covers up to her chin, and nestled in the warmth of the downy-soft duvet. She didn't have to budge until eight.

An image of Natalie Benchfield popped into her mind and she willed it away. This morning was for rest. No corpses. No police work.

She heard the door open and close, and the delicious smell of fried bacon wafted under her nose.

"You're not going to make me move, are you?" she said sleepily, one eye open.

"Heavens, no." Kurt's tone had a familiar pied-piper quality to it. He crawled into bed and lay on his side facing her. "But I brewed a pot of Starbucks Breakfast Blend and warmed those giant jelly rolls that Tessa made. Emily cooked up some bacon and made a fruit bowl of strawberries, bananas, and blueberries. But you've still got forty-five minutes before you have to start getting ready for church. If you'd like to sleep in, we'll save you some."

Brill opened both eyes, and Kurt flashed her that charming Kevin Costner grin that usually accompanied his acts of kindness.

"My mouth is watering now. I'll never be able to go back to

sleep." She sat up and swung her legs over the side of the bed, then slowly stood and stretched her lower back.

Kurt grabbed her robe off the chair and helped her slip it on, then pulled her into his arms and held her. "Have I told you today that I love you, Mrs. Jessup?"

"I'm not sure. Up until now, I've been comatose."

He cupped her face in his hands and pressed his lips to hers. "I love you. Always have and always will."

"I love you too—so much."

"I promise you'll never have to doubt it ever again. Come on, let's eat breakfast while the jelly rolls are warm."

Brill went out to the kitchen, Kurt on her heels, and saw that the table was set with the floral place mats and white dishes she used when they had company. "How nice. You even put roses in the bud vase."

"I'll bring everything to the table," Emily said.

"Did someone call Vanessa?"

"I'm here." Vanessa walked through the doorway, Carter on her hip.

She strapped him in the high chair and then sat at the table. "Ethan's going to meet us at church."

"What about Drew?" Kurt said.

"Drew won't go. I think he's mad at God."

"Give him time." Brill took a sip of orange juice. "I saw the murder scene and how shaken he was by Tal Davison's death. He's probably processing the whole thing. I'm sure it was traumatic."

Emily set the fruit bowl on the table, then brought a platter of bacon and a basket of jelly rolls and bagels. She sat next to Carter.

The baby reached out and tried to touch her, his smile lighting up the room, but she didn't seem to notice.

"You feeling okay, sweetie?" Brill said.

"I'm fine."

"Why the long face?"

Emily looked up and wrinkled her nose. "I read in the newspaper about the girl that got shot. She wasn't that much older than me."

So much for putting police work on hold, Brill thought. "What happened to her is a tragedy. She was in the wrong place at the wrong time."

"But a gang member did it, right?"

Fear had stolen the sparkle from Emily's bright blue eyes. Was she remembering her horrible ordeal with Eduardo Mendez?

"Emily, gangs typically do drive-bys to intimidate rival members or someone related to a rival member. That's not what happened in this case."

"So the gangs aren't back?"

"We can't say that for sure yet, but it doesn't seem likely. How about we say grace and enjoy this wonderful breakfast while it's still warm?"

❋　❋　❋

Ethan buttoned his dress shirt and tucked it in, then fastened the belt on his trousers.

"*Somebody* is trying to impress the family." Drew stood in the doorway, his arms folded across his chest.

"I'm not sure a blue shirt and tan trousers qualify as *impressive.*

Now this new tie"—Ethan held up a blue, red, and tan paisley tie—"that's another story."

Ethan sat on the bed and slid on his favorite loafers.

Drew stared at him, a silly grin on his face. "You polished your shoes."

"So?"

"I've known you all my life. I can't remember the last time you polished a pair of shoes. Or wore a tie. You've got it bad, Cuz."

Ethan laughed, then picked up a pillow and threw it at him. "I don't need this harassment. I'm going to church with the Jessups. I thought I should look worthy to have their gorgeous daughter on my arm."

"She's gorgeous, all right." Drew seemed to study him. "Can I ask you a personal question?"

"Go ahead."

"If she *wasn't* such a knockout, would you be as willing to accept the baby as part of the package?"

"Sure. Carter's great, and he's part of Vanessa."

"He's also part of someone else. Can you handle that?"

"Obviously I can, Drew, or I wouldn't be pursuing her for all I'm worth."

Ethan went over to the mirror and started to comb the tangles out of his curls.

"What if the baby's father decides he wants back in the picture? He has rights."

"He won't be back."

"You don't know that."

"Yeah, I do."

"Who *is* the dad, anyway?"

Ethan pushed his round glasses higher on his nose and locked gazes with Drew in the mirror. "No one you know."

"Have you ever met him?"

"Actually I have."

"Did you like him?"

"I had mixed feelings. Look, the guy is out of the picture by choice, and it's permanent. Carter will never know him."

"Does he pay child support?"

"It's none of your business, Drew. Back off."

"I'm just watching out for you. Kids cost a fortune. I don't want you getting in over your head just because Vanessa's hot."

Ethan walked over to Drew and stood face-to-face. "Don't refer to Vanessa that way again. Show some respect. My attraction to her goes way beyond chemistry."

"Are you in love with her?"

"There's *something* serious going on. It's hard to get her off my mind."

Drew put his hands in the pockets of his cargo shorts and looked down, his feet rocking from heel to toe. "You've got grad school ahead of you. Do you think it's smart to get sidetracked right now?"

"I can handle it."

"Can you?"

"What's that supposed to mean?"

"I just don't want you to do something you'll regret."

"Like what?"

There was a long, awkward pause.

Finally Drew said, "I'm sure you know it would complicate things if your relationship with Vanessa got too … *physical.*"

"Give me a little credit, will you?" Ethan held tightly to his cousin's shoulders and looked him squarely in the eyes. "I'm not going to change my mind about saving sex for marriage just because I'm falling for Vanessa—not that it's any of your business."

"I thought you might feel differently since—"

"Since what—she's already been with someone?"

Drew shrugged. "I guess so."

"Well, you guessed wrong. I'm done answering personal questions."

Drew flopped on the bed. "It's just that you've never shut me out of anything before."

"I'm not shutting you out. But we're both adults now. I'm not going to climb up to the tree house and tell you everything that's going on in my life. My relationship with Vanessa is private. Understood?"

"Understood." Drew put his hands behind his head. "Actually, I like Vanessa. You two look good together. I'm happy for you."

Tessa Masino breezed in the front door to Nick's Grill, Antonio right behind her. She stood for a moment, cooling herself under the ceiling fan, and admired the dark green vinyl booths and faux wood table-tops that looked as fresh and new as they had when Nick remodeled a couple years back. This year's addition of an oak laminate floor had warmed the place up immeasurably.

She put her lips to Antonio's ear. "I would be beside myself if you had this same flooring put in our kitchen. It could be my birthday present."

Antonio chuckled. "More like Christmas, anniversary, Mother's Day, and birthday thrown into one."

Nick waved and hurried over to them. "Welcome, friends. The Sunday special is a grilled salmon pasta that'll knock your socks off. Big chunks of salmon, veggies, and penne pasta tossed together in a light creamy sauce and served in a pastry shell. Key lime pudding for dessert."

Tessa put her hand on her heart. "Sounds so good."

"No chance you're going to let me have a triple bacon cheeseburger deluxe and sweet potato fries?" Antonio said.

Tessa rolled her eyes in response and walked over to the counter, where Gus and Maggie were already seated.

"Hello, hello," Tessa said. "How was church?"

"We joined the seniors' Sunday-school class today." Maggie took Gus's hand. "My other half kept the discussion lively."

Antonio slid onto the stool between Tessa and Gus and slapped Gus on the back. "How's it going, friend?"

"Really can't complain, but I always do."

"So what do you know?"

Gus stroked his white mustache. "It's mighty sad the authorities found another shooting victim—a kid to boot."

"I should say so." Tessa shook her head. "I'm just sick over it."

"Kinda odd her parents hadn't reported her missin', though."

"Downright criminal," Antonio said. "Who loses sight of a kid that age for two days? They ought to be charged with neglect."

"According to WSTN," Maggie said, "the parents thought the girl was with her grandmother."

"Thought?" Antonio looked over at Maggie. "Isn't it their job to *know?*"

"This girl might have lied to both," Tessa said. "She wouldn't be the first thirteen-year-old to play family members against each other."

"Still doesn't explain what her backpack and trash were doin' on the front porch of that vacant house," Gus said.

The corners of Antonio's mouth curled up. "Maybe she had a secret powwow with the red shadows."

"Please don't get him started, Antonio." Tessa exhaled loudly enough to show her disgust.

"Don't worry"—Gus waved his hand—"I'm not gonna tell you what I think."

"Since when?"

"Since now. Those of us who believe that the red shadows are behind the unexplained crimes in this town are wastin' our breath discussin' it with those of you who don't."

It's about time, Tessa thought. She bit her lip and resisted the temptation to respond.

Nick walked behind the counter, a bar towel draped across his shoulder. He bent down and spoke softly. "I just found out the name of the little girl who was shot: Natalie Benchfield."

"Who told you?" Antonio said.

"I can't say, but it's someone in the know. Keep it to yourselves. Maggie, what's wrong?"

"I know that name. The Benchfields are customers. They come in on Saturdays. They had a middle-school-age daughter and a son that needed a booster seat. I remember the name because Mr. Benchfield always paid by credit card—and because I felt sorry for the daughter. People always made over her baby brother. I made it a point to compliment her."

"Oh, yeah," Nick said. "I think I remember. Wasn't she a little blonde?"

"Uh-huh. Tiny thing. Cute as a button except for the heavy eye makeup adolescent girls seem to like. I can't believe she got killed in a shooting."

Gus squeezed Maggie's hand. "When'd you see her last?"

"Just a couple weeks ago. She'd just gotten braces and seemed pretty proud of them, like it was a rite of passage or something."

"I remember our Sabrina at that age." Tessa sighed. "I would have been devastated if something like this had happened to her."

"Yes, but we would never have lost track of her for two days," Antonio said. "I don't mean to sound judgmental, but her parents should've known where she was."

Brill stood at the window in her office, her hands clasped behind her back. Below, on the well-manicured grounds of city hall, a boy in a red shirt threw a Frisbee to a sleek Irish setter that leaped in the air to catch it. Two young women walked side by side on the sidewalk, pushing babies in their strollers. Through the trees she could see beyond the hazy foothills to the Great Smoky Mountains silhouetted in the distance.

A knock at the door startled her and she turned around.

"Come in, Trent."

"We finished reviewing the phone records and the past month's emails of each of the victims. There were no red flags except for this, and I'm not sure it's even related to the shootings." Trent walked over to her and handed her a folder. "Look at these emails between Natalie Benchfield and someone who refers to himself as Vincent."

Brill read several of the exchanges and glanced up at Trent. "Natalie was emailing back and forth with a man she met in a chat room?"

"Sure was. Some of it's provocative. Her parents don't seem to know anything about it. Said they trusted her and didn't put any parental controls on her computer. This Vincent character said they should set up a time to meet."

Brill sighed. "And did they?"

"She gave him her cell number the day before she left home. Her phone records show that she got a five-minute call from an untraceable number—a prepaid cell phone—on Thursday afternoon just after school let out. It's the last call she got before her dad took her phone away."

Brill shook her head. "Are you thinking what I'm thinking?"

"Yeah. It's possible Natalie had already arranged to meet Vincent *before* she got into the fight with her dad."

"Then it's possible she provoked the fight to give her an easy way to leave the house." Brill read another page of the email dialogue. "Clearly, Vincent whoever-he-really-is was looking for more than friendship. It's hard to say from their back-and-forth just how naive Natalie was or wasn't."

"I'm guessing *wasn't*. On page five she gives him a detailed description of the undergarments she was wearing."

"She was thirteen, for heaven's sake." Brill shook her head and handed the file to Trent. "Have you told her parents?"

"That's my next stop."

"All right, let's pursue this as a possible child molestation case. Talk to the medical examiner and let's see if we can get a DNA match to someone in our sex-offender database." Brill looked out through the blinds on the glass wall to the busy detective bureau. "This girl might have been the victim of two separate crimes."

Late Sunday evening, Ethan stood on the porch at Drew's and gave his mother an extra-long hug, the flowery fragrance of her hair reminding him of Vanessa's.

"If you two need anything," Lisa Langley whispered, "and I mean *anything,* you call us."

"We will, Mom."

Lisa turned to Drew and cupped his face in her hands. "Are you sure we can't talk you into coming to Maryville with us for a few days?"

"Thanks, Aunt Lisa. But I've got a final on Tuesday. You'd just have to run me back over here."

Tom Langley shook Drew's hand and then pulled him into a bear hug. "Lots of people are praying for you, Drew. You're going to get through this."

"Thanks, Uncle T. I know I will."

A second later, the four of them converged, and it was hard to tell who was hugging whom.

"You and Mom be careful on the road," Ethan said. "As soon as we can, Vanessa and I will drive over to see you."

"That'll be great," Tom said. "Okay, Mama, let's get out of here and let these young men wind down. Drew, I hope you do great on your final. And Ethan, I hope you get off to a good start on the job. I told Ralph if he doesn't treat you right, he'll have to answer to me."

So why doesn't he answer to you for not treating Drew right?

Ethan walked out on the porch, the sky overhead a blazing mantle of lava pink, and stood with Drew as his parents walked to their car, waving as they drove off.

"That wasn't so bad, was it?" he said to Drew.

"Not at all. I didn't realize how much I've missed them. Thanks for giving them a heads-up about my not wanting to talk about the shooting."

"They weren't looking for details," Ethan said. "I think they just wanted to see for themselves that you were all right."

"So did I pass inspection?"

Ethan turned and followed Drew inside and flopped on the couch next to him.

"Yeah, I think they can drive back to Maryville now and stop worrying about the two of us fending for ourselves."

"Good. It was nice getting together with them, but I feel guilty taking you away from Vanessa the evening before you start your job."

"Somebody had to do it. I'd never leave her on my own." Ethan smiled. "I did enjoy going to church with her family and having lunch with them. But it was great seeing my parents, too. And now I need to go call her and get to bed early so I don't sleep through my alarm in the morning."

"You seem pumped about working for Uncle Ralph."

"Yeah, it'll be okay."

"It'll be better than okay, Ethan. I'm glad that you two get along great."

"Well, it bugs me that you don't have a relationship with him."

"It's nothing new. Why is it bothering you all of a sudden?"

Ethan shrugged. "Maybe because you're hurting. You're his brother's son, Drew. The same as me. How can he ignore you?"

"Because he and Dad parted ways a long time ago. I've accepted it."

"I guess I haven't." Ethan put his hand on Drew's knee. "You going to be okay alone all day tomorrow?"

Drew nodded. "Yeah, don't worry about me. I've got some serious studying to do. I doubt I'd open the door even if the president himself rang the bell."

CHAPTER 11

Ethan parked in front of Langley Concrete Company and took the keys out of the ignition, then sat for a few moments, savoring the fiery streaks of hot pink and purple that painted Monday morning's sky. When was the last time he was up before the sun?

The air was still cool, but the forecast called for sunny skies and temperatures in the mid eighties.

He grabbed a big bottle of water and his lunch pack off the passenger's seat and got out of the car, proud of himself for making two peanut butter and jelly sandwiches the night before. He'd thrown in a bag of chips, a package of Oreos, and a couple of granola bars for snacks.

He heard a motor and saw a black truck pull into the parking lot. The young bearded driver waved at him, then pulled into the space next to him and got out.

"Hey, Ethan. Good to see you, man."

The voice was familiar and unmistakable.

"Stedman! The beard threw me for a minute. I like it." Ethan walked around the front of the car and shook Stedman Reeves's hand. "What've you been up to?"

"Oh, working mostly. Same old."

"Still dating that cute gal with the Mustang convertible?"

Stedman laughed. "Actually I'm free of entanglements at the moment. I hear you're going to be working with us again all summer."

"Yeah, that's the plan."

"Ralph mentioned that you stayed in touch with Vanessa while you were away at school."

"I did. Saw her and Carter every chance I got. We're going to see how things go over the summer. So where do we start this morning?"

"Misty Meadows—get used to the name. We've got foundations and driveways to pour for the entire housing development. We'll be working there all summer. First we need to get your paperwork done. Come inside. Tonya's got it ready."

"Who's Tonya?"

"She keeps the office running smoothly and takes care of the scheduling. She tries to be a tiger, but she's really a pussycat."

Ethan followed Stedman inside and was hit with the aroma of fresh-brewed coffee. A fifty-something woman sat at the reception desk, working at a computer. Her bleached-blonde hair was chin length and straight, her roots dark, her mascara heavy. She looked at Ethan over the top of her glasses, the name *Tonya* displayed in glittery letters across the front of her T-shirt.

"You must be Ralph's nephew Ethan." Her voice was deep and husky. "I'm Tonya Mason."

"Nice to meet you." Ethan shook her hand and noticed that her nails were long and painted pink and she had multiple jeweled rings on her fingers.

"I've got all the paperwork you need to fill out. We're only doing the legal stuff. We can bypass the personal information and job history. Would you like a cup of coffee while you sit down and take care of this?"

"Uh, sure. Where's the pot and I'll help myself?"

Tonya removed her glasses, which hung from a gold chain around her neck, and handed him a clipboard with some papers attached. "Here, you get started on this and I'll bring you a cup. How do you like it?"

"Cream and sugar please."

She walked over to a built-in cabinet against the wall, where Ethan spotted the coffeepot. He noticed she was wearing designer jeans and high heels.

"Uncle Ralph has made some improvements to the office since I was here last summer. Looks nice. I like the wood floor."

"I'm crazy about it," Tonya said. "It's the same red oak laminate Nick used down at the Grill. Doesn't show a thing and easy to clean. That old carpet was nasty with stains. You boys aren't exactly neat, if you know what I mean."

Ethan looked around the room. Three metal desks, three computers. Light wood paneling on the walls. Plaid curtains on the windows. His uncle's photographs of the Great Smoky Mountains hung in all the right places. Nice.

"Ralph said you boys are going to be up to your elbows in the Misty Meadows project."

Ethan rubbed his hands together. "Yeah, I'm ready to get dirty. That's what he's paying me for. My paychecks will all get recycled to the University of Memphis. I'm just grateful for the job."

Tonya handed him an insulated cup filled with coffee. "Ralph's so proud of you he's busting his buttons. Don't let it go to your head.

Now hurry up and get that paperwork signed. I need you two out of my hair. I've got work to do."

"Yes, Ms. Tonya," Stedman said with mock reverence in his voice. "May I please use the bathroom? I promise to put the lid down."

"See that you do. And you"—she turned her gaze on Ethan—"sit over there. Press hard so the ink will show up on the copies."

Ethan set his clipboard on an empty desk and sat in the swivel chair. He looked over at Tonya, who was obviously enjoying this. "It's clear who's boss around here. Just curious … what happens if Stedman forgets to put the lid down?"

She set her glasses on her nose, the corners of her mouth twitching. "I'll shoot him, and then dispose of the body."

Vanessa sat at the kitchen table and sipped a cup of coffee, listening to the sound of Emily playing with Carter out on the screened-in porch. Through the bay window she could see the foothills half-lit with the first rays of dawn.

Brill breezed into the kitchen, dressed in her uniform, her red hair still wet and straight as a pin. "Oh good, I'm glad to have a few minutes alone to talk to you." She poured a cup of coffee and sat across from Vanessa, wearing a toothy grin much like Emily's when she had a secret she was dying to tell. "Your dad and I had a discussion last night, and we think you should forget about working a summer job and enjoy the time with Carter. You need a break."

"Not having to study is a break, Mom. I want to contribute. It's not cheap having the two of us here."

"We're doing fine." Brill took a sip of coffee. "Wouldn't you like a chance just to unwind and be with Carter whenever you want?"

"Sure. But I knew the sacrifices I'd need to make when I chose to raise him as a single mom."

"Of course you did. But your deciding to take online classes has left a surplus in the college fund. We want you to keep using that money all summer to cover living expenses for you and Carter. You've worked really hard. We want you to unwind and be ready to tackle your senior year."

"That's very generous of you and Dad." Vanessa studied her mother's face. What *wasn't* she saying? "Hmm … I suppose that would also give me more time to spend with Ethan."

Brill covered her smile with her hand. "Okay, so we have an ulterior motive. We like Ethan. We want you to have the chance to see where the relationship's going."

"That's right." Kurt came into the kitchen and stood behind Brill, his hands on her shoulders. "If you wait tables all day, you're going to be exhausted. You'll be torn between giving Carter the attention he needs and Ethan the attention he wants. Both are important. And we don't want you neglecting yourself."

Vanessa's eyes brimmed with tears. Could they have given her anything that would have meant more? "I can't believe you. This is so generous."

"Your father and I are proud of you, honey. We honestly weren't sure how you'd do, trying to balance your studying and taking care of Carter. You've amazed us. We want you to take the summer and enjoy the two men in your life."

Vanessa snatched a napkin out of the holder and dabbed her eyes. "Well, if you're serious, you won't have to ask twice. I'll call the restaurant and tell them I don't need the job after all. They had a list of applicants a mile long. I won't be hard to replace."

❖ ❖ ❖

Vanessa lay on her side atop the powder blue comforter on her bed and caressed Carter's back. She could tell by his breathing that he was in a deep sleep.

She smiled. Her energetic baby boy was exhausted from crawling all over the house and pulling himself up on the furniture. He would probably be walking by the end of the summer. How would she keep up with him?

Her thoughts drifted to Ty Nicholson, and she wondered what name he was using now. Did he ever wonder about his son? What she'd named him? What he looked like?

Sometimes she was so full of love for Carter that she longed for someone to share the joy of parenting with. Ty was not that person. If she'd listened to him, Carter would never have been born.

She stroked the baby's hair and was transported back to the delivery room, to the night of July twenty-third …

"Vanessa, he's beautiful! He's beautiful!" Emily had sounded breathless as she repeated the words over and over.

Someone wearing green scrubs placed the baby on Vanessa's abdomen. There he was: the son she had carried for nine months and whose every move she had felt. The child she had wondered about and fretted over and considered giving up for adoption but couldn't bear to part with. The child she was committed to raising as a single parent. He had been born, still connected to her by the umbilical cord and breathing on his own. The moment was surreal—magical—and she had captured it in her heart so she could revisit it again and again.

Something else that was forever embedded in her memory was Emily's presence during labor and delivery. Every reservation she'd had about a ten-year-old being present for the birth was dispelled by her sister's jubilant reaction.

"He looks like *you.*" Emily's bright blue eyes were almost as wide as her smile. "I didn't know he would be so cute. I thought babies were all wrinkly and red."

"I did too. But his coloring is perfect. *He's* perfect." Vanessa exchanged glances with Emily, who looked adorable in her much-too-large green scrubs. "You did really great as my labor coach. I'm proud of you. So do you still want to be an obstetrician after all that?"

"More than ever." Emily's face beamed. "I couldn't believe how cool it was when Carter was born. I got all tingly and I cried and laughed at the same time. I never did that before."

Hadn't Emily surprised even the doctors and the nurses with her level of energy and exuberance throughout the process? They were patient with her continual chatter and questions and just detailed enough with their responses.

Vanessa figured they broke every rule in the book to accommodate Emily, who never once seemed out of place. Could the bond the two sisters now shared ever be broken—or fully understood by anyone else?

What happened after that was a blur. But she remembered the nurses cleaned up the baby, measured and weighed him, then wrapped him in a receiving blanket. Vanessa held Carter while the nurse put a little blue cap on his head.

"There you go, darlin'," the nurse said. "He's all yours."

All yours. The thought sent her heart racing and her mind reeling. She was at the same time delighted and terrified—as if a part of her had reached a mountaintop while another part had plunged into the depths of the sea.

Had she ever been more afraid in her life than when they wheeled her out of the hospital, her newborn son in her arms, their future uncertain? By then her mother and father were nearly as giddy as Emily over the prospect of having a baby in the house …

Carter breathed in, his exhale a sigh, bringing Vanessa back to the present.

She snuggled closer to him and pressed her lips to his warm, soft cheek. Could she ever love anyone or anything more than she loved this child?

Thank You, Lord, for my son. For Emily. For parents who love me and their grandson. Thank You for loving me and providing for me, even though I did this all wrong.

Vanessa rolled over on her back, her hands behind her head, and watched the ceiling fan go round and round. Was Ethan having a good first day on the job? Would Drew be okay by himself? Maybe she should take Carter for a stroll before lunch and check on him.

CHAPTER 12

Vanessa pushed Carter's stroller on the sidewalk along Spring Creek Boulevard, the tree branches above her forming a thick, leafy canopy, glints of sunlight visible through the cracks. The air was balmy with the promise of summer, and her heart fluttered with thoughts of Ethan.

Was he the kind of man she could spend the rest of her life with? Perhaps it was presumptuous to ponder it at this stage of their relationship. But wasn't it wise to consider it now—before things got more serious?

Ethan had character. Hadn't he proven himself to be a trustworthy friend—unselfish, truthful, reliable? Wasn't he consistently patient and tender with Carter? Was there anyone more tenacious about studying or more willing to work to pay his tuition? Ethan set a goal for his career. He honored his parents. And he put God first.

It wasn't hard at all to imagine him as her husband, her lover, her best friend. A daddy to Carter. A spiritual leader. A beloved member of her family. In every way, Ethan was the type of Christian man she wanted to marry.

If there was anything that gave her pause, it was that Ethan had been true to his commitment to save sex for marriage, and she hadn't. Would he be able to forget about Ty Nicholson when he shared her bed? When he saw her stretch marks and all they represented? Would she?

Neither her repentance nor God's forgiveness could undo the fact that she had already experienced the carnal pleasures that God had reserved for marriage—and that she had gotten pregnant. What if Ethan thought it didn't bother him and found out after they were married that it did?

Or what if he wasn't the lover Ty was? Would it matter to her? Was she awful for thinking of such things? If only she had stuck to her moral values, this wouldn't even be an issue.

Lord, I want whatever You want for me. That's what really matters.

Vanessa turned into the driveway of the familiar two-story red-brick house and carried Carter's stroller up the steps and onto the porch. She rang the bell and waited several seconds before hearing footsteps inside.

The door opened, and Drew Langley stood smiling at her. "Hey. I didn't expect to see *you* today."

"I hope we're not interrupting you."

"I was studying for my English lit final, but I need a break."

"Carter and I were out for a stroll and wanted to bring you some brownies. They're in my backpack. If you'll open the big flap, you'll see the plastic bag, right on top."

Drew stepped outside and squeezed past the stroller, then slipped in behind her. "Wow, I love brownies. Great timing. Thanks."

"You're welcome." She waited as he opened the flap and removed the bag. "I enjoy baking but sure don't need the calories."

"Since when do you have to worry about calories? There's not an ounce of fat on you; isn't that right, Carter?"

She smiled. "I'd like to keep it that way."

Drew came back around and stood just to the left of the front door. "You want to come in?"

"Thanks, but we're really just out for a—"

BANG!

Terror seized her, and she froze.

BANG!

Drew fell backward against the house, his hands clutching his neck and dripping with blood.

Tires squealed.

Vanessa screamed in horror. She fumbled to get the door open, then pushed the stroller into the house and down the hall to Ethan's room and slammed the door shut. She grabbed a chair and wedged the back of it under the doorknob, then turned and covered Carter with her body, the baby clutching her blouse and squalling. She held him close, her heart seeming to pound out of her chest. Or was it his?

Seconds passed. Her ears hurt from Carter's screams. Was it safe to move? Was the shooter gone?

Vanessa removed the chair, cracked the door, and shouted, "Drew …? Drew, can you hear me?"

She pulled Carter out of the stroller and into her arms and realized she was sobbing and shaking. "Shh, it's okay, baby. It's okay."

She stroked his back until they both quieted down, then tiptoed into the living room. The front door was still wide open. She hid behind the fold of the drapes so she could see outside.

"Drew, can you hear me …? Drew …?"

Vanessa looked up the street one way and then the other. She darted out onto the porch where Drew lay next to the blood-spattered bag of brownies, his neck oozing blood, his head lying in a red pool. She felt his pulse. Nothing.

❖ ❖ ❖

Vanessa sat on the couch in Drew's living room, her face in her hands. Why hadn't she seen something? Heard something useful? Drew was killed right in front of her, and she couldn't even help the police.

"Would you like me to repeat the question?" Trent Norris said.

"Uh, yes. I'm sorry. It's hard to stay focused at the moment."

"How many shots did you hear?"

"Two." Vanessa lifted her eyes. "I'm sure. The second shot hit Drew."

"Then what happened?"

"It's kind of a blur. I heard tires squealing, and I pushed Carter into the house and into a bedroom and closed the door and put in chair in front of it. I wanted to run out the back door"—she started to cry—"but I was so scared the shooter would turn around and come back. I felt less vulnerable in the house."

"Did you see the vehicle drive off?"

"No, I just heard the tires squeal. I didn't see the car or the driver. I was facing Drew with my back to the street."

"You didn't hear other shots in the distance?"

"No, but Carter was screaming."

"When you walked down Spring Creek, you approached Drew's house from the east. Do you remember seeing a vehicle parked in the vicinity with someone sitting in the driver's seat?"

Vanessa shook her head. "I really don't. But I was deep in thought and enjoying the walk. I'm no help at all. It happened so fast. One minute he was alive, and the next minute he was dead. It doesn't seem real." Tears streamed down her face.

Brill walked over to the couch and sat next to her. "Trent, I think we've got all we need from Vanessa. We can bring her in later and try to help her remember details."

Vanessa rested in her mother's embrace, her gaze falling on her own bloody footprints that led to the couch. "I wonder if whoever killed Drew thought he knew something about Tal's murder."

"Why would you think that? Did Drew say something?"

"No, but I was uneasy that the shooter might've thought Drew saw something. I even brought it up to Ethan. He said you would've told us if you were concerned."

"Of course I would. Drew was in bed at the time of the shooting, honey. The lights were out in the apartment. There was no reason to assume the shooter thought Drew saw anything more than the other witnesses who spotted the truck." Brill held her tighter. "I would never have put you or your friends at risk."

Vanessa nodded and sat up straight. "I know, Mom. Can I go now?"

"Sure. Give me a few minutes and I'll take you home. Your dad just called. Emily put Carter down for a nap. He's fine."

"How can he be fine? That poor child saw and heard everything. What if it scars him for life?"

"It won't, honey. He's too little to process what happened. He was more than likely reacting to *your* fear."

Vanessa looked around the living room. "Where's Ethan?"

"Two of my officers are in the kitchen talking with him. We're just trying to determine if he's noticed anything strange since he moved in here. Did he mention seeing or hearing anything odd?"

"No, and I'm sure he would have. Mom, I need to be with him."

"We're almost finished questioning him." Brill took her thumb and wiped a tear off Vanessa's cheek. "Ethan's taking it hard. It's obvious he and Drew were really close."

"Like brothers. I can't imagine how his aunt and uncle are going to cope with getting a phone call that their only child was shot and killed. What a disastrous ending to their twenty-fifth anniversary cruise."

Tessa Masino sat next to Antonio at the counter at Nick's Grill, sipping her coffee, waiting for her order.

"Four people dead and we're not even shocked anymore," Gus said. "We're gettin' to be too much like the big city folks, if you ask me."

We didn't ask you, Tessa thought. *But for once, you're right.*

"I'm not blamin' the police chief," Gus added, "but y'all can't dispute that we've had nothin' but trouble since she got here. Some of it followed her from Memphis. That ex-con she helped put away sure shook things up."

"None of it's her fault," Antonio said.

"I know." Gus tipped his glass and crunched a piece of ice. "Just statin' the obvious."

"Most of the violence here is the result of gangs and drugs," Tessa said. "Same as everywhere else."

"So they say." Gus raised his white eyebrows up and down. "I'm not going to tell you again what I think."

That'll be the day, Tessa thought.

"Regardless of who's doin' it, crime's out of control." Gus crunched another piece of ice. "Chief Jessup needs to get the sheriff involved. Sam Parker ... now he's a force to be reckoned with."

Tessa bit her lip, then looked down the counter at Gus. "The crime situation hasn't improved under Sheriff Parker's watch either. Times are changing. Sophie Trace isn't the safe little haven it once was. That's just the world we live in."

"Yeah, well, the police chief's family is involved *again.* Like I said, I'm not *blamin'* her, but it's weird."

"I'm sure she's not happy about it either," Antonio said. "That sweet daughter of hers didn't deserve to witness a murder."

Tessa shook her head. "Those bullets were just inches away from Vanessa and Carter. Makes my skin crawl."

"At least this time the shooter only struck on Spring Creek Boulevard," Maggie said. "I heard on the news they think he fired at least a dozen times. It's amazing no one else was hit."

"It's downright frightening this person can strike anywhere in town," Tessa said. "And in broad daylight."

Gus arched his eyebrows. "Yep."

"The police will find out who is doing this, Gus." Tessa waved her hand dismissively. "And it'll be a flesh-and-blood person, not some mythical red shadow."

"That's the spin the cops will put on it."

"Whoever it is," Antonio said, "he sure is bold to strike in broad daylight. It's like he wants to be caught."

"There has to be more to it than that." Tessa held out her cup as Jo Beth came by with the coffeepot. "I trust Brill to get to the bottom of it."

※   ※   ※

Brill stood at the window in her office and looked down at the empty parking spaces. She heard a knock on the door.

"Why are you still here, Chief?" Trent said.

"I need time to think before I go home."

"I'm sure glad Vanessa and Carter weren't hurt."

"So am I, but what about the four that *were?*" She paused and fought back the emotion that was just below the surface. "It's unacceptable that four young people have been shot dead on my watch."

"There was nothing you could've done. No one saw this coming. It doesn't make sense."

"I won't rest until it does."

"We're spread thin on the investigations."

"I know." She turned around and leaned on the glass, her arms folded across her chest. "I've asked Sam Parker to help us. He's got the manpower. And he's thorough."

"I guess beggars can't be choosers, but I could go the rest of my life without rubbing elbows with Sheriff Parker again."

"I want this shooter badly enough that I don't care who I have to get to help us. And the Natalie Benchfield case is complicated. We need to know who shot her, but we also want to find this Vincent character and find out if she hooked up with him."

Trent nodded. "We've contacted the state police to help us find him from his email address. We'll get him."

"In the meantime, we need to follow every lead to help us nail down the shooter." She looked out the window at the last vestiges of light in the western sky. "I want you and your detectives to meet with the sheriff and me in the morning at nine."

"Where?"

"My office. Come prepared to give a solid overview of where we are with each of the four victims."

"Yes, ma'am. Not a problem. Are you geared up to endure the sheriff's patronizing attitude?"

"As ready as I'll ever be." Brill smiled wryly. "I loathe inviting his big boots onto my turf, but the truth is we need him."

"And he'll be only too glad to remind you of it."

Brill arched her eyebrow. "So be it. But even *he* doesn't have the resources the state police do. That might keep him just humble enough to be tolerable."

Trent laughed. "Oh, I doubt that. I'll see you in the morning. Don't stay too late."

"I won't. I just need to get quiet and deal with the feelings I've stuffed all day. My daughter came *this close* to dying." She held up her thumb and forefinger, an inch between them. "My grandson, too. How many times can my family get that close to death and manage to escape it?"

"I guess as long as the Lord allows it, ma'am."

"I thought you were going to stop calling me ma'am." She locked gazes with Trent. "You're right. But it's my job to do everything in *my* power to keep them safe."

CHAPTER 13

Vanessa nestled with Ethan on the glider on the Jessups' screened-in porch, her head on his shoulder, her arm linked in his. He hadn't said ten words in the past half hour. Not that she needed him to talk. She didn't feel like it either. Every time she closed her eyes she saw Drew's pallid face and vacant eyes—and the bag of brownies spattered with his blood.

How was she supposed to reconcile that one second Drew was standing there, full of life—and the next he was dead? Or shake the bone-chilling reality that she and Carter were so close to the bullets?

She had only recently stopped having nightmares after being accosted by the ex-con who stalked her mother. But this? Would she ever close her eyes again without looking into the face of death?

Ethan breathed in and let out a long sigh. "Drew's parents get in from London at ten thirty in the morning."

"Did you decide to drive to Knoxville to meet their plane?"

"Yes. But I have no idea what to say to them."

"They probably just want to throw their arms around you. You're like a second son to them." Vanessa stroked Ethan's arm. "I imagine that will be a source of comfort."

"I don't know if I can be strong for them."

"You'll help each other."

Ethan was quiet for a moment, then tightened his hold on her. "I can't believe how close I came to losing you."

"But you didn't. We'll get through this together."

Ethan took off his glasses and set them on the side table, then rubbed his eyes. "I'm overwhelmed. It's just too much to process."

"Why don't you get some rest?"

"It was nice of your parents to offer me your brother's room tonight. I'm not sure what to do. If I move back in with Uncle Ralph and Aunt Gwen, Drew's parents might get their feelings hurt. You know my uncles are at odds."

"Maybe this will bring them together."

"I wouldn't count on it. Both are proud and stubborn."

Vanessa looked up at Ethan, seeing the angst pooling in his eyes. "What started the whole thing in the first place?"

"Uncle Richard went off on Uncle Ralph after Drew's baby sister died. Richard apologized later and said it was just his grief talking. Ralph wouldn't accept his apology."

"Do you know why?"

"Just that Ralph didn't think he was sincere."

"Then why doesn't Richard try again?"

Ethan shrugged. "Who knows? They're both stubborn. Sometimes I think they keep the conflict going because it's all they have still holding them together."

"How sad. It seems like twins should be close." Vanessa brushed her fingers through Ethan's fine curls. "You think Drew's parents will be able to go back home after what happened?"

"I hope so. It's still home. That's where the good memories are. But my parents will invite them to stay at their house as long as they want."

"The trek back and forth from Maryville is going to get old when they're arranging their son's funeral."

"My parents will help. I don't want to talk about *them.*" Ethan stroked her cheek and looked into her eyes. "I want to talk about *us.* There's so much I want to say to you."

"Like what?"

His eyes welled and his chin quivered. "I'm so sorry you had to see what happened to Drew. But I'm thankful you're all right …" His voice trailed off.

"At least Drew didn't suffer. I doubt he knew what hit him."

"I can only imagine what was going through your mind."

"All I could think about was protecting my son." Vanessa relived the moment, emotion tightening her throat. "I was terrified the shooter might come back looking for us. I've never been that scared, not even when that guy who was stalking Mom grabbed me."

"I wish I'd have been there for you. It kills me to think of you and Carter hiding in my room with the back of a chair wedged under the doorknob."

Vanessa held more tightly to his arm. "Your being there wouldn't have softened the horror of seeing Drew shot to death. Be glad you *didn't* see it." A tear spilled down her cheek.

"I'm sorry, honey. I really am."

Ethan pulled her into his embrace, and Vanessa began to cry, and then cry harder, not sure which weighed more heavily on her, what had happened or what almost did.

Brill stood at the bathroom sink, dressed in her ivory silk pajamas, and rubbed cleanser on her face. She rinsed it off and patted her face dry, the raw truth staring back at her in the mirror. She couldn't miss the fine lines that fanned out from her eyes or the accordion creases around her mouth—or that the expensive night cream she got duped into buying hadn't "reduced the appearance of wrinkles" to her satisfaction.

Kurt seemed oblivious. His flirting with her made her feel womanly and desirable—in total contrast to how she felt as the buck-stops-here police chief who had zipped up four body bags in as many days.

She couldn't quite shake the image of Drew Langley's lifeless stare. How was she supposed to accept that four young people died on her watch? Or that the shooter was still out there and liable to strike again? Or that her daughter had been through another frightening experience—this time with her baby son so close to the line of fire?

And what were the odds Drew and his roommate died randomly by the hand of the same shooter, but on different days and in different locations? And yet everything pointed to a drive-by in both instances. The bullets that killed all four victims came from the same gun.

"You coming to bed?" Kurt stood in the doorway.

"Yes, I'm through in here."

She started to leave and he blocked the doorway and pulled her into his arms.

"Honey, I'm so sorry these shootings are happening. I can't believe Ethan's cousin is dead. Or that Vanessa and Carter were right there when it happened. Sends chills up my spine."

"That's two of us." Brill nestled in his embrace and let it comfort her. "I want us all to avoid being out front until we get this shooter.

That includes going out for walks. I don't want to overreact. I just want everyone out of the line of fire. I'm still not over how close Vanessa and Carter came to being victims."

"Do you think it was just coincidence that both Drew and his roommate got hit?"

Brill pushed back and looked into Kurt's eyes. "I don't know yet. That's *some* coincidence. Everything points to random shootings. But I think we have to dig deeper."

"How?"

"Retrace our steps. Talk again to the victim's friends, coworkers, and family members."

"Drew's parents will be here tomorrow." Kurt kissed her forehead. "Are you going to question them?"

"Of course. They might know something, though I'm not holding my breath. I'll tell you one thing: I dread looking into the eyes of any more parents who have lost a child. This is one week when I'd gladly give this job to someone else."

Ethan started to turn out the lamp in Ryan Jessup's bedroom when his cell phone rang. The display indicated Stedman was calling. Should he answer it or wait until tomorrow?

He stared at the number for a moment, then put the phone to his ear. "Hey. Sorry I didn't call you back. Time got away from me. I thought I'd wait until morning."

"Not a problem," Stedman said. "How're you holding up?"

"I'm numb. I don't think it's hit me yet."

"I'm really sorry, man. Don't worry about work. You just take care of you. Did your cousin's parents cut their cruise short?"

"Yeah, they flew from Athens to London, then caught a flight home. I'm picking them up at ten thirty in the morning. How did Uncle Ralph seem after my call?"

"Distracted. A little blunt like he gets once in a while. You think he'll go to the funeral?"

"I don't know. He hasn't spoken to his brother in years."

There was a long stretch of silence, and he heard Stedman breathing on the other end of the line.

"I was just about to crash when you called," Ethan said. "I appreciate your checking on me."

"I heard on the news that the first guy to get killed by this mystery shooter was your cousin's roommate. Why didn't you say something?"

"I didn't want to talk about it." Ethan set the alarm clock for six. "I figured Tonya already told you."

"Well, she didn't. So do the cops think it was just a coincidence that your cousin and his roommate were shot by the same gun?"

Ethan raked his hand through his hair. "I don't know. They'll have to pursue it."

"Pursue it how?"

"That's their problem, Stedman. Right now, I just want to get some sleep, okay? It's been a tough day."

"Yeah, sure. Sorry. Let me know if there's anything I can do."

"I will. Good night."

Ethan disconnected the call and set his phone on the nightstand. Of course it was a coincidence. It had to be. Why would anyone deliberately target Drew?

CHAPTER 14

Ethan sat at the oak table in the Jessups' kitchen, looking out the bay window, his hands wrapped around a warm mug of coffee. Between the houses across the street he could see the misty foothills beginning to take shape in the light of dawn. A mockingbird sat atop the bushes, reciting his proud litany of impersonations for an audience of One.

An audience of One. Ethan thought of Drew and tried to imagine him face-to-face with his Creator—no longer wounded or in pain. It wasn't fair that his parents were left with only memories and grief and the lifeless shell of their only child.

Ethan was vaguely aware that someone had come into the kitchen. He turned and saw Mrs. Jessup, dressed in her uniform, pouring a cup of coffee.

"Good morning," he said.

"I tried to be quiet so I wouldn't bother you." She put two teaspoons of sugar in her coffee and stirred.

"It's okay. I'm basically numb."

She sat at the other end of the table and took a sip of coffee. "I know this probably sounds rote, but I really am sorry for your loss. I can only imagine how hard this must be. I know you and Drew were close."

"Closest thing to a brother I ever had." Emotion rose in his throat, and he washed it down with a sip of lukewarm coffee.

"We're going to find out who's responsible, lock him up, and throw away the key. But that won't bring Drew back. I'm so sorry you have to go through this."

"Thanks. I'm sorry Vanessa had to see it. I can't even imagine how I would've handled it if something would've happened to her …" Ethan's voice cracked, and his eyes welled. "Or Carter."

"Me, either." She took a sip of coffee and looked out the window.

How did she stay so cool?

"What time are you leaving for Knoxville?" she asked.

"Nine. Uncle Richard and Aunt Becca get in at ten thirty. I'd rather be early than late. I'm hoping the traffic will thin out by then."

"It should."

Ethan felt as if a mountain were sitting on his chest. How was he going to get up, get to his car, and drive? What was he going to say to his aunt and uncle? All he really wanted to do was crawl back under the covers and close his eyes.

"Are you going by yourself?"

"Yes, ma'am."

She locked gazes with him. "Ethan, I think it's time you called me Brill. Every time you call me ma'am I feel like the police chief or just plain old."

"I'm sorry. I was raised here in the south, and that's the way I was taught."

Brill smiled. "So was I. But you're a friend of the family now. Kurt and I would be very comfortable with you using our first names."

"I might have to practice."

"I'll remind you."

He nodded and stared at his hands. "I'm worried about Vanessa. I think she's trying to be strong for me. But what she went through yesterday was horrific. She can't be all right, just like that."

"I agree. Vanessa's barely had time to get over the last ordeal. But her faith is strong. And maybe it helps her to comfort *you*. We all want to be there for you and help you through this."

"I know you do. I appreciate it."

"You're welcome to stay here as long as you want."

"Thanks, that's kind of you. But I've decided to stick with my original plan and spend the summer with Uncle Ralph and Aunt Gwen. Drew's folks will understand. And if they don't … well, I'm not getting in the middle of the feud between Uncle Ralph and Uncle Richard."

"How does your dad handle his brothers being estranged?"

"He hates it. Dad tried for years to talk sense into Ralph and get him to accept Richard's apology, but he just wouldn't do it. And Richard refused to apologize again. So rather than risk losing his relationship with both brothers, Dad decided not to take sides. Should be interesting at the funeral home. I don't know how many years it's been since they've said a word to each other."

"It's unfortunate"—Brill stared out the window—"but maybe Drew's death will bring the family together."

"He'd be so happy if it did," Ethan said. "I wonder if people in heaven know what's going on down here."

"I've wondered the same thing. I lost both my parents to illness and my in-laws in a tragic automobile accident. All of them were believers so I know where they are. But I wonder about them—what they see and what they know."

Ethan's eyes stung, and he blinked to clear them. "When does it stop hurting?"

"Everyone's different, Ethan. All I can tell you is that it does."

"Do you ever stop missing them?"

Brill seemed to stare at her coffee mug. "No. But the aching goes away."

"Good." Ethan studied her. She really *did* understand the pain he was feeling. But did anyone understand how alone he felt? He couldn't remember a time when Drew wasn't part of his life. It was as though he had lost a part of himself.

"I'll be praying for you today. Let me know if there's anything I can do to help." She downed the last of her coffee and stood. "We're getting the sheriff's department involved this morning. The extra manpower may help us speed up the process. We *are* going to find the shooter and make sure he never gets the chance to do this again."

"Thanks, Brill. I know you'll do your best."

"I won't rest until we get him."

❉   ❉   ❉

Vanessa finished dressing Carter, then picked him up and gave him to Emily.

"He always smells good," Emily said. "Well, except for when he needs his diaper changed."

"I just gave him a bath and rubbed him down with baby lotion. He's fresh as a daisy and extremely huggable."

"I'll play with him as soon as I get home from school." Emily's eyes seemed to search hers. "You look sad."

"I'll be fine."

"I've never seen anybody dead before. Was it really awful?"

"Yes, it was really awful. I'd rather not talk about it."

"Okay." Emily fiddled with a button on her blouse. "I'm sorry Ethan's cousin died. But I'm glad you and Carter didn't. Is that okay? To be glad, I mean?"

"Yes, I'm glad too, but that doesn't mean I'm not upset and sad about Drew."

"He didn't even get to eat the brownies you made."

Vanessa's mind flashed to an image of Drew clutching his bloody neck and the bag of brownies falling to the porch. She blinked it away.

Emily sat Carter on the floor and gave him his toy tool bench and plastic hammer, then stood up tall. "I would've been soooo sad if you and Carter had gotten shot."

Vanessa tilted Emily's chin. "But we didn't. So let's not even go there."

"But I have to. I need to picture it in my mind and then realize it *isn't* real. That's how I've learned not to be afraid of everything that scares me."

"Seems a bit extreme, Emily."

"Well, it works. If I picture you dead and then I see you standing right there, I'm relieved—and not scared anymore."

Vanessa tugged her ponytail. "Whatever. Too graphic for me."

"Of course, I don't really know what you would look like dead because I've never seen anybody dead. But I just use my imagination and—"

"I got it, Shortcake. You don't have to draw me a picture."

"I'm *really* glad nothing bad happened to you. I like it so much better now that you're home. I got lonely when you were at college. But if you hadn't gone to college, you wouldn't have had Carter. So I guess it's good you went."

"I guess it is." Vanessa forced herself not to smile at Emily's rambling. "You're going to be late for school if you don't get going."

"I'm going. Bye, Carter. Auntie Em is going to school now. I'll see you soon and we'll play patty-cake."

Carter flashed a gaping smile that revealed his two bottom teeth and held up his arms, cooing.

"Oh, all right. Who could resist that face?" Emily reached down and picked him up. "I wish I didn't have to go to school so I could babysit you all day. But I have to go now. Go see Mommy."

Emily put Carter in her arms. And for a split second, Vanessa was eleven again, passing baby Emily off to her mother.

"The bell rings in ten minutes!" Kurt hollered from the bottom of the stairs.

"Coming!" Emily looked up at Vanessa. "I think you should stay home until Mom gets the shooter."

✳   ✳   ✳

Ethan stood at the front door with Vanessa. Why was it so difficult not taking her with him to Knoxville to pick up his uncle Richard and aunt Becca?

Vanessa's eyes searched his, and it seemed as though she had her foot in the door to his soul. "I wish I could go with you." She combed her fingers through is hair. "Are you sure you're up to doing this? Seeing Drew's parents is going to be emotional."

"I'm going to have to face them sometime," he said. "I'd just as soon get it behind me. Frankly, I'm worried about *you*. What you witnessed was gut-wrenching, Vanessa. I don't want you downplaying what happened to you just because you know I'm hurting."

"I'll be all right. What I saw still doesn't seem real. Maybe it never will."

"I want to be there for you, if it does."

He put his arms around Vanessa and held her close, her head resting on his chest.

"I hear your heart racing," she said.

"See how you affect me?"

She pushed back and looked up at him. "Or your adrenaline is off the chart. I know you're nervous about what to say to your aunt and uncle."

"I just don't want to fall apart, that's all. They need me."

"You need each other. All three of you probably *need* to fall apart. Just be real about it. Should be easier after that."

Ethan kissed her forehead. "You're starting to sound like me."

"Well, I've been around you long enough. You're starting to rub off on me."

"That's a scary thought." He smiled in spite of himself.

"So what happens after you pick up your aunt and uncle from the airport?"

"I'll drive them to the house and get that out of the way, and then I'll drive them to Maryville. My parents will help them make Drew's funeral arrangements."

Vanessa sighed. "It's going to be awkward for your uncle Ralph. He's the odd man out."

"That's his choice. But he won't feel that way when I'm around. And I'm going back to work as soon as I can. I need to stay busy, and I need the money."

"You'd better get going. I'll be praying that you're safe on the highway, and that you'll be a comfort to your aunt and uncle."

"Thanks." Ethan traced her eyebrow with his thumb. "Do me a favor … stay inside today."

"I'm not going anywhere."

"Good. The more I think about Drew and his roommate being shot by the same gun in two separate incidents, the more I question whether this was really random."

"Then how do you explain the other victims?"

Ethan held her face and looked into her clear blue eyes. "I don't have answers. It's just weird, that's all. But you're an eyewitness, and *that* makes me nervous."

"I didn't see anything. I had my back to the street."

"Just don't go out, okay?"

CHAPTER 15

Brill sat at the conference table in her office, next to Detective Captain Trent Norris and across from Sheriff Sam Parker and Detectives Beau Jack Rousseaux and Spence Marcum.

"I appreciate each of you taking the time to read the case files and meet with me. I want to be sure we're all on the same page. Before we begin, I would like to thank Sam for agreeing to help us investigate these shootings. We always appreciate what he brings to the table."

Sam smiled. His gold tooth was almost as obvious as his utter glee that she had found it necessary to enlist his help *again*. "I assure you, Chief Jessup, the pleasure is mine. I'm always happy to step in when your department gets inundated."

Brill could almost feel Trent bristling. But Sam's condescending attitude was a small price to pay for the extra manpower. Could anyone dispute that the sheriff was as efficient as he was obnoxious?

"We don't have enough officers to investigate four shooting deaths," she said. "We don't want to leave any stone unturned and will gladly accept your help."

Sam's mustache moved slightly, and she figured he was smirking.

"I've asked Trent to summarize what we know so far," Brill said. "I promised not to keep you too long, so I'll turn it over to him."

Trent opened his folder and looked down at his notes.

"Victim number one: Tal Davison. Caucasian male. Age twenty-one. Junior at Stanton College. Shot in the chest on the sidewalk in front of his apartment building at 504 Stoneleigh, at approximately ten forty-five last Thursday night. No witnesses. Davison went inside the apartment after being shot and was found unconscious by his roommate, Drew Langley, who tried unsuccessfully to revive him and called 9-1-1.

"Victim number two: Skyler Roberts. Caucasian female. Age twenty. Sophomore at Stanton. Body discovered on the balcony of her apartment building at 480 Essex by her roommate, Olivia Jones, around eleven a.m. on Friday, when Jones returned after spending the night with relatives in Knoxville. The victim died of a bullet wound to the head. Medical examiner puts the TOD between ten p.m. and midnight the night before.

"Victim number three: Natalie Benchfield. Caucasian female. Age thirteen. Student at Sophie Trace Middle School. Body was discovered next to a vacant house at 507 Fifth Street at approximately six p.m. Saturday by the next-door neighbor. Blood spatter suggests the victim had been shot in the neck while sitting on the front steps. Died in the side yard where she collapsed. The ME determined the victim had been dead between forty and forty-eight hours, which puts the TOD in the time frame of Thursday night's shooting."

Trent turned the page. "Victim number four: Drew Langley. Caucasian male. Age twenty-one. Junior at Stanton. Shot in the neck at his parents' home at 720 Spring Creek Boulevard, at approximately eleven thirty yesterday morning. A friend, Vanessa

Jessup, was standing on the front porch with the victim at the time of the shooting and was not injured. Jessup did not see the shooter or the vehicle."

Trent paused for a moment and then continued. "Also, our third victim, Natalie Benchfield, may have been the victim of an additional crime. Evidence suggests that she planned to meet a man she met on the Internet, known at this time only as Vincent. We're working with state police to trace his email address in an effort to locate him. The medical examiner has not released results of the girl's autopsy, but we could be looking at a child molestation case, too."

Trent scanned the page, turned it, and continued. "Regarding the vehicle, various witnesses have described the truck used in both shootings as a late-model red Ford F-150.

"We've narrowed down the gun. Ballistics determined that the rifling profile of the nine-millimeter Luger-type bullets recovered from each of our victims is unique to Smith and Wesson's second and third generation semiautomatic pistols, which includes all four-digit model numbers.

"That about covers it. Any questions?"

Sheriff Parker leaned forward on his elbows, peering over the top of his glasses, his steely gaze resting on Brill. "Your family does have a way of bein' in the wrong place at the wrong time. How'd your daughter happen to be at the scene at the time of the shooting?"

"Vanessa is dating the victim's cousin," Brill said. "She took her baby for a stroll and stopped by the victim's house to deliver some brownies she had baked. It's all in the report, Sam." *You're not going to make me defensive. Move on.*

Sam rubbed his chin. "Yes, I read the report. I have a few questions. Thursday night's shooting took place within an area of five square blocks near the college. Was there anything significant about that?"

"We don't think so," Trent said. "And after this second shooting occurred along Spring Creek Boulevard, it seems unlikely that either shooting was intended to establish any sort of pattern. It appears the shooter fired randomly in both cases."

"Then you've concluded that Drew Langley was not specifically targeted in yesterday's shooting?"

"We haven't reached a conclusion." Trent glanced over at Brill and then at the sheriff. "But the shooter fired at least a dozen shots along Spring Creek Boulevard after the victim was hit. If Drew Langley was the intended target, it seems unlikely the shooter would have continued to fire and draw attention to himself."

"What do you know about Langley?"

"He was a junior at Stanton on a full scholarship," Brill said. "Dean's list. Good family. No known enemies. No drug use. Squeaky clean."

Sam moved his gaze from her to Trent and back to her. "What about the roommate—Davison?"

"His father is an alumnus and big financial contributor. And the CEO of Davison Technologies. Parents divorced. Liked to hang out with his college buddies. Known to drink too much, but no drugs. No known enemies. We haven't found a reason why either of these young men would be targets."

Brill's temples started to throb. Did she really need Sam Parker second-guessing everything she did?

"You would have me believe that college roommates got shot with the same gun, days apart and at different locations, and it was just coincidence?"

"We haven't finished our investigation, Sam. All we're saying is that we don't have anything yet to suggest otherwise."

"I beg to differ." The sheriff arched his eyebrows. "Davison went inside the apartment after he was shot. Maybe the shooter was afraid he told his roommate who did it."

Brill shook her head. "It's unlikely the shooter would come to that conclusion when the press reported from day one that there were no eyewitnesses."

"The only eyewitness I'm talkin' about is the victim." Sam's eyes turned to slits. "It's not implausible that Davison could've seen who it was who shot him and told his roommate before he died."

"But Davison never regained consciousness after Langley discovered him in the apartment. The media made that clear."

"Maybe the shooter's not takin' any chances."

"Maybe," Brill said. "It just seems unlikely."

Sam leaned back in his chair, his arms folded across his chest, an annoying smirk pasted on his face. "There's somethin' about that pesky word *unlikely* that drives me up the wall. Of course, there is another possibility that I'm sure has crossed your mind." His face was suddenly somber. "The shooter might've been aiming for someone else."

Brill felt a cold chill crawl up her spine. "Meaning Vanessa?"

"Think about it, Chief Jessup. Is there anything you're not telling us?"

✸ ✸ ✸

Tessa Masino stood at the door to Nick's Grill. The green and white striped awning of the Toffee Emporium next door seemed to glow in the noonday sun.

"Will you hold your horses?" Antonio said as he hurried to catch up.

Tessa opened the door to the Grill and was hit with the delicious aroma of Nick's spicy red sauce.

Antonio followed her inside. "Mmm. Today's special doesn't smell low fat."

Nick came over to them, put his hand on Tessa's shoulder, and shook hands with Antonio.

"Today's special is a low-fat veggie ravioli smothered in red sauce that'll knock your socks off. Comes with a green salad and sourdough garlic bread."

"Oh my, that's what I'm having," Tessa said. "What could be better than guilt-free ravioli?"

Antonio smiled. "Seems like an oxymoron."

Tessa went over to the counter, where Gus and Maggie Williams were already seated. "Hello, hello."

"Hey," the Williamses said in unison.

Antonio straddled the bar stool between Tessa and Gus and slapped Gus on the back. "How's it going, friend?"

"Really can't complain, but I always do."

"So what do you know?"

"I'd rather you tell us what *you* know," Gus said. "Has to be a lot goin' on at the police chief's house."

Antonio took Tessa's hand. "There is. They're all relieved Vanessa and that little baby are all right. And devastated that her boyfriend's cousin was killed."

"All Vanessa was doing was bringing brownies to a friend, for heaven's sake." Tessa shook her head. "I spoke with her, and she's beyond shocked. I'm not sure it's sunk in yet."

"God help her when it does," Maggie said.

Tessa sighed. "I don't understand how the shooter could strike in broad daylight without *someone* seeing his face."

Gus leaned forward on the counter. "Ah, that's right. The truck windows were tinted, and no one saw the driver—if there even *was* a driver."

"Don't start with the red-shadows nonsense." Tessa held up her hand.

"All right. But it's not like the spirits of the Cherokee haven't tried to warn us time after time that we stole their land."

Jo Beth stood behind the counter, her green pad in hand. "Y'all ready to order?"

"Specials for us," Gus said.

Antonio nodded. "Same here."

"Coffee all around and a Coke for Gus?"

Everyone nodded.

"Okeydokey. I'll be right back with your drinks."

Jo Beth started to leave but stopped when Maggie called her name.

"I've been meaning to ask you," Maggie said, "how do you manage to get your hair in a braid? It's beautiful."

"Thanks. My husband does it for me. He loves to brush it. I'm fixin' to get it trimmed. I've never had it cut short."

"Where did you get such gorgeous, thick dark hair?" Tessa asked. "It's quite enviable."

Jo Beth smiled. "Thanks. My father's Cherokee."

Tessa looked at Gus, noticing that his face had gone almost as white as his mustache. She wondered if he was taking inventory of all the times he had made reference to the red shadows in Jo Beth's presence.

"You should be in one of those Herbal Essences commercials," Tessa added.

"Thanks. But I don't think I'm glamorous enough for that. Y'all sit tight. I'll place your orders and be right back with your drinks."

Jo Beth went through the double doors, and Gus sat quietly, his hands folded on the counter.

Antonio nudged Gus with his elbow. "Cat got your tongue?"

"How was I supposed to know Jo Beth was half Cherokee?" Gus's face was bright pink.

"Why don't you ask her if her dead ancestors are riding around in a red Ford F-150, shooting Anglos?" Antonio chuckled. "Maybe she'll give you the inside scoop."

Maggie linked arms with Gus and looked embarrassed for him.

Tessa started to say something and then didn't. Why make him feel worse than he already did? If this didn't make him think twice about that silly legend, what would?

Clint Ames slid onto the stool next to Tessa. "Hey, friends. What'd I miss?"

"Oh, nothing worth repeating," Antonio said. "What do you know?"

"Not a thing. And if you don't believe *me*, just ask my wife." Clint laughed and set his sunglasses on the counter. "Have you ordered?"

Nick suddenly appeared at the end of the counter. "A customer just heard on the radio that the police think they found the truck used in the shootings."

"Where?" Tessa said.

"It was parked at Woodall's Grocery overnight. It's stolen. Registered to a man in Pigeon Forge."

CHAPTER 16

Ethan sat in his car and looked out across the milky layers of blue gray foothills to the silhouette of the Great Smoky Mountains that faded in and out of the afternoon sky. Overhead, a hawk soared effortlessly, its wings outstretched, its red tail catching glints of sunlight.

A squirrel crawled up on the hood of his car and stared at him through the windshield, then scurried away.

He slowly drew in a breath and let the tightness in his throat begin to relax. Hadn't he shed enough tears today? Shown enough emotion? Felt enough empathy?

He waited a few minutes more, then got out of the car and trudged over to the construction site where his uncle Ralph was talking with Stedman Reeves. Another man on the crew was hosing off a driveway of freshly poured cement.

Ralph looked up. He hurried over to Ethan and spoke softly. "How'd it go?"

"It was tough. Uncle Richard and Aunt Becca are devastated. They can't think straight. I wouldn't trust either one of them to drive right now. I'm glad they're staying with my folks."

"Did you take them by their house, the way you planned?"

Ethan blinked away the stinging in his eyes. "Yeah, the front porch is still roped off with yellow crime scene tape, but the police allowed us in the back door."

"How long were you there?"

"I don't know, maybe twenty minutes. They went in Drew's room and sat on the bed for a long time. Uncle Richard insisted on seeing the crime scene, so Detective Rousseaux showed it to us." Ethan paused and gathered his composure. "Drew's blood was still there—on the front of the house, and on the porch. Vanessa's bloody footprints, too."

"Did it upset him?"

"Yeah, we all lost it. But in a strange way it helped to see it and understand exactly what happened."

Ralph gently rubbed Ethan's back. "I'm glad Vanessa's all right. And her little boy."

"Me too …" Ethan's voice cracked. "I just want Brill to get whoever did it."

"So you already dropped Richard and Becca off in Maryville?"

"Yeah. When I left, Mom was trying to get them to take a nap. They looked like zombies. I think they were exhausted before they added jet lag to it."

"It's a crying shame they have to go through this."

"Why don't you tell them that?"

Ralph's face turned expressionless. "Don't get on my case about it, okay? It's complicated."

"But isn't this the perfect opportunity to put your differences aside?"

"I don't see that happening."

Ethan sighed. "What if it had been Uncle Richard who was shot and killed instead of Drew—and you never got another chance to make peace?"

"It's not that simple, Ethan."

"Well maybe it's time you stopped making it so complicated!"

Ralph seemed to study him. "I know you're upset, but don't try to psychoanalyze me. You've never had to deal with brother issues."

"I'd gladly trade you. Drew was the closest thing to a brother I'll ever have. And it really gripes me that you and Uncle Richard are letting whatever differences you have rule your life."

"It's not your problem, Ethan. Like I said, it's complicated."

"And losing a son isn't?" Ethan's eyes watered, and his uncle's face grew blurry. "Are you just going to ignore the situation—let your twin brother bury his only child without any acknowledgment?"

"I'm not the only brother he's got. My presence won't do anything to ease Richard's grief. And this is not the time to dredge up our personal history. He has enough to deal with."

"That's a cop-out and you know it! You're letting your stubborn pride ruin the chance to put it behind you." Ethan exhaled loudly enough to show his utter disgust and then waved his hand dismissively. He didn't want to embarrass his uncle in front of the work crew.

"Look," Ralph said, "I'm sick about what happened to Drew. I really am. But his death doesn't undo anything."

And you're not about to let it. Ethan bit his lip and stuffed his hands in his pockets. "I got my things from Drew's house. I just came by to see if it's okay if I go ahead and move in with you and Aunt Gwen."

Ralph patted him on the back. "It's more than okay. We've

looked forward to it for months. Why don't you plan to take a week off until you're sure your head's on straight?"

"If it's all the same to you, I'd rather come back to work. I'll cope with Drew's death better if I stay busy."

❖ ❖ ❖

Brill stood at the window in her office and stared at nothing. Unless they got fingerprints or trace evidence from the stolen truck, she had nothing. Zilch. But how dare Sam Parker imply that she was hiding something!

She was vaguely aware of footsteps and then a knock at the door. She turned around and saw Trent Norris in the doorway.

"What's up?"

"I've got the autopsy report on Natalie Benchfield." Trent walked across the room and handed it to her. "No big surprise on the cause of death. She bled out from the gunshot wound to the neck."

"What about sexual assault?"

"The ME said the results were inconclusive. So even if we find this Vincent she was corresponding with, we're not going to nail him for this one."

"Maybe not, but if he's a registered sex offender whose parole prohibits contact with a minor, we can get him for that. And if he was there when the poor child was shot and just left her to die, I want his head on a stick."

Trent arched his eyebrows. "We're still waiting on trace. But unless we find his DNA or fingerprints on the girl or her belongings, he'll deny he was ever there."

"Then we'll let him think we have his DNA and get him to confess." Brill sighed. "How close are we to tracing his email to his home address?"

"The state police thought they'd know something by today—tomorrow at the latest. I'll keep you posted."

"Thanks, Trent."

"You look beat up. How's Vanessa holding up?"

"Better than I expected. I think she's trying to be strong for Ethan. He's really taking it hard."

"I'm sure he is. But I can't even imagine how Vanessa felt when she heard the shots and saw Drew Langley get hit. Imagine standing there with a helpless baby, wondering if you're next."

Brill tucked her hair behind her ear. "I *have* thought about it—off and on all day. Kurt and I could be planning a double funeral. Makes my skin crawl."

"Why don't you cut out early and go be with your family? It's going to be a rough week, especially if we're going to attend the funerals. Tal Davison's should be huge. His father is actually shutting down the plant on Friday so workers can pay their respects. Pigeon Forge and Sevierville have already volunteered to send officers to help with traffic and crowd control."

"Good."

"I'm nervous that the shooter hasn't been caught. I wonder if that will deter people from coming out."

Brill turned and looked down at the grounds around city hall. "They may not line up along the route to the cemetery. But people always turn out in droves when someone dies a tragic death, especially young people. I imagine we'll have our hands full on Thursday for

Natalie Benchfield's funeral. Every middle-school kid in town will probably be there."

"Let's hope the critics stay home. There's no shortage of people who are outraged that Natalie's parents only got a slap on the wrist."

"Let's just hope the Benchfields' poor judgment was a result of being exasperated by a rebellious adolescent and not a serious character flaw."

"Skyler Roberts's funeral is Thursday afternoon in Atlanta. Any idea what Drew Langley's parents are planning?"

"Drew's funeral will be Saturday at two o'clock at my church, Cross Way Bible Fellowship. I'm dreading it. I know Vanessa will be emotional, which will make it hard for me to maintain a professional demeanor."

"You're allowed to be human, Chief."

"You say that, but people expect a show of strength. No one feels safe with the shooter still out there. They want a leader, not a parent with the same fears they have."

"Can't you be both?" Trent arched his eyebrows. "During the disappearances, you addressed the community as our police chief *and* as a wife and mother. People appreciated that."

"True. But this time I'll have to work hard to keep my emotions in check."

"Can't be any more emotional than Sean O'Toole's funeral last year, and you got through that." Trent nodded toward the door. "Why don't you go home? I can handle things here."

"Thanks, Trent. I think I will."

Ethan sat in his car across the street from his cousin's house and watched investigators cleaning up the crime scene. Who was it that had gunned down his cousin like a wild animal and defiled this place that held such happy, innocent memories? How many times had he slept over in the attic room? Camped out in the backyard? Come to birthday parties? Barbecues? Thanksgiving dinners? How many Christmas Eves had they all sang around the piano—everyone except Uncle Ralph and Aunt Gwen, who declined each invitation?

How could Uncle Ralph hold on to his stubborn pride when his twin brother was suffering so?

Ethan rested his forehead on the steering wheel and thought of Vanessa standing at the front door, Carter in the stroller, as the bullets whizzed past her and penetrated Drew's neck. He blinked away the image of the dried red pool on the stoop—the very lifeblood of his closest friend, who was more like a brother than a cousin. With just six months difference in their ages, he couldn't remember a time when Drew wasn't part of his life. Now he felt as if his heart had a hole in it, and he couldn't understand how his uncles had withstood their estrangement all these years. Had it been like a death for *them?* Did they grieve the loss and go on, pride and indifference filling the void?

Warm tears rolled down Ethan's cheeks. The inescapable fact that he would not see Drew again in this life was bearable only because he had no doubt he would see him in the next. But the pain of missing him was only one day old and already seemed oppressive.

Lord, I can't do this.

A lifetime of memories ran through his mind, his dreams turning to vapor. How was he going to find the strength to cope with the gaping hole Drew left behind? Drew was supposed to be there to see him graduate. Cheer him on through grad school. Stand up as best man at his wedding.

Ethan wiped his tears with the bottom of his shirt. He had to pull himself together. How could he function if he gave in to the sorrow that seemed to consume him? Drew's parents needed him to be strong. Vanessa needed him to hold her up through the drama of Drew's funeral and burial. He needed to work for Uncle Ralph to help pay his tuition. Would he be able to do any of that if he allowed his grief to become debilitating?

You will keep in perfect peace him whose mind is steadfast, because he trusts in you.

The words from Isaiah seemed almost audible. He breathed in slowly and let it out and then did it again. He would have to save his tears for when he was alone. He needed to go see Vanessa and make sure she was coping.

※　※　※

Ethan sat on the glider on the screened-in porch at the Jessups', holding tightly to Vanessa's hand. Where had she found the presence of mind to make such a delicious dinner when she had a final to study for, a baby to care for, and trauma to cope with? Just being with her was comforting.

"Did I mention the pork chops were *really* good?" he finally said.

"About a dozen times." She put her head on his shoulder. "My mother was a good cook when she had more time. I've been stealing her recipes. Cooking dinner is my one big contribution to living at home. My parents *really* appreciate it since they both work. It's so much healthier than eating out—and cheaper."

"Well, dinner was delicious."

The silence returned. Ethan debated whether or not to bring up the obvious. Finally he said, "How'd you do today, dealing with everything?"

"I stayed busy, which isn't hard to do when you're chasing a baby. I guess we're going to have to get a gate for the stairs when he starts to walk."

"When does that usually happen?"

Vanessa fiddled with a button on his shirt. "All babies are different. The average is around a year. But you've seen him. I think he's going to walk early."

"He's beautiful like his mother, and such a happy little guy. You've done a great job with him."

"My family's pitched in. Emily's been invaluable. She's almost as good as having a nanny."

Ethan listened carefully to the thickness of her words. "How are you feeling *emotionally?*"

"It's hard to describe. When I woke up this morning, it felt like something heavy was sitting on my chest. If it hadn't been for Carter, I'm not sure I would've had the strength to get up. I've felt drained all day. It's hard to think."

"Me, too. It's the grief."

Vanessa sighed. "It takes an enormous amount of energy to do anything."

"I know." Ethan stroked her hair. "It'll go away eventually. But there's no way around it."

"Please tell me it doesn't last long."

"Everyone's different. It has to run its course."

Neither of them spoke for a few minutes.

Finally Vanessa said, "I woke up in a cold sweat during the night. I dreamed some guy was chasing me. I was running as fast as I could, pushing Carter in the stroller. I could almost feel the guy's breath on my neck. It was horrifying."

Ethan kissed her cheek. "You've been through a frightening experience. It's going to take time before the fear goes away."

"It would help if my mom would catch the shooter."

"That might not happen for a while. We need to play it safe in the meantime."

"What are you saying?"

"I don't want to add to your fear, but I'm nervous. What if someone wanted Drew dead—for the same reason he wanted Tal Davison dead? And what if he thinks you saw him? What's to stop him from coming after you?"

"I didn't see anything. I just heard tires squeal."

"The shooter doesn't know that. It freaks me out to think he could be looking for you."

Vanessa squeezed his arm. "You're overreacting. I'm sure the shooter watches the news, and the media reported that I didn't see anything. Besides, Mom said they haven't found anything to suggest the shooter targeted Drew."

"Yet. She said *yet.* "

"Ethan, you're scaring me."

He turned and looked into her eyes. "I'm sorry. I'm just not convinced that you're safe. I don't think you should leave the house until the police know more."

CHAPTER 17

Brill sat at the kitchen table with Kurt, having a dish of black-cherry ice cream. She looked out the bay window at the glowing lava-pink streaks on Tuesday night's sky, the silhouette of the Great Smoky Mountains barely distinguishable in the ghostly haze.

"You seem pensive," Kurt said.

"You know I don't do well when there are so many unknowns in a case. But I'm also irritated with Sam Parker."

"What *now?*"

Brill stuck her spoon in a mound of ice cream. "He's playing devil's advocate and suggested that it's possible Drew's shooter missed his target, and that he was really aiming for Vanessa. He wanted to know if there's something *I'm* not telling him."

Kurt rolled his eyes. "How'd you respond?"

"You mean besides wanting to wipe the condescending smirk off his face?"

"Take it easy, red." Kurt half smiled. "Sam can be a real pain. But I suppose it's a fair question since you *have* been stalked by someone you put in prison and who tried to hurt Vanessa to get back to you."

"And he's behind bars. For heaven's sake, Kurt, I would never withhold information in a murder case. I don't believe what's going on now has *anything* to do with me or Vanessa … but it might have something to do with Drew." She glanced over at the doorway and lowered her voice. "Four people are dead, and Drew was at two of the murder scenes, one of them as a victim. We can't just ignore that possible connection."

"So how do you proceed? Are you thinking he was into something illegal?"

"I didn't say that. I'd just like to dig a little deeper with Drew's parents and with Ethan."

"What are you after?"

Brill pulled her spoon out of the ice cream. "I'm not sure. But if these roommates were targeted, there must be something in their apartment, computers, or phone logs that would give us a clue as to why."

Kurt's gaze collided with hers. "If they were murdered, then the so-called *random* shootings might have been a smokescreen for something bigger?"

"I think it's a possibility."

"Did you discuss it with the sheriff?"

"I was just about to when he suggested Vanessa might have been the target. He already made it clear he doesn't think the roommates being shot was a coincidence. We agree on that. But while he's busy trying to connect it to Vanessa and ultimately *me,* I'll talk to the Langleys and see if that yields anything. Sam doesn't need to be involved unless I find something suspicious."

❖   ❖   ❖

Stedman turned off the eleven o'clock news. So the red truck was stolen. What was going on? How many people were going to die? He picked up his cell phone and dialed Grant Wolski's number.

"Hello."

"It's Stedman. We need to talk."

"I'm in the middle of something."

"I'll wait."

"I told you not to call me."

"Yeah, well, that was before Davison's roommate got shot. Don't worry, I'm using a prepaid cell phone. I want to know what's going on."

Stedman heard muffled voices, and it sounded as though Grant covered the receiver.

"If you hang up on me, I'll just keep calling." Stedman switched the phone to his other ear. "I'm not going to stop hounding you until you give me an answer."

"It's not your concern," Grant said flatly.

"Not my concern? *I'm* the one who agreed to kill Davison, and now he's dead—only *I* didn't do it. And whoever *did* keeps on killing people. I don't want this to come back to me."

"Your hands are clean. Forget about it."

"I can't. We had a deal, Grant. I was psyched up to shoot Tal Davison and get out from under this debt. Do you have any idea how hard that was? Now I've got that weighing on my conscience, *plus* I still owe you a small fortune that keeps going up a thousand bucks a day."

There was a long moment of dead air. The only sound was Grant's breathing on the other end of the line.

"You still there?" Stedman said.

"Yeah. It's too bad things didn't go the way we planned. There's nothing either of us can do about that. Doesn't change the fact that you owe me."

"Fine. But if this comes back to me, I'm telling the cops everything I know."

"That would be a big mistake."

"No bigger than being implicated in something I didn't do."

"Just sit tight and let this thing play out."

Stedman's temples throbbed. "Play out *how?* Four people are dead. Whatever's going on, it's not what I signed up for!"

There was a long pause, and it sounded as if Grant got up and moved to another room.

Finally Grant started speaking. "All right, look ... you made a valid point. This isn't what you signed up for. Let's just forget the deal. Forget the debt. And you find someone else to play poker with. I don't want to hear from you again."

"Are you saying I don't owe you anything?"

"You heard me."

He's willing to let sixty grand go—just like that? "I'd like it in writing."

"Forget it, Stedman. There's nothing in writing that says you owe me. If I say you're off the hook, you're off the hook. There *is* one condition, though, and I need you to hear me—and hear me well: Open your mouth to *anyone* about the deal we made, and it'll be the last time you ever do."

Grant's 'one condition' stopped him like the crack of a whip. "So now you're threatening me?"

"Call it whatever you want. It's out of my hands."

"What's that supposed to mean?"

The phone went dead.

Stedman laid the phone on the arm of the chair, his heart hammering, his mind racing. Why did he get the feeling he had just traded one problem for a much bigger one? If he kept his mouth shut, what was to keep Grant or whoever was behind the shootings from implicating him? Maybe he should just go to the cops and tell them what he knew.

Stedman crushed a Pepsi can and tossed it in the recycle bag. Tell them what? That he agreed to kill a man for Grant Wolski and someone else beat him to it? That he was a pathetic gambling addict who had pawned his integrity and his moral compass so he could pay a debt and come back to the poker table?

As a dog returns to its vomit, so a fool repeats his folly. Why did he remember this Bible verse now when he hadn't been to church in ages?

Suddenly he craved a cigarette, even though he had kicked the habit two years ago. If he went to the police and told them what he knew, could he be charged with conspiring to kill Tal Davison, even though he didn't go through with it? Then again, Grant was a well-respected supervisor at Davison Technologies. Would anyone even believe him capable of conspiring to kill his boss's son? And if Grant denied it, what then? Would the police try to link Stedman to the men in the red truck?

Stedman looked out into the dark night. Could his conscience handle more people dying because he didn't speak up?

Vanessa sat in the stillness, slowly rocking Carter, not ready just yet to turn loose of him for the night.

What if Ethan was right? What if whoever gunned down Drew was going to come after her? The sound of gunfire and the look on Drew's face when the bullet hit him flashed through her mind with frightening clarity.

She realized she was squeezing Carter the way she would a teddy bear, her heart pounding, her skin clammy.

Lord, protect us. Please don't let any more bad things happen to this family.

"Hey, I didn't hear Carter cry."

Vanessa lifted her gaze and saw Emily standing in the doorway. "What are you doing up?"

"I went to the bathroom and saw the lamp on." Emily walked over and stood facing Vanessa. "I'll rock him. You can't be tired tomorrow. You have to study."

"Thanks, but I got him up because I *needed t*o hold him."

Emily was quiet for a moment, then her eyes narrowed. "I know you're freaked that you saw Ethan's cousin get killed. But you've still got finals to deal with. You have to stay focused."

"You sound just like Mom."

Emily caught a yawn with her hand. "Dad says Mom and I are cut from the same cloth."

"I think Dad's right."

"I like rocking Carter."

"I know you do." Vanessa reached up and squeezed Emily's hand. "But it calms me when he sleeps in my arms."

"And you need lots of calming?"

"Something like that. It affects me like Pouncer's purring affects you."

"Oh." Emily sat on the side of the bed, her hands folded in her lap. "I just want you to know I'm here for you—if you ever want to talk about what happened."

Like I'm going to dump all my fears on an eleven-year-old. "That's sweet of you, Shortcake. It means a lot."

"You probably think I'm too young to understand what you're going through, but I'm not. I know what it's like to keep thinking about scary things that happened."

"So how do *you* deal with it?"

Emily sighed. "I just give it to God and stop thinking about it until I feel brave. Then I close my eyes and go back to whatever scared me—only this time, I picture Jesus there with me. When I see Him, I stop being afraid. The memories don't scare me anymore."

"All this happens just in your imagination?"

Emily nodded. "It feels real though. Tessa says I'm just changing my perspective. But I forgot what that word means."

"Perspective just means the way you look at things."

"Oh yeah. I remember now."

"Did Tessa teach you to do that?"

"Uh-huh. She does it too. The Bible says God never leaves us, so He *had* to be in the room with us when Eduardo held the gun to my head. So now when my mind flashes back, I see Jesus there with us, and thinking about it doesn't freak me out."

Vanessa smiled to herself and wondered what Ethan would think of Emily's psychology lesson.

"Sounds like you've learned some coping skills," Vanessa said.

"Maybe you should try it and save yourself all the trouble."

"Maybe I will. Right now I can barely believe what's happened."

"I never met Drew. Was he nice?"

"Yes, he was. He and Ethan were like brothers."

"It makes me sad when Ethan cries."

"You saw him cry? Then you were eavesdropping again. Emily, why do you do that? You know better. People have a right to privacy."

Emily shrugged. "Sorry. I'm just curious."

"One of these days it's going to get you in trouble."

Emily slid off the bed and onto her feet, stifling a yawn. "If you're going to rock Carter, I'm going back to bed. If you start to think of scary things, remember what I said. It really will help."

Ethan sat in the window seat in his bedroom at Uncle Ralph and Aunt Gwen's house and looked out into the night. He spotted the Big Dipper and the North Star and thought back to when he and Drew were boys and used to lie on their backs in front of their camping tents, gazing up at the summer sky, trying to remember the stars and constellations.

How could Drew be gone—just like that? It didn't seem real, except for the aching in his gut, a nagging reminder that he wasn't dreaming and it was a reality he had to face. Uncle Richard and Aunt Becca asked him if he wanted to come to the funeral home for a private viewing—a chance to say good-bye to Drew … but could he handle it? Could he bear to see the bullet wound that had taken his cousin from him and scarred Vanessa's memory with a horrible image that might haunt her for the rest of her life?

Ethan's vision blurred with tears. He needed to be strong for Vanessa. For his parents. For Uncle Richard and Aunt Becca. He needed to hide his emotion from Uncle Ralph and Aunt Gwen. Why waste his grief on them or be pulled into the feud that had split the family for a decade and a half? Any tears he allowed himself to shed needed to be done right here—in the dark of night.

Ethan looked up at the stars and wondered if Drew could see them from heaven. Where was heaven anyway?

Lord, I know he's with You. That's all that matters.

Suddenly the loss seemed overwhelming and the emptiness deep and raw. Ethan felt the knot in his throat tighten, as if it were being pulled in two opposite directions. He took in a breath, surprised when it turned to sobbing. He heard the woeful sound, but it seemed as if he were listening to someone else. Finally he went over to the bed and buried his face in the pillow—and wept.

CHAPTER 18

The next morning, Brill sat at the conference table in her office, the case files spread out in front of her. Four corpses and no leads. She sighed. Not a promising beginning to the day. She heard a knock and looked over just as Trent came in, carrying a manila folder.

"Chief, we just got a break on this Vincent character who emailed Natalie Benchfield. The DNA on the Coke can found near her backpack is a match to a registered sex offender, Hans Bowerly—the same guy the state police, just a few minutes ago, tracked down through his email address. Lives in Stanton's Ferry. He's in custody and will be transported here around noon."

"Okay, let's get this show on the road. What do we know about him?"

"Caucasian male. Thirty-seven. Sentenced to ten years for possession of child porn and indecency with a child. Currently on parole with the standard prohibition against being with a minor unsupervised. We've got him on that much."

"Great work, Trent. I want to be there when you question him. Be sure to let Sam Parker's office know."

"Speaking of Sheriff Parker"—Trent pursed his lips—"were you ever able to blow off his smug attitude?"

"Not entirely. I could understand him suggesting that Vanessa might've been the target. But he's out of line for implying I would withhold anything about my past that might impact a murder investigation."

"Don't worry, Chief. Rousseaux, Marcum, and I know that."

"I think that Vanessa was in the wrong place at the wrong time," Brill said, "and that the two roommates were involved in something—or knew something—that got them killed."

Trent nodded. "We're with you. Thing is, there's nothing on their computers or phones that points anywhere. We searched the apartment high and low. There's just nothing to link Davison and Langley to anything, shady or otherwise. They didn't even hang out with the same friends."

Brill sighed. "So we've got four dead kids and no leads on the shooter."

"Other than he stole a red Ford F-150."

"And no one saw him do it."

"Right."

"Okay, come get me when Hans Bowerly arrives. Let's find out if he was with Natalie when she was shot—and if he saw anything."

Stedman stood with Ethan at the Misty Meadows work site, waiting for the second cement truck to arrive.

"I'm really sorry about your cousin," Stedman said.

"Thanks." Ethan pushed his hands in the pockets of his cutoffs. "It's hard to take. Drew was like a brother to me."

"Do the cops have any suspects?"

"I don't think so. You know Vanessa saw the whole thing?"

"Yeah, I heard that on the news. Did she see the guys in the red truck?"

"No, she had her back to the street. You said guys, *plural*. Where'd you hear that?"

"Just a figure of speech." Stedman quickly reverted to his poker face. "I don't think the media reported how many there were. No one's ever come forward. No witnesses, right?"

"Not yet. The police are trying to find a connection between Drew and his roommate, though. It's a little uncanny that the same shooter got to both of them."

"You think they were into something illegal?"

Ethan shrugged. "I can't imagine it. Drew was straight as an arrow."

"What do you know about the roommate, Tal Davison?" *Other than Grant wanted him dead?*

"Not much. He was a student at Stanton. His father's the CEO of Davison Technologies. He'd only been Drew's roommate a short time. I never met him."

Stedman looked down at the ground and moved a stone with his sneaker. "His old man was responsible for a lot of layoffs. You think someone wanted to get back at him by going after his son?"

"Seems like a stretch. That doesn't explain Drew or the other two victims."

"Yeah, you're probably right." Stedman raised his head and looked out at the mountains. *Shut up before he gets suspicious.*

"Frankly, I don't know what to think. I can't imagine anyone wanting Drew dead. But what are the odds of this happening by chance?"

"It's a pretty safe bet it didn't."

"Yeah, that's what I think." Ethan exhaled loudly. "Why don't we talk about something else? Tell me a little more about what you're up to these days."

"Oh, same old—minus the girlfriend."

"No women?"

Stedman flashed a sheepish grin. "Sure. The queen of hearts, spades, clubs, and diamonds."

"Are you still into playing online poker like you were last summer?"

"Sure. But it's a lot more fun with live players. I found some guys here who like to play." *Why did I tell him that?*

Ethan raised an eyebrow. "I thought playing poker for money was illegal—unless you're just betting nickels and dimes."

"Cops have more important things to do than bust up card games where guys are betting for fun. It's not like we're playing for millions. Anyway, I've backed off. Last time I played, I had four jacks, ace high, and lost to a straight flush. I couldn't believe I didn't win with a hand like that."

"No kidding. Did you bet it all?"

"Yeah, but not to worry"—Stedman flashed a phony grin—"I found a way to get it all back."

"Still Mr. Lucky, eh?"

"Something like that."

Brill leaned on the window sill in her office and let the warm sunshine melt over her. In the distance, beyond the towering trees that shaded the grounds around city hall, the Great Smoky Mountains looked as if they'd been painted on the horizon, the backdrop for a giant stage production.

"Chief, Hans Bowerly just arrived. We put him in the second interview room."

Brill turned around and saw Trent standing in the doorway. "Is he cooperative?"

"He hasn't lawyered up yet." Trent smiled wryly. "I'd like to get him to talk before he wises up."

"Let's go."

Brill followed Trent across the bustling detective bureau and down the hall to the second interview room.

Hans Bowerly, a husky guy with a full head of mousy brown hair, sat at the oblong table, cracking his knuckles. He wore jeans and a Key West T-shirt—and an apprehensive expression.

"I'm Police Chief Jessup, Hans."

"I came here willingly," he said, "but I didn't do anything wrong."

"We just want to ask you a few questions about your relationship with Natalie Benchfield."

"I already told your detective that I hardly knew the girl."

Brill pulled out a chair and sat across the table from Hans and next to Trent.

She stared at her hands for thirty seconds—just long enough to make the suspect uncomfortable. Finally she said, "I'm here to listen. Captain Norris will ask you some questions."

Trent folded his arms across his chest. "Let's start with you defining what you mean by, 'hardly knew the girl.'"

"I emailed her a few times," Hans said. "I had no idea she was only thirteen. She told me she was eighteen."

"Really?" Trent lifted his eyebrow. "Because we were able to access Natalie's hard drive. I've got a printout of a recent online back-and-forth you had with her."

"Hey, that's private. You—"

"*After* Natalie told you she was thirteen, you initiated a long and rather graphic discussion about her undergarments, et cetera. Would you like me to read it to you?"

"No." Hans wiped the perspiration off his upper lip. "But I never asked her to meet me. I swear."

"Did you call Natalie on her cell phone?"

"You won't find *my* number on her phone records." Hans smirked.

"Look, wise guy"—Trent leaned forward on his elbows and put his nose in front of Hans —"we know you used a prepaid cell. We're going to nail you. I suggest you cooperate with us while we're willing to listen, or you're going back to jail."

"So what if I *did* call her—which you can't even prove. We never got together. It's against the conditions of my parole. You think I want to go back to that pit?"

"Then tell me this." Trent held his gaze. "How is it that your saliva DNA ended up on a Coke can next to her backpack at a vacant house on Fifth Street?"

Hans's face turned sizzling pink. "I-I don't know. I haven't been to Sophie Trace in months."

"Oh, you were here, all right," Trent said, "and with Natalie Benchfield. So why don't you stop with the innocent act? You're in up to your ears."

"I want a lawyer."

"Fine." Brill folded her hands on the table. "We can stop right here and get the court to appoint you a lawyer. But if you help us, we can do a lot more to keep you from going back to jail than your lawyer can."

"What do you want?"

"Information."

"What kind of information?"

"A description of the shooter."

"You don't think I was—"

"Oh, but we *do,*" Brill said. "We think you were sitting with Natalie on the front steps of that vacant house at the time she was shot—and that you dumped her body in the side yard and left her there to die. Your parole violation is enough to get you sent back to jail. And unless you help us, you're not going to get out until you're an old man."

Hans's chin quivered. "I didn't know what to do. We were sitting on the steps, *just talking,* and this truck comes out of nowhere. I heard shots, and the next thing I knew, there was blood everywhere, and I realized Natalie had been shot." Hans combed his hands through his hair. "I knew if I got caught with her, I'd go back to jail."

"So you dumped her in the side yard and left her to die?" Trent said.

"No. She was crying and wanted to go home. I tried to keep pressure on her neck and stop the bleeding, but she got away and ran around to the side of the house. I chased her and she passed out cold."

"Why didn't you call 9-1-1?"

"She was choking, man." Hans's eyes glistened. "She wasn't gonna make it, no matter what. She was dying."

Trent threw his hands in the air. "You couldn't be sure of that. Did you even try to help her?"

"I told you I tried to keep pressure on the wound and she pushed me away. After she passed out, it was hopeless."

"So now you're a doctor?"

"You weren't there." Hans looked at Trent defiantly. "I'm telling you, she was a goner. I had to either get out of there or go back to jail. What would *you* do?"

"I would've at least dialed 9-1-1 while I was hightailing it out of town." Trent got up in Hans's face and grabbed him by the collar. "That child lay on the ground decomposing for two days. Two days! She was barely recognizable to her parents, did you know that? And all because you couldn't be bothered to dial three lousy numbers and get her some help."

Hans started to tremble. "I didn't want to leave her like that. I thought someone would find her."

"You *thought?* All you thought about was not getting caught. You weren't worried about whether Natalie was going to live or die. What kind of garbage leaves a helpless little girl to bleed to death?"

"Detective, back off." Brill grabbed Trent's arm and pretended to pull him off Hans. "Why don't you take a break? You need to calm down."

Trent let go of Hans's collar and gave him a slight shove. "Whatever. I'm done with this loser anyhow."

Trent pushed back his chair and left the room, muttering to himself.

Brill waited half a minute and then said, "Sorry. My detective captain is passionate about victims—especially children."

"He didn't have to treat me like dirt. I told you what happened. This is harassment. I'm not saying anything else without a lawyer present."

"You don't get it, Hans. A lawyer isn't going to let you answer my questions. And unless you do, I'm not going to persuade the parole board that you shouldn't go back to jail. It's your choice. What's it going to be?"

Hans seemed trapped in a long pause. Finally he said, "All right. Forget the lawyer. What else do you want to know?"

Brill slowly rose to her feet and started pacing. "What time did you and Natalie meet on Thursday night?"

"Around ten. But it's not what you think," he quickly added. "She called me from a pay phone and asked me to meet her at the vacant house. Said her parents kicked her out and her grandmother wasn't home, and she was scared. Look, I know I was out of line in those emails, but it was just talk. I didn't go there to do anything to her."

"Did you drive?"

"Yes, but I parked one block over and walked."

"What happened when you got there?"

"Natalie was sitting on the front porch drinking a Coke and offered me one. She told me she'd been hiding there all evening. Said she was in big trouble for using too many minutes on her cell phone and didn't want to have another fight with her parents. She asked me what she should do."

"What'd you tell her?"

"I told her that her parents were probably more worried than mad. And she should call them and tell them she wanted to come home. Of course, that's not what she wanted to hear. She wanted to come home with me. I told her that wasn't going to happen, and she started to pout and went down and sat on the front steps."

"You expect me to believe that you, a convicted child molester, told a thirteen-year-old girl to go home to her parents when she was willing to get in the car with you?"

"Look, I thought about taking her with me, okay? But I learned my lesson. I don't want to go back to jail. I decided before I ever went there that it was not going to be like that."

"What happened next?" Brill asked.

"You know how girls that age can be drama queens. She went on and on about how her parents would never forgive her and she'd be grounded for the rest of her life. I figured if I listened until she was through venting, I could talk her into going home. There was no way I was taking her anywhere with me. And I couldn't just leave her there all night."

"Were you sitting next to her on the steps, facing the street?"

"Yes."

"Did you see the shooter's vehicle approaching?"

"First I heard it. I remember because it slowed down, and I was nervous that the police might be out looking for her and I'd get caught violating my parole. I looked up, relieved it was just a red truck. Then I heard shots and a few seconds later realized Natalie had been hit."

"You're not wearing glasses. Do you wear contacts?"

"No, my eyesight's fine."

"And you were, what, thirty feet from the street when Natalie was shot?"

"What's your point?"

"My point"—Brill got steely quiet and let her gaze bore into his conscience—"is that you could've seen who fired the gun."

CHAPTER 19

Brill walked in the front door of her home and out to the kitchen, glad to see Kurt sitting at the table, reading the newspaper.

"Mmm, something smells good. Where are the girls?"

"Vanessa put a meatloaf in the oven and is resting, and Emily's watching Carter. And dear old Dad"—he flashed a grin—"is taking advantage of all the help."

"It's only going to get better with Emily out of school tomorrow for the summer." Brill walked over to the refrigerator and opened the door. "You want something to drink?"

"I've got a Coke, thanks."

She reached in the fridge and got a bottle of water, then sat at the table across from Kurt. She twisted off the cap and took a sip of water. "How did Vanessa seem today?"

"Quiet. I can only imagine what she must be feeling. Had to be terrifying to see Drew killed right in front of her. I think she's more rattled than she's letting on. She's holding back for Ethan's sake."

"Poor thing," Brill said. "I don't need to tell you how badly I want to get this guy. We're using all the resources we've got to find a connection between Drew and Tal and the shooter. If there's a connection, we'll find it."

"*If?*" Kurt's eyebrows came together. "There's no way you can think these shootings were coincidental."

"No, but we did a thorough check of their incoming and outgoing calls and emails"—Brill loosened her tie and slid it off—"and nothing leads us to believe either roommate was involved in anything questionable. They didn't even share the same friends."

"There *has* to be a connection, Brill."

"My gut says you're right, but the facts we have don't bear it out. On the surface, both shootings appear to be random, though even Sam and Trent aren't buying it." She looked out at the hazy foothills, determined to finish updating Kurt on the case and then forget about it until tomorrow. "We did get a break, though. The state police tracked down the guy who emailed Natalie Benchfield. He is a registered sex offender out on parole. No surprise."

She told Kurt everything that had happened from the time she and Trent began interrogating Hans Bowerly until he confessed to meeting Natalie.

"We had another reason for bringing him in, Kurt. The front steps of that vacant house aren't far from the street. We hoped he got a look at the shooter."

"Did he?"

"It was dark, but he saw the passenger fire the gun—a man with a beard and mustache. Thick, dark hair. He thinks he was young."

"That's not a detailed description."

"Facial hair is easy to grow and remove, so it might not help us. But it's more than we had before. And if the shooter doesn't think he was seen, he might not change his looks. We've released the description to the media. Someone might know something about this bearded man—or might have seen him."

"What's going to happen to Hans Bowerly?"

"He'll cut a deal for helping us and won't be sent back to jail for violating his parole. There's no proof that anything illicit took place between Natalie and him, so we can't charge him with anything."

"So where do you go from here?"

"Good question. We've got a stolen 2008 red Ford F-150 with no identifiable fingerprints or DNA. We've got a mystery shooter with a mustache and beard, but otherwise too vague for an artist's sketch. And from the rifling profile, we know the weapon was a Smith and Wesson second or third generation semiautomatic pistol. But without fingerprints or DNA, we're essentially stalemated. We need to start digging deeper into the personal lives of Drew Langley and Tal Davison. There has to be something there to connect the two roommates to the shooter."

"Hi, Mom." Vanessa walked into the kitchen and put her arms around Brill. "Did you find out anything new?"

"We've now got a partial description of the shooter."

"Really?"

Brill gave Vanessa the description she had released to the media.

"Though having a general description of the shooter is helpful," Brill said, "we're still going to have to dig more deeply into the personal lives of Drew and his roommate."

Vanessa sat in the chair next to her dad. "Ethan doesn't believe Drew was involved in anything shady."

"That may be true, but if these were intentional murders and not random shootings, we've got to figure out why someone wanted them dead."

"I feel so bad for Drew's parents," Vanessa said, "and for Ethan."

Brill studied her daughter's face. "Honey, if Ethan told you something about his cousin that could help the investigation, even if it was private, you wouldn't keep it from me, would you?"

"Of course not. I'd insist that Ethan come to you with it."

"Good."

Brill's phone vibrated. She took the phone off her belt clip and glanced at the incoming caller name and number. "Excuse me. I need to take this—yes, Beau Jack, what is it?"

"You're not going to believe this, Chief, but I think we might have recovered the Smith and Wesson used in the shootings."

"What?" She locked gazes with Kurt. "Where'd you find it?"

"In the Dumpster behind the Toffee Emporium," Beau Jack said. "We got an anonymous call from a man who said we would find it there, wrapped in a towel. We're about to take it back to the station and dust it for prints."

"See if you can find out who placed that call."

"I'm already on it."

She glanced up at the kitchen clock. "I'll see you in ten minutes."

❖   ❖   ❖

Ethan sat with Vanessa on the screened-in porch at the Jessups' house, waiting to find out if the gun the police found would lead to the person who killed Drew.

"I don't know what's taking my mother so long," Vanessa said.

"We probably should go ahead and eat dinner without her. I've been through this enough to know she may not get home for hours."

"I sure hope the gun leads to the killer." Ethan squeezed her hand. "I've always tried to be there for grieving people, but I've never really understood how it feels to lose someone until now."

Vanessa sighed. "I remember when my grandparents died in the car wreck. We were all sad for a long time, and it didn't seem real then either. We just need to get Drew's funeral behind us. The next few days are going to be hard. Too bad it had to come right on top of Memorial Day weekend." Vanessa stood and arched her back. "I'm going to go get dinner on the table. Would you mind rounding up the family?"

"Be glad to. Your meatloaf smells delicious."

Ethan followed Vanessa to the door, where she almost ran headlong into her dad.

"I was just coming to get you," Kurt said.

"Have you heard from Mom?"

"No. But we might as well eat. Your mother is liable to be tied up for a while."

"You're reading my mind. I was just coming inside to get it on the table."

"How can I help?" Kurt said.

"Pour the iced tea. Ethan, would you get the meatloaf out of the oven and set it on the stove?"

"Yes, ma'am. You don't have to ask me twice."

Ethan followed Kurt and Vanessa into the kitchen, where Emily was strapping Carter into his high chair.

How natural it was being with Vanessa's family. It seemed so unfair that he had waited months for school to be out so he could

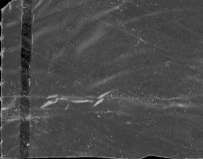

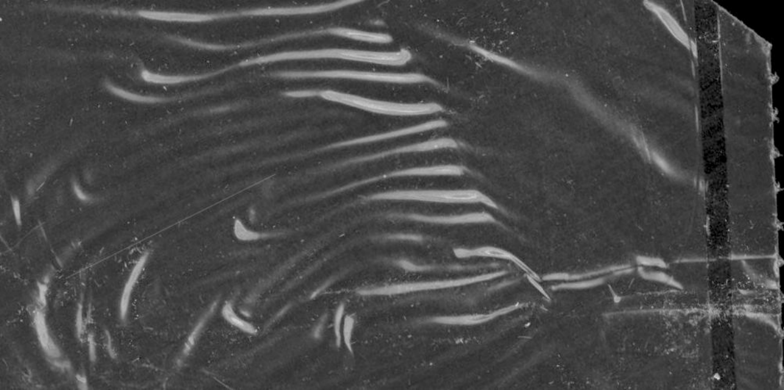

spend the summer getting to know them better—and now tragedy had once again taken center stage.

❖   ❖   ❖

Brill stood at the window in her office, a cup of coffee in her hand, and looked at the flaming pink sky above city hall.

She heard footsteps and turned around just as Trent Norris breezed into her office.

"The gun's registered to an Edgar R. Ortega of Irvine, California," he said. "It was stolen six months ago, but it's definitely been fired recently. We've asked ballistics to put a rush on it, and we should know soon whether the bullets we retrieved from our victims came from this gun."

"Good work."

"There's a bonus." Trent flashed a half-moon smile. "We did get a complete thumbprint and several partials. They don't match anyone's in the system—yet."

Brill took a sip of coffee. "Let's make sure we actually have the murder weapon and this isn't some kind of stunt. But regardless, we need to refocus on Tal Davison and Drew Langley. Let's start digging into their personal lives and revisit the parents with the idea that these young men may have been targets and not random victims. I know it's a difficult time for the families with the funerals this week and Memorial Day weekend coming up, but this can't wait."

❖   ❖   ❖

Ethan did another lap around the kitchen, Carter riding on his shoulders and giggling with delight.

"Okay, buddy, that's it for tonight." Ethan set Carter on the floor, and the boy crawled to Vanessa and pulled up on her legs.

"Wow, that was fun, wasn't it, baby boy?" Vanessa stroked Carter's hair, then looked up at Ethan. "He loves it when you play with him. I know you really didn't feel like it tonight. But thanks."

"I love it too. And it sure beats moping around."

Emily crushed a Coke can and threw it in the recycle bag. "Would you like me to take Carter upstairs and put on his pj's?"

"Thanks, Shortcake. That'd be great. I'd like to walk Ethan out to the car."

"Come on"—Emily held out her arms to Carter—"let's go find Barney."

Vanessa watched Emily take Carter out of the kitchen, then locked arms with Ethan and strolled toward the front door. "You need to get to bed."

"You're probably right. I have to be up at five and on site at six."

"I wish you'd take a little time off—at least until Drew's funeral is over."

"I'll do better if I stay busy." Ethan opened the front door and followed her out on the stoop. "But I really do need the college money. If I don't work, I don't get paid."

"Isn't your uncle Ralph's attitude toward his brother hard to take?"

"Yeah, but it's always been hard for me. At least he's consistent." Ethan put his arm around Vanessa's shoulder. "I don't want to talk to him about it anymore. I said what I had to say."

"Won't it be awkward at work, tiptoeing around Drew's death?"

"Not really. We're all busy. But Stedman's there, and I don't have to pretend with him. He's sympathetic about Drew, and he's gone out of his way to be nice."

❖ ❖ ❖

Tessa stood staring out the kitchen window, and was startled when Antonio's voice interrupted her thoughts.

"I'm sorry, what did you say, dear?"

"I was just wondering," Antonio said, "where you put those delicious sugar cookies you baked this afternoon."

"I hid them." Tessa shot him an impish grin. "They're for my Bible-study group tomorrow, and it was the only way to make sure there would be some left for the ladies."

"Aw, come on, love. I'm not that bad."

"Oh yes you are … actually, I did save you a bedtime snack." She dropped the curtain and walked over to the oven and opened it.

Antonio laughed. "I never thought to look in there."

"I knew you wouldn't." She reached in the cold oven and took out a small plate covered with plastic wrap, then poured a glass of milk and set both on the table in front of him.

Antonio kissed her cheek. "You're amazing. So what were you fixated on over there?"

"I was just praying for the Jessups. And for Ethan. It's such a hard week for them."

"I'll say."

"Ethan just left, but Brill's still not back. Something must be going on."

Antonio glanced up at the clock. "Well, the news will be on in a few minutes. Maybe the cops cracked the case. It'd sure be nice if they got the shooter before the two funerals tomorrow. It must be just awful for the parents to bury their daughters and not even know who killed them."

"I'm not sure it would be any easier if they knew who did it. But there can't be any closure until they get the shooter."

"You know"—Antonio took a bite of cookie—"we get irritated with Gus for blaming Brill for everything, but it really is hard to fathom what's happened in this town since she took over. I'm not sure Chief Hennessey would've had the experience to tackle it, much less solve it."

"The Lord knew exactly who we needed to lead," Tessa said. "All those years she worked vice on the Memphis force prepared her perfectly for it."

"I can't argue with that. But I sure don't like the fact that we're starting to have crime like the big city."

❖ ❖ ❖

Brill scanned the ballistics report and handed it back to Trent.

"We can't be more certain than a hundred percent," she said. "We've got our murder weapon. Now if we could just figure out whose fingerprints are on it."

"Well, like you said, Chief, we need to start digging into Davison's and Langley's personal lives. Somebody out there wanted them both dead. We need to find the connection."

Brill looked out the window into the dark night. "I admit I'm baffled at the moment. We've got two young men who have never been in trouble and whose phone records and computer histories reveal them to be honest, hardworking college students."

"Their bank statements and credit cards, too," Trent said. "At least from what Beau Jack's pulled together so far. I just don't see any indication that either of them was involved in using or dealing drugs—or anything that looks suspicious. Nothing out of the ordinary about their lifestyles, except for Davison's having a Hummer. And we know his dad bought it for him. I guess we need to revisit their friends and see where that takes us."

Brill willed away a yawn. "We'd better get started before the holiday weekend bogs down our efforts."

CHAPTER 20

Ethan walked into the office of Langley Concrete Company at 5:40 a.m. and spotted Tonya Mason standing at the built-in counter, pouring a cup of coffee.

"It's just me," he said. "Coffee smells great."

"You timed that just right," Tonya said. "You like cream and sugar, right?"

"Yes, thanks." Ethan walked over and stood next to her. "You come in this early *every* day?"

"Yep, same as you." She handed him an insulated cup filled with coffee. "But only because I can take off early. This body is getting too old to put in twelve-hour days. Cindy comes in at one and works till six. I don't think you've met her yet. Listen, before I forget, I just wanted to say how sorry I am about your cousin."

"Thanks. I appreciate that."

"Ralph, bless his stubborn heart, doesn't say much about it. But I know it's eating at him."

Good, Ethan thought.

The door opened, and Stedman shuffled in, his eyelids heavy.

"Morning," he said. "Caffeine. I need caffeine."

Tonya laughed. "You aren't worth diddly-squat till you've got a shot of coffee in your veins."

Stedman came up behind her and gave her a peck on the cheek. "Thanks, Ma."

Tonya poured him a cup of coffee. "All right. That's all the pampering you two are getting from me. I've got work to do, and Ralph will be expecting you at the site."

Stedman patted Ethan on the back. "How're you doing?"

"Fine, if I don't think too hard about it."

"I heard on the news that Drew's funeral is Saturday."

"Yeah. I guess the services for the two girls that got killed are today. And Tal's is tomorrow."

The door opened and closed. "Morning all. Did you know the cops found the gun used in the shootings?"

Ethan turned around and saw one of the crew workers with a newspaper under his arm. "Was it in the *Gazette?*"

"Front page."

"Can I see that?" Ethan asked.

"Sure."

Ethan took the newspaper, and the headline jumped off the page. He quickly scanned the article.

Police Recover Gun Used in Deadly Shooting Sprees

Sophie Trace Police Chief Brill Jessup told reporters late last night that her department has recovered the weapon used in two separate shootings that claimed four victims, three Stanton College students and an eighth grader at Sophie Trace Middle School.

Chief Jessup would not comment further, citing the

ongoing investigation, other than to say that the weapon, a Smith & Wesson semiautomatic pistol, was surrendered to police by an anonymous source and that ballistics has verified it is the same gun that took the life of Tal Davison (21), Skyler Roberts (20), Natalie Benchfield (13), and Drew Langley (21).

A source inside the police department said that fingerprints were found on the gun but police have made no arrests in the case.

Sheriff Sam Parker was unavailable for comment, but a source in his department said that Sheriff Parker and Police Chief Jessup believe that the deaths of Davison and Langley, who were college roommates, were more than coincidence, and an investigation is under way to find a connection in the shooting deaths, which occurred several days apart and at different locations.

A memorial service for each of the victims is being held this week (see times and locations in Section B, page 2).

Ethan handed the newspaper back to the worker and finally remembered his name. "Thanks, Judd. I knew about the gun last night but didn't know the information had been released to the press."

"So what's the deal?" Stedman said. "What kind of gun was it?"

"A Smith and Wesson pistol of some kind." Ethan shrugged. "I don't know much about guns."

"It was a semiautomatic," Judd said. "The shooter knew what he was doing. I hope they get the sucker and hang him out to dry."

"They ought to just ban those kinds of guns altogether," Tonya said.

Stedman's eyebrows came together and ridges formed on his forehead.

"What's the matter?" Ethan said. "You're not in favor of banning certain guns?"

"That's an issue all by itself. I just feel bad about your cousin getting shot. Must be hard for you to hear all this."

"Yeah, kind of," Ethan said. "I'm going to drive over to Misty Meadows. See you there?"

"I'm right behind you."

At noon straight up, Stedman walked into Rambo's Bar and Grill and saw Grant Wolski sitting in a booth by himself, eating a big sandwich.

He slid into the booth across from Grant. "I figured you'd be here. We need to talk."

"Are you crazy?" Grant said. "I told you to stay away from me."

"Did you hear the cops have the gun that was used in the shootings?"

"So what?" Grant said.

"It's the same kind of gun you showed me."

"I got news for you. There're a lot of them out there."

Stedman lowered his voice. "Don't mess with me, Grant. You handed me two Smith and Wesson pistols and said to choose. Someone used the *other* one to kill those four people, right?"

"What *is* it about 'it's not your concern' that you don't understand?" Grant looked around the room. "I let you off the hook for the money and told you to stay away from me. Now get out of here. I mean it."

Stedman leaned forward on his elbows. "Look, man, four people have been killed, and one of them is a thirteen-year-old. Are more people going to die? Because I don't want this on my conscience."

"Don't make this your problem."

"I can't just pretend I don't know anything."

"You *don't* know anything."

"Then why don't you fill me in? Because I've got a bad feeling about this."

"Oh, so *now* you've got a bad feeling?" Grant slid his sandwich aside and pushed forward with his elbows until his face was in front of Stedman's. "Funny ... you didn't have a bad feeling when you agreed to kill a man to pay a lousy poker debt."

"We both know what I agreed to do. And I have to live with it the rest of my life. Why don't you tell me what *you* did?"

"You have no idea what you're sticking your nose into."

"So why don't you enlighten me?"

"Go back to work, Stedman. Forget we had this conversation." Grant moved his gaze around the room. "You don't want to be seen here with me."

"Why—did *you* do it?" Stedman was kidding, and he was surprised to see Grant's face turn a deep shade of pink. His mind raced in reverse, and suddenly he was hot all over.

"It was *you,* wasn't it?" he whispered. "You had the other gun. You're the one who wanted to get back at Win Davison. You killed his son yourself."

"You just won't leave it alone, will you?"

Stedman felt as if his heart fell into a heap. How could he have been so stupid? "Now I get it.… You made sure I left my fingerprints on both guns so you could set me up. You never intended for me to kill Davison at all. You just wanted to frame me for it."

"Keep your voice down. Just back off, and the cops will never know whose prints they are. Open your mouth to anyone—and I mean *anyone*—about any of this, and you're going down for the shootings. It's out of my hands. Now beat it."

✦ ✦ ✦

Brill sat between Trent and Sam Parker in the reserved seating at the Sophie Trace Civic Center and listened to the pastor from First United Methodist Church attempt to comfort Natalie Benchfield's parents. The only distinguishable sound besides his voice echoing in the huge old building was sniffling. There were no empty seats—and probably no dry eyes, not even Sam Parker's.

What was it about a child's death that seemed to render everyone helpless? A mountain of grief … and nowhere to hide from it.

She wondered if Natalie's parents were riddled with guilt because they didn't call and check on their daughter after she left home mad and told them she was going to her grandmother's house. Would they be forever saddled with the "I hate you's" that Natalie shouted in anger but didn't live long enough to take back?

Brill's mind wandered back to when Vanessa was thirteen and going through a sassy, rebellious stage. How grateful she was that no harm had come to her daughter. Could there be anything more frightening to a parent than having a child out of control? Or more gut-wrenching that having a child's life cut short?

Judging from the tone of the memorial service, it seemed as if the Benchfields were not religious people. Without the assurance that they would see Natalie again in eternity, how did they summon the courage to say good-bye?

Brill decided not to think about it and turned her thoughts to the case—and finding the killer. All they had was a stolen red Ford F-150, a stolen Smith & Wesson semiautomatic pistol, and Hans Bowerly's glimpse of a young man with a dark beard and mustache. Now that the information had been released to the media, maybe someone would come forward with another piece of the puzzle.

CHAPTER 21

On Friday morning, Brill looked in the mirror and tugged at her uniform jacket until the epaulets were properly positioned on her shoulders. She felt a twinge of sadness, remembering Detective Sean O'Toole's funeral last summer. Hadn't most of the occasions that had required her to wear her dress uniform involved paying honor to the dead?

Kurt came and stood behind her. "Impressive. A pretty redhead in dress blues. Turns me on."

She laughed. "I hope you're the only one who'll see me that way. But I would like to be impressive. This is probably the biggest funeral this town has seen since Chief Hennessey died. I'm sure the mayor and city council will be watching my every move to be sure I don't offend Win Davison."

"I know he's a powerful guy," Kurt said, "but this isn't about him, it's about his son."

"Yes, but it's hard to separate the two, especially since Tal's death was the end of the line for a male heir. And don't forget we're expecting the turnout to be high. We've got officers from Sevierville and Pigeon Forge helping with crowd control. Community Church holds about a thousand. And there're almost that many employees at Davison Technologies who got the day off. Hard to say how many will show up."

Kurt kissed her cheek. "Just don't let Win Davison intimidate you. Everyone knows you were just doing your job when you questioned him. For heaven's sake, you questioned all the parents in the same way."

"Yes, we did." Brill sighed. "And I feel so bad for them. I had hoped to make an arrest by now so they wouldn't have to bury their kids with everything still up in the air."

"Your department's been working around the clock. What more can you do?"

"Nothing. But I needed a big break in the case by now, and we don't have it."

Kurt stroked her cheek. "Then be content to look impressive, Chief, and hold your head high. There's no doubt in *my* mind that you'll crack the case. You've certainly proven to the community that determination and hard work bring results."

"Tell that to Davison. I'm sure he won't miss this opportunity to tell the media about his disappointment with my department's investigation."

"Would anyone really expect anything else from him or the other parents of the victims? No one is going to be happy until the shooter is found—you, most of all."

"True. It's just that, as hard as my department has been working, I hate to see their efforts diminished."

Kurt brushed the hair out of her eyes. "He might be too somber today to say anything. Even a big shot like him needs space to grieve."

Ethan hosed off a driveway of newly poured concrete, his mind on tonight's visitation at the funeral home. He knew it would be comforting to Uncle Richard and Aunt Becca, but all he wanted to do was hide until it was over.

"How're you doing?" Uncle Ralph's voice was uncharacteristically soft.

"I'm okay."

"I wish you would've taken the day off."

Ethan shook his head. "I'd rather be busy. I've got the long weekend off. That'll be hard enough."

"You're welcome to join Gwen and me for our cookout on Monday. Tonya and her husband are coming. Also a few neighbors."

"Thanks, but I made plans to spend Memorial Day with Vanessa, though I have a feeling we're both going to crash for the rest of the weekend after Drew's funeral tomorrow."

"Maybe you should. But if you change your mind, bring her with you."

Is he really going to talk about a cookout and ignore the obvious? "The visitation tonight starts at seven." Ethan didn't try to hide his indignation. "Mom and Dad are taking Uncle Richard and Aunt Becca over there about six thirty, and—"

"Tom called and told me. He's already raked me over the coals, so save your breath."

"I guess none of this matters to you."

"Hey"—Ralph took Ethan by the chin and turned his head—"it *does* matter to me—more than you know. I'm sorry for what Richard is going through, but it doesn't change the unfinished business between us."

"It could if you wanted it to." Ethan pulled away. "The only thing standing in your way is your pride."

"Maybe so, but it's not that simple."

"You've made it complicated. It doesn't have to be."

Ralph sighed. "Ethan, I know this frustrates you. But there's so much more to it than you understand. Richard and I don't even know each other anymore. I haven't said a word to him in so long I wouldn't even know where to begin."

"I have a feeling just saying, 'I'm really sorry about Drew,' would cover most of it. Would that be so difficult?"

"No, but it would open a door I'm not prepared to walk through."

"That is so lame."

Ralph's eyes glistened and he blinked a few times, then patted Ethan on the back. "It's my fight, not yours. I've got to handle it my way and on my timetable."

"Well, at the rate you're going, that means never."

❖   ❖   ❖

Brill stood with Trent and Sheriff Parker at the Davison Family Cemetery, which was at the edge of a rolling meadow surrounded by hazy foothills. The afternoon sun was hot, but the shade of a big oak tree and a gentle breeze made standing outside bearable, even in uniform.

Mayor Lewis Roswell and several city council members stood across from her, the gorgeous mahogany casket between them, the family seated in folding chairs under the green canopy.

The officiant said a few words and prayed over Tal Davison's body, after which each member of the family filed by and, with thoughts unspoken, laid a flower atop the casket. Cynthia Davison wept inconsolably and was helped along by a tall, handsome man, presumably her boyfriend. Win Davison, his arm linked with his pregnant wife's, bowed his head, still as a stone, and finally added one last flower to the mix before escorting his wife to their seats.

Brill wondered how difficult it must be for a high-profile person like him to withhold his feelings at such an emotional moment.

Three of Tal's sisters began singing "Amazing Grace," and the sweet innocence of their angelic voices was soon joined by those gathered. Brill mouthed the words, but her eyes clouded over as she imagined how grieved she would be if she were standing at *her* son's grave, laying his murdered body to rest.

She blinked to clear her eyes and looked out over hundreds of people gathered at the grave site, wondering if the killer was there— the same shooter who had killed Drew in cold blood and whose bullets had missed her daughter and grandson by inches.

❖ ❖ ❖

Ethan walked out of Langley Concrete Company at ten after six and saw Stedman sitting in his truck, his head tilted back, his eyes closed. He walked over to take a closer look.

"Hey, you okay?"

Stedman jumped at the sound of his voice. "Uh, yeah. I've just got a banger of a headache. Guess I'm not used to the heat yet."

"Sorry. You should probably go sit in air-conditioning and take some Excedrin or something."

"I will. I didn't want to leave without saying I'll be thinking of you tonight and tomorrow. Hope it's not too painful."

"Thanks, I appreciate that." Ethan glanced over at two young boys riding their bikes down the street and laughing together. "I wonder if the shooter has any idea the grief he's brought on the families of the victims—or if he even cares."

"It's hard to say. Maybe he had his own agenda and never thought past himself."

"Well, if he wanted to be famous, he got his wish. I pity him. I just hope I get the chance to see him held accountable. Drew was like the brother I never had, and putting him in the ground will be the hardest thing I've ever done. I want his killer to know that. I want him to know what he took from me—and my aunt and uncle."

Stedman's eyes teared up, and he looked away. "I have to work tomorrow or I'd come to the memorial service."

"I know you would," Ethan said. "That means a lot to me. Go home and take care of that headache. I've got to go shower and clean up."

Stedman started the truck. "I know this sounds dumb, but if there's anything I can do, I'm here for you."

Ethan patted his arm. "Thanks."

As Stedman pulled out of the parking lot, Ethan was struck by the fact that even a coworker seemed more affected by Drew's death than Uncle Ralph did.

Stedman sat at the kitchen table, his hands wrapped around a can of Coke, his mind replaying the conversation he'd had the day before with Grant Wolski. If Grant wanted to hurt Win Davison, why didn't he just kill the guy's son without telling anyone? Why did he go to the trouble of involving Stedman and then interfering at the last minute to do the job himself? Someone occupied the driver's seat that night. Were the two of them planning to frame Stedman? He remembered handling the gun and had no doubt his fingerprints would be on it.

Stedman stroked his beard. The man the cops brought in for meeting that young girl at the vacant house said the passenger in the red truck, who also fired the gun, was young and had a dark beard and mustache. That description didn't fit Grant in the slightest. Had he disguised himself with the intention of framing Stedman?

But why? Why not do his dirty deed and be done with it? He didn't have a criminal record, and the police would have no obvious reason to suspect him of anything. And if Stedman became a suspect, he wasn't going to take the blame without telling his side of the story. Why would Grant risk his name being added to the mix? None of this made sense.

Stedman got up and paced at the kitchen window. And what did Grant mean when he said it was out of his hands? And that Stedman had no idea what he was sticking his nose into? Was it a conspiracy? Were there others who were disgruntled with the layoffs at Davison Technologies? Or who had a personal grudge against Win Davison? Did it even bother Grant that three other people had died?

Stedman felt a cramping in his gut. The only thing he was sure of at the moment was that he'd better not draw attention to himself by shaving his beard—and that he'd better keep his mouth shut.

❖ ❖ ❖

Ethan stood at his cousin's casket and stared at the young man, who looked asleep. If it were possible for a dead person to look good, Drew did. Somehow the mortician had managed to get his coloring right—so much so that Ethan was tempted to shake him and wake him up.

Ethan felt a hand squeeze his shoulder, and then he heard his dad's voice.

"People have started to arrive," Tom said softly. "Would you like a few more minutes?"

"No. I'm okay, Dad."

Ethan took comfort in his father's touch for a moment longer, then walked over and stood next to his mother, prepared to help greet those who shared their grief.

Uncle Richard and Aunt Becca, eyes red rimmed and voices quivering, hugged the first arrivals and spoke quietly.

Ethan shuffled from one foot to the other, not quite knowing what to do with his hands. Why did he feel so confused? Part of him wanted to curl up and weep, and part of him wanted to pick up the ceramic vases in the room and smash them against the wall.

He shook hands with a white-haired man wearing thick glasses who introduced himself as Hayford Slocum. He watched the man's mouth move but didn't hear a word he was saying. Mr. Slocum patted Ethan on the shoulder and then moved on to his dad.

Martha Slocum hugged Ethan and said she had been his Sunday-school teacher when he and Drew were preschoolers. Her tears were as real as the scent of perfume that thickened the air around them.

More consolers came and went, but Mrs. Slocum's scent remained for quite some time.

Ethan was pleasantly surprised at how comforting it was to hear others who had known Drew share their fondest memory. At times the laughter was almost healing and, for a moment, he forgot where he was and what they were doing. Until Vanessa showed up.

Ethan went over to her, took her by the hand, and led her to Drew's casket, nervous about how she would react.

She stood silent for a long time, seemingly studying Drew's face. "I was dreading this," she said. "But he looks so much better now. I'm glad I saw him."

"Yeah, he really looks like Drew." Ethan took a clean handkerchief out of his pocket and wiped the tears off her cheeks. "I wasn't expecting that either."

"I can't believe the line of people," she said. "Did you get started late?"

"No, hundreds of people showed. It's amazing. What did you do with Carter?"

"Emily has him outside. So how are you holding up?"

He brushed the hair off her wet cheek. "Better than I thought I would. I haven't been to many of these. I guess I didn't realize how comforting it would be."

"It sure was when my grandparents died," Vanessa said. "I'll never forget how special it was that all those people came out to pay their respects."

"Speaking of that, I probably should go back and stand with my folks."

"Go ahead," Vanessa said. "I'm fine. By the way, is your uncle Ralph coming?"

Ethan shook his head. "No, he's stubborn as ever. It's sad, too, because he would've liked Drew. I think the two of them could've had a relationship if things had been different between my uncles."

"Is your uncle Ralph sad about Drew?"

"I'm sure he is—but not enough to face his brother."

"They've sure got some major pride issues going on. How do your aunts handle it?"

"No better than the rest of us." Ethan kissed her forehead. "I'll stop by the house when I'm done here."

CHAPTER 22

Ethan sat next to Vanessa on the glider, watching Carter sleep in her arms, and listened to the sounds of nature, glad for the refreshing breeze that flowed through the screened-in porch at the Jessups'.

He enjoyed the moment and tried not to think about what tomorrow would bring. The hum of crickets and the earthy smell that scented the night air reminded him of the times he and Drew camped out in the backyard when they were kids—and then up in the hills when they were older. Good memories. Memories he never wanted to lose.

"What are you thinking about?" Vanessa said.

"The crickets got me thinking about camping with Drew. The first time we tried it, we were really little, maybe six or seven. Uncle Richard pitched a pup tent in the backyard, and Aunt Becca made us *provisions*. It was a big deal. We tried to act brave, but every sound sent us shrieking and laughing, hiding our heads in our sleeping bags. I was sure Bigfoot was out there and we were going to be his next meal. My aunt and uncle decided if *they* were going to get any sleep, we would have to move our campsite into the living room."

"Did it work?"

"Yeah. We both fell asleep pretty fast once we were inside with the door locked." Ethan smiled. "But we talked about that campout for a long time. And the monsters lurking in the shadows got bigger every time we told it."

"Like a fish story?"

"Exactly." Ethan's smile faded, and he let out a long sigh. "I've never had to let go of anyone I loved before. It's harder than I imagined."

"It really is. At least you'll be able to comfort your patients when you're a counselor. God won't let your sorrow be wasted."

"Life experience would be a great thing to have if you didn't have to *experience* it first."

"Ethan, you should post that on your Facebook page. It's rather profound."

"Profound, eh?"

"Yes, I'll have to ponder it awhile."

"While you're pondering, would you mind if I hold Carter?"

"Heavens, no." Vanessa gently moved Carter into Ethan's waiting arms.

"He's so cute when he's sleeping," Ethan said. "It makes me feel strong when I've got him—and in control. It's a lot better than feeling like a scared little boy."

"Dealing with death strips us down to our most vulnerable state, doesn't it?"

"Well, listen to you." Ethan nudged her with his elbow. "Now it's your turn to sound profound."

Vanessa was quiet for a minute, then said, "I've been debating something in my mind since we left the funeral home. I really don't want to wear black tomorrow."

"So don't."

"I want to wear white, but I don't want to offend anyone."

"My family is pretty hard to offend, Vanessa."

"If we have to lose Drew, the least we can do is celebrate his going home for eternity. I think he'd want us to, don't you?"

Ethan stroked a lock of her hair. "Absolutely. I've been so down that I honestly hadn't thought about what Drew would want. But you're right."

"So it's all right with you if I wear white?"

"Of course." He slipped his arm around her. "You just talked me into wearing a white shirt."

"Good." She laid her head on his shoulder. "It's going to be very emotional. It'll help me to keep it all in perspective."

Tessa looked out the bedroom window and watched Vanessa stroll with Ethan to his car and then disappear in his arms. For a moment, in the light of the moon, it seemed as if the two silhouettes were one.

"You spying on the lovebirds?" Antonio said.

Tessa felt her cheeks warm. "I thought you were asleep."

"I woke up and realized you weren't next to me."

"Sorry, I'm restless. I think I'll go downstairs and make myself a cup of tea."

"You thinking about tomorrow?"

Tessa went over to the bed and sat on the side. "I suppose I am. I feel so bad for Ethan and his family—and for the Jessups. They've had more than their share of grief in the past two years. I want to go to Drew's funeral to support them. But I'm dreading it. It's difficult enough when friends our age pass on. But nothing about burying young people feels right."

Antonio took her hand. "I'm glad to know Drew was a believer. That has to help. But the grief his parents feel is different than anything we've been through."

"I wonder what all this stress is doing to Vanessa's relationship with Ethan."

"What do you mean, love?"

"Well, grief doesn't leave much room for romance. I'm afraid the mood of the summer will be dark and heavy instead of light and airy."

Antonio chuckled. "Light and airy? I've never thought of it that way."

"Okay, happy and carefree. You know what I mean. They just shouldn't be heavy laden when they're trying to fall in love."

"Doesn't seem fair, does it?"

"No." Tessa sighed. "Ethan will have to go back to the University of Memphis at the end of August. It'll be here before we know it."

"Guess you won't get to play matchmaker."

"Oh, I'm just going to pray." Tessa squeezed his hand. "I think God has plans for these two. And if I'm right, things will fall into place just as they should."

Antonio lifted an eyebrow. "And you're just going to leave it alone and let God act without your help? That'll be the day."

"I do think I'll go downstairs and make some tea." Tessa stood, suppressing a smile that threatened to give her away. "We're going to eat at Nick's tomorrow before we go to the funeral, aren't we?"

"We should have time, since the service starts at two. Why?"

"Oh, I was just thinking it might be crowded since it's a holiday weekend. We should probably get there early."

"No wonder you can't sleep," Antonio said. "Why are you wasting your brain power on that?"

"You're right. I think I'll get my Bible and have a nice quiet time with the Lord. I'm sure Gus will find a way to blame Brill for the shootings and somehow tie it all to the elusive red shadows. I probably should make sure I'm prayed up so I don't end up bickering with him."

❋ ❋ ❋

Brill sighed and swung her legs over the side of the bed. She sat for a moment, then set her bare feet on the floor and shuffled over to the window. The side yard was totally lit up with moonlight. Pouncer scurried along the wood fence, chasing away an orange and white cat that belonged to the family two doors down.

Why hadn't she taken something to help her sleep? It was too late now. If she took a sleep aid, she'd never be able to function in four hours when it was time to get up. How she dreaded facing such a stressful day feeling washed out from the get-go.

Had Vanessa been able to fall asleep? The media would be waiting for her tomorrow like a pack of wolves, pressuring her for a firsthand account of Drew's shooting death and her own ordeal of scrambling to protect Carter. At least she had some experience with being pursued by them and knew to keep her head down and avoid responding to their barrage of questions.

Brill put her hand on the back of her neck and massaged

the muscles. Why was she so uneasy about Vanessa being out in public?

"Honey, why are you standing at the window?"

She turned to the voice, and Kurt's eyes looked like two black coals in the light of the moon.

"My mind's racing," she said. "I want to be sure I've covered everything for tomorrow."

"Tal Davison's funeral went smoothly, and Drew's will be a lot smaller."

"I know. I'm concerned about Vanessa. The media will be all over her, pressing her for the gory details of Drew's shooting. I think I'll have Rachel Howell keep an eye on her for the day."

"I can take care of Vanessa."

"Are you sure?"

"Where'd that come from?" Kurt sat up in bed.

"I'm probably being paranoid, but if someone wanted to get to her, she'd be an easy target."

"Honey, you made sure the media reported that Vanessa didn't see the vehicle *or* the shooter. Why are you worried someone would want to get to her if she isn't a threat?"

Brill turned her back to him and looked up at the moon. "The problem is I don't know what constitutes a *threat* since we don't know why these young people were killed. I don't think it was just coincidence, but we still can't find a common thread."

"What does that have to do with Vanessa?"

"Nothing, I hope. But until we know more, I just think it would be wise to take extra precautions today."

"What *precautions?*"

"Keep your voice down, Kurt. All Vanessa needs is for you to overreact." Brill walked over to the bed and sat next to him.

"Sorry," he said. "But I had let go of the idea that Vanessa might be in danger."

"I had too, but now I'm not so sure. I'm not too keen on her being out in the open, especially with the media singling her out. Rachel was wonderful when she accompanied me to Memphis for Zack's funeral. She's the best shot in the department, and she's a black belt in karate. Other than Trent, I can't think of anyone I would trust more to watch Vanessa's back."

Stedman sat in the La-Z-Boy in his moonlit living room. The ticking of the cuckoo clock his grandmother gave him seemed exaggerated and annoying. He got up, stopped the pendulum, and listened to the silence, which was soon replaced by the drip-drip-drip of the kitchen sink.

He flopped on the couch and stretched out. How much trouble was he in? His fingerprints were all over the Smith & Wesson someone turned over to the police. If the cops came looking for him, what could he tell them? There was no record of the deal he made with Grant. No alibi for the time of the shooting.

Stedman sighed. The more he thought about it, the more convinced he was that Grant had switched the deck and dealt himself a straight flush and Stedman four jacks. Grant set him up to bet big and lose big. Were the other players in on it?

None of it made sense. Why did Grant need to frame Stedman?

He could've gotten away with killing Win Davison's son without anyone knowing or suspecting him. He was a model employee.

Stedman sat up and threw a couch pillow in the fireplace, sending last winter's ashes in all directions. How had he gotten himself into this mess?

Your gambling's an addiction, son. Get help before they own you.

Father David's words resounded in his head and both angered and frightened him. They owned him, all right. The question was, had they sold him out?

CHAPTER 23

Brill straightened her suit jacket so the four-starred epaulets were square on her shoulders, then placed her hat atop a head of thick red hair. The police chief in the mirror was a stark contrast to the late Chief Hennessey.

There were those who felt her taking the helm in a town of thirteen thousand was a comedown from heading up a detective division in a major city. She didn't see it that way—not that it mattered. The job was what it was.

The only reason she sought the position was to get away from Memphis and the painful memories associated with Kurt's affair. Could she have ever imagined what a challenge it would present almost from the moment she was sworn in?

But even in the shadow of Chief Hennessey's legacy, she had proven to the community that she was capable of solving cases and seeing difficult investigations through to completion. Could anyone dispute that she had dealt with more violence in two years than he had in thirty?

She saw the angst in the blue eyes staring back at her in the mirror. Would anyone even care about her successes today when she stood by and watched a *fourth* set of parents bury their murdered child?

Kurt's reflection appeared next to hers in the mirror. "Vanessa's up. She's sitting out in the kitchen."

"Thanks. I'll go talk to her." Brill put on her lipstick and blotted it. "I'll catch up with you at Drew's parents' house after the funeral."

Kurt kissed her on the cheek. "You'll get this guy. Don't let Drew's death destroy your confidence."

"If anything, it's fueled my determination."

"Now you're talking."

Brill squeezed his hand, then turned and walked out to the kitchen, where Vanessa sat at the table, feeding Carter.

"Hi there, big guy." Brill went over to Carter and brushed his fine hair with her fingers. "How's the cutest grandbaby on the planet?"

"Starved," Vanessa said. "He's a little eating machine."

Brill hugged Vanessa. "How are *you* doing this morning?"

"So-so. I feel a little hollow, like something's been ripped out of me. Maybe it's just empathy for what Ethan and his family are going through."

"I don't know, honey"—Brill pulled out a chair and sat—"you've been through a traumatic ordeal yourself. It has to be weighing on you. Listen … I made a decision to do something I think is wise. I've asked Rachel Howell to escort you to Drew's funeral today."

"Rachel? Why?"

"I have no doubt the media is going to be relentless in their quest to get you to talk about the shooting."

"They know I can't talk about the case while the investigation is open—not that I would anyway."

"But that won't stop them from trying. I'd like Rachel to run interference. She can help shield you from them."

Vanessa held her gaze. "There's more to it than that, isn't there?"

"It can't hurt to give you a little extra protection as long as the shooter is still out there."

"That'll make Ethan happy. He's been worried about my safety since Drew was shot."

"Really? You didn't mention it."

"I thought Ethan was being overprotective. You said you weren't too concerned that I was at risk since I didn't see the shooter or the car."

"I *wasn't* that concerned in the beginning," Brill said, "because I was convinced we would discover that Drew and Tal Davison were involved in something illegal. But they had completely different cell phone directories, email contacts, even friends. If they were involved in something illegal, we would've expected to find a common contact somewhere."

"Maybe their deaths were just an eerie coincidence."

"Maybe. But since we don't know yet, I'd feel better if Rachel Howell accompanied you to the funeral."

❖   ❖   ❖

Ethan stood at his bedroom window at Uncle Ralph and Aunt Gwen's and watched the morning sun spread like warm butter across the hazy foothills. He felt strangely alone. For the first time in his life, he was the only child in the Langley family. He and Drew had been inseparable, and now his presence at any family gathering would be a stark reminder to everyone else that Drew was gone.

Ethan took off his glasses and wiped his eyes. He had to pull himself together. He needed to help Uncle Richard and Aunt Becca get through the most horrible day of their lives.

He walked over to the closet and took out the white dress shirt he had borrowed from Uncle Ralph and the dark blue suit he had worn to the sweetheart ball when he was a senior in high school. And a blue and red striped tie.

He liked Vanessa's idea of wearing white to celebrate Drew's going home for eternity. It would be a hard day for her, too, and he wished he didn't have to wait to see her until the family and friends gathered after the funeral.

There was a knock at the door.

"Come in."

"It's me." Uncle Ralph opened the door and stepped inside. "I was just wondering how you were doing."

"I'm not sure how I'm supposed to be doing when I'm about to bury my best friend and only cousin. Okay, I guess. Thanks for lending me the white shirt."

"No problem. Listen … I just wanted to say I'll be thinking of you today. I know it'll be a tough one."

"You should be saying this to Uncle Richard."

"Ethan … "

"It's not too late. He and Aunt Becca are too sad to fight with you. I think they'd just appreciate knowing you care, that's all."

"I told you I care. That's not the issue."

"I'm sorry, but the *issue* doesn't seem that important right now."

Uncle Ralph's face looked flushed. "I don't know what Richard's told you, but there's no way he wants me there."

"Then shame on both of you—" Ethan threw his hands in the

air, disgusted that his eyes teared up and a knot of emotion stole his voice.

Ralph exhaled loudly. "I know my feud with Richard is a huge disappointment to you, Ethan. But it has nothing to do with you and me. I love you like you were my own. And I'll always regret that I never got to know Drew."

"Yeah, well, you *should* regret it." Ethan took off his glasses and tossed them on the bed. "But you're going to have much more serious regrets if you don't make peace with Richard. He's your twin brother, for heaven's sake. You've wasted fifteen years of your lives— all because you won't accept his apology!"

"Hey, watch that tone, bud. This is your uncle Ralph you're talking to. I don't take that from anybody."

Ethan paused to gain his composure. "I didn't mean any disrespect. I'm just caught between two uncles I care very much about."

"Yeah, I know. I hate that." Ralph squeezed his shoulder and was quiet for half a minute. Finally he said, "Take it easy, okay? I'll see you tonight. I hope things go as well as they can."

Tessa pushed open the door at Nick's Grill, hearing thunder rumbling in the distance, and hurried inside, a sudden breeze seeming to push Antonio in on her heels.

A second later Nick stood with his arm around her and his hand extended to Antonio.

"Welcome, friends."

"Oh my, what smells so delicious?" Tessa said.

A grin slowly spread across Nick's face. "Low-fat, low-calorie, no-guilt personal-size pizza made with veggie sausage on a thin, crunchy crust. You choose three veggie toppings. It'll knock your socks off."

Antonio gave him a high five. "Now you're talking."

"Comes with my homemade pizza sauce," Nick said, "and low-fat mozzarella. I'm proud of this one. It's really tasty."

"That's what I'm having," Tessa said.

Antonio laughed and nudged her toward the counter. "I might have two."

Tessa made her way to the counter and saw Gus and Maggie seated in their usual places. "Hello, hello."

"Hey there," Maggie said. "You two look nice. Oh, that's right; you're going to Drew Langley's funeral after this."

Tessa nodded and took her seat.

Antonio slid onto the stool between Tessa and Gus and slapped Gus on the back. "How's it going, friend?"

"Really can't complain, but I always do."

"So what do you know?"

"Not as much as I'd like to," Gus said. "Why do you suppose someone would turn the shooter's gun over to the police and not give a hint as to who it belonged to?"

Antonio shrugged. "Guess they thought the police would be able to figure it out."

"So *has* that police-chief neighbor of yours figured it out?"

"How would we know?" Tessa said. "We're not privy to her police business."

Gus's eyes narrowed. "I think it's *everyone's* business when four people die of gunshot wounds and no one's been arrested. Doesn't sound to me like the cops know squat."

"These things take time"—Tessa looked down the counter—"and I think you should refrain from second-guessing Brill when you don't have all the facts."

A smile appeared under Gus's mustache. "I have my own idea about who's behind the crimes in this town."

"Yes, we know," Tessa said, "and each time you've been proven wrong."

"Have not."

"Have too."

"Have not. The stuff I'm talkin' about can't be proven one way or the other."

Clint Ames slid onto the stool next to Tessa and put his sunglasses in his shirt pocket. "What stuff?"

"All right, you know what *I* think?" Antonio raised his hands and brought them down on the counter with a thud. "I think Gus stopped believing the red-shadows legend a long time ago—and doesn't want to admit it because he enjoys rabble-rousing. Am I right?"

Gus's face went blank. He opened his mouth and then closed it without saying a word.

A clap of thunder shook the building, and no one said anything.

Finally Tessa became aware of Jo Beth McCauley standing on the other side of the counter.

Jo Beth cleared her throat, as if to make her presence known. "I'm ready to take y'all's orders, whenever you're ready."

"Gus and I are each having the special," Maggie said, louder than she needed to.

Tessa gave a nod. "Same for Antonio and me."

"Topping preferences are up on the board. You each get three." Jo Beth wrote down everyone's choices and then said, "Coffee all around and a Coke for Gus?"

Four heads nodded in agreement, and Jo Beth turned and went through the swinging doors, her long dark braid reminding Tessa of their conversation about her Cherokee heritage.

"What time's the funeral?" Maggie asked.

"Two." Antonio glanced at his watch. "We're praying that Vanessa gets through this day in one piece. It's not fair that she barely got over one trauma and now has another to deal with."

Tessa kept her eye on Gus. He just stared at his hands.

Nick held his army green umbrella over Tessa and Antonio and ran with them to their car as the heavens opened up and torrents of rain blew across Third Street. He got them situated in the car and then ran back inside, waving at them from the door as a clap of thunder shook the building and rattled the windows.

He folded the umbrella and hung it on the coatrack, figuring the Masinos would not be the only customers needing his help. He noticed Gus was still sitting at the counter. He grabbed a bar towel and wiped the rain off his arms, then walked over to Gus and slid onto the stool next to him.

"Boy howdy, it's sure carrying on out there. Going to wreck

holiday plans for a lot of folks." Nick could feel the tension coming from Gus. "You're awfully quiet, friend."

"That oughta make you happy," Gus said.

"Come on, you know better than that."

Gus planted his elbows on the counter, his chin on his palms, and exhaled. "I still can't believe Antonio turned on me—and in front of everyone."

"Your old buddy didn't turn on you."

"What would *you* call it?"

Nick saw a flash of lightning out of the corner of his eye and waited for the crash of thunder and its lengthy reverberation. Should he try to sugarcoat it or just say it straight out?

"Gus, how long have we known each other?"

"I don't know … more than twenty-five years."

"Have I ever lied to you?"

"Not that I know of."

"Misled you in any way?"

"No."

"Then listen to me: I think you need to be honest with yourself about Antonio's question."

"What, that I don't believe in the legend anymore—or that I like rabble-rousing?"

Nick lifted an eyebrow and held Gus's gaze. "Both."

"Hey, it was a nosy question, and I don't owe him an answer."

"Well, *I'd* sure like to know—because I don't think anyone wants to shut you up; they just want you to change the subject."

Gus took his straw and poked at the ice cubes in his glass. "Okay, so I'm on Chief Jessup's back again. I don't think it's wrong for a citizen of this town to question what she's doin' when there're four bodies and no suspects."

"Fair enough. But it's more than that, Gus."

"Like what?"

"Like you find a way to twist the facts of every case until the subject comes back to the legend, one way or the other."

"So?"

"So it's wearing us out."

Gus winced. "Aw, don't say that."

Nick reached over and gently gripped Gus's wrist. "It has to be said, friend. Let's be honest with each other. Was Antonio right? Do you *really* believe the red-shadows legend—or is rabble-rousing the only way you know how to get involved in the conversation?"

Gus sat quietly, his cheeks flushed, and seemed to stare at nothing.

Nick tried to discern whether Gus's silence was a sign of anger or of embarrassment.

A minute passed. Finally Gus said, "I'm not a stupid man, Nick. I keep up with what's goin' on around the globe. I watch cable news half the day." Gus let out an exaggerated sigh. "So why is it so hard for me to just talk to folks without stirrin' the pot?"

"Not everyone is social. Sometimes you have to learn to be. So tell me the truth: Do you really believe in the legend?"

Gus rubbed his mustache. "Nah. It's just somethin' I grew up with that's always intrigued me. And it's fun when I can use it to get the best of Tessa." Gus chuckled. "She's somethin' when she's flustered."

"You've been faking it all this time?"

"Pretty much. Though I wasn't so sure after Billy Dan swore he saw the red shadows when he was kidnapped. For a while I toyed with the idea that they might be real. But now I think the roofie they gave him made him see things that weren't there."

"Is that so hard to admit to your friends?"

Gus tipped his glass and crunched a piece of ice. "It's more complicated than that."

"How?"

"Y'all didn't grow up with the legend like I did. There's somethin' special about keepin' to it. It's as much a part of this town's history as our name."

"That doesn't have to change, Gus. The legend can be history. It just doesn't have to dominate our lunch conversation, especially since we all know it's just talk. Why don't you draw on some of that cable-news knowledge and talk about something else?"

"I told you I'm not social."

"You talk to Maggie just fine. We're your friends, Gus. Just be yourself and leave the legend at the barbershop."

There was a long stretch of uncomfortable silence.

"You've got a lot of nerve, confrontin' me with this," Gus finally said.

Nick stood and gave Gus a gentle pat on the back. "But that's what friends do. I've got to go greet customers. Are we okay?"

"We will be. Thanks for not sayin' anything in front of Maggie."

"I saw her go into the kitchen," Nick said, "and figured she was checking to see if we're still living up to her standard. I miss having her waiting tables. You stole her right out from under my nose, you know."

Gus turned and looked up, a twinkle in his eye and a grin beneath his mustache. "Not too bad for an old duffer with the social skills of a fire ant."

CHAPTER 24

Stedman sat in his truck and pulled the last few Oreos out of the wrapper, his gaze fixed on the Great Smoky Mountains and the vivid rainbow that formed a perfect arch from one end of the sky to the other. He wondered if Ethan could see it—and how well his family was holding up with his cousin's funeral just fifteen minutes away.

"Was it something I said?"

Ralph Langley's voice was loud and his laugh intrusive, but Stedman tried not to show his annoyance.

"Hey, Ralph. I just felt like being by myself rather than waiting out the storm with the guys."

"I was just checking on you. Now that the sun's out, it feels like a steam bath out here. I was hoping you didn't have another of your headaches."

"No, I'm fine. Just waiting for the cement trucks. I wonder how Ethan's doing." *And your brother's family—not that you care.*

"It's a terrible thing that's happened to my nephew. I told you my brother Richard and I have been out of touch for a long time, right?"

"That's what you said."

"I couldn't very well go to my nephew's funeral with so many unresolved issues. It'd be awkward for everybody."

"I suppose so."

"Some people might think I'm being cold. It's not that I don't care. I just don't think this is the time to break the ice. I mean, we haven't said two words in fifteen years."

"Ralph, you don't owe me an explanation."

"Yeah I do." Ralph patted his shoulder. "I look like the bad guy in all this, and I'm really not. Though it really doesn't matter what people think. Today's not about me. I don't have a relationship with Richard, and I'll never have one with Drew. But Ethan's like a son to me. I can't get him off my mind."

"Ever try making peace with your brother?" Stedman said.

"Sure I have. It's complicated. Richard said some cruel things to me and apologized. But I believe he meant what he said, and I'll never be close to him again."

"I'm not close to my brother either. I just think Ethan and Drew were close the way *brothers* are supposed to be. They had something special, you know?"

Ralph sighed. "Yeah, they did."

"You suppose the rainbow is some sort of sign—like God telling everyone that Drew's okay?"

"I don't know. They sure don't get any prettier than that." Ralph glanced at his watch. "I'm going to call and make sure the cement trucks are ready to roll. We've still got driveways to pour before we shut down for Memorial Day."

Stedman crushed the Oreo wrapper and stuffed it in the sack. He wondered if Ralph would be surprised to know that he wasn't the only one holding on to something he felt guilty about.

Ethan sat with his parents in the second row of Cross Way Bible Fellowship and listened to the organ playing familiar hymns that he knew would make the older adults happy. Drew would have preferred something contemporary.

He looked up through the huge cross window and saw blue sky. At least they wouldn't have to deal with bad weather when they went to the cemetery for the burial.

Burial. How he dreaded the thought of that final good-bye. He could file by Drew's coffin and place a rose on it. But no one could decide for him when or how he was going to say good-bye. Or even *if.*

He glanced at the silver blue coffin and cringed at the thought of Drew being enclosed. Drew loved the outdoors—wide-open spaces. It seemed so wrong. Then again, it was just his body. Couldn't his spirit soar in another realm?

He remembered the two of them as kids, capes tied around their necks, running down the street with their arms extended and pretending to fly like Superman, the wind tickling their faces.

His thoughts shifted to a breezy day the previous August when he and Drew had golfed together before they had to go back to school. Drew won by three strokes, but it was never about the score. It was always about spending time together. They promised to play again as soon as they came home for summer break. How could they have known they would never get that chance?

Ethan brushed off the tear that spilled down his cheek. He heard his mother and Aunt Becca quietly weeping and thought his heart would break. It was surreal—Drew in a casket, wearing a suit and tie, the collar of his shirt hiding the bullet hole in his neck.

Lord, how am I going to get through this? Why did you let Drew die so young—and so violently? And why did Vanessa have to see it? Hadn't she been through enough?

He figured Vanessa was sitting with her dad and Emily somewhere behind him. Chief Jessup sat with the mayor and the sheriff across the aisle. She looked somber. They all did.

The organ music stopped, and Pastor Gavin Bonner came out and stood at the pulpit. The church was suddenly pin-drop still, almost as if everyone had breathed in and forgotten to exhale.

"My dear friends," his deep voice resonated, "we gather today, not only to mourn Drew Langley's death, but to celebrate his life— and his going home to be with His Lord and Savior …"

Ethan almost smiled when he spotted the cuffs of his white shirt and remembered his conversation with Vanessa the night before. He hoped Drew could see him because he knew he'd be impressed—and perhaps a little amused—at the sight of Ethan wearing a borrowed white shirt and stuffed into a suit and tie.

"As we walk Drew to the gates of eternity and part ways for now, we have the assurance that a glorious future awaits every person who has put his or her faith in the Son of God …"

Ethan tuned out Pastor Gavin's words. He couldn't afford to lose it. Not here. Not now.

He wondered what Drew was doing at this moment and if he had any memory of how he had died—or if all the things of earth were washed from his knowing. Did he see what was happening here? Did he know how loved he was? Or was all this for the living?

Tessa listened to Pastor Gavin, her thoughts wandering, her gaze moving from Brill to Vanessa and back to Brill. The sadness was heavy and almost tangible, and she wished it were possible to pick up the burden and carry it awhile to give the mourners a rest.

Twenty-one years old. What a waste. What might Drew Langley have contributed had he been allowed to live out his life?

And yet You, O Lord, had ordered his steps since before time began. You know him intimately and have called him into Your presence. Your timing is not our timing. Your ways not our ways. Father, comfort those who love this young man. Give them strength and the proper perspective.

Tessa sighed and held more tightly to Antonio's hand. Brill would find the killer. She had no doubt of that. What must be going through Vanessa's mind? Was the memory of the shooting terrifying?

Tessa could still see vivid images of the night she and Antonio and little Emily and Jasmine were held at gunpoint. Not that she welcomed the intrusion to her thoughts, but she could imagine Jesus there with them now, and the images no longer woke her up at night, her sheets soaked with anxiety. Fear no longer held her captive.

Lord, give Vanessa the grace to let go of the fear and not to be crippled by the memory of Drew's death. And Lord, be with his parents. And with Ethan. The emptiness in their hearts must seem unbearable.

Antonio squeezed her hand, almost as if he could read her mind.

Tessa studied Brill, who looked very official in her dress uniform but a decade older somehow. How grieved she must be that four young people were cut down while she was in command—and that it hit so close to home.

Brill shifted her weight in the pew, her eyes searching the left side of the church. There they were. She finally spotted her family, glad to see Rachel Howell sitting next to Vanessa. Emily had linked arms with Kurt, her head on his shoulder. They all looked somber.

Pastor Gavin's deep voice brought Brill back to the moment.

"And so it is with mixed emotions that we give the soul of Drew Maxwell Langley back to His Creator, who never once had him out of His sight. Lord, we do not pretend to understand the reason this young man has been taken from us, but we trust in Your infinite wisdom, Your unfailing love, and Your master plan that surpasses all understanding …"

Brill folded her hands in her lap and pretended to be listening but decided she could maintain her composure only if she didn't hang on every word Pastor Gavin spoke. The sniffling and sobbing of Drew's relatives was hard to take and fueled her commitment to finding the person or persons responsible for his death.

She'd been over it a hundred times in her head. If Drew and Tal had been involved in something illegal—or if they had information that could have incriminated someone else—it was not evident in their emails, in their phone records, or on anything found in their apartment. How could two college kids manage to cover their tracks like a couple of professionals?

A young man with a guitar strapped round his neck walked over to a microphone and began singing "It Is Well." But was it? Would it ever be until justice was served?

Brill saw Vanessa wipe the tears off her cheeks and Kurt slip his arm around her. She glanced over at Ethan. He sat still as a stone, his hands folded in his lap, his face expressionless. She could almost hear the sound of his heart breaking in two.

When does it stop hurting? he had asked her.

Everyone's different, Ethan. All I can tell you is that it does.

Brill blinked to clear the moisture from her eyes, keenly aware that unless she could bring closure, it might take forever.

CHAPTER 25

Stedman pushed open the door to his side of the duplex his grand-mother was renting to him for a fraction of what he would pay elsewhere. He took off his work boots and socks, walked barefoot to the kitchen, and tossed his keys on the table. He reached in the refrigerator, which was empty except for leftover Chinese takeout and his last can of beer. He popped the top of the can and took a big gulp, Thursday's conversation with Grant at Rambo's playing over and over like a stuck CD.

It seemed obvious that Grant intended for Tal Davison's death to send a message to his big-shot father. But why did Grant—or whomever he was conspiring with—decide to shoot indiscriminately, knowing innocent people could be hit? And why go after Drew Langley? What did his death have to do with anything? And why the phony deal to make sure Stedman's fingerprints were on the gun—unless he was trying to pull something? But what? And why?

The hype over the funerals had to be pressuring the cops to make an arrest. What if the anonymous person who turned in the gun decided to tell the police whose prints were on it? Grant told him he had nothing to worry about as long as he kept his mouth shut. But how could he believe a guy who tricked him? What if he *was* being set up? Was he going to sit back like a dupe and let it happen?

He leaned against the sink and looked out the kitchen window, hoping his grandmother would not pick now to come over. He chugged the beer and crushed the can. How could he have gotten himself mixed up in this? He was ashamed that he'd ever agreed to kill a man. But he didn't do it. Was he even capable of it? Hadn't he followed Tal Davison for blocks, cowering behind the steering wheel, unable to get up his nerve? He was not going to be somebody's scapegoat for four murders!

There must be something he could do to protect himself. He glanced up at the clock. Grant would be playing poker tonight. Maybe it was time to start searching for whatever it was Grant *wasn't* telling him.

Ethan stood out in the backyard of his uncle Richard and aunt Becca's house, his hands in his pockets, and looked out beyond the giant oaks to the silhouette of the Great Smoky Mountains that dominated the evening sky. He could almost feel Drew's heartbeat beneath his feet, hear his voice in the breeze. They had stood together on this very spot a hundred times. How could he be gone?

A warm hand touched his back.

"How're you doing?" Tom Langley asked.

"I'm pretty empty, Dad. How about you?"

"That about covers it. Sure you don't want something to eat? The church women brought enough to feed an army, but it's been sitting out awhile and the girls want to get it in the refrigerator."

"Thanks. But I'm really not hungry."

"The funeral was nice."

"Very. But I'm disgusted with Uncle Ralph for not at least sending flowers."

"You've got enough on your plate without worrying about that situation."

Ethan looked into his dad's face, which bore Richard's gentleness and Ralph's determination. "I'm the only nephew now. It feels weird."

"I know, son. I'm so sorry."

Ethan's eyes brimmed with tears, and the Great Smoky Mountains became a blurred mass of gray, like the inkblots pictured in his psychology textbooks. "I can't imagine my life without Drew."

"You two were inseparable. I can only imagine how hard this is for you."

"Why did it have to end like *this,* Dad? I mean, why couldn't Drew have died trying to save someone's life? I hate it that people will remember him as a murder victim—a statistic."

"His family won't."

"I doubt Vanessa will ever be able to think of Drew any other way."

His dad looked at him knowingly. "Then we'll just have to tell her about the Drew we knew and loved. But you're the psych major. I don't need to tell you how to handle things." He popped Ethan with his knuckle. " So … you really like this young lady. I can tell."

"I do—a lot."

"Is it serious?"

"I'd like it to be." Ethan exhaled. "All I planned to do this summer, besides work for Uncle Ralph, was enjoy Vanessa's company—and Carter's—and see where that would take us."

"Good. Sounds promising."

"Come on, Dad. Drew's murder didn't exactly set the mood for romance."

Tom put his hands on Ethan's shoulders. "Listen to me: True love can bloom in any season. It's the hardiest living thing on the face of the earth."

"Yeah, if grief doesn't kill it."

"It won't unless you let it. Drew died, Ethan. You didn't. As long as you're still breathing, you've got a future to plan for. And if it were me, I sure wouldn't let that beautiful young woman slip through my fingers."

"I feel guilty even thinking about my own happiness right now."

"That'll pass. You can't just stop living because Drew was taken from us."

Stedman drove down Main until he was out of downtown, then turned right on Robin Road and left on Bluebird. He drove slowly past the dark green bungalow at 520 and didn't see lights on or Grant's Explorer in the driveway. Poker games were held in the back room at Rambo's and typically went on until the wee hours of the morning.

Stedman drove one block over and parked along the curb under a big shade tree, relieved when the moon disappeared behind the clouds. He waited until he was sure no one was in sight, then got out, grabbed a bag out of the bed of his truck, and moved stealthily in the dark through the side yard, toward the alley.

A frenzied dog yapped somewhere nearby. That's all he needed. He slipped surreptitiously behind what appeared to be a detached garage, then crossed the alley to the privacy fence behind Grant's house. He released the latch on the heavy wood gate and pushed—relieved when it opened with no resistance.

The lights came on next door, and then the back porch light. Stedman ducked down behind a large garbage can and didn't breathe. He heard a woman's voice, but the thumping of his heart was so loud he couldn't make out what she was saying. Suddenly this seemed like a bad idea.

Stedman sat on his heels, considering what he was about to do and the consequences if it backfired. What choice did he have? Grant wasn't volunteering any information.

The porch light went out. The dog stopped barking. Stedman's pulse quickened.

Okay, lady. Go back to bed and let me do what I came to do.

He waited for a solid minute, then zipped across the yard to Grant's back door. It was locked. Stedman took a hammer out of his bag and tapped the window until it broke, then reached inside and slid the bolt lock. The door opened. He was in!

Ethan sat on the glider with Vanessa on the back porch at the Jessups', listening to the crickets, glad to be away from friends, neighbors, and strangers expressing their condolences. The earthy scent of the night air was soothing, and he hated the thought of leaving.

He squeezed Vanessa's hand. "I should probably go and let you get some rest. Carter will be up with the sun."

"Emily will help me. Stay a little longer. It's so nice just sitting with you. It's the only peaceful thing about this day."

"Okay. I was just trying to be sensitive. I'm in no hurry to leave. It's great being out here with you."

"Not exactly the way we planned the summer, is it?"

Ethan blinked the stinging from his eyes. "I still can't believe Drew's gone. I keep expecting him to walk through that door."

"I know. I just want to erase the murder scene from my mind and remember how he looked before." Vanessa leaned her head on his shoulder. "I wish I could have been with you today. It was a real drag having Rachel Howell following me around."

"Well, I'm glad she did. And I'm glad you've agreed to stay home until your mom gets the shooter. I think it's a wise precaution."

"I don't know how long I can stand it. Being stuck at home makes me crazy. You know how I was last summer."

"Carter will keep you busy during the day." Ethan stroked her cheek. "And I'll come over in the evenings."

"I know Mom will figure out who's doing this. She always does. I just hope it doesn't take all summer."

"She's got her work cut out for her. I've racked my brain, trying to figure out why someone would want Drew dead. I knew him better than anyone, and I'm totally baffled."

❖   ❖   ❖

Stedman closed the back door at Grant's and let his eyes adjust to his pitch-black surroundings and his body to the refrigerated air.

He groped his way through the kitchen and dining room and

found the living room. He pulled the drapes, took his flashlight out of his bag, and moved the beam of light slowly around the room. Grant's place was tasteless. The guy didn't even have pictures on the walls.

"Okay, where's your computer?" he mumbled. "Everybody has one."

Stedman went back to the kitchen and searched for a desk. Nothing. He walked down the hall and stood in the doorway of a bedroom crammed with boxes and assorted junk. He moved on to a larger bedroom and spotted a laptop on a desk in the corner. He pulled out the chair and sat.

He rubbed his hands together. "Here we go."

He turned on the computer and when it finally booted up, he saw that it had been set to ask for an account password. Why would Grant do that unless he had something to hide?

Stedman typed in the word *Grant* and was denied access. He typed in the word *lucky,* but that was rejected too. *Poker* didn't work either. He tried dozens of words that made sense to him—all rejected.

He put his elbows on the desk and combed his hands through his hair. What now? He took a huge risk coming here. Failure was not an option.

Should he just take the laptop with him? What if Grant figured out he broke in and stole it? What if he called the cops and used the incident to accuse Stedman of the shootings? All they'd have to do is compare his fingerprints with those on the gun. It's not as though he had an alibi.

Stedman sat for a moment and summoned all the determination he had. How hard could it be to figure out the password for this stupid computer?

He typed in every word related to poker he could think of and was rejected, then on a whim typed in *poker face*—and bingo!

Stedman's pulse raced so fast he felt light-headed. He clicked on to Windows Mail and saw six opened messages in the in-box. There was one new message. He clicked on to it: a personal note from Brett Wolski about a family barbecue.

Stedman went to the bottom and clicked on to the oldest message and started reading. He moved up and read another and then another. Most of the emails appeared to be exchanges between Grant and their poker buddies, but Stedman's name wasn't mentioned in any of them.

He went to the sent box and read a few emails and didn't see anything interesting there either. Maybe Grant did all his scheming in person—the way he had done with Stedman—so there wouldn't be any correspondence to link him to anyone.

Stedman clicked on to deleted mail and put it in alphabetical order, looking for familiar names. Grant had sent more emails to William Roseland than anyone else—a guy he worked with and who also played poker with them. Stedman started with the most recent and skimmed each of the emails to William, and none alluded to anything shady—and not a hint of conspiracy.

Stedman sighed. He pulled up Grant's documents and read down the list. Most of what he saw appeared to be personal letters to credit card companies regarding his late pays. This guy's life was less interesting than his. His eyes stopped on a folder titled SPECIAL PROJECT.

He clicked on. The folder contained only two documents. One was an email, dated May 1 of this year, addressed to Grant and a guy named Roy Dupontes from Win Davison. *Win Davison?* Grant was just a supervisor at Davison Technologies. What special project would he be working on for the CEO? Stedman clicked on the email and read it: *Meet me in my office at 6:00 p.m. Delete this after reading. WD.*

So why didn't Grant delete it? Stedman opened the other document, a lengthy memo Grant sent to himself, and read every word, line by line. And then read it again.

He was suddenly hot all over and felt as if he were nailed to the chair, a wave of nausea threatening to deposit the contents of his stomach onto Grant's keyboard. He had to get out of there. He had no business knowing any of this! But at least now he had some leverage.

He held the flashlight above the printer, then fumbled with the buttons and turned it on. He set it to print one copy and pushed the button.

The sound of a car door slamming sent a chill crawling up his spine. He turned off the flashlight and stepped over to the window, peering out between the blinds.

A police car was parked out front, and two officers were walking toward the house! The dog next door was yapping again, and he wondered if its owner had called the cops.

Stedman's pulse raced. He reached for the copy and cringed when he saw an orange button flashing on the printer. A paper jam! That's all he needed.

He tugged at the trapped paper and it tore. He stuffed the torn piece in his pocket, swearing under his breath, then grabbed his bag and groped his way through the inky blackness faster than he thought possible, slipping out the back door and through the gate. He crossed the alley and ran down the side yard toward his truck, hoping the cops hadn't spotted him.

He shot out of the darkness into the warm glow of the streetlight and climbed in the front seat of his truck. He fumbled to get the keys in the ignition, sweat dripping down his temples, the pounding of his heart filling the silence. He was relieved when the truck started the first time.

Stedman pulled away from the curb, careful not to leave any tread marks on the pavement, keenly aware that if those involved in the cover-up figured out he knew, he was a dead man.

CHAPTER 26

Brill stumbled out to the kitchen, her silk pajamas feeling cool against her skin. She poured a cup of milk and put it in the microwave, then sat at the table in front of the bay window. She looked out into the moonlit night, surprised to see Ethan's car parked out front.

She got up and walked into the dining room and peered out through the sheers on the French door. Vanessa and Ethan sat on the glider, her head on his shoulder, and appeared to be sound asleep. Poor things had an emotionally exhausting day. Should she wake them? Surely Ethan's aunt and uncle would be worried.

Brill cracked the back door and spoke softly, "Vanessa, honey, wake up ... Ethan ...?"

Ethan stirred first and looked disoriented.

Vanessa stretched and then looked over at Brill, her eyes at half-mast.

"You two fell asleep." Brill opened the door wider. "It's almost midnight. I thought Ethan's aunt and uncle might be worried."

"I'm sorry. I meant to be out of here long before now." Ethan yawned. "I'd better go. Aunt Gwen is probably walking the floor." He kissed Vanessa's cheek. "Don't walk me to the car. I'll call you tomorrow. Just get some sleep."

"Okay." Vanessa held his hand as he stood, and then he pulled her to her feet. "You can walk me to the stairs," she said.

"All right. Good night, Brill. Thanks for waking me up."

Brill gently grasped his forearm and gave it a squeeze. "Be good to yourself. You've been through the mill."

"I will. I'm going to sleep in and go to late church."

"Good."

Brill went inside behind Vanessa and Ethan and then turned into the kitchen to let them say their good-byes in private.

She took her milk out of the microwave and sat again at the table, wide awake and wishing she had the case files at home so she could study them—not that she didn't have every detail filed in her head.

She took a sip of warm milk just as the front door opened and closed. She looked out the window and watched Ethan walk to his car, his grief fueling her commitment to finding the shooter. But how many restless nights would pass between now and then?

❖   ❖   ❖

Stedman locked the front door to his duplex and left the light off. He went into the kitchen and looked in the refrigerator before remembering he was out of beer. He grabbed the Coke bottle he had filled with water and went over to the table and sat. He unscrewed the cap and took a drink. Was he shaking? He ought to be shaking. Grant was right. He'd had no idea what he was getting himself into.

Stedman took the small piece he tore off the memo out of his shirt pocket. Grant's name was on it but nothing on front or back that made sense. Nothing incriminating.

He spat out a swear word and kicked the chair across from him with his foot. It fell backward and hit the floor. Grant would have found the paper jam by now and deleted the entire folder from the computer. What good was knowledge without proof? *Stedman's* fingerprints were on the gun. If he went to the police, Grant Wolski, Roy Dupontes, and Win Davison would deny everything. He couldn't prove otherwise. And until he could, there was no point involving the authorities in something that could blow up in his face.

He wadded up the paper and threw it across the room. Once Grant told the others that someone broke in and tried to print that memo, they would be sure to destroy any other evidence that might link them to this. And what price would Grant pay for not destroying the memo as instructed?

Stedman sat back in the chair, his shirt soaked with sweat, and took a gulp of water. Not only did he have to worry about being framed, but now he had to play dumb when Grant accused him of breaking into his house.

❋ ❋ ❋

Ethan pushed open the front door at his uncle Ralph's, his suit coat slung over his shoulder, not surprised to see his uncle sitting in his easy chair, eyes wide open.

"Come in, Ethan."

"Sorry, I would've called," Ethan said, "but I fell asleep, sitting on the back porch with Vanessa. Her mother just woke us up a few minutes ago."

"Hey, it's none of my business what you and Vanessa do."

Ethan sat on the ottoman and looked Uncle Ralph in the eye. "As long as I'm living with you it is. But I wasn't *doing* anything. That's not how it is between us."

"I'm not your conscience," Ralph said. "I'm just your uncle. I love you, and I was worried. That's all."

"Did Mom and Dad call before they went back to Maryville?"

Ralph nodded. "Your dad said everything went as well as it could, under the circumstances."

"The funeral was nice. I couldn't believe how many people came."

"If that was supposed to be a dig, don't start." Ralph cracked his knuckles. "I've already been down this road with Tom, and I refuse to feel guilty for not going. There's no way Richard wanted me there."

"Would it have killed you to send flowers?"

"He didn't want my flowers either." Ralph bit his lip and laced his fingers together. "Don't judge me. This is harder for me than you think."

I sure hope so. "Did Dad tell you they buried Drew next to baby Abigail?"

"Yeah, I thought they might."

"It's hard to believe Uncle Richard and Aunt Becca have buried both their children."

Ethan remembered standing at that cemetery, a six-year-old clutching his mother's hand tightly, wondering why crib deaths happened and wishing everyone wasn't so sad. He'd never seen his father or either of his uncles cry before that day, and he never forgot it.

"You were there when they buried the baby," Ethan said. "I remember."

Ralph seemed to stare at nothing. "How're Richard and Becca holding up?"

"Their faith is strong. I'm sure they'll be okay. But I've never seen them this broken." Ethan stood. "I'm exhausted. I'd really like to go to bed."

"Yeah, sure. I'm glad you're all right. I was starting to worry. I know you're disappointed in me, but it didn't seem like your style to punish me."

"You're right." Ethan draped his suit coat over his arm. "I really did fall asleep, or I would've been home at eleven like I told you."

Ralph half smiled. "I'm sorry things started off badly. But I'm really glad you're here for the summer. I've looked forward to this for a long time."

"Me, too. Good night."

"Good night."

Ethan walked down the hall and into his bedroom and closed the door. He slipped out of his clothes and into his pajama bottoms, then stood at the window and looked up at the moon that had been slipping in and out of the clouds all evening. The entire night sky was softly lit, and so was the landscape.

He wondered what it was like to be in the presence of God. Were those who had died in the faith asleep until the resurrection of the saints—or were they already rejoicing? The separation was torturous. Drew had never been more than a phone call away before.

Drew's contagious laughter echoed in his mind. Why would anybody want him dead? The desire to know was becoming an obsession. But tonight, all he wanted was to fall asleep and forget about it.

CHAPTER 27

Tessa Masino pushed open the glass door at Nick's Grill, Antonio right behind her, and was hit with the delicious aroma of freshly brewed coffee, warm bread, and something distinctly spicy.

The waiting area was packed out with families still dressed in church clothes and tourists wearing the smart green and white Sophie Trace T-shirts the chamber of commerce sold for five dollars each.

Nick Phillips waved from the counter and motioned for them to head that way.

Tessa smiled at a tiny boy with blond curls who was holding a yellow balloon and walked over to the counter where Gus and Maggie were already seated. She wondered if Gus was pouting after Antonio put him in his place.

Nick gave her a one-armed hug and shook hands with Antonio. "Today's special is a veggie meatball sandwich, served on homemade Parmesan bread. Comes with a side dish of tomato and feta cheese pasta. I promise you, it'll knock your socks off."

"*Veggie* meatballs? Pleeease." Antonio rolled his eyes. "My Italian grandmother just turned over in her grave."

"My veggie meatballs taste like meat." Nick winked at Tessa. "If you try it and don't like it, choose something else—on the house."

"Risk-free eating. I like that." Antonio slid onto the stool next to Gus and acted completely natural. "So how's it going, friend?"

"Really can't complain. But I always do."

"So what do you know?"

"I heard Drew Langley's funeral was nice." Gus tipped his glass and crunched the ice.

"It was," Antonio said. "The church was packed. The pastor had nice things to say."

"That's good. Never have figured out how pastors get through services like that one without showin' emotion."

Tessa looked down the counter at Gus. What had gotten into him? No sarcasm? No pointing a finger at Brill? She caught Maggie's eye and looked away.

"Maggie and I are drivin' over to Gatlinburg this evening. Thought we'd have dinner at the Whistlin' Dixie. Brill Jessup's boy works there, doesn't he?"

"He will when he gets back from Costa Rica," Tessa said. "He's the night manager during the summer."

"I hear he's a fine young man."

"He is. Starts law school in the fall." Antonio turned to Gus and snapped his suspenders. "Okay, bud. Who are you and what'd you do with Gus Williams?"

"What?"

"I've known Gus for thirty years, and you're an impostor."

"Aw, can't a fella be nice without gettin' all this flack?"

Jo Beth set two mugs on the counter and filled them with coffee, then put several tiny tubs of creamer in Antonio's palm and walked away.

Antonio smiled sheepishly. "I liked the *old* Gus—just didn't want him turning every conversation into a debate about the legend. I apologize if I came on a little strong."

"Apology accepted. So has the police chief gotten any new leads on the shooter?"

"Brill doesn't confide that kind of thing in us," Antonio said. "But not according to the news."

"Well"—Gus looked down the counter—"Tessa usually has the inside scoop on the Jessups."

Tessa felt her cheeks get hot. "I really don't know anything more. I took a casserole over there last night. Brill and Kurt seemed somber. Vanessa and Ethan were upstairs getting the baby ready for bed. Emily was a little clingy with me. She probably doesn't know how to verbalize what she's feeling."

Gus poked the ice in his glass with his straw. "Hard to believe that four people died in this town and the shooter got away with it."

"The victims have been buried," Tessa said. "But the case certainly hasn't. Brill's not going to rest until justice is served."

Stedman paced in front of the refrigerator, wondering why he hadn't heard from Grant. Had he not discovered the paper jam? Did he not suspect it was Stedman who had broken in? He heard a car door slam and stepped over to the window to pull back the curtain. A white Ford Explorer was parked out front. The doorbell rang.

Stedman breathed in slowly and exhaled. He might as well get this over with. He went in the living room and looked through the peephole. The man at the door wore sunglasses, but he could tell it was Grant Wolski. He opened the door, and in the next instant, Grant grabbed him by the collar and shoved him.

"Who do you think you are, breaking into my house and hacking into my computer?"

"What are you talking about?"

"Oh, drop the innocent act." Grant kicked the door shut with his heel. "I just found the memo you tried to print out stuck in my printer. I ought to call the cops and tell them whose fingerprints are on the gun!"

"You won't. And there's no need to raise your voice. I heard you."

"Well, you sure didn't *listen*. Do you have any idea what you've stuck your nose into?"

"I do now. Did you really expect me to just sit back and let you frame me?"

Grant sighed. "We weren't *going to* frame you unless it backfired and we needed a fall guy. But we didn't. It was working. Why couldn't you leave it alone? Why'd you have to hack into my computer and stick your nose into things that are none of your business?"

"I had a right to know what was going on since my neck was on the chopping block. Don't worry. I'm not going to say anything."

"It doesn't matter. They won't be willing to take that chance!"

"How will they even know that *I* know—unless you tell them?"

There was a long stretch of steely silence, and Stedman wished Grant would take off his glasses so he could see his eyes.

"Listen, man, let's just keep this between us," Stedman said. "I'm not going to tell anyone."

"Then why did you want a copy of it?" Grant threw his hands in the air. "What were you going to do with it—take it to the cops?"

"Why would I do that? My fingerprints are on the gun. I just wanted it to protect myself, in case *you* went to the cops. For crying out loud, Grant. I know you get that. Isn't that the reason you wrote that memo to yourself? And didn't delete the one from Win Davison?"

"I tried to keep you out of this. You should've listened. These people killed Drew Langley *just in case* he knew something. Does that tell you anything?"

"Can't you tell them I'm not a threat?"

"Of course you're a threat, moron!" Grant lowered his voice. "You're the only outsider who can name the people involved. I swore on my mother's grave I wouldn't tell anyone."

"You didn't tell me. I found out on my own."

"Only because I got careless. In their minds, that's the same thing. There *will* be consequences." Grant hit Stedman in the gut with his fist and then shoved him with both hands.

Stedman fell backward and landed on the couch. "Are you worried for yourself—or are you threatening me?"

"I already told you: It's out of my hands. I was trying to protect you when I told you to stay out of it. Now you're on your own."

"Meaning what?"

Grant turned and opened the front door. "You'll find out soon enough."

Ethan sat on the back steps at the Jessups' and watched the hummingbirds fighting for a place at the feeder, aware of Emily giggling and squealing as she pulled Carter through the sprinkler in his wagon. For a moment, he almost forgot the grief that seemed to have put his life on hold.

"Dad's about ready to put the burgers on the grill." Vanessa came outside and sat next to him. "Wait until you taste my mother's potato salad. Actually it's my great-grandmother's recipe, but it's so delicious."

The corners of Ethan's mouth twitched. "There're only two kinds of potato salad: good and better."

"Well, Mom's is the *best.*"

"I guess we'd better get those two munchkins into dry clothes," he said.

"They can wrap up in a towel. We're going to eat on the porch, and I'm sure they're not done playing in the water."

"They're going to be shriveled."

Vanessa laughed. "Emily won't call it quits until her lips turn blue."

"Yoo-hoo." The singsongy female voice came from across the yard.

Ethan turned and saw Tessa and Antonio Masino coming in the gate, each carrying a plastic container.

"Hello, you two." Tessa waddled toward them, dressed in a pink shift and sandals. "We brought baked beans to go with dinner. And cherry cobbler squares for dessert."

"Here, I'll be glad to take those in for you." Ethan stood, gave Tessa a one-armed hug, and shook Antonio's hand.

"That's all right, dear," Tessa said. "I'll carry this in. I want Brill to taste the beans and see if we need to add a little more brown sugar before we serve them."

Antonio smiled and handed his container to Ethan. "You'd better take these. I can't be trusted not to snitch one. Tessa outdid herself."

Ethan followed Tessa up the back steps and out to the kitchen.

Brill opened her arms and gave Tessa a big hug. "Welcome."

"It was nice of you to ask us. We don't usually make a fuss over three-day weekends, what with our Sabrina and her family in England now."

"We'll, we've adopted you. You're family."

Ethan set the plastic container on the countertop and went back out on the screened-in porch, glad for a nice breeze. Vanessa had set the table for six adults and Emily and Carter. It was a little tight, but it would be nice eating outside. He thought of his uncle Richard and aunt Becca and how hard it must be for them to have an empty place at their table.

Emily came in the porch door, carrying Carter, who was wrapped in a white fluffy towel.

"Here"—she handed Carter to Ethan—"take Baby Moses for a minute so I can use the bathroom."

"Baby Moses?"

"It's just an expression." Emily laughed and disappeared through the door and into the house.

Ethan looked into Carter's deep blue eyes that were just like Vanessa's and instantly evoked a smile from the baby.

"I guess it's just us guys."

Ethan loosened the towel so Carter's arms were free, and the baby had Ethan's glasses in his grip before he could be stopped.

"Man, you're fast."

Ethan gently pried the tiny fingers from his glasses, then reached in his pocket, took out his key ring, and offered it to Carter as a peace offering. The squeal of delight told him he'd made a hit.

What was it about holding Carter that made him feel strong? He had never forgotten the wonder of having felt Carter kick when Vanessa was pregnant or the thrill of having held him right after delivery.

"Da da da da." Carter seemed proud of his new sound.

"I heard that." Emily laughed. "He called you da da."

"I've got news for you, Shortcake. He'd call *you* da da at this stage of his development. He's probably just getting even for you referring to him as Baby Moses."

"I only do that when he's wrapped in a towel." She held out her arms. "Okay, I'll take him now."

"Who says I want to give him back?"

"Hold him, then. He likes you. I can tell."

"Think so, eh?"

"Yep. So are you and Vanessa courting?"

Ethan smiled and looked down at Emily. "Interesting choice of words."

"Tessa calls it courting. Is that the same as dating?"

"I've never looked up the exact definition in the dictionary," Ethan said. "Your sister and I are *building a relationship.*"

"Well, whatever you call it, I'm glad. Vanessa needs something happy. And that'll make Carter stay happy."

Ethan sensed there was more to it than that.

"Emily … are you worried that Drew's death is going to spoil things between Vanessa and me?"

Her face turned pink. "Kind of. I mean, I'm *really* sorry what happened to him. But Vanessa is sad all the time. And you are too."

Ethan tilted her chin and looked into her eyes. "Listen to me … nothing is going to change what Vanessa and I have started. We just need a little time to grieve. It's important that we let ourselves *feel* the sadness so we can let it go. It won't go away if we pretend it's not there and try to move on too quickly. Does that make sense?"

Emily nodded. "It was that way when Poppy and Grammy died in the car wreck."

"Then you understand."

"Sure."

Carter giggled and held out his arms and let his weight fall toward Emily. She caught him. "Okay, little man. Let's get you situated in your high chair." She cocked her head and held Ethan's gaze. "I'm really glad you're here for the summer. I like it when you come over."

"Thanks. I enjoy it too."

"My parents like you," Emily said. "And Tessa *really* does. I can tell. Her eyes get all sparkly when Vanessa talks about you."

"Sparkly, eh? That's a good thing."

Emily flashed a toothy grin. "Definitely. Tessa spends a lot of time with God and prays for our family. If she didn't feel good about you, I don't think you'd stand a chance with my parents."

"Sounds like I'd better be sure I'm on Tessa's good side."

"Oh, I think you're on Tessa's *great* side."

CHAPTER 28

Ethan, arm in arm with Vanessa, strolled out to his car, the night air thick with humidity and the scent of wet earth, the moonlit foothills visible between the houses across the street. He turned around, leaned against the car, and pulled Vanessa into his arms.

"I had a wonderful time spending the day here," he said. "I actually forgot about Drew when we played Monopoly. It felt so good to laugh."

"It did." Vanessa nestled in his arms. "We should do it again tomorrow."

"Did you get the feeling that Emily was matchmaking?"

"Do you think?" Vanessa chuckled. "It occurred to me that she's never seen me romantically involved with anyone. She never even met Ty."

"I think she's getting a kick out of us."

"They all are. Did you see Mom nudge Tessa when you sold me Park Place?"

"I wanted the Reading Railroad. I thought it was a fair trade."

"Oh, pleeease. No one else would've done that when I already had Boardwalk. Emily would've died first."

Ethan smiled. "Okay, so I showed a little favoritism." He kissed the top of her head and inhaled the flowery scent. "What can I say? I love you."

He winced. Why had he let something so precious just slip out like that? Couldn't he have waited for some knight-in-shining-armor moment? Given her jewelry? Taken her someplace special?

"I love you, too," she whispered. "I've wanted to say it before now. But with all that's happened, there never seemed to be a right time."

Ethan, certain that the pounding of his heart must be audible, pressed his lips to hers and let his actions say what his words lacked. He did love her. And she loved him. The magnitude of that glorious fact made his knees suddenly weak.

He slowly pulled back from Vanessa and let his weight fall against the car, feeling almost giddy. He wanted to laugh and cry at the same time but did neither. Breathless, he reached out and stroked her cheek, Vanessa smiling with her eyes.

He was aware of his phone vibrating but wasn't about to ruin the moment by answering it.

"When did you know?" Vanessa said.

"I guess a part of me knew the first time you placed my hands on your pregnant tummy and let me feel Carter kick."

Vanessa laughed. "When I looked like a hippo, and you said I was the loveliest hippo you'd ever seen?"

"You were."

"Love *must* be blind. No one else could've seen me that way."

"I thought you were beautiful. Now you're ravishing."

Ethan pulled her close, letting her warm, soft lips melt into his, then cupped her face in his hand and gazed into her eyes.

"I love you, Vanessa. It's so great hearing myself say what I've thought a thousand times. And I'm falling in love with Carter, too."

"I can tell. He adores you."

"I want us to enjoy the summer and see where it leads. But I want you to know that I'm hoping it leads to something permanent."

Her crystal blue eyes brimmed with tears.

"Honey, what's wrong?"

"Nothing's wrong. Suddenly everything is wonderful. I'm just afraid something will happen to mess it up."

"Nothing is going to mess it up. Let's start the summer over right here. Let's put God in the center. He has a plan. And if that includes us being together, He'll clear a path." Ethan tightened his arms around her, feeling more protective than he ever had before. "Lord, we want *Your* will for this relationship. Vanessa and I commit ourselves to You and to each other and Carter. We pray that You'll help us to make our relationship all it's meant to be—and that we will be a reflection of You. In Jesus' name we pray. Amen."

"Amen." Vanessa laid her head on his chest. "Do you have any idea how wonderful it is having a godly man to love? You're a gift. God is so good to allow me a second chance to do this right."

Ethan's phone vibrated again and he let it go. The direction of his life had just changed, and he wanted to savor the moment. How could anything anyone else had to say be more important than this?

❖ ❖ ❖

Stedman squeezed his cell phone. Why didn't Ethan answer? Why hadn't he called back? He peeked out the curtains and wasn't sure what he was looking for. Grant said there would be consequences. What did that really mean?

He picked up the Smith & Wesson pistol. If only he hadn't handled the other one and left his fingerprints all over it. If only he hadn't agreed to kill a man. Father David warned him his gambling would be his demise. But could even the parish priest have envisioned him caught in *this* web?

Four people were dead—all to cover up the death of one. The conspirators had nothing to lose. They didn't come this far only to get derailed. Guys like Win Davison paid to stay on track. When money was no object, there was nothing it couldn't buy—including a man's soul.

Why did that memo have to get jammed in the printer? No one would ever believe the ugly truth without evidence!

Stedman's hypocrisy taunted him. Would naming the conspirators alleviate his own guilt, just because he never followed through? Nothing could change the fact that he had purposed in his heart to kill a man. He was no better than Grant and the others and no less guilty. But he wasn't willing to take the fall for them.

He glanced at his watch. It was late. How big a window did he have before the conspirators decided he was a liability? Was he crazy to consider what he was about to do? Was it fair to Ethan? What choice did he have?

❈   ❈   ❈

Brill went out to the kitchen to get a glass of warm milk, surprised to see Vanessa sitting at the table.

"Honey, why aren't you asleep? Is anything wrong?"

"No. Just the opposite."

"Would you like a cup of warm milk?"

"No, thanks."

Brill poured a cup of milk and put it in the microwave, then went over and sat next to Vanessa.

"So what's keeping you up?"

Vanessa smiled, her eyes twinkling. "Ethan loves me. He told me tonight."

"I see. And do you love him?" *As if I didn't know.*

"Very much. We've both been holding back saying it because of the circumstances. It just sort of popped out of Ethan, and then I responded. And before we knew it, we were praying that God would be in the center of it and direct it the way *He* wants. It was amazing." A tear trickled down her cheek. "After my fiasco with Ty, I never dreamed God would give me a second chance."

Brill tilted Vanessa's chin and wiped the tear with her thumb. "I'm so happy for you. Not surprised, but happy. Ethan just might be the answer to my—and your father's—prayers. He seems crazy about Carter, too."

"He is. We just want to take the summer and let our relationship blossom."

"I'm sorry you have to deal with grief at the same time."

"Me, too. But this feels bigger than the sorrow." Vanessa laced her fingers together. "Maybe falling in love will trump all the bad. It did today. We had so much fun. He loves being with our family."

"The feeling's mutual. And in case you didn't notice, Emily adores Ethan."

"Believe me, I've noticed. Lately, she's been talking about Carter needing a daddy."

"He does. But I think your father has been a wonderful stand-in, and he can assume that role as long as necessary. I'd like to think you and Ethan know not to get in a hurry, just because of Carter."

"Don't worry. We won't. Ethan's got a lot of schooling ahead. There's an awful lot to consider if this is the real thing."

"If?"

Vanessa giggled. "Okay, it *is* the real thing. I meant to say *if* we decide we want to move forward."

"Move forward with what?" Kurt stood in the doorway, wearing his terry bathrobe, his arms folded across his chest.

"Ah, perfect timing." Brill patted the empty chair on the other side of her. "Come sit for a minute and let Vanessa tell you why she can't sleep."

Ethan gripped the wheel of his Camry and glided down Main Street, the hazy foothills looking ghostly in the light of the moon. His phone vibrated, and he remembered he hadn't checked his messages.

He glanced at the display and put the phone to his ear. "Stedman, it's late, man. What's up?"

"We need to talk—in person."

"Something wrong?"

"Yeah. And I need your advice."

"All right. Why don't we meet first thing in the morning?"

"Actually I was thinking now—at the outdoor theater in Shady Park."

"It can't wait until morning?"

Stedman exhaled into the phone. "No. Look, I'm in a little trouble. I don't have anyone else to turn to."

"Can't you talk to your grandmother?"

"Not about this."

"If you're looking for gambling money," Ethan said, "I'm the wrong guy to—"

"I don't want money. Just be there—please? I've got information Vanessa's mother needs to know. I may not get another crack at this."

The phone went dead.

Ethan checked his messages, and they were all from Stedman. What was going on? What kind of weird phone call was that? Why didn't he take whatever it was to the police? Stedman's tone sounded urgent. He was asking for help. How could he just leave the guy hanging?

CHAPTER 29

Ethan stopped at a red light at Main Street and Second. Beanie's Coffee Shop was still going strong, but mostly everything else downtown had closed, even tourist shops.

The light turned green, and he drove several more blocks and turned left on Stanton Boulevard. He spotted the gazebo at Shady Park and pulled into a space at the end of the parking lot, noting that his Camry was the only car in the lot. He got out and walked down the stone pathway that led to the outdoor theater, then climbed up in the bleachers and waited in the dark for Stedman.

He took out his phone. He might as well send Vanessa a text message. He decided not to change tonight's mood by mentioning his covert meeting with Stedman. What could he tell her anyway? He texted the words *I'll never tire of saying I love you* and hit the Send button.

"There you are."

Ethan jumped, his hand over his heart. "Good grief, man. Couldn't you cough or something? I didn't hear your truck pull up."

"I know." Stedman sounded out of breath. "I parked it a couple blocks away and jogged over here. I wanted to be sure I wasn't followed."

"What's going on?" Ethan said. "Why are you being so secretive?"

Stedman sat next to him on the bleacher and leaned forward, his elbows planted on his thighs, his hands clasped between his knees. "I have important information the police chief needs to know."

"Why didn't you tell her yourself?" Ethan asked.

"Keep your voice down." Stedman sat up straight and peered into the darkness. Finally he said, "If I go to the police, there's a plan in place to frame me."

"What are you talking about?"

Stedman spoke barely above a whisper, "One of my poker buddies, Grant Wolski, conspired with two other people to kill Tal Davison. And they figured out a way to frame *me* for it, just in case they needed a fall guy."

"You know who killed Tal?" Ethan grabbed his shirt with both hands. "Then you know who killed my cousin! Who was it? Tell me right now!"

"Shhh! Just hear me out. I need your help."

"For what?"

Ethan listened as Stedman told him about losing the poker game and owing Grant sixty thousand dollars.

"I thought I'd died and gone to heaven when I was dealt four jacks. I was so sure I was holding the winning hand that I bet money I didn't have and couldn't get. I thought it was odd that Grant trusted me for it, but I didn't think I'd need it."

"You were wrong, man. When are you going to get help for your gambling problem?"

"Look, I don't need a lecture. I've got a bigger problem." Stedman's voice shook. "I was so desperate to get out of debt with Grant that I agreed to do something really low—actually lower than low."

Ethan listened as Stedman told him everything that had happened from the time he struck a deal with Grant until he sat in his truck, gun in hand, unable to pull the trigger and kill Tal Davison.

"That's when two guys in a red truck sped in front of me, shot Tal right where he stood on the sidewalk, and sped away. I panicked and drove off, hoping no one saw me there."

"Did you get a good look at the two guys?"

Stedman shook his head. "Happened too fast. The passenger did the shooting. I let Grant believe I did it until the police found that college girl shot. Then I confronted him with the truth—that I didn't have the guts to kill Davison and I sure didn't kill the girl. He said it was my problem and since I reneged on my end of the bargain, I still owed him the sixty thousand dollars. Said it would go up a thousand bucks a day for every day I didn't pay."

"Sounds like a real sweetheart."

"It was depressing. But after the thirteen-year-old was found dead, and then your cousin was killed, I started to panic. I called Grant and told him I didn't want all these deaths on my conscience. He said it wasn't my concern. That's when I lost it. I told him it *was* my concern, that I had agreed to kill a man to be relieved of my debt—and that someone beat me to it—and now I had a bigger debt piling up *and* a guilty conscience. I told him that's not what I signed up for. He got quiet, and then did something that caught me completely off guard: He agreed with me. He said we should forget the deal. Forget the debt. And that he didn't want to hear from me anymore. I could hardly believe it."

"Just like that?" Ethan said.

"Yeah. Weird, huh? I was so relieved that I stopped worrying about it until the details started to come out. The shooter was described as a young man with dark hair and a beard and mustache. The weapon was a Smith and Wesson semiautomatic pistol. And the police found fingerprints on the gun. It all pointed to me. I had a bad feeling, and I wanted answers."

Ethan listened as Stedman described his encounter with Grant at Rambo's.

"He said if I backed off, the cops would never know whose prints were on the gun. But if I told anyone, I was going down for the shootings. None of it made sense, and I didn't trust him. I couldn't just sit back and let someone use me as a patsy. I decided to break into his house and see if I could find something that would answer my questions."

"Did you?"

Stedman raked his fingers through his hair. "Yeah. I hacked into Grant's computer and found a Special Project folder in his Word documents. Inside was a copy of an email, dated May first, to Grant and some guy named Roy Dupontes—from Win Davison. It said, 'Meet me in my office at 6:00 p.m. Delete this after reading.' I also found a detailed memo Grant wrote and emailed to himself about what happened in that meeting."

"And …?" Ethan said.

Stedman started cracking his knuckles, his hands trembling. He seemed trapped in a moment of silence, as if he were battling with himself about whether or not to continue. Finally he said, "*Win Davison* orchestrated the shootings. He ordered the hit on Tal!"

"What? Why would he kill his own son?"

"He found out Tal wasn't his biological son. Apparently a guy that Mrs. Davison had an affair with, Paulson McGiver, contacted Win with DNA proof that Tal was McGiver's son and threatened to expose the truth unless Win paid him a million dollars."

"So he had Tal *killed?*"

"And McGiver. The guy lived in Nashville. I'll bet if Chief Jessup checks with the Nashville police, she'll find out he was murdered this month."

Ethan paused, trying to grasp the magnitude of what Stedman had just told him. "How could Win do that? Tal was the only son he'd ever known. He must've had feelings for him."

"You'd think. But Grant's memo indicated that Win was disgusted with Tal because he was starting to hedge about taking his rightful place in the family business. Tal told him he was considering the police academy, and Win took it as a slap in the face and an embarrassment to the family. I guess he thought he could save face all the way around if he just had Tal eliminated."

Ethan wiped the perspiration off his forehead. "That's the same twisted thinking that drives honor killings."

"Win went on to remind Grant and Roy that they owed him big and it was payback time. Their orders were to team up and take out Tal and make it look like he was a victim of some drunken hoodlums shooting up the neighborhood. They needed to find someone to frame in case it backfired so the police would never get close to Davison."

"This is unbelievable. Are you saying you were *it?*"

Stedman nodded. "That part wasn't in Grant's memo, but I've been piecing it together. Grant knew I was on a losing streak and rigged the poker game, knowing full well that if I was dealt four jacks I'd bet big, lose big, and be desperate to make good on the bet and keep my place at the poker table. His offer to cancel the debt if I killed Tal was a ruse so he could set me up.

Ethan shook his head. "Talk about a risk. What was Grant going to do if his plan backfired and the police believed you were set up? Once they started digging, they'd be bound to find out Win Davison was involved."

"Grant would never let that happen. He could always tell police that he masterminded the hit on Tal to get back at Win Davison for laying off so many of his workers. Frankly, that's a lot more believable than the truth. A jury would be sympathetic. He'd probably get the minimum."

"But he would still go to jail."

"For a while. But Grant loves playing the odds. He didn't plan on getting caught. That's why he's so mad at me for sticking my nose in this."

"Did you forward Grant's memo to your computer?"

Stedman sighed. "No, I never thought to do that. I tried to print it out, but the printer jammed just as the cops showed up, and I had to split. There was a lot more to it than I just told you. And when I got home, I wrote down everything I could remember. But I can't prove any of it."

"Was there any indication why they killed Drew?"

"Yeah, they thought he might have known about the friction between Tal and his dad, and Win didn't want to chance that it would ever come up in the police investigation. He said Drew was a liability."

Ethan tightened his fists and fought the urge to use them on Stedman. "I'm going to the police."

"No!" Stedman gripped his wrist. "If they think I said anything to you, they'll kill us both. Grant came by my duplex this morning and threatened me."

"He threatened to kill you?"

"No. He claims he tried to protect me, and that whatever happens to me now is out of his hands. They've already killed five people. What would you think?"

Ethan shoved Stedman and rose to his feet. "I knew your gambling would get you in trouble, but I can't believe you let yourself get involved in *this*. Why did you call me here? You think I feel better knowing Drew was murdered just because he *might* have known about the conflict Tal had with his dad?"

"No. I thought of a way to take down Davison without losing my life. But I need your help." Stedman took a folded piece of paper out of his shirt pocket and handed it to Ethan. "I need you to give this to Vanessa's mother. It's every detail I can remember from the memo. And tell her about my deal with Grant. You have to persuade her that I'm being framed—and that Win Davison and the others involved can't know I said anything. They have to believe the conspiracy was uncovered by the *police.*"

❋   ❋   ❋

Ethan stopped at the red light at Cherokee Parkway and had no recollection of driving the last six blocks. Why should he get involved in this? Stedman got himself into this mess. Guys like him would never learn as long as people kept bailing them out. Then again, this was really serious, and there didn't seem to be another way out. If Stedman went to the police, the plan to frame him would be set in motion. He would go to jail, and Davison would get away with killing Drew.

Ethan looked in his rearview mirror for the umpteenth time. He wasn't being followed. There was hardly a car on the road. No one knew he had met with Stedman. Or that he was the only other person besides the conspirators who knew Win Davison was behind the shootings.

Ethan considered Stedman's plan and tried to be objective. Even if Ethan agreed to go to Brill and tell her everything, could she act on it? Would she? Would she be willing to arrest Win Davison and make him believe the *police* uncovered the conspiracy? Could she even find enough evidence to charge Davison? And if she did, wouldn't his defense attorneys have him out on bail within hours? Wouldn't Davison then rely on the very plan he and Grant and the others had put in place—and let Stedman take the fall? All the evidence pointed to Stedman being the shooter. Any accusations he made against Win Davison or Grant Wolski would be regarded as hearsay as long as there was no evidence to back it up. And hadn't the conspirators had ample time to destroy whatever evidence they missed before?

Ethan sighed. He really didn't want to get involved. But could he stay silent, knowing Stedman's life was on the line? He needed to sleep on it. Pray about it. One thing he knew for sure: He wasn't going to let Davison get away with killing Drew.

❖　❖　❖

Before she went back to bed, Brill walked upstairs with Vanessa to steal a glimpse of Carter. She walked over to his crib and laid her hand on his back and felt him breathe.

"I can't believe how much I love this little guy," Brill said. "Having the two of you living here has turned out to be an enormous blessing."

Vanessa came and stood next to her, putting one arm around Brill's waist. "You and Dad and Emily have been wonderful. I could've never made it without you. I can't believe I've only got one more year of school. Once I have my teaching degree, I'll be able to support us."

"I'm proud of you, honey. I know it hasn't been easy, but I don't think I've ever heard you complain."

Vanessa picked up Carter's little hand and studied his fingers. "I've never once wished I'd made a different choice. But I can never thank the three of you enough for all you're doing to help with Carter."

"Well, it works both ways. That little scamp has pulled this family together. I can hardly bear the thought of you leaving us. I know it's inevitable. You need some time to be on your own."

Vanessa was quiet for a moment, and then said, "What if I don't have time to be on my own?"

"I'm not following you, honey." *Or maybe I am.*

"Mom, what if the feelings Ethan and I have for each other lead to marriage? Would it be a mistake if I never experienced my independence? Would I regret it the rest of my life?"

Brill smiled. "I never did. I married your dad right out of college. Living on campus is all the independence either of us ever had. And you had two years of that."

"True."

"Your dad and I were head over heels in love. It's a miracle we passed our finals. All we could think about was being together."

Vanessa suddenly seemed far away.

"Where'd you go?"

"Mom, can I ask you a personal question?"

"Go on."

"Do you think Dad's having an affair had anything to do with the fact that he married so young and never really dated around?"

Brill was rendered mute for a moment by her daughter's candor. "I'm not entirely comfortable discussing this with you, Vanessa. The woman was someone your dad had a crush on in high school. They ran into each other at Starbucks at a time when I was paying more attention to my career than to your father. He was vulnerable, and he stepped out of bounds. I don't think the outcome would have been any different if he'd dated a hundred women."

"Okay. It's just something I've wondered about. So you don't think either of us would regret not having that time to be on our own?"

Brill took Vanessa's hand and walked with her over to the bed and sat. "I can't tell you or Ethan how you would feel. All I can tell you is that your dad and I were crazy in love and there was no better place for us than to be together. I never regretted marrying your father right out of college. And I don't think he had any regrets either. Why don't you ask him?"

"I might—just to get a male perspective."

"I couldn't be happier that you and Ethan love each other." Brill picked up a lock of Vanessa's hair. "Just don't get ahead of yourselves. Let things unfold naturally. If it's meant to be for a lifetime, you'll know."

"How?"

"You just will."

Vanessa got up and stood at the window, looking up at the moon. "Do you have any idea how good it feels to have hope for the future in the midst of all this gloom and doom?"

"I do. I'm glad you have Ethan to love."

"It's wonderful—and a little scary. It was hard losing Ty. But I think I'd die if anything happened to Ethan."

CHAPTER 30

Stedman stood at the kitchen counter, spreading a thin layer of margarine across the last heel of bread and wishing he had the fifty bucks he blew on lottery tickets in the past month.

He looked through the window at the fiery pink morning sky and heard his grandmother's TV blaring. Had she noticed his truck missing yet? It seemed smart to park it around the block and stay out of sight—at least until Ethan made up his mind whether or not he was willing to go to Chief Jessup with the conspiracy information. It had to be overwhelming for Ethan to find out that his cousin had been eliminated—and about the deal Stedman made with Grant Wolski.

Stedman certainly couldn't defend himself. Agreeing to kill a man so he could keep gambling toppled the scales of moral indecency. But how did it come to that? When did gambling cease to be entertainment and become a fix he couldn't do without? The thrill of winning was like a shot of cocaine—and he always needed another. Hadn't his gambling compulsion alienated his girlfriend, his parents, and his grandmother? Hadn't it cost him his financial freedom and his integrity—and likely his job? The only thing left to lose was his life—and that was certainly in question.

What would he do if Ethan decided not to get involved? How long could he stay at home with the lights out before Grant and the others figured out he was hiding there, crouched in the dark like a kid scared of what might come out of his closet?

Then again, what right did he have to expect anyone else to get sucked into something this dangerous? What if he hadn't been careful enough? What if somehow Grant knew about his late-night meeting with Ethan? What if Davison had already put a price on their heads?

Stedman sighed. Or what if he was just being paranoid? He welcomed the first rays of sun through the window. At least now he could see what he was doing. He poured a glass of water, then folded the piece of bread and butter and walked over to the kitchen table and sat. He remembered it was Memorial Day and had a sinking feeling that on this day next year, his family might be putting flowers on *his* grave.

Click. Click. Click.

What was that? He stopped chewing and listened intently. There it was again! Someone was jiggling the handle on the door!

He wiped his hands on his T-shirt and grabbed the gun he had gotten from Grant and intended to use on Tal Davison. He darted into the living room and crouched down behind the couch, his hands shaking, the blaring of his grandmother's TV drowning out the thumping of his heart. At least if he had to shoot, she would never hear it.

❖   ❖   ❖

Ethan stood on the back deck at his aunt and uncle's house, a mug of coffee in his hands, and watched the sun peek over the milky white foothills, turning the backyard into a shimmering carpet of green. He could tell it was going to be another hot day.

His late-night encounter with Stedman gave him a headache, and he never did fall asleep. Could he afford not to share this information with Brill, even if it ruined the holiday for the Jessups? Unless he intervened on Stedman's behalf, Win Davison and those he paid to kill Tal and Drew were going to get away with it.

Ethan took a sip of lukewarm coffee and moved his gaze beyond the misty hills to the Great Smoky Mountains. How did a straight arrow like Drew get pulled into this sick drama? Would he ever be able to accept Drew's death until he had the answer?

He downed the last of the coffee. Stedman needed his help. As disgusted as he was with the guy, did he have the heart to turn his back on what had obviously been a difficult confession and a plea for help?

Ethan heard the glass door slide open.

"There you are."

He turned toward the voice and saw his uncle Ralph standing in the doorway.

"I wanted to catch you before you left. I know you and Vanessa want to take it easy today. But if you're out and about, stop by."

"Not today. But I promise we will after things calm down and we feel more sociable, okay?" *Plus I'm about to wreck the day for the Jessups.*

"If you change your mind," Ralph said, "you're welcome to drop in unannounced. We're having three couples over. You know Tonya and Hank Mason. The other two are neighbors. There's plenty of food, and we're not going to run out of homemade ice cream."

There was a long moment of uncomfortable silence.

Finally Ralph stepped outside. "Look, Ethan. I hate this tension between us. You know I'd do just about anything for you. You're the son I never had, and I love you like you were my own. But we're different when it comes to how we deal with family issues."

"Uncle Ralph, you don't *deal* with family issues. You've turned a deaf ear for fifteen years."

"You're entitled to your opinion, but I don't need to hear it."

"Okay, what about forgive us our debts as we forgive our debtors? The *Lord's* prayer doesn't leave much room for opinion."

"I don't need a guilt trip, Ethan. My disagreement with Richard is complicated."

"Not really. Uncle Richard said some hurtful things and apologized—but that wasn't good enough for you."

"I told you it's not that simple."

"Keep telling yourself that. But you could put an end to this feud, if you wanted to. You won't accept Richard's apology—and it's crippling the whole family!"

"Ethan"—Ralph shook his head—"you really don't know what you're talking about."

"Then tell me what I don't know because I'm sick of it! Your brother lost his son, and it's absolutely cold of you to ignore it."

"That's exactly what Richard *wanted* me to do." Ralph's voice quivered. "Oh, he's not going to admit it to the rest of the family, but it's the truth."

"What are you talking about?"

Ralph's face turned pink, and he looked away. "Just forget it. I've said too much."

"Or not enough. Since this wall between you and Uncle Richard has affected me my whole life, don't you think I deserve to know whatever it is you're not saying?"

"It's ugly, Ethan."

"How can it be any uglier than your indifference?"

"Well, I don't want to talk about it."

"I don't really care what *you* want, Uncle Ralph. You're hurting the rest of us, and it's got to stop. This has gone on for fifteen years. Get *over* it!"

Ralph put his hands in his pockets and looked down at the ground.

"I'm sorry if I made you mad," Ethan said. "I've just lost the closest thing to a brother I'll ever have—and yours is across town and you won't even talk to him. Don't expect any sympathy from me."

"You have no idea why I've stayed away from Richard's family."

"All I need to know is that he apologized."

"No, he didn't!" Ralph said. "Not really. He said the words, but his heart never changed."

"About what? Let's get this out in the open."

"I don't think … look, I'm sorry I said anything. Just forget it."

Ralph turned to go, and Ethan grabbed his wrist. "I don't want to forget it. Please … tell me what it is that's hurting you so much. Why can't you forgive Richard?"

"It's not me who won't forgive! It's him."

"What are you talking about?"

"It's no secret that Richard blamed me for baby Abigail's death. Gwen and I were babysitting her at the time, and Gwen ran to the store while the baby was down for a nap. I was watching football when she died in her sleep. I guess he needed to blame someone."

"The doctor said it was a crib death. He knows you weren't responsible. He said some things in his grief that he didn't mean."

"Well, he also said something he absolutely *did* mean."

"What?"

Ralph's chin quivered. "He said … that I already *killed* one of his kids … and to stay away from Drew."

The words pierced Ethan down to his soul. He couldn't imagine the Uncle Richard he knew saying something that cruel. "I am *so* sorry, Uncle Ralph. That must've been devastating."

"Do you think?" Ralph paused to gain his composure. "*That's* why I didn't have a relationship with Drew. It's not that I didn't want it."

"But Uncle Richard apologized, didn't he?"

"He said the words, but I didn't believe him. His apology gained him favor with the family. And I got blamed for the rift."

"Do Mom and Dad know this?"

"They know. They think *I* need to forgive Richard, and I think it's the other way around."

"Why don't you just talk to Richard about it? People change."

"What difference does it make now? He doesn't have to worry about me being around Drew anymore." Ralph stood slump-shouldered and didn't lift his gaze. "Sorry to dump all this on you, but you wanted to know. I'm going to go out to the kitchen and help Gwen get things ready for the cookout. I hope you have a relaxing day with Vanessa."

❖ ❖ ❖

Ethan drove past Stedman's duplex, surprised to not see his truck parked in the driveway. Where else would he be? Why hadn't he at least returned Ethan's phone calls? Or answered his texts?

Ethan glanced at his watch. It was already seven thirty. Maybe Stedman left to get a breakfast biscuit or something. His mouth watered at the thought, and he suddenly regretted turning down Aunt Gwen's offer to fix him bacon and eggs. There was a McDonald's on Forest Parkway. Why not get a quick breakfast and wait there for Stedman to call? It would be easier to think on a full stomach.

He drove around the block and pulled up in front of Stedman's duplex. He grabbed a notepad and pencil out of the glove box and scribbled a note telling Stedman what time he had come by and to call him so they could talk about Ethan's decision.

He folded the note and looked up and down the street and didn't see anyone. He got out of the car and jogged around to the right side of the duplex, behind the bushes badly in need of trimming, to the door adjacent to the driveway.

He bent down and pushed the note through the metal mail chute. As he stood, the air was flooded with the distinctive stench of body odor—and a second later his neck was in a vice.

He clawed at someone's hairy arm, gasping for air, his glasses falling off his face, his head feeling as if it would explode. Seconds passed and everything started to turn to gray fuzz, then the attacker loosened his grip and grabbed him by the hair. Ethan felt the tip of a knife pressed against his neck.

"Listen to me. I'm only going to say this once: Whatever you think you heard ... whatever you think you know ... *forget* it"—he moved his lips to Ethan's ear and slid the knife ever so slightly across his throat—"or I'll deliver your girlfriend and her baby to you piece by piece." The guy yanked his hair. "Is that clear?"

Ethan managed to form the word *yes* before he ran out of wind.

"I'm going to let go of you now. If you make a sound—so much as a whimper—I'll slice you from ear to ear and let you bleed out right here. I have no real reason to let you live, other than I'm feeling generous. Understand?"

Ethan felt his head bob slightly.

"I want you to face the door and count out loud to fifty. If you repeat any of Stedman's crazy, mixed-up accusations—to anyone, cops or not—I'll filet your girlfriend and her kid. And then I'll come after you. Do you get that?"

"Yeah. I-I get it."

"On the other hand, if you forget about Stedman and the pack of lies he told you, life will go on just like before, the danger will have passed, and we can all breathe easy. Isn't that what we want?"

Ethan forced his head to move up and down, but everything in him screamed in defiance.

"You can't win this hand, kid. Take my advice and fold before you lose everything. Now start counting …"

Tessa, dressed in the pink cotton robe Antonio bought her for Mother's Day, hobbled to the end of the driveway and picked up the newspaper. She looked out past the houses across the street. A huge billowy cloud hung above the Great Smoky Mountains, its rim glowing with the morning sun that had slipped behind it, a handful of white rays fanning out across the expanse.

Her heart leapt. It was a poor soul who believed this painting had no artist but Mother Nature.

She heard a familiar meow and looked down at Abby rubbing against her legs. "Did you think I was talking to you, sweet girl?"

A car approached, and she recognized it as Ethan's. She waved, but he didn't wave back and drove past the Jessups' house. How odd.

Tessa opened the newspaper and read the headline: Shooter Still at Large.

"I can't bear to read another word about it," she mumbled. "I'm sure Gus will give us an earful."

She folded the paper in half and walked back into the house, where Antonio sat on the living room couch, watching the activity at the birdbath on the other side of the sliding glass door.

Tessa handed him the newspaper, and he handed her a cup of coffee.

"Is it hot out yet?" he asked.

"No, it's glorious. I have half a mind to walk down to the park and take a stroll before the throngs of picnickers arrive."

"If you'll wait until I've had my fill of coffee, I'll go with you." Antonio shot her a playful grin. "I can use you for a cane."

Tessa waved her hand. "We can use each other. Before we go to Nick's, I want to make lemon bars to take to the Jessups' this evening when we go back to play Monopoly."

"We could just stop by the dairy and pick up some banana-split ice cream. That'd save you from being on your feet."

"What else have I got to do?" Tessa said. "By the way, I just saw Ethan drive down the street. He didn't wave at me, and he drove right past the Jessups' house. Very strange."

"You sure it was him?"

"Yes, quite sure. It's not like him to be rude. He must've had his mind on something else."

CHAPTER 31

Ethan drove up the winding road to the Stanton Valley Overlook, certain that he hadn't been followed. He pulled down the rearview mirror and examined his neck. His skin was still red and blotchy where the guy had choked him. Would the marks turn to bruises tomorrow? How would he explain them? He was glad he wore a golf shirt. At least the collar would hide the worst of it for now.

His attacker's words played over and over in his head with terrifying realism. *Whatever you think you heard … whatever you think you know … forget it. Or I'll deliver your girlfriend and her baby to you piece by piece.*

Ethan quickly blinked away the gruesome images that popped into his head. What choice did he have but to keep silent? The conspirators would have made sure all the evidence was destroyed. They had killed before, and they would do it again. There was nothing he could do to help Stedman now. He had to do whatever it took to protect Vanessa and Carter.

He picked up his cell phone and hit Redial, distraught when the voice mail message came on.

"This is Stedman. Sorry I can't take your call. Leave your number, and I'll call you back." *Beep …*

"Stedman, it's Ethan. I've left five phone messages, man. Why aren't you calling me back? I really need to hear from you as soon as you get this message."

Ethan's hand shook so hard that he had difficulty getting his phone back on the belt clip. What if Stedman didn't get his messages? What if they killed him? What if Ethan was the only one left besides the conspirators who knew Win Davison was behind the shootings? What if Drew's killers were going to get away with it?

You can't win this hand, kid. Take my advice and fold before you lose everything.

Ethan's heart hammered, fear holding him as tightly as the man with the knife.

A couple of chipmunks scurried across the hood of his car, one in pursuit of the other. For a split second he wished he had Carter with him and wondered if the child had even seen a chipmunk yet.

How could this be happening? How could he be put in the position of letting Drew's killer go free to save Vanessa and Carter? Why should he have to cheat one to save another?

Lord, there has to be a better way. You don't want me to give in to fear.

But he had given in. He was consumed with it.

❖   ❖   ❖

Vanessa, wondering why she hadn't heard back from Ethan, sent him another text message. He planned to come over around noon and it was ten after. Had she ever been so eager to see anyone in her life? Now that they had declared their love for each other, it was as though all of her pent-up feelings had come to the surface and were bubbling over.

"What's taking Ethan so long?" Emily flopped on the glider next to Vanessa.

"He's probably taking things nice and slow today. It is a holiday, after all. It's a time to relax, not rush. Where's Carter?"

"Dad took him in the stroller and went over to the Masinos'. Mom is making that yummy Mexican casserole I love for dinner. And we get to have chips and salsa. Mom made it mild so Antonio won't get heartburn." Emily leaned her head against the back of the glider and sighed. "I love being out of school for the summer, but I'm already missing Jasmine, Angeline, Amy, and Madison—James Lee, too, but he is *not* my boyfriend. We're both good at math, that's all. Why are you smiling?"

Vanessa hadn't been aware that she was. She picked up Emily's hand and squeezed it. "I just get a kick out of your chattiness. You remind me of me at eleven."

"Well, I hope I'm like you when I'm twenty-one."

"Thank you, Emily. What a sweet thing to say."

"You're nice. Madison's sister yells at her all the time."

Vanessa's phone chimed, and she looked at the text that had come in from Ethan: *Something came up concerning Drew. Can't be with you today. Forgive me. I love you.*

"What?" Vanessa said, staring at the phone.

"What's wrong?"

"Ethan's not coming."

"How come?"

"Something came up about his cousin. I'm not really sure what, but he said he can't make it."

"Are you going to cry?" Emily said.

"Of course not." *I sure feel like it, though. Couldn't he have at least called to tell me?* "I'm just disappointed, Shortcake. I was so looking forward to it. Tomorrow he goes back to working six days a week."

"Yesterday was fun."

Vanessa smiled to cover her sadness. "Yes, it was. I was just hoping for an encore."

❖   ❖   ❖

Ethan left his car in a grocery-store parking lot a block from Stedman's and jogged to the alley behind his duplex. He slowly opened the chain-link gate, looking all around for any sign of life. He heard the TV next door and remembered that Stedman's grandmother lived there.

He walked stealthily to the side door where the attacker had caught him off guard. Stedman's truck was still not in the driveway. Where was he? Why didn't he return his phone messages?

Ethan rang the doorbell and listened. He didn't hear footsteps. He rang the bell again. Nothing.

He turned the handle, shocked when the door opened. He stuck his head inside.

"Stedman, it's Ethan. Are you there?"

He stepped inside, the floor creaking beneath his feet, and shut the door behind him.

"Stedman!"

Ethan walked slowly through the kitchen and into the living room, and then down the hall to the bedrooms. The bed was unmade in the master bedroom and the bathroom was trashed out, but there was nothing to indicate whether or not Stedman had come home last night.

Ethan slipped out the front door and rang the bell next door. He saw a light flash on and off when he rang the bell and figured Stedman's grandmother had it rigged so the light would alert her when someone was at the door. He rang the bell again. The TV went off.

A tiny old woman with tight silver curls and stern eyes opened the door. "Whatever you're selling, I can't afford. Whatever you're preaching, I've heard before."

"Ma'am, I'm a friend of your grandson Sted—"

"What's that you say? Speak up."

Ethan raised his voice to just under a shout and spoke slowly. "I'm a friend of your grandson Stedman. I need to get ahold of him. He's not home. And he's not answering his phone. Do you know where I might reach him?"

The old woman folded her arms across her chest, her wiry gray eyebrows coming together. "He's probably over at the Indian reservation," she hollered, "throwing his money away at the casino. Or out playing poker with those high-roller friends of his. I stopped keeping track of Stedman a long time ago after he stole my grocery money. Are you one of his gambling buddies?"

"No, ma'am. We work together. I really need to talk to him. Do you know if he came home last night?"

"Aren't you the nosy one?" She pursed her lips, her eyes turning to slits, and seemed to study him.

"Sorry if I'm bothering you. I'm a little worried about him. He's waiting to hear from me. About an important matter. He's not answering his cell phone. I just wanted to be sure he's okay."

"My grandson is certainly *not* okay. If you know him at all, you know he's addicted to gambling. He'll lie, steal, or cheat to get money. Please don't give him any. Tell him to call Gamblers Anonymous." She started to shut the door, and Ethan stuck his foot in it.

"Wait. Please! This is really important. Do you know where he might go—if he just needed to get away and think? I *have* to find him."

She softened her tone. "Do you think Stedman's in some kind of trouble? I worry every day the police are going to come knocking on my door."

Should he tell her anything? How could he put her at risk? The less she knew the better.

"I don't know that he's in trouble, ma'am. I just want to speak with him."

"What'd you say your name was?"

"Ethan Langley."

"I'm Audrey Reeves." She offered him her hand. "Nice to make your acquaintance. Stedman's my only grandchild, you know. He was a good boy until the gambling got ahold of him. He used to come stay with me part of every summer. Our favorite thing we did together was to go for nature walks. When he got older, we found a trail in the foothills that led up to a stream and a pretty waterfall. We used to take a picnic lunch and go up there. Never saw another soul."

"And you think he might've gone there?"

The woman's gray eyes grew wide. "If I could walk worth a hoot, that's where I'd go. You want to go look for him?"

"I'd like to, ma'am. Can you tell me how to find it?"

Brill stood at the kitchen counter and sprinkled grated cheddar over the chicken enchilada casserole. She placed foil over the top just as she heard Kurt's footsteps approaching.

"What's this about Ethan not coming over today?" he said.

Brill licked the salsa off her finger. "Something came up related to Drew, and he's not going to be able to make it. He didn't say *what*— just that it had to do with his cousin. Vanessa is so disappointed. After last night, she could hardly wait to see him."

Kurt put his arms around Brill, his cheek next to hers. "*I'm* disappointed. I admit it was fun having Ethan here yesterday. He adds a new dimension to our Monopoly games."

"He really does." She closed her eyes and relished Kurt's closeness and the manly scent of Polo that drew her in. "I can't imagine what came up on Memorial Day that was so important he couldn't make it over here, but I'm guessing he's as disappointed as we are. Vanessa is upstairs sulking. Why don't you go give her a pep talk?"

"Thanks, but I don't need a pep talk." Vanessa stood in the doorway, Carter resting on her hip. "I'm sure whatever Ethan had to do was important. I'd just feel better if he called and filled me in on the details." Vanessa stuck her finger in the salsa. "Mmm. No one makes it like you do, Mom."

Carter giggled and reached out for Brill to hold him.

"You really know how to melt Grandma, don't you?" Brill lifted him into her arms and spun around a couple times until he laughed out loud.

"Hey, what's for lunch?" Emily came into the kitchen, her hair pulled back in a ponytail, her bathing suit on.

"There're cold cuts for sandwiches," Brill said. "And a fruit salad."

Vanessa opened the refrigerator. "I'll make lunch if someone will watch Carter."

"I'll take him," Emily said.

Brill laughed. "*My* turn. I'm going to go put my bathing suit on and get in the pool with him."

Emily pressed her lips together and stifled a laugh. "Mom, it's a *kiddie* pool."

"It's plenty big enough for two. In fact, why don't you join us?" Brill tugged her ponytail.

"Oh brother, I think Dad ought to get a picture of this."

Kurt winked at Brill. "Why not? We could submit a picture for the community page of the newspaper. People would love to see our sassy redheaded police chief playing in a kiddie pool with her daughter and grandson."

"If you want to live to be forty-six," Brill said, "I suggest you put that idea back where it came from."

"You're cute when you're paranoid."

Brill locked gazes with him and smiled in spite of herself. "Kurt, I'm serious."

"I'm just having a little fun with you, honey. I'm not going to photograph you in the pool. But I'll bet there's not a police chief in East Tennessee who looks as good as you do in a bathing suit."

She laughed. "Since I'm the only *female* police chief in East Tennessee, I'll bet you're right."

Ethan sat in his car at the Gas 'N' Go station at Main and Ninth and typed Vanessa a text message: *Busy day. Miss you. Love coming your way, Ethan.* He hit the Send button.

How long could he stay in touch with her and avoid lying? That's where he drew the line. He wasn't going to lie to her.

Audrey Reeves turned out to be a sweetheart. She was deeply hurt that Stedman had stolen money from her. But if she knew that her grandson had agreed to kill a man in order to pay his gambling debt? She'd be devastated.

Ethan unfolded the paper with the directions Audrey had so painstakingly written out. Was Stedman hiding somewhere? Or had he been murdered and his body disposed of? There was nothing on his side of the duplex to suggest there had been a struggle. Had he even made it home last night? Audrey said his truck was not in the driveway at six this morning when she went out to get the newspaper.

Ethan had a sick feeling that Win Davison might have taken care of the *problem,* and that now the only problem left was Ethan, whom the conspirators assumed knew far too much. Why try to threaten him into submission? Why didn't they just kill him? Why take the chance that he would go to Chief Jessup? Then again, what could he tell her? All evidence pointed to Stedman's guilt. They had set him up well. And with his history, not even his grandmother would think it implausible that he might resort to murder to pay his gambling debt. After all, he had *agreed* to it.

Ethan studied the directions and crude map Audrey had sketched out. It was a long shot, but it was worth a try.

CHAPTER 32

Tessa sat at the counter at Nick's Grill and ate the last bite of a grilled salmon filet before wiping her mouth with a napkin.

"Goodness, Nick. I think you outdid yourself."

Nick Phillips smiled and slung a white bar towel over his shoulder. "There's just nothing better than Alaskan cold-water salmon. Had to charge a little more, but I'm glad you think it was worth it."

"Tastes like chicken to me." A grin appeared under Gus's white mustache. "Just kidding. It's real good. I may be losin' my marbles, but my taster still works."

Maggie locked arms with Gus and took a sip of coffee just as Jo Beth came by with a fresh pot and gave everyone warmers.

"Y'all have plans for Memorial Day?" Jo Beth said.

"Maggie and I went out to the cemetery this mornin' and put flowers on my relatives' graves." Gus hooked his thumbs on his suspenders. "I've had ancestors buried out there since before the Civil War. A couple of them died in that war."

"The War between the States was so sad," Tessa said. "To think that citizens of the same country were killing each other."

"Still are," Gus said. "They're just not suitin' up. I guarantee you the war against crime has never been won."

Antonio nodded. "I wonder how many people are murdered every year in this country."

Gus pushed his glasses higher on his nose. "Last I heard, it was a little over sixteen thousand."

"Where'd you hear it?"

"On the Internet," Gus said. "I was just surfin' and one thing led to another, and I ran across it on NationMaster.com. Real interesting site."

Tessa looked down the counter at Gus. "*You* surf the net?"

"Sure do. Why do y'all look so shocked?"

"Tessa and I never have gotten into computers." Antonio took her hand. "Our daughter and son-in-law want us to learn so we can email them and our little granddaughter in England. Computers are overwhelming. We've just never done it and wouldn't even know where to start."

"Nothin' to it," Gus said. "I could set you up. We could drive over to Best Buy and pick one that suits you and get you up and runnin' in no time. Email's the easiest thing in the world."

Tessa stared at Gus. "Well, I'm surprised *and* impressed. How did we not know you were into computers?"

"You never asked."

"Never asked what?" Clint Ames slid onto the stool next to Tessa and took off his sunglasses.

"Our friend Gus has been holding out on us," Antonio said. "He surfs the net."

"Doesn't everybody?" Clint said.

"Tessa and I don't. But Gus says he can set us up and show us how to email our daughter."

"You know how to plug in all those wires?" Clint said. "I always have to get one of my sons to help."

Gus shrugged. "Sure. I've been doin' it for years."

"I can't believe you never mentioned it," Tessa said.

"I'd rather rabble-rouse than talk about myself. I'm tryin' to do better."

Maggie patted his arm. "So anybody got plans for today?"

"I'm working," Clint said. "We're filled up at Hazy View. Every cabin, chalet, and campsite."

"Tessa and I are going over to the Jessups' this evening for dinner and another round of Monopoly."

Gus looked over the top of his glasses. "The police chief plays Monopoly?"

"All the time," Antonio said. "Why is your jaw dropped?"

"I'm just tryin' to picture Brill Jessup playin' Monopoly like a regular person."

Tessa rolled her eyes. "Well, for heaven's sake, Gus, of course she's a regular person."

"I never pictured her that way before—like you never pictured me as a computer geek. There's a lot more to me than meets the eye, and I reckon that's true of her, too."

"Hey, look this way." Nick went over to the flat screen TV and turned up the volume. "Something's going on …"

"Again, the Stanton County Sheriff's Department has identified the body of an apparent hit-and-run victim as forty-one-year-old Grant Wolski of Sophie Trace. Wolski's body was discovered by a cattle rancher just before eleven this morning about two miles east of town on Brenner Creek Road. Sheriff's deputies said they believe

Wolski may have been intoxicated. He smelled strongly of whiskey, and an open container was found in his SUV, which was found parked on a gravel road a short distance from where he was struck.

"Sheriff Sam Parker said his department has no suspects at this time but has already launched a full investigation and ordered an autopsy.

"Wolski was an operations supervisor at Davison Technologies. He's divorced and has two sons that live with their mother in Washington State.

"We return now to our regularly scheduled programming and will bring you breaking news as we have it …"

Nick reached up and turned down the volume.

"A hit and run?" Tessa said. "Who would do such a thing?"

Antonio took her hand. "At least it's not another shooting."

Ethan stopped his car, a trail of white dust behind him on the gravel road. According to his odometer, he had gone eight-tenths of a mile off Deer Path. Isn't that what Audrey Reeves told him to do?

He rolled down his window; the only sounds outside were the buzzing of insects in the tall grass and the cawing of a crow. The sun was high and hot, the foothills wrapped in a milky blue haze. He picked up the directions Audrey had given him, unfolded the paper, and started reading out loud.

"Go eight-tenths of a mile. Look for the lone sycamore tree in the pines." He glanced up and spotted it at the edge of the forest about thirty yards to his right. "Go to it and keep walking straight into the woods about a hundred yards. You'll come to a rushing stream. Waterfall about thirty yards upstream. Look for Stedman there."

Ethan memorized the directions, folded the paper, and put it in the pocket of his cargo pants. Did he even know what he was going to say to Stedman if he found him?

He looked in his rearview mirrors for any sign that he might have been followed, then got out of the car and walked through the tall grass toward the lone sycamore tree, his eye drawn to a bright yellow goldfinch perched atop a thistle.

Lord, give me wisdom. I want Drew's killer caught and convicted. I can't accept that I have to keep quiet and let these guys frame Stedman— or kill him—in order to protect Vanessa and Carter and myself. Show me a better way. There has to be a better way.

Ethan stopped at the sycamore tree. The forest was dark and considerably cooler. He looked around. How was he supposed to continue on a hundred yards to the stream without a trail to follow? He took the paper out of his pocket and reread Audrey's directions in a spot of sunlight filtering through the canopy. Yes, that's what it said to do.

Ethan sighed. The trees were thick. If he wound his way around them, could he be sure he was going in the right direction? Why hadn't he thought to bring a compass?

He heard a loud swooshing noise and felt a gush of wind on his neck. He ducked and looked up in time to see a huge owl light on a distant tree branch. His mind played in reverse, to an incident that happened when he was ten …

"There's a humongous nest up there," Drew said. "Let's go see what's in it."

Ethan went over and stood next to his cousin at the base of a giant leafy tree in the woods behind Uncle Richard and Aunt Becca's house. "It's getting dark. We should go."

Drew let out a husky laugh and started climbing. "Last one up there's a rotten egg."

Ethan followed, clutching the tree trunk with arms and legs. The two raced upward, bark flying in all directions, exchanging playful taunts all the way to the top.

"I won," Drew said, sounding as if he had just enough air left to get the words out.

"No fair. There wasn't even room to pass you." Ethan crawled up on a thick branch and sat. "Can you see what's in the nest?"

Drew took a tiny flashlight out of his back pocket and shone it on the nest. "It's empty."

"After all that? Are you sure?"

"Yep."

"What's that moving farther out on the limb?" Ethan stood and grabbed the branch above his head with both hands so he could get a better look. "They're baby owls! Three of them! See if you can reach them!"

Drew lay on his stomach and inched forward. "I wonder if they'll sit on my arm like my parakeets do."

In the next instant, a gigantic owl swooped down and hit Drew's back with its talons, almost knocking him off the limb and screeching so fiercely that he started to bawl.

"Go!" he hollered. "Let's get out of here!"

Ethan didn't have to be asked twice. With the parent owl still screeching and scolding, the two ten-year-olds made their descent in record time. The second their feet hit the ground they wound their way out of the woods and ran lickety-split back to Uncle Richard and Aunt Becca's house.

Drew's shirt was ripped, but his back wasn't badly scratched. The only injury Ethan had was to his ego, when Drew pointed out that he had wet his pants. Considering what an exciting discovery they had made, neither bawling nor pants-wetting seemed dishonorable ...

Ethan came back to the present, the memory of Drew so vivid and real that emotion was just under the surface. He wanted Win Davison held accountable—not Stedman.

He looked out at the maze of trees and willed himself to take a step and then another and another, weaving in and out of the trees, trying to move forward in the direction of the stream.

A twig cracked somewhere behind him. He stopped, his heart pounding. Was he being followed? He hid behind a tree ... as if that would do any good. Was it possible the guy who attacked him put a tracking device on his car while he stood robotically at Stedman's door, counting to fifty?

Dread flooded him. What if they wanted him to lead them to Stedman? What if they planned to execute both of them?

Brill walked down the familiar corridor, her sandals squeaking on the shiny floor, and remembered how intimidated she had been the few times she met Sheriff Sam Parker on his turf. She stopped at the first open door and knocked.

Sam sat at a round table in the corner, his hands clasped behind his head, a row of teeth visible under his mustache.

"Come in, Chief Jessup. Have a seat." Sam had a smile in his voice, too.

Brill shook his hand, then sat in a vinyl chair, feeling vulnerable dressed in crop pants and a blouse instead of her uniform.

"I'm sorry to interrupt your holiday," Sam said. "But some information has come to light in my investigation of today's hit and run that you need to be aware of."

"You said it was urgent." *It had better be.*

Sam opened a file folder that contained some photographs. "I want you to take a look at a piece of evidence we recovered in the victim's SUV."

Sam handed her an eight-by-ten photograph of what appeared to be the bottom half of an email message. The top portion had been torn off.

"I think it's clear enough that you can read the words," Sam said. Brill started reading:

Sorry to shock you like this, but the reason I know Stedman Reeves shot Tal Davison is because I gave him the gun and promised to cancel his sixty-thousand-dollar gambling debt if he would do it. What can I say? I wanted Win Davison to know what it was like to lose something he cared about.

I wanted him to suffer for being so callous about laying people off and watching their dreams go down the toilet.

Stedman did a good job. He made Tal's killing look like the result of a random shooting spree. But he nearly freaked when he found out he accidentally killed two girls in the process. He was in a lot more trouble than he bargained for and started to worry that Davison's roommate might have seen something. He decided he couldn't take any chances and killed him, too.

The reason I'm emailing you is to tell you that Stedman's losing it! His guilty conscience has finally sent him over the edge, and he's turned on me. He's threatened to kill me for getting him involved. He's crazy enough to do it, so I'm going to find a place to lay low for a while. I'll call work Tuesday and say there is a family emergency and I need to use some vacation days. If you need me, call my cell. I wanted you to know in case something happens to me.

Grant

Brill sat back in her chair, her mind racing with the implications. "Well, Sheriff … that's the *last* thing I expected to hear today."

Sam's grin got wider. "We bagged the black paint and metal slivers we found on the victim to see what kind of vehicle was used in the hit and run. Just so happens this Stedman Reeves is driving a black Nissan Frontier. Looks to me like I found your shooter."

CHAPTER 33

Brill breezed into her office. Trent Norris waited for her at the conference table, a cup of Starbucks set at her place.

"Is that for me?" she said. "You're reading my mind."

Trent flashed a half-moon smile. "Thought you might need it, Chief. Sorry the holiday got messed up, but if Reeves is our shooter, it's a small price to pay."

"Were your sons disappointed you had to cut your fishing adventure short?"

"Well, sure. But they each caught three stripers—big ones at that. Their mother's taking them to Water World this afternoon. I think they're over it."

Brill took a sip of coffee. "Oh, this is so good, Trent."

"Two sugars, just like you like it." He sat back in his chair, his arms folded across his chest. "So was Sam Parker gloating the whole time?"

"Don't you know it? If his grin had gotten any wider, it would've pulled that gold tooth right out of his mouth." She smiled. "Okay, fill me in."

"I've got Rousseaux and Marcum working with sheriff's deputies to locate this Stedman Reeves character. We got an APB out for his arrest and a warrant to search his duplex. Reeves's grandmother is his landlady and lives in the other half of the duplex. Rousseaux showed her the warrant, and she let him in. The door was open but there was no sign of forced entry. She doesn't think Stedman came home last night. Said a young man came looking for him this morning, and she told the guy the same thing."

"Did she get the young man's name?"

Trent pushed out his bottom lip and shook his head. "She couldn't remember. Said he had long, sandy hair and the personality of a hedge apple. She wasn't helpful, but officers and deputies are still over there. Maybe the warrant will uncover something. But get this: Reeves works for Langley Concrete."

"What a coincidence. That's where Ethan is working this summer. His uncle owns it."

"I remember you saying that. I've got officers on their way to talk with Ralph Langley, and we have a warrant to search Reeves's locker at the business location."

"I think we should talk to Ethan."

"I agree. He's at your place today, right?"

Brill shook her head. "Actually, he isn't. Something came up related to his cousin, and he couldn't join us. Vanessa should be able to reach him and get him to come down here. On second thought, I'll get his number and call him myself."

�֍   �֍   ✖

Ethan sat on the trunk of a fallen tree and looked at the dense forest around him. Surely he had gone a hundred yards by now. Where was the stream? Had he wandered off course, weaving his way around the trees? Or had Audrey Reeves deliberately sent him on a wild goose chase?

A twig snapped a second time, and Ethan's heart nearly pounded out of his chest. Someone was definitely there. How much more of this could he take?

He got up and stood behind a tree—not that he was any less conspicuous, but he felt less vulnerable. Was it worth all this tension just to tell Stedman about the unconscionable threat to Vanessa and Carter—and that he couldn't go to Chief Jessup and do what Stedman had asked?

Ethan stepped away from the tree, his hands clenched at his sides. "Who's out there?" he hollered angrily. "Stop following me like a coward and show yourself!"

Leaves rustled, and then a young buck sprang into the air, leaping over the fallen tree Ethan had just sat on, and ran into the woods, its white tail waggling.

Ethan staggered backward into a tree, his heart hammering, his knees about to give out. At least it wasn't someone Davison had sent to kill him.

The LORD is with me; I will not be afraid. What can man do to me?

The verse from Psalm 118 popped into his head. He took in a deep breath and exhaled slowly. And then did it again. Was he going to let fear dictate his actions? He came out here to find Stedman. If he turned back, where would he go? Was he prepared to go home early and lie to Uncle Ralph and Aunt Gwen about why he wasn't with Vanessa? Or sit around at their cookout and make small talk with the guests? Could he go see Vanessa and pretend nothing was wrong? What kind of precedent did that set for an open and honest relationship? Was he capable of facing Brill and pretending he didn't know who was behind the shootings?

His cell phone vibrated and surprised him. He hadn't been able to get a cell signal since he left the car. The display screen blinded him for a moment, and then he saw that Chief Jessup was the caller. He decided to let the call go to voice mail.

He waited a minute and then retrieved the message and played it back.

"Ethan, it's Brill. I know you took the day to deal with something personal concerning Drew, and I'm sorry to intrude on that. I'm going to cut to the chase. A man you work with, Stedman Reeves, is now a suspect in both shootings. It's imperative that we find him. We also think he's responsible for the death of a man named Grant Wolski, who was found dead in a hit-and-run accident this morning. We found evidence in Wolski's vehicle that implicates Stedman as the shooter. He's considered armed and dangerous, and no matter how well you think you know him, I strongly urge you to stay away from him. If you know how we can find him, I need to know ASAP. Either way, we need you to come down to the station and tell us everything you know about him. Your uncle and the other workers on the crew are cooperating fully. Please call me back on my cell when you get this message."

Ethan stared at the phone, trying to let her words sink in. Grant Wolski was *dead?* According to Stedman, he was the key player in the entire setup. There was no way that hit-and-run was an accident. But could Stedman have done it? Would Grant's death have benefited Stedman in any way?

Ethan wiped the perspiration off his forehead. He didn't see how. Why would Stedman kill the one eyewitness who could verify his story? With Grant out of the picture, it was Stedman's word against the fabricated evidence to the contrary.

He checked to make sure he still had a signal, then keyed in Stedman's number. He would leave a hundred messages for Stedman if he had to. Eventually the guy would get tired of Ethan bugging him and would call back. Did Stedman know the police were looking for him?

The phone rang three times, and Ethan waited for the voice-mail greeting to click on.

"Hello, Ethan."

"Stedman! Why didn't you return my calls?"

"I was busy disappearing. Some guy got into my duplex this morning and was nosing around. I hid, and he never knew I was home. But he had a knife. He walked through the place and then left. I decided to get out of there."

"Smart move. I went by your place, hoping we could continue our conversation from last night. You weren't there, and I started to leave a note at your door when some guy grabbed me from behind and threatened me at knifepoint."

"Threatened you how?"

"He said that unless I forget all the lies you've been telling me, he would—" The words caught in Ethan's throat. Could he even say them? Did he even want to?

"He would *what?*"

"He would deliver Vanessa and Carter to me—piece by piece. And then he'd come after me." He hated that his voice was shaking.

Stedman sighed into the receiver. "I am so sorry, man. How'd those guys even know we talked? That's exactly what I was trying to avoid."

"Well, we need to continue that conversation someplace private—not on the phone."

"Where are you now?" Stedman said.

"Lost. It's a long story."

Ethan explained how he had gone to Stedman's grandmother's door, convinced her that Stedman needed his help, and gotten directions to the one place he might have gone.

"I did what she said and got as far as the woods." Ethan sighed. "I tried to continue on a hundred yards, but I'm not sure I followed a straight line. I don't see the stream. I just need to get out of here."

"Well, you're in luck. Grandma knows me pretty well."

"What do you mean?"

"I'm right where she said I'd be. Stay put. I'll find you. Hang up and let me call you back so I can listen for the ringing in the woods. Don't answer it. Maybe you're closer than you think."

"All right. But hurry. I just now got the signal back."

❖ ❖ ❖

Vanessa sat on the glider, Carter asleep in her arms. Her father came out on the screened-in porch and sat next to her.

"You okay?"

"Not really." Vanessa stroked the baby's back. "Ethan liked Stedman. He's going to feel betrayed if it turns out that Stedman killed Drew. I just wish he'd call me. I don't understand why he's avoiding me."

"I wouldn't be so quick to take it personally," Kurt said. "The poor guy has to be on overload. And it's not unusual for a man in his situation to need a little space to think and work out his feelings."

"But that's not how it's been. Ethan shares his feelings with me and has been very open with me—until today."

"He's been texting you today, hasn't he?"

Vanessa nodded.

"Which means he has you on his mind. Maybe he's chosen to text rather than call because he just doesn't want to talk about whatever it is he's doing. Since it has to do with Drew, it's probably depressing."

Vanessa glanced at her dad sheepishly. "I'm being selfish, aren't I?"

"I just think you need to be more realistic, honey. The full weight of losing Drew is bound to hit Ethan between the eyes at some point. I think you have to cut him some slack if he's private about some of it."

Vanessa nestled closer to her dad. "You're right. I keep wanting to push the sadness away and just enjoy being in love."

"That's understandable. You two have been through the mill. But you both need time to catch your breath."

Emily came outside and sat on Kurt's lap, putting her arms around his neck. "How come you're whispering?"

"We're not whispering. We're just not talking loudly enough for you to eavesdrop." Kurt tickled her ribs, evoking a shriek that caused Carter to stir.

"Shhh," Vanessa scolded. "If he doesn't get his nap, he'll be grouchy as an old bear."

Emily put both hands over her mouth. "Sorry."

"Vanessa and I were talking about grief," Kurt said. "And how sometimes people prefer to keep their feelings private."

"Oh." Emily stroked Carter's hair and seemed to be processing. "Ethan has grief. I can tell. I remember when Poppy and Grammy died and I felt so sad and didn't want to move or do anything. It was like I swallowed a giant rock."

"That's certainly one way to describe it." Kurt looked over at Vanessa and winked.

"Did Mom arrest the shooter yet?" Emily asked.

"We aren't absolutely sure that Stedman Reeves *is* the shooter. He's innocent until proven guilty." Kurt tugged her ponytail. "But no. The police are still looking for him."

"I wonder why Ethan didn't call Mom back," Vanessa said. "He of all people would want to cooperate with police so they could arrest Drew's killer."

❖ ❖ ❖

Ethan's phone rang four times before going to voice mail. He cupped his hands around his mouth.

"Stedman!" he shouted. "Can you hear me?"

Ethan's voice resounded in the forest. Surely Stedman would hear him if he were anywhere nearby.

Father, I need Your help. I have to make a big decision, and I don't have much time to think about it.

Ethan felt light-headed, the severity of Brill's phone call beginning to sink in. How involved could he get in this mess before he could be charged with obstruction of justice—especially when he had a working cell phone and a direct line to the police chief?

He hated that he was being intimidated into doing something he knew wasn't right. Could he really look Brill in the eye and deny that Stedman came to him with this story? Could he let an innocent man get the death penalty and Drew's killer live happily ever after—without at least telling the police what he knew?

Then again, Stedman wasn't exactly innocent. Didn't he admit he had planned to kill Tal Davison? What if he did kill him and was lying about it? What if he did what Grant Wolski had asked so he could get out from under his gambling debt—and then panicked that Drew might know something and decided to kill him, too?

What if Stedman fabricated the elaborate story about being framed, hoping Ethan was gullible enough to help him convince Brill? What if he got in his truck and ran down Grant Wolski so the guy couldn't contradict his story?

Ethan picked a piece of bark off the tree and held it in his fingers. That didn't add up. If Stedman was guilty, why would Win Davison bother sending one of his goons to intimidate Ethan?

Lord, give me wisdom. If Stedman's telling the truth, what's happening to him is wrong. I can't just wash my hands and walk away.

"Hold it right there! Put both hands behind your head."

Stedman seemed to appear out of nowhere, and Ethan was staring down the barrel of his gun.

"Come on, man. You know I'm not armed," Ethan said.

Stedman patted him down. "Sorry. I can't be too careful right now. I wouldn't put it past the cops to talk you into taking me back at gunpoint."

"The cops may be the least of your worries," Ethan said. "It's already started. Grant Wolski was killed this morning by a hit-and-run driver."

"*What?*"

"Oh, it gets worse—the police think *you* did it. *And* they found something in Grant's car that convinced them you shot Tal Davison and my cousin. They're turning Sophie Trace upside down looking for you. There's an APB out for your arrest. They think you killed five people."

Stedman seemed to stare at nothing. "I guess I shouldn't be surprised. This is probably the nail in my coffin. Grant was sure there would be consequences for his failure to delete that email from Davison and for keeping a record of what was said in the meeting. But this is brilliant. Davison must've decided he could get rid of Grant in the hit and run, make it look like I did it, *and* plant evidence in Grant's SUV that made the police think I was the shooter. Do you even know what the evidence was?"

"Brill didn't say."

"I thought you said you didn't talk to the cops."

"I didn't. Brill's left me a detailed phone message. And she's called two more times. I'm going to have to return her calls at some point." Ethan looked over Stedman's shoulder and saw nothing but trees. "Is there some place we could sit and talk?"

"Sure. The waterfall Grandma told you about isn't far. Follow me. I'm sorry I pulled you into this, man. I just thought you were the one person who could get the cops to listen. But now that Davison and his cronies have succeeded in framing me, there's no need for you to get involved. They got what they wanted. They won't bother you anymore."

"Don't count on it. I'm the only other person who knows they pulled it off. Which makes *me* the threat."

CHAPTER 34

Brill sat next to Trent on the couch in Ralph Langley's living room, her eyes fixed on a handful of feisty hummingbirds fighting over the feeder outside the window, her ears attuned to Trent's questioning of Ethan's uncle Ralph.

"How long has Stedman worked for you?" Trent said.

"He started eight years ago this month. He's a good employee. About the only thing I've ever gotten on his case for is coming in late. He likes to play around on the casino sites on his computer and doesn't always know when to call it a night."

"So he's a gambler?"

"Yeah, he is. Anyone who's been around Stedman for long knows that about him. But like I said, he's a good employee. It doesn't really interfere with his job that much."

"And what is his job, Mr. Langley? Is he foreman?"

"No, I still manage things on-site. But Stedman's the highest paid employee on my payroll. He's a big asset, especially since he also speaks enough Spanish to help me with my Hispanic workers."

Trent gave a nod. "Ever hear him mention a guy named Grant Wolski?"

"Not that I recall."

"Ever hear Stedman talk about playing high-stakes poker?"

312

Ralph tented his fingers and seemed focused on them. "I don't think poker's legal in Tennessee."

"That's not what I asked you, sir."

Ralph's cheeks were suddenly flushed. "I overheard him setting up games over the phone a few times. I figured it was his business. It's not like he has a casino in his garage. It's just a bunch of competitive guys who like to play for money."

"What makes you say that?"

"I guess because that's what Stedman said. I'm not a gambling man myself. I really didn't pay much attention to it. Am I in trouble for not reporting him?"

"Mr. Langley"—Brill turned her gaze to him—"we're just here to find out what you know about Stedman."

"What's he done? Why are you asking these questions?"

Trent glanced over at Brill and then at Ralph. "We have reason to believe he was involved in the shootings—and a hit-and-run death this morning."

"Stedman? No way!"

"The evidence suggests otherwise, sir. Let's stay focused. Do you know any of his friends?"

Ralph's face was suddenly expressionless. "He had a girlfriend, Holly something—Miller ... Morgan ... *Morton*. That's it: Morton. They broke up months ago. I never really met his guy friends."

"In eight years, you've never met any of his buddies?" Trent said.

"I really haven't. I met his grandmother—Audrey Reeves. She rents him half her duplex."

"What kind of relationship does Stedman have with her?"

Ralph raised an eyebrow. "Oh, I think Audrey's his conscience. She's quite a character and keeps Stedman on the straight and narrow. He's not on speaking terms with his folks, and I've never asked why. I don't like to pry."

Trent wrote something on his ruled pad. "Have you noticed any mood changes in Stedman lately? Did he seem tense to you?"

"Now that you mention it, he's had trouble staying focused. Forgets things. Has to be told more than once what needs to be done. He's had a couple of those bad headaches he gets every now and then. Hasn't been very social with the work crew either."

"How long has this has been going on?"

Ralph scratched his chin and seemed to be contemplating. "Several weeks. Definitely worse in the last two. I cut him some slack. Like I said, Stedman's been a good employee for eight years. I figured he was just working through something."

"What kind of relationship does he have with Ethan?" Brill said.

"Good. They worked together all last summer, and they're off to a good start this year. Stedman's been very sensitive to Ethan since his cousin was killed. There's just no way I can believe that Stedman shot any of those people. There has to be some mistake."

"Do you know if Ethan and Stedman pal around outside of work time?"

Ralph looked from Brill to Trent and back to Brill. "You're kidding, right? Every second Ethan has off the clock, he spends with Vanessa. You see him more than I do. You probably should be talking to him about this. Stedman might confide things in Ethan he'd never say to his employer."

"We're trying to get in touch with Ethan," Brill said, "but he's not returning the calls. I know he had something personal he had to take care of today regarding Drew."

Ralph's eyebrows came together. "I don't think so. He's spending the day with Vanessa. He told me himself, right before he left the house this morning."

"What time was that?"

"Seven, seven fifteen. I thought it was early for him to be intruding on you folks. Ethan was so eager to get going that he didn't even want his aunt to fix him breakfast."

"The thing is," Brill said, "Ethan planned to come over much later than that—around noon—but he sent Vanessa a text message and said something had come up concerning Drew and he had to cancel."

Ralph sighed. "I'd sure like to know what's going on."

You and me both, Brill thought. She looked at her watch. Why hadn't Ethan returned her phone calls? She'd already left three messages. Maybe he turned his phone off.

Ethan sat cross-legged on a large, flat rock, watching the spring run-off spilling over the top of Deer Path Falls and plummeting twenty feet into a clear, round pool, rainbow mist cooling his face.

"How did you and your grandmother find this place?"

Stedman sat facing him, his gaze intrusive. "It's been so long I don't even remember. Someone she knew owned the property. *We* named the falls Deer Path. Hardly anyone even knows it's here."

Ethan smiled wryly. "I had a map, and I couldn't find it."

"Could we just cut to the chase?" Stedman said. "Before I can figure out what I'm going to do, I need to know what you're going to tell Chief Jessup."

"Did I mention that in her phone message she said you were considered armed and dangerous and not to approach you?"

Stedman's eyes turned to slits. "So why *did* you?"

Ethan picked up a twig and drew a heart on the rock, Vanessa's perfume pervasive in his memory. "I don't happen to think you're dangerous. And I don't think it's right to let the wrong guy go to prison—or get the death penalty—for this. You agreed to do something despicable, but when it came down to it, you couldn't pull the trigger—because you're not a killer. You might be charged with conspiracy to commit murder, I don't know. What I *do* know is you shouldn't be charged with capital murder in the deaths of five people."

Stedman's eyes brimmed with tears, and he looked down and began cracking his knuckles.

"This goes way beyond my wanting Win Davison to pay for killing Drew," Ethan said. "It's a matter of principle. I can't turn my back on an innocent man because I'm being threatened."

"Believe me, the threat's real."

"I'm sure. The guy was very graphic about what he intended to do to us. He also said that I couldn't win this hand, that I should take his advice and fold before I lose everything."

"Sounds like good advice."

"I guess that depends on what you've got in your hand."

"What do you mean?"

Ethan looked at the round pool beneath the waterfall and remembered how clean he felt the day he made his profession of faith and was baptized. Why should a King's son cower in fear when he had been granted the power of his Father's authority? Didn't he have angels protecting him? Wasn't every step he would ever take recorded before he was born? Didn't his heavenly Father have a purpose for his life? Was he going to let those pathetic pawns of darkness bully him into silence? He looked into Stedman's eyes. The guy wasn't perfect, but he wasn't evil like them. And Ethan wasn't going to sacrifice him without a fight. If right was right, it was right all the time—not just when it was convenient.

"You may not understand this," Ethan said, "but I believe in playing the hand I've been dealt. You know I'm a Christian. I gave my life to Christ, and I belong to Him. Nothing happens to me that He hasn't allowed for a purpose. I'm not going to be intimidated into doing the wrong thing."

Stedman's eyes widened. "Look, I agreed to kill a man. I'm no better than they are. You don't owe me anything."

"I owe you the truth. It took courage for you to admit what you *almost* did. We need to tell Brill the truth and let her take it from there."

"Don't be a hero, Ethan. It's dangerous."

"It's the right call. Let's put our cards on the table and see who's got the stronger hand. That's the last thing Win Davison is expecting us to do. God's on the side of truth, Stedman. Right now, that's the best defense we've got."

"Come on, man. If the cops get their hands on me, it's all over."

Ethan looked out into the forest. "I said we should put our cards on the table. I didn't say where."

CHAPTER 35

Vanessa walked barefoot along the flower beds in the backyard, sprinkler hose in hand. Why did this Memorial Day seem so long without Ethan being there with her? After their mutual declaration of love last night, could his absence be any more disappointing? She heard the screen door open and shut.

"There she is. There's Mommy." Emily strolled toward her with Carter clinging to her like a chimpanzee. "He just woke up from his nap."

Vanessa took Carter into her arms and gave Emily the sprinkler hose. "How's my handsome baby boy?" She kissed his nose, and he flashed a smile the size of the Grand Canyon.

Emily held the hose on the flower bed and put her hand in the spray. "Are you sad Mom had to leave and won't be here when we eat her yummy casserole?"

"I'm always a little sad any time Mom can't be with us on a holiday. But if they think Stedman Reeves is the shooter, she has a good reason to be working."

Emily locked gazes with Vanessa and seemed to pry the lid off her comfort zone. "Did Ethan call you back yet?"

"Emily, don't be a pest."

"That's what little sisters are for."

"Not today. He hasn't called, but he's sent me three text messages. He must be thinking of me."

"Ethan's *always* thinking of you. He sold you Park Place, for heaven's sake. Who else would do that? It practically guaranteed you would win."

Vanessa smiled. "True."

Vanessa's cell phone chimed, and she took it out of the pocket of her sundress. It was a text message from Ethan. *I'm stepping out in faith. Pray for a good outcome. I need you to trust me and Him. I love you. Ethan.*

"What did he say?"

"He said, 'Tell Emily to mind her own business.'"

"I'll bet he said something mushy."

"No, he didn't."

"Then why are your eyes all twinkly?"

Vanessa smiled without meaning to. It was the fourth time that day he'd said he loved her. Was her sheer delight that obvious? "Here, take Carter. Why don't you play with him in the pool?"

"I can't right now. Jasmine's coming over, and Dad's letting us make peach ice cream."

"All right. Would you mind turning off the water? I think I'll take him out in his stroller."

❖ ❖ ❖

Ethan climbed up the side of the rock formation, Deer Path Falls visible on his left. Stedman reached the top and offered Ethan his hand, then pulled him up the rest of the way. The two climbed over some large boulders and onto a smooth, flat oval rock that looked about six feet across at the widest point. The spring runoff moved swiftly past them, crashing into the boulders in the stream, creating swirls of white foam before plummeting over the edge of the cliff.

"So this is where the waterfall originates," Ethan said.

Stedman nodded. "The cell signal is clear up here, but we have to deal with the water noise."

"Sorry your phone's dead."

"I forgot to charge it when I got home last night. I had other things on my mind."

Ethan sat for a moment and caught his breath. "This is incredible."

"You sure you want to do this, man? Once you make that call, there's no turning back."

Stedman was right. This was the point of no return. *Was* he sure? The words of Ephesians 6 resounded in his head and seemed almost audible.

Therefore put on the full armor of God, so that when the day of evil comes, you may be able to stand your ground.

"Yes, I'm sure," Ethan said. "Let's dig our heels in and tell the truth. What these guys are doing is worse than wrong—it's evil. We can't let them get away with it."

"I can't believe you're helping me."

Ethan took his phone off the clip and looked at it for a moment. "Let me pray before we do this." He put his hand firmly on Stedman's shoulder, feeling more bold than embarrassed.

"Lord God, you are the way, the truth, and the life. You're *always* on the side of truth. Of that we can be sure. What's happening to

Stedman is a lie—a scheme right out of Satan's handbook. It's evil. It's destructive. It has to be stopped.

"But the two of us are no match for these guys. And the minute we talk to the police, things are going to get dangerous. Lord, we can't do this without You. Protect us from evil. And help us convince Brill that Stedman didn't kill those five people. Let truth prevail and justice be served. In Jesus' name we pray. Amen."

Ethan took his hand off Stedman's shoulder. "I didn't ask if you minded me praying. There's just no way I'd open this door without getting God involved."

Stedman's face was flushed. "It's okay."

Ethan took a deep breath. "All right, here we go." He pulled up Brill's voice message and then pressed the number eight to reply. He glanced over at Stedman. "It's ringing. Let's hope it doesn't go to voice mail—"

"Hello, Ethan! I've been trying to reach you. Did you get my messages?"

"I did. Sounds like you had a big break in the case."

"Then you know we're trying to find Stedman Reeves. Do you know where he is?"

"Actually I do. He's here with me."

"With *you?* Where are you? Is he holding you against your will?"

"No. We're sitting on a rock next to a rushing stream. It's a little hard to hear you."

"Ethan, what's going on? This is serious. This man is dangerous."

"What if I told you that Stedman's been set up—that he didn't do the shootings and didn't kill Grant Wolski?"

"I'd say you don't have all the information. You can't believe anything he tells you."

"But isn't it possible *you* don't have all the information? Brill, I was threatened by some guy at knifepoint and told not to say anything about this—that if I did, they'd kill Vanessa and Carter. That's why I didn't come to you with it."

"Who threatened you?"

"I didn't see his face. But he sure didn't want me to back Stedman's story."

"What story? Ethan, talk straight with me. What are you trying to say?"

"That *Win Davison* is behind the shootings. He ordered the hit on Tal when he found out he wasn't his biological son—*and* because Tal didn't really want to work for him. He had Tal's biological father killed too. A guy named Paulson McGiver, who wanted a million dollars not to go public with it. He also ordered the hit and run on Grant Wolski and planted evidence to implicate Stedman. And he killed Drew because he thought he knew that Tal didn't want to work for Davison Technologies. It's all connected."

"Do you know how preposterous that sounds?"

"I do. Brill, you have to hear this from start to finish or it won't make sense. It all started with a poker game. Stedman got in over his head and lost sixty thousand dollars to Grant Wolski, and—"

"Did you say *sixty* thousand?"

"I did."

"That's an exorbitant bet for a young man who probably makes half that in a year. Not to mention it's illegal."

"It's illegal, but you know it goes on. Look, Stedman was holding four jacks and bet money he didn't have. He never thought in a million years he would lose that hand. He was ruined. Later, Grant came to him and told him what he could do to pay the debt. That's where the setup began. Here, I'll let him tell you himself." Ethan handed the phone to Stedman. "Just tell the truth."

"Hello, Chief Jessup."

Ethan sat and listened, praying silently as Stedman told Brill every detail of what had happened from the time he made the deal with Grant to kill Tal Davison until this morning when the man with the knife was snooping around his duplex.

"But without the memo I saw," Stedman said, "I can't *prove* anything I just told you … no, ma'am, I can't come in and make a statement. You don't understand. Davison doesn't need me anymore. He won. You all think I did it. You'll have to arrest me, and I couldn't make bail even if it was offered, which I doubt. Once I'm in jail, Davison will find a way to have me killed, and that'll be that. Except for one thing: *Ethan* knows … yes, I believe the threat is real. The guy's already responsible for six killings. Ethan won't be safe if Davison thinks he's a threat, and neither will your daughter and grandson, so—"

Bang! Bang! Bang!

Ethan felt a bullet whiz past his ear and looked over at Stedman in time to see him lunge forward and the cell phone slide down the rock and into the water.

Vanessa nestled on the couch, Carter content to cuddle in her arms. What was it about riding in the stroller that turned him into such a little lovebug? She heard footsteps, and then her father came into the living room.

"Honey, we've got a situation." Kurt's face was ashen, his eyes wide. "Your mother just called, and—"

The doorbell rang.

"That's probably the police," Kurt said. "I need to answer it."

"What?" Vanessa said. "Dad, what's happened?"

Kurt hurried to the door, and Vanessa heard voices. It felt as if her heart had stopped. Had someone died? Had something happened to her brother in Costa Rica?

Ethan's text message came rushing back to her.

I'm stepping out in faith. Pray for a good outcome. I need you to trust me and Him. I love you, Ethan.

Vanessa sat frozen. What had he done? She felt her heart pounding against Carter's chest and held him tightly, dreading the next voice she would hear.

"Hello, Vanessa."

Officer Rachel Howell came in the living room and sat on the love seat across from her.

"Your mother asked me to come over and stay with you until we're able to check some things out."

"What things?"

Kurt hustled Emily into the living room, and they sat on the couch next to Vanessa.

"Ethan and Stedman Reeves just called your mother and gave her new information that might lead to the arrest of the person they allege is responsible for the shootings *and* today's hit and run."

"But isn't Stedman your suspect?"

"We have reason to believe he may have been set up."

"Why are you here?" Vanessa said.

Rachel shot Kurt a glance and then held Vanessa's gaze. "Before your mother had finished listening to Stedman's side of the story, she heard gunfire. The phone went dead. There's no signal."

Vanessa felt as if someone had reached inside her and pulled her heart out. Finally she found her voice. "Didn't they tell Mom where they were?"

"Ethan said they were sitting on a rock by a rushing stream. That's it."

Kurt sighed. "That has about a million possibilities."

"I'm sorry," Rachel said. "Without the GPS locator in his BlackBerry, we have no way of knowing where they are."

Emily reached over and took Vanessa's hand, looking up at her with the most compassionate blue eyes Vanessa had ever seen. "Don't be scared. I just prayed for a guardian angel to be with him. I did that when we didn't know where Mom was, and *she* came home."

Vanessa brushed off a tear that trickled down her cheek.

"The good news," Rachel said, "is we're working this case concurrently with the sheriff's department. An APB has been issued, and Sheriff Parker has his deputies searching for their vehicles. Every available law enforcement officer in the county will be helping."

"Honey, Ethan's smart," Kurt said. "He'll use good sense."

"I still don't understand why Rachel's here."

Rachel folded her hands in her lap and cleared her throat. "Late last night, Stedman shared with Ethan his concern that he was being framed for the shootings and said it involved someone high profile. He wanted Ethan to take his concerns to Chief Jessup under the radar."

"Why didn't he do it himself?"

"Stedman feared for his life. He had been warned to keep his mouth shut. I don't have all the details. But I do know that Ethan was threatened at knifepoint and told that, if he opened his mouth"—Rachel lifted her gaze—"you and Carter would be killed, and so would Ethan."

Two gunshots reverberated in Vanessa's mind, and for a split second she relived the horror of that dreadful moment when Drew was gunned down and she fled with Carter, terrified the shooter would come back for them.

"What if they shot him? What if they killed him just like they killed Drew? Lord, please don't let this happen!" Vanessa started to sob. "Don't let Ethan die. I've never loved anyone this way. Please don't let him die."

CHAPTER 36

Brill got out of her squad car, glad for the towering trees that lined both sides of Azalea Lane, their branches meeting in the middle and creating a green, leafy canopy overhead.

She walked toward the cottage-style house she and Kurt fell in love with the moment they saw it. Had they really lived here two years? It seemed like only yesterday she was telling the movers where to put the mountain of boxes that contained what was left of her life—and wondering if she had made a big mistake pulling up her roots and transplanting them to the other end of the state.

Who driving by would ever guess the suffering her family had endured in the privacy of these walls? And yet hadn't the Lord used every heartache to His glory? Wasn't her marriage stronger? Her family closer? Her faith unshakable?

Vanessa had matured in every way since Carter was born. But could she handle losing both men she loved in less than a year's time?

Lord, You're in control. I trust You. But I'm scared to death for Vanessa if Ethan's dead.

Brill put her hand on the knob and took a slow, deep breath. She opened the door and was greeted with a gust of cold air and the fragrance of this week's roses.

In the next instant Kurt's arms were around her, and she let herself rest in the blanket of his comfort and strength, regretting she could only stay a few minutes.

"Rachel is out in the kitchen," Kurt said. "Vanessa's upstairs."

"How is she?"

Kurt pulled her a little closer and kissed the top of her head. "How would you be? She won't let Carter out of her sight. Emily won't either and didn't argue about calling Jasmine and telling her we'd make ice cream another time."

"Thanks. It's just until the threat is over." *Over?* Unless she could make a solid case against Win Davison, would it ever be over?

"Tessa and Antonio insisted on being here as planned," Kurt said. "They will take care of serving dinner and cleaning up, and gladly play Monopoly with Emily and whoever else wants to join them."

Brill smiled. "They're such a blessing. What would we do without them?"

"They've sure held us together a few times when we were coming apart at the seams. How are *you* doing?"

"I really have a bad feeling about Ethan. I heard *five* gunshots before the phone went dead. If Stedman's right, Davison's a desperate man who's on the brink of losing his precious empire. He'll stop at nothing."

"You think he's serious about this threat to come after Vanessa and Carter?"

Brill pushed back and looked into Kurt's eyes and saw her own fear staring back at her. "I'm not taking any chances. Let me go give Vanessa a hug, and then I have to get back. I need to meet Sam Parker in his office in fifteen minutes."

"How're you two getting along?"

"I put up with a lot from Sam. But he's good at what he does. There's no question I need his help. I'm going to ask him to question Win Davison. Davison has a chip on his shoulder when it comes to me. Sam's known him for years and knows how to turn on the charm before he goes for the jugular. The two of them should have an interesting time trying to manipulate each other."

Ethan crouched down behind two large boulders, clutching tightly to Stedman's gun, his hands shaking, his hope dwindling. How did Davison's henchman know how to find them? Ethan was so sure he hadn't been followed.

Stedman lay in a heap on the flat rock where he and Ethan had sat talking to Brill just minutes before, blood pooled under his left shoulder and streaming into the water.

Ethan now understood how desolate Vanessa felt in those moments after Drew had been shot and killed. What should he do? The forest would start getting dark as soon as the sun dipped lower into the afternoon sky. He thought of Stedman's grandmother and wondered how she would take the news.

The sound of the fast-moving water made it difficult to hear twigs snapping, leaves rustling—anything that would alert him that someone was approaching.

Lord, how could this happen? I was so sure You wanted me to help Stedman. Why didn't You just close that door? Why did You let me walk through it and fail?

He thought of Vanessa and the joy they had felt after voicing their feelings for each other. Would he ever see her again? Hold her in his arms? Would they have the chance to let their love grow and see where it would take them? Not until this moment had he ever seriously considered his own death and how it might come. This was certainly not what he would have chosen—and not at twenty-one.

Lord, if I'm going to die, at least help Brill put Drew's killer behind bars. Don't let our deaths be for nothing. And help Vanessa. Don't let her get bitter. Don't let it change the sweet person she is.

Ethan blinked the stinging from his eyes. He couldn't imagine Vanessa as a bitter person, but how could she accept his death, especially after losing Ty? He tightened his grip on the gun, glad Stedman had put in a new clip. He might have to shoot his way out of here, but it would only be for show. He had never handled a firearm other than a hunting rifle.

What if he ended up face-to-face with the guy who killed Stedman? Could he even pull the trigger? Ending someone's life probably wasn't nearly as difficult as living with having done it. Did he want to be saddled with that burden? Hopefully, it wouldn't come to that.

He stared at the water crashing against the rocks, then moved his gaze to Stedman's body—and did a double take. Stedman's eyes were open! He was looking around as if trying to figure out what had happened.

Ethan waved, then put his finger to his lips, hoping Stedman wouldn't call out. He climbed up on the flat rock and crawled over to where he lay.

"I thought you were dead, man. You've been shot. You were talking to Chief Jessup about being framed. If you remember, blink twice."

Stedman blinked two times.

"Okay, don't talk. Just listen. I know it's hard to hear with the sound of the water. You've been shot in the arm, and I need to see how serious it is. But we need to get out of the open. Whoever shot you probably used a rifle with a scope. If I help steady you, do you think you can make it over to those trees?"

Stedman hesitated, then nodded.

"This is going to hurt, but we need to move quickly." Ethan stood and took Stedman's good arm and pulled him to his feet and then caught him just as he gasped and almost lost his footing.

He wrapped Stedman's uninjured arm around his neck and helped him across the rocks and onto the bank, then lowered him gently to the ground at the edge of the forest, resting his back against a tree.

Stedman screamed without opening his mouth, his face covered in beads of sweat.

"Let me take a look at the wound," Ethan said. "I'll try not to hurt you. Just relax."

He laid down the gun and gingerly examined Stedman's arm.

"Looks like the bullet went all the way through your upper arm and came out the other side. The bleeding is already slowing down. I think you're going to be all right, but I need to get you to a hospital."

"Man, it hurts." Stedman winced, his breathing rapid.

Ethan unbuttoned his golf shirt. "This will do for a bandage. It's not sterile, but it's safer than leaving the wound exposed."

He took off the shirt and wrapped it gently but snugly around Stedman's bicep. "That should help stop the bleeding. I need to cut your T-shirt off you and make a sling."

Ethan took out his pocketknife and carefully cut Stedman's T-shirt, pulling it away from his wounded shoulder, and then slid the shirt off over his head. He ripped it into strips and tied them together to form a sling, then ever so carefully tightened the sling around Stedman's neck until the wounded arm was secured.

"There," Ethan said. "Nice and snug. Your arm won't hurt as much if you're not moving it."

"Thanks …" Stedman's voice was barely audible.

Ethan sized up the situation for a moment. Did he really want to leave Stedman behind with the shooter out there somewhere? Would he be able to find his way out of the woods—or be able to lead a rescue team back in? He had to try.

Lord, help me! I'm so turned around.

Ethan glanced at his watch. "Stedman, I have to make a decision. I don't think you're strong enough to walk out of here. I need to go for help. And I need to do it while it's light enough for me to find my way out of these woods."

"I'm going with you."

"It's too risky. You could die."

Stedman grabbed his wrist and locked gazes with him. "It's risky either way. If you get lost … we could *both* die."

❖ ❖ ❖

Brill sat next to Trent at the round table in Sam Parker's office. Sam sat across from her, his bushy white eyebrows arched, a toothpick stuck between his lips.

"That's quite an allegation," Sam said. "Even if it's true, there's not a shred of proof. If you go get Win Davison and bring him in, he'll lawyer up and be back on the lake in less than an hour."

"That's why I think we have to play this carefully." Brill folded her arms on the table. "You have a relationship with Win. I don't. I'll never get him down here to answer questions without a lawyer present. The only way that's going to happen is if we work together."

"Define *work together*, Chief Jessup."

"I need you to think of a way to get Win to come in and talk to us. And I'd like you to conduct the interview."

Sam looked over the top of his glasses. "Are you suggesting I should take the lead on this?"

"Actually I'm *asking* you to."

Sam sat back in his chair, his arms folded across his chest. "Well now, that's a surprise. You're willing to let me do things *my* way?"

Brill could almost feel Trent bristling. "This is not about turf. It's about justice. I believe Win Davison might be responsible for the murders of six people, beginning with Tal. Grant Wolski knew about Paulson McGiver's murder, and Nashville PD confirmed it. Cynthia Davison admits to having an affair with McGiver and knowing that he was Tal's biological father. Everything Stedman said is falling into place. I think we have to consider Win Davison our prime suspect. Let's hope Ethan and Stedman aren't two more of his victims. I don't care how powerful he is. He needs to be knocked off his throne and locked up."

Sam's eyes narrowed. "And you think I'm powerful enough to get it done?"

"You're cunning. And right now we need a fox, not a lion."

"I'll take that as a compliment." Sam tapped his fingers on the table and seemed to be thinking.

"You're very good at what you do, Sam. I need to know if you're with me on this."

Trent shifted his weight.

Sam plucked the toothpick from between his lips. "I suppose I could pretend to take the bait planted in Grant Wolski's vehicle and tell Win that we're currently interrogatin' the man we believe is responsible for the shootings and the hit and run. Technically, that'll be true, won't it?" Sam laughed. "I'm all for lettin' him think we took the bait and have Stedman Reeves in custody."

"Good. How soon can you pick him up?"

"Assumin' he's at his lake house, twenty minutes."

Brill stood. "I'll stay out of your way. I would like to observe the questioning, if that's all right with you."

"No problem." Sam put his palms on the table and rose to his feet, standing a foot taller than Brill. "Y'all know that if Win framed Reeves, he likely did an airtight job of it. Reeves is the perfect patsy. He's a gamblin' junkie who admittedly agreed to whack a guy to pay off a bad bet in an illegal game. His court-appointed attorney won't be any match for Win Davison's—assumin' it ever gets that far. We may never get this thing off the ground."

"Thanks for agreeing to try. And just so you know, this is personal. My daughter Vanessa is in love with Ethan Langley, who's one of the finest young men I've ever known."

Brill felt emotion tighten her throat. Had Sam noticed? All she needed was for him to patronize her now—when she felt the most vulnerable.

Sam seemed to study her, and the tautness left his face. He walked around the table and stood facing her.

"My baby, Lisa Beth, is nuts about a guy named Corley," he said softly. "It'd break her heart if something happened to him, and seein' her hurt would do me in."

"Then you understand how I'm feeling right now."

Sam squeezed her shoulder. "Let me go pick up Win Davison. In the meantime"—Sam turned to a forty-something man who reminded her of Kurt—"I'm going to have Deputy Pierce look at our new computerized map of Stanton County and locate the areas of white water where Ethan and our only witness could've found a strong cell signal. Let's put together a search-and-rescue mission and see if we can't find them alive."

❖ ❖ ❖

Brill strolled along the sidewalk around the Stanton County courthouse, Trent at her side. They had walked around once already without either saying anything. What was there left to say?

"I need a cigarette." Trent took a cigarette out of his pocket and lit it, turning his head as he took the first puff and exhaled a stream of white.

"I thought Sam was genuinely on board." Brill glanced over at Trent. "You know we need his help. Win Davison's not about to talk to us without an attorney present—not after the brouhaha he created because we questioned him when Tal was shot."

"At least now we know why he poured on the indignation when

we questioned him. I can still see the jerk pounding the table with his fist, demanding justice."

"We're going to do everything in our power to make sure that's *exactly* what he gets," Brill mused. "You know, I remember thinking at the time that he acted more like a demanding CEO than a grieving father. But it honestly never occurred to me that he had anything to do with Tal's death."

Trent took another puff of the cigarette before dropping it on the sidewalk and crushing it. He picked up the butt and threw it in the trash receptacle.

"Much better," she said.

"You're worse than my wife." Trent unwrapped a Tootsie Pop and stuck it in his mouth.

"You're no good to me dead."

"Right now, I don't seem to be much good to anybody."

Brill smiled. "Why don't you stop pouting and go find me some evidence so we can nail Win Davison to the wall? I want you and Beau Jack and Spence to work with Sam's deputies. Once we have the search warrants, this takedown is going to go fast."

CHAPTER 37

Brill stood at the two-way mirror outside the interrogation room at the Stanton County Sheriff's Department, watching Sam Parker and Deputy Pat Milstead begin their questioning of Win Davison.

"Thanks for comin' in," Sam said. "Deputy Milstead is just going to take a few notes so I don't forget anything. We're sorry to intrude on your holiday weekend. But seein' as how we may have your son's killer in custody and it may not take long to get him to confess, I thought you should be here for that."

"I appreciate that." Win took a sip of coffee. "What did you tell me his name was?"

"Stedman Reeves. He's a concrete finisher by day, a gambler by night."

"I was surprised to hear you've got him in custody. The media is reporting him still at large, and those hounds are usually right on your heels."

"We're trying to keep this under wraps," Sam said, "until we're sure Reeves is our man."

"Well, you must be pretty sure if you've arrested him."

"He's in custody, but we haven't charged him with anything yet."

"You said this Reeves got himself into some kind of trouble."

Sam nodded and folded his hands on the table. "Pitiful. He said he lost sixty thousand bucks in a high-stakes poker game to a fella named Grant Wolski. Reeves couldn't pay up. Said this Wolski told him he needed a job done. That if Reeves would eliminate your son, the debt would go away. He agreed to do it. But before he could get up the nerve, he claims two guys in a red truck pulled in front of him and shot Tal right there on the sidewalk and sped away."

"I'm sure he'd say just about anything to save his hide."

"Well, I'm sure he would," Sam said. "But Grant Wolski can't tell us his side of the story. He was killed today in a hit-and-run accident."

"Yes, our human resources director called and told me." Win traced the rim of his cup with his finger. "I'm sure you know Mr. Wolski was a supervisor at Davison Technologies."

Sam nodded. "Can you think of any reason he would want to kill your son?"

"Actually I can. A number of the workers in his division had to be cut in the layoffs. I guess he took it hard and wanted to get back at me. There's no other explanation for why he would want my son killed. Tal was such a great kid."

"Yes, I'm sure he was." Sam stroked his mustache. "I'm sorry for your loss, Win. I know you had high hopes for him."

"I did. Tal was going to come work for me after he graduated. It's something we'd talked about since he was twelve."

"And he was excited about it?"

"Ecstatic. He knew what a privilege it was."

"Wasn't it your grandfather who founded the company?"

"Yes, it was. Of course, technologies have changed throughout the years, and we've adapted and kept up. Tal would have been such an asset in that regard. Plus, he had a great business head on his shoulders."

Sam's eyebrows came together. "Hmm … where did I get the idea that Tal planned to go to the police academy?"

Win's expression went blank, but he didn't miss a beat. "I can't imagine. Tal knew it was his birthright to step into my shoes one day—the fourth generation to run the business. We were both pumped about it."

"So Tal wasn't plannin' to go into law enforcement?"

"Of course not. No offense, Sheriff, but his first year's bonus alone would be more than your annual salary."

Sam pursed his lips. "Well, it's a fact no one ever got rich in law enforcement. I just wish I could remember why I thought that. It's not like me to file something away and not remember where it came from."

"I *would* like to get back to my wife and our guests at the lake. Could we move on to the reason you wanted me here?"

Sam pushed his glasses higher on his nose. "Sure. I just need you to help me clear up a few things."

"Go on."

"Reeves claims there was a conspiracy to kill your son, and that he was set up to take the fall."

Davison rolled his eyes. "Nice try. But he admitted that he agreed to kill Tal. Anything he says now is just a last-ditch effort to keep from getting life in prison—or the death penalty."

"That's kinda what I thought. But his allegation about there bein' a conspiracy to kill Tal piqued my interest."

"What conspiracy? Wolski got Reeves to kill my son in exchange for canceling his gambling debt."

"That's what they agreed on, yes. But what if it didn't go down that way? What if there's more to it?"

"I can't believe Reeves is wasting your time with all this nonsense. Where's his attorney?"

"He doesn't want an attorney. Seems confident that we're going to find him innocent."

"Did he give you specifics on this *alleged* conspiracy?"

"He surely did. Got into great detail, as a matter of fact."

"Now *my* interest is piqued. What did he say?"

"I'm not really at liberty to talk about his statement."

Win leaned forward, his elbows on the table. "Then why did you bring it up? This is my son's death we're talking about! You can't keep me in the dark!"

"Well, I can tell you Reeves named people in high places. When it gets out it ought to shock the socks off the folks in Sophie Trace."

Where are you going with this, Sam? Brill thought. *If you push him too hard, he's going to lawyer up.*

"What do you mean by high places?"

"That's all I can say right now. Have some more coffee. Deputy Milstead, would you get us another cup? Cream and sugar for Mr. Davison. I drink mine black."

"Yes, sir. I'll be right back." Pat got up and left the interview room.

Win wiped his upper lip. "Look, Sheriff, I came down here in good faith. What is it you need from me? Spell it out so I can go home and enjoy what's left of my holiday weekend."

"I just need you to help me brainstorm this conspiracy notion. I'm not convinced Reeves killed your son."

"You actually believe his story about a red truck cutting in front of him and someone shooting Tal?"

"I certainly haven't ruled it out. Some things just don't add up."

Win folded his arms across his chest. "Like what?"

"Like who killed Tal's roommate, for starters. If Wolski wanted to get back at you, he succeeded when he had Reeves kill your son. It makes no sense that Reeves would kill Tal's roommate four days later."

"It would if Reeves was nervous that Drew Langley could ID him."

"The media reported that Langley was in his room, listening to music on his iPod, and wasn't aware of anything that happened outside."

"But he tried to revive Tal. Tal could've told him who the shooter was."

"Except Tal never regained consciousness. The media reported that, too."

"So Reeves didn't want to take any chances." Win sighed. "You're making this much too difficult."

"Well, the pieces don't fit."

"I don't see why"—Win's voice went up an octave—"when *everything* points to Reeves being the killer. A witness said the shooter had dark hair and a beard. Reeves admitted that he agreed to kill Tal and *why*—and *who* put him up to it. For cryin' out loud, his prints are on the gun! What more do you need?"

"How'd you know Reeves's prints are on the gun?" Sam folded

his arms across his chest and peered over the top of his glasses. "We haven't told the media yet."

That's it, Sam. Make him squirm! Brill leaned against the glass outside the interview room.

"I—well, I, uh …" Win's face turned crimson. "Naturally, I just assumed they were Reeves's prints found on the gun since he admitted he shot Tal."

"He admitted he *agreed* to it. He denies goin' through with it."

"Obviously he's lying."

"And you've never met Reeves?"

"Of course not."

Sam rubbed his chin. "Then how'd you know he had dark hair and a beard?"

Win seemed trapped in a long pause. Finally he said, "Since you brought him in, I'm assuming he fits the description."

"Or the description fits him."

"What do you mean?"

"Maybe the shooter disguised himself to look like Reeves so he could frame him."

"All these *maybes* are wearing me out, Sheriff." Win looked at his watch. "Could we wrap this up soon? I'd really like to get back to the lake."

"All right. We did find something that should blow all the maybes right out of the water."

"Well, why didn't you say so? What was it?"

"Something Reeves forwarded to himself this past Saturday night from Wolski's computer. He admitted breaking in. Said he was looking for evidence to prove his innocence."

The color and expression drained from Win's face.

Sam sat back in his chair and clasped his hands behind his head. "It was a copy of a memo Grant Wolski had written to himself after a meeting you had with him and a fella named Roy Dupontes in your office the night of May first. Do you recall that meeting?"

"I have a lot of meetings, Sam. I don't recall that particular one."

"Let me see if I can refresh your memory. You had just been contacted by a man named Paulson McGiver, who produced DNA evidence that Tal was *his* biological son and not yours. He tried to extort a million dollars from you to keep him from going public with it. Then three days later he's found facedown in a ditch with a bullet in his head. And lo and behold,"—Sam shook his head—"we discover that bullet came from the very same gun that killed Tal—"

"Stop!" Win held up his hand. "I want to call my lawyer."

Sam rose to his feet, bracing his palms against the table, and put his face in front of Win's. "Yeah, I thought you might."

CHAPTER 38

Ethan trudged through the forest, along the creek bed, holding Stedman's uninjured arm around his neck, trying to support his weight. He spotted a clearing flooded with sunlight about forty yards in front of them.

"You need to rest," Ethan said. "Let's see if we can make it to that fallen tree."

Ethan helped Stedman lower himself into a sitting position and then sat next to him, listening to himself pant. Could Stedman sense his doubt that they were headed in the right direction?

"How're you feeling?" Ethan said.

"A little woozy. But I'll be all right. We need to keep moving. I wish we could take that patch of sunlight with us the rest of the way. But the forest is going to get dense again before we get out of here."

"How can you be sure where we are? It all looks the same to me."

"Because that break in the canopy is the only one along this creek. Trust me, this is the way to Deer Path." Stedman winced and grabbed his shoulder. "We'll come out near the place where I hid my truck."

"I never thought to hide my car," Ethan said. "I guess it's my fault we were shot at."

"Not really. Davison's men probably put a tracking device on my truck. I'm not safe anywhere. At least I was able to tell Chief Jessup what I know. Let's hope she believed me and will act on it." Stedman motioned toward the clearing. "We'll have to skirt the sunlight. It'd be quicker to cut through it, but I don't like the idea of being that vulnerable, do you?"

"No. I'm all for playing it safe."

Ethan sat in the quiet and enjoyed the patch of blue sky above the clearing, knowing that the thick branches of the forest canopy would soon block out most of the light. He felt as if he had walked into a creepy fantasy novel, and Stedman's grandmother was the only one besides Davison's goons who knew where they were.

Brill had to have heard the gunshots before Stedman dropped the cell phone into the water. Had she told Vanessa? Was Vanessa doing what he had asked in his last text message? Was she praying and trusting—or was she too distraught?

Ethan glanced at his watch. "We've been on the move for twenty-five minutes. How long will it take us to get to your truck?"

"Another half hour, maybe longer. We're moving at a snail's pace. Sorry I'm too weak to walk without your help."

Bang!

Ethan pulled Stedman to the ground, his heart pounding wildly, and crouched behind the fallen tree.

He pressed his fingers to the stinging on his neck and felt blood.

Another bullet shot past him and ricocheted off a huge pine tree.

Stedman swore. "I was hoping we had ditched this guy. You're bleeding. Let me see."

Ethan turned his head so Stedman could examine his neck.

"It's hard to get a good look without more light, but I think the bullet just grazed you."

"Aren't you going to shoot back?" Ethan said.

"Not yet. I don't want to waste ammunition. I doubt he even knows I have a gun. Maybe I can take him by surprise."

"Do you even know how to shoot that thing?"

"Good enough to make him think I do. I just don't know how close he is. If he's got a rifle, he's probably shooting from a distance. No point in wasting bullets we might need."

Ethan's heart sank. "Are we just supposed to hunker down here like a couple of sitting ducks?"

"What choice do we have?" Stedman's eyes were wide, the gun shaking in his hand.

Ethan peeked over the top of the horizontal tree trunk and saw nothing but trees and darkness.

Lord, we don't want to kill anyone. But we don't want to die either. Please get us out of here.

Brill paced in front of the glass wall in Sam Parker's office, waiting for an update from search and rescue regarding Ethan and Stedman.

"How're you holdin' up?" Sam said.

"I'm encouraged now that we got the warrants for Win Davison's two homes and his office—and also Wolski's house and Dupontes's apartment. Let's hope we find enough evidence to put Davison and Dupontes away permanently. Of course, if it means Win moves Davison Technologies to Chattanooga, we're going to have nine hundred unemployed citizens and a ruined local economy. People may tar and feather us to show their gratitude."

Sam shook his head. "Win's father is still involved in the business as a consultant. Win's oldest daughter could take the helm in four or five years when she gets out of college. As proud as that family is and as long as they've had roots down here, I don't see them closin' it down or movin' it either. I think Win enjoyed threatening to do it because it made him feel powerful."

"I hope you're right."

"Can I get you somethin' to drink?" Sam said.

"No, thanks. I'm fine."

There was a long stretch of comfortable silence.

Finally Sam said, "Brill, we've had our differences. But I really appreciate what you did today."

"All I did was ask the right person to flush out Win Davison. We both know he wouldn't have come in and talked to *me* without his lawyer."

"Because he knew he couldn't manipulate you. You refuse to be intimidated." Sam's grin appeared under his mustache. "I ought to know. I've sure tried."

Brill flashed him a wry smile and folded her arms across her chest. "Ours hasn't been a match made in heaven. But I respect what you bring to the table, Sam. I always have. Today was a perfect example. I told you I needed a fox and not a lion. You were terrific."

"What—you don't think I can roar, too?" He let out a hearty laugh and for the first time she saw Sam the man.

"I'd like to think this could be a fresh start in our professional relationship," Sam said. "To tell you the truth, we make a great team.

I admit I had my doubts when you first came on the scene. I didn't think my deputies would take you seriously."

"Chief Hennessey's boots were too big for the little woman, eh?"

Sam arched his eyebrows. "Something like that. You have to understand, there's never been a female police chief in Stanton County until you came along. I guess it was just a matter of teachin' us old dogs new tricks."

"So am I officially one of the good ol' boys?"

"Who wants another good ol' boy?" He offered her his hand. "You're the chief of police—and a darned good one."

Vanessa sat on the glider on the screened-in porch, Carter asleep in her arms, feeling as if she were in a world of her own. She was vaguely aware of Rachel Howell sitting behind her at the patio table, thumbing through a magazine. And the clanking of dishes in the kitchen. She heard the door open and close.

"Would you mind if I joined you?" a voice whispered.

Vanessa looked up and saw Tessa's kind face.

"Not at all."

Tessa sat beside her, and Vanessa couldn't help but think that Ethan should be sitting there.

Tessa took her hand and squeezed it. "Ethan may be missing, but God has him in His sight. I've felt for a long time that the Lord had His hand on the two of you—well, actually, the three of you. Ethan is right where God wants him."

Vanessa moved the glider faster. "It's so hard to think that way when he might already be dead. I'm scared, Tessa." A tear spilled down her cheek. "I love him so much."

"I know you do. We all do. We need to keep praying that he's all right and will get to safety on his own, or that search and rescue will find him."

"It's a long shot that they'll ever spot him from a helicopter. There's white water everywhere, but there are so many trees."

"Brill said they're checking the areas where Ethan and Stedman could have gotten a strong cell signal. That narrows it down some."

Vanessa sighed. "Why does God have to test our faith? I mean why do I need another trial? Why does Ethan? Haven't we been through enough?"

Tessa strengthened her grip on Vanessa's hand. "It seems that way. But is faith really faith until it's tested? It's one thing to claim we have it. It's another to actually put it into practice."

"But why is all that necessary?"

"I suppose because we're not puppets, honey. We have free will. And choosing to have faith is the very crux of having a relationship with God. Unless we put our faith in Him, we make everything He promises us in His Word null and void. We know from Scripture that without faith, it's impossible to please God."

Vanessa put her cheek next to Carter's. "It's strange, but in his last text message to me, Ethan said he was stepping out in faith, and that I should pray for a good outcome. He said he needed me to trust him and God."

"It sounds to me like Ethan knew exactly what he was doing."

"I feel so helpless," Vanessa said.

"You are helpless, but He is able. We just have to sit tight and let God be in control."

※   ※   ※

Ethan sat on his heels behind the fallen tree trunk and listened for anything that would indicate they were being tracked. Since they had been following the creek bed from a short distance, the sound of the rushing water wasn't loud enough to drown out other noises.

"How long are we going to wait here?" Ethan said. "The forest is losing light by the minute."

"We should probably move on." Stedman, his face soaked with sweat, repositioned his wounded arm in the sling.

"You really need a doctor. You're too weak to be traipsing through the woods, dodging a hit man with a rifle."

"I'll be fine. Let's go."

"Wait!" Ethan turned his head and listened. "Do you hear that?"

"Yeah. The woods are vibrating—it's a chopper, man!"

"They must be looking for us! I'm going to run over there in the clearing and wave my arms." He turned to go and was yanked back by his back pocket.

"And get yourself shot," Stedman said. "It's too dangerous."

"Well, so is staying out here with a hit man in the shadows. I'd rather take my chances of getting rescued. If the guy starts shooting at me, pelt him with gunfire and try to hold him off long enough for me to get the attention of whoever is in that chopper. This might be our only chance."

Ethan broke free and took off running toward the clearing, the sound of the chopper now distinct.

Lord, let them see me! Let them see me!

He pushed himself with every ounce of strength he had, images of Vanessa and Carter flashing through his mind. He wanted to live his life. To enjoy being in love. To see what the future held. He didn't want to die in a dark, obscure forest and become a banquet for wild animals.

He reached the clearing and raced into the light, waving his arms just as the search-and-rescue helicopter flew across the hole in the canopy and disappeared beyond the treetops.

Ethan slowed to a stop, his hands on his knees, his side feeling as if he had been kicked by a mule. He labored to catch his breath, the hot sun beating down on his bare back, the helicopter's eerie reverberations taunting him. Had the search-and-rescue crew seen him? Or had he come into view a second too late?

Shots rang out. Ethan felt a searing pain in the fleshy part of his calf and almost fell to his knees.

A barrage of gunfire followed. Had Stedman answered the onslaught?

Ethan hobbled out of the clearing and into the dark forest and collapsed. Would Davison's hit man keep advancing until he had killed them both?

"Ethan!" Stedman's voice echoed across the clearing. "Stay where you are. I'll find you!"

Ethan tried to respond, but the pain took his breath away, and he couldn't find his voice. He sat on the ground, rocking back and forth, and held his palm directly on the wound, applying pressure.

Lord, we'll never get out of here without Your help.

Maybe they weren't supposed to make it out alive. Maybe this was to be his final resting place. God must have a plan for all this. Even if they were never found, maybe the fact that he and Stedman had gone missing would rouse enough outrage from Brill to demand Win Davison be investigated. The pain in his calf was so intense and consuming that he didn't have any fight left.

He closed his eyes and tried to imagine Vanessa in his arms, her perfume filling his senses, her long silky hair falling down to the middle of her back. Just when she seemed so real he could almost touch her, the ground seemed to vibrate. He didn't move. Didn't breathe. A deep rumbling sound reverberated in the distance. The chopper! Was it coming back? Had the search-and-rescue crew seen him? Or were they just making another pass?

Ethan tried to get up on his feet, but the stabbing pain in his calf dropped him back on the ground. Maybe he could crawl out into the clearing, but could he make it in time to be seen? Would he take another bullet?

What was the alternative—dying out here? He turned over on his belly and pulled himself toward the clearing with his arms, every movement making his calf feel as if it were being ripped off.

Lord, give me strength to keep going.

He spotted a fleck of yellow and realized it was his golf-shirt-turned-bandage moving slowly along the perimeter of the forest in his direction. Stedman must be trying to get to him.

The chopper sounded close now. Would Stedman be brave enough to step out into the sun and wave his arm?

Ethan kept pulling himself with his arms toward the clearing, but the terrain was slightly uphill, and his strength was dwindling.

Through a crack in the trees, he could see the chopper hovering overhead. And someone with binoculars peering down.

"Don't leave," Ethan tried to shout and realized he was barely audible. "We're here. We're here …"

The chopper slowly began to descend. His heart hammered with hope. He saw dried grass blowing in all directions and heard the engine go off.

A few seconds later he heard the door open and then an amplified male voice.

"Stedman Reeves, Ethan Langley, this is the Stanton County sheriff's search-and-rescue team. If you're there, show yourselves."

"Here!" Stedman's voice called out. "Over here!"

Stedman staggered out into the clearing and two search-and-rescue people ran over to him. Stedman pointed in Ethan's direction. It was over.

Thank You, Lord.

Ethan laid his head on the forest floor and inhaled the smell of damp earth. He heard footsteps pounding the ground, coming in his direction. He could hardly wait to see Vanessa.

CHAPTER 39

Ethan faded in and out of wakefulness, aware of voices and clanging noises and the soles of shoes squeaking on tile.

"Mr. Langley, you're in St. Luke's Hospital. You've had surgery to remove a bullet from your calf. The surgery was successful, and you're in recovery. I'm giving you morphine to help control the pain. Do you need something for nausea?"

Ethan shook his head, his eyes still closed.

"You'll be in recovery another hour, and then we'll take you to your room. Your family is waiting there for you. I'll keep checking to see if there's anything I can do to make you more comfortable. Just rest."

It was all coming back to him. The chopper flight. The oxygen mask. The IV. Relief from the excruciating pain.

Was Vanessa here waiting? Did she know Stedman was being framed? Had Brill begun to take action against Win Davison? Or were her hands tied from lack of evidence?

Ethan felt a sharp pain in his calf and remembered trying to escape the forest, Stedman badly injured and on the verge of collapse. Was the hit man still at large? Was the threat over, or would he still be looking over his shoulder and worrying about Vanessa and Carter?

How he loved them! He had known that on some level since Christmas break. But it wasn't until he thought he would never see them again that he realized how intertwined they already were.

A knock startled him.

"Mr. Langley's parents are asking how much longer he'll be in recovery," said a man with a deep voice. "I told them another hour, and that you would call us just before you headed upstairs with him. But they wanted me to check."

"Asking me a hundred times won't speed up the process, but it'll make them feel better. Remind them that the cafeteria is open. Be kind. They've been through a lot today."

Ethan wondered if his parents were waiting alone or if Uncle Richard and Aunt Becca had come too. How horrible for his family to have this crisis right on top of Drew's passing.

And what about Uncle Ralph? Was he walking the floor alone? With both of his right-hand men down, he must be beside himself. How had he reacted to Stedman's involvement in this mess? Ethan wondered if Stedman was at St. Luke's—and whether he'd required surgery too.

Vanessa must be frantic with worry. Had Brill told her about the threat? Would Brill have even let her come here to the hospital? Or would he have to wait until he was strong enough to go to the Jessups' house to see her again?

Ethan felt his limbs tingle as the morphine started to work.

Lord, thank You that I'm alive. Please keep Vanessa and Carter safe—and help us stop Win Davison.

Ethan felt as if he were floating on water … drifting … disappearing …

✦ ✦ ✦

Brill stood outside Roy Dupontes's apartment with Sam Parker, Trent Norris, and Deputy Milstead, waiting as the sheriff's SWAT team prepared to serve an arrest warrant on Dupontes, whom they now believed to be responsible for all five shooting deaths, for the hit and run, and for wounding Ethan and Stedman.

So much had happened that almost none of it seemed real yet. The news that Ethan was out of surgery and expected to make a full recovery trumped everything else. But there was much to ponder, not the least of which was the unexpected breakthrough in her professional relationship with Sam.

"We did a good thing today," Sam said.

Brill glanced out at the blazing pink western sky. "The people of Sophie Trace should sleep a lot better tonight. I know Vanessa will."

Trent folded his arms across his chest. "How could a guy as sharp as Win Davison be stupid enough not to erase his hard drive? Or destroy the DNA report?"

Sam's grin turned his eyes to slits. "A warrant is a beautiful thing. Powerful people never think they'll get caught."

"Imagine how different things would be," Brill said, "if Win had just taken a deep breath and worked through his disappointment about Tal not being his biological son. If he was so hung up about bloodline, he could've let the boy go into law enforcement instead of working for Davison Technologies. Admittedly, my perspective is a bit slanted in that regard. But the world did not have to end for Win Davison because he didn't have a *male heir to the throne*. He has six daughters who might want to pick up the ball someday."

Trent pursed his lips. "I think Win's motivation to kill Tal went way beyond the bloodline issue, Chief. If the truth got out, it would create a scandal, and everyone would know his first wife cheated on him and conned him into giving her love child an inheritance. He didn't want to face the humiliation. And he wasn't about to let Tal's biological father extort money from him either. Win's answer to every problem is either solve it or eliminate it."

Pat glanced over at the apartment. "It's hard enough trying to figure out people who you expect to be unscrupulous. But what gets into an otherwise decent guy like Stedman Reeves that he would agree to kill a man to keep from losing his place at the poker table?"

Sin, Brill thought. *Why are we so surprised?*

Sam turned his head and spit. "In my thirty-five years in law enforcement, I've seen time and time again what happens to people when they're obsessed with wanting more of something—or someone. Never comes to any good."

Sam put his walkie-talkie to his ear. "Sheriff Parker here, I've got my ears on, over.... All right, let's put the lid on the pot. Go!" He lowered his walkie-talkie and looked over at the others. "SWAT team's on the move."

Brill gently bumped Trent's shoulder with hers. How odd it was for both of them to be on the periphery instead of calling the shots. Yet wasn't it strangely freeing to share Sam's turf without the wall of defensiveness and possessiveness between them?

Lord, protect the SWAT team, she prayed. *Help us get this guy.*

The four of them stood like statues for what seemed an eternity and just listened.

Finally, Sam put the walkie-talkie to his ear. "Sheriff Parker here, over.... Is that so ...? When I said let's put the lid on the pot, I didn't expect you to take me literally." Sam threw his head back and roared. "In the closet, you say? ... Recently ...? Great. Good work, Smitty. Put it all into evidence, and don't make any mistakes. I'll see you at the jail. Out."

Sam put his walkie-talkie on his belt, still chuckling. "Seems ol' Roy Dupontes didn't hear the SWAT team enter his apartment. He was sittin' on the john with the radio blarin', probably listening to the news to find out how much damage he inflicted on Reeves and Langley. Of course he denies even knowin' Win Davison. But there's a good-sized arsenal in his closet, including a recently fired rifle. Ballistics will tell us whether it fired the bullet removed from Ethan Langley's calf.

"And now that we've retrieved the memo off Wolski's hard drive, Dupontes looks good for all the shootings. Davison's hard drive should cough up everything else we need." Sam smiled and winked at Brill. "All in all, I'd say we had a banner day."

❊　❊　❊

Ethan lay with his eyes closed, the cool clean sheets soothing to his skin, and listened to the bustling activity in the hospital corridor.

His parents and Uncle Richard and Aunt Becca had finally left. Could they have looked any more exhausted and still been beaming when the doctor reassured them that he was going to be fine?

He heard a knock on the door and then the sound of it swinging open, footsteps softly approaching. Fingers brushed the curls off his forehead, and warm lips touched his cheek. A familiar flowery fragrance made him open his eyes.

Vanessa stood over him, lovely as an angel, her eyes glistening with unshed tears.

"Hi," she whispered.

"Hi, yourself."

"I was so worried we'd never find you."

"God knew where I was." Ethan squeezed her hand. "I love you, Vanessa. I've been waiting all day to say it."

"I love you even more than I did last night." She brushed a tear off her cheek. "I don't know why, but that seems so long ago."

"Maybe because this was one of the longest days of our lives." He brought her hand to his lips. "I had no idea how much I would miss you if you were absent from my life. But I realized today that you could never really be absent. You're already a living, breathing part of me—so is Carter."

"Sounds serious."

"It's *very* serious."

Ethan held her hand to his cheek, looking into her crystal blue eyes.

"Are you two done so I can come in?"

Emily stood in the doorway, looking adorable in white crop pants and a pink blouse.

"Sure, come in," Ethan said, "but I assure you your sister and I will never be done."

Emily grinned. "You know what I mean."

"So who's watching Carter?" Ethan said.

"Tessa and Antonio. They're watching him at our house so Dad could drive Vanessa and me over here. Dad's parking the car." Emily bent down and studied the bandage on his neck. "Why do you have *that?* I thought you got shot in the leg."

"That's where the first bullet grazed me. That wasn't so bad. The one in my calf was another story. It was almost enough to make a grown guy cry."

Emily cocked her head. "The guys in my family already cry—mostly when they're happy. I'm sorry you got shot. It must've been scary having a hit man chasing you."

He moved his gaze to Vanessa and then back to Emily. "I guarantee you, once is enough."

"They're all behind bars," Vanessa said, "except for the man who died in the hit and run. I called your uncle Ralph before I came over here to see if he'd heard anything on Stedman. He said Stedman was released on a personal recognizance bond of a thousand dollars, so he won't have to pay anything as long as he doesn't jump bail. He'll be here in the hospital overnight and then stay with his grandmother—at least until he finds out what the judge decides."

"Do you know what he's being charged with?"

Vanessa tucked her hair behind her ear. "Criminal attempt at murder—or something like that. I got the impression that, because he brought this out in the open, he'll get probation."

"I'm not sure Uncle Ralph will hire him back unless he goes through a program and kicks his gambling habit. If the judge doesn't require it, I'm sure Uncle Ralph will."

"Doesn't Stedman have a mom and dad?" Emily asked.

"Yes, but they haven't spoken in a long time."

"Like your uncle Ralph and your uncle Richard?"

Vanessa nudged Emily with her elbow. "It's none of your business. Where did you hear that? Have you been eavesdropping again?"

Emily's face turned as pink as her blouse. "I'm trying to do better. I just can't help myself."

"Can't or won't?" Vanessa's eyebrows came together. "That's private business."

"It didn't sound private, since everyone in Ethan's family already knew about it." Emily batted her eyes. "And we're practically like Ethan's family now."

"Nice try," Vanessa said. "But you're not going to charm your way out of this. You owe Ethan an apology."

"I'm sorry." She looked into his eyes and seemed to be searching for something. "You're going to be a psychologist. How am I supposed to stop eavesdropping?"

"You *really* want an answer? Because you have to really want to do it."

Emily nodded.

"Just decide *ahead of time* that whenever you're tempted to do it, you're going to walk away. You have to be bigger than the problem, so that it never has the chance to get bigger than you. God will help you, if you ask Him."

"That makes sense. But it might be harder than it sounds, since I've been doing this my *whole* life."

Ethan forced himself not to smile. "I never said it was easy. But it's a lot easier than the consequences if you know things you shouldn't and speak out of turn and hurt someone's feelings—or their reputation."

"Are you listening to this?" Vanessa tugged her ponytail. "You're only eleven. There's hope for you yet."

Emily pressed her lips tightly together, but they finally gave way to a big grin. "Just think: Someday Ethan's going to get paid for that kind of advice. Cool!"

"Not unless I get out of here and back on my feet," Ethan said, "so I can earn my tuition money."

There was a knock, and he saw Kurt standing in the doorway.

"Hey there," Ethan said. "Come in. Join the party."

Kurt came over and shook his hand, holding it a little longer than he normally would. "Great to see you, man. You gave us quite a scare."

"I'm sorry I couldn't say anything. The creep that threatened to hurt Vanessa and Carter wasn't messing around."

Kurt nodded. "You did the right thing by calling Brill. Turns out he's the same guy who shot you and Stedman. Ballistics matched his rifle to the bullet removed from your calf. He confessed to all the shootings when he thought Davison was going to cut a deal. I came to tell you it's over."

Ethan squeezed Vanessa's hand. "What a relief. Thank You, Lord."

"Did the doctor say how long it would take for the leg to heal?" Kurt asked.

"It's just a flesh wound, so I'll be out of commission for a couple weeks, but I should be able to ease back into things after that. I'm definitely not down for the summer."

CHAPTER 40

The next day, precisely at noon, Tessa breezed into Nick's Grill, Antonio close behind, and hurried over to the counter, where Gus and Maggie Williams were already seated and watching the news.

Before she could say anything, Nick Phillips came through the double doors of the kitchen and put his arm around her, offering Antonio a hearty handshake.

"Welcome, friends. What a difference a day makes, eh?"

Tessa put her hand on her heart. "I'll say. I'm not even hungry. I just wanted to be with friends."

"WSTN just announced that the mayor, Chief Jessup, and Sheriff Parker are going to address the community at two. They're carrying it live."

"*Hello,*" Gus said. "We're over here, in case anyone cares."

Antonio chuckled, then slid onto the stool next to Gus and slapped him on the back. "How's it going, friend?"

"Really can't complain. But I always do."

"So what do you know?"

"I think I'd rather hear what *you* know. How's Chief Jessup's family holdin' up?"

"Doing better than you might think, considering what they've been through."

"Antonio and I took them some apricot muffins this morning," Tessa said. "Now that Ethan's safe, they all seem fine."

Gus tilted his glass and crunched a mouthful of ice. "I'll tell you what: I can't help but respect a young man who refused to be bullied into sellin' out an innocent guy, especially when it meant takin' a huge risk. Some people might argue it was foolish, but it tells me what he's made of. He's gonna fit right in at the Jessups'."

Tessa looked down the counter. "Well, for heaven's sake, Gus. Was that comment meant to reflect favorably on *Brill?*"

"I suspect it was." Gus winked.

"I'm still aghast that Win Davison is the one who had Tal killed," Maggie said, "and that five others died because of his twisted plot to cover it up. Let's hope this scandal doesn't kill the town's economy, too. If Davison Technologies closes its doors, I don't see how we could survive the domino effect of having another nine hundred people out of work."

Gus took her hand in his. "Darlin', after everything that family's done to build the business for three generations, they're not gonna board it up and call it quits."

"Then who's going to run it with Win in prison?"

"Maybe Win's dad will step up again for a while. Or maybe they'll hire a CEO that doesn't have ice in his veins and find out people are more productive when they respect their boss. And don't forget he's got a bunch of daughters in the wings. The Davisons are not gonna let this be the last thing people remember about them."

Nick nodded. "Gus is right. There may be a ray of hope in all this. I can't imagine that Win will be missed. And I have a feeling most people who work there would welcome new leadership as long as their jobs were secure."

"I hope you're right," Maggie said.

There was a momentary lull in the conversation.

"I'd like to change the subject for a minute, if I may." Antonio nudged Gus with his elbow. "So when can you take us to Best Buy to get a computer?"

Gus stroked his mustache. "I'm free after lunch."

"Great. So are we."

"Oh dear," Tessa said. "I wasn't expecting this to happen so soon. I need time to adjust. What if I can't learn it? I'm not very good with electronics."

"You can learn to email," Maggie said. "It's simple."

"Sabrina and Phil will flip if they get an email from us." Antonio put his arm around Tessa. "Just imagine: We could communicate with them at any hour on any day—all the way to London. Jessie, too. I say we go for it." Antonio glanced over at Gus. "But you're going to be our techie, right?"

Gus swatted the air. "Sure. Don't y'all worry about a thing."

"Hi, everybody." Clint straddled the stool next to Tessa. "So what'd I miss?"

"Well, it looks like Antonio and I are getting a new address." Tessa enjoyed baiting him for a moment.

"Aw, you're not leaving Sophie Trace, are you?"

"No, we're getting an *email* address. How about that?"

Clint smiled. "You're finally coming out of the dark ages. Good for you."

Jo Beth came through the swinging doors, filled the coffee mugs,

and took orders. Gus and the others pored over Antonio's drawing
of a kitchen computer nook and made suggestions about printers,
scanners, and copiers.

Tessa sipped her coffee and observed, keeping one eye on the
TV and the amazing turn of events unfolding in the shooting case
and the other on Gus, who seemed to have come alive since Antonio
challenged him not to be disingenuous. Had she ever seen such an
about-face in a person before? Could she have ever imagined Gus
taking the lead and teaching Antonio and her anything—much less
how to link up with their daughter at the push of a button?

Her cell phone rang. She rummaged through her purse and
found it.

"Hello."

"Tessa, it's Emily. Are you at home?"

"No, Antonio and I are at Nick's having lunch and making plans
to get a computer. Can you believe it?"

"Wow, that's awesome. Now you can write Jessie, and she can
send pictures so you won't miss seeing her grow up."

"I'm excited about that. I've missed them so. What can I do for
you, sweetie?"

"Would you show me how to make those yummy lemon bars? I
want to take some to Ethan at the hospital."

"Sure I will. Antonio and Gus are going to be busy for a bit after
lunch. Could you come over at one thirty?"

"Okay, thanks. Oh, I almost forgot … could I borrow the
ingredients?"

Tessa chuckled to herself. "Of course you can. See you soon."

"Love you. Bye."

Tessa started to respond, but the connection was dead before she could return the sentiment. She put the phone back in her purse and pasted Emily's "love you" in the scrapbook of blessings. Life had certainly changed since the Jessups moved in next door and she had become a surrogate grandmother. There wasn't a doubt in her mind that God had brought this family to Antonio and her because they each had something the other needed—and that her prayers for each of them mattered.

She was suddenly aware of coffee being poured into her cup.

"You look lost," Jo Beth said.

Tessa lifted her gaze. "Oh, I'm not lost, honey. I'm just deep in thought. Never in my life have I been more comfortable with where I am."

Brill sat at her desk and looked out beyond the shade trees that graced the grounds around city hall to the bank of storm clouds that had rolled in over the Smokies and hidden the mountains from view. A flash of lightning zigzagged across the sky, followed by a booming clap of thunder that reverberated and shook the windows.

She sensed someone in the doorway and turned in time to see Trent knock on her open door.

"Got a minute?" he said.

"Sure. Come in."

Trent walked over and stood in front of her desk. "There's something I want to give you." He reached in his pocket and took out a pack of cigarettes. "I won't be needing these anymore. I quit. This time I mean it." He handed the cigarettes to her.

"I'm proud of you, Trent. Why the change of heart?"

"I don't know exactly when it clicked. But hearing about Stedman Reeves's gambling habit and what it did to him turned my stomach. I don't want *anything* to control me like that. I don't want to be one of those people I've seen who still lights up when he's carrying an oxygen tank and his chronic cough turns him inside out. Or while he's on chemo for lung cancer. Or right after he gets out of the hospital after a heart attack. That's not how I want to end up."

"Good for you."

Trent put his hands in his trouser pockets and seemed to stare at nothing. "I've made all kinds of excuses, but the bottom line is I knew the risks going in. I *let* the habit take hold. And the only way I'm going to kick the habit is to take back control. So ... let me go on record to say: I'm taking control of my life again. Or I guess I should say, I'm letting God have control of my life again. And I'm asking you to hold me accountable."

"All right, I will."

"Even if I have to find a support group, I'm serious this time. I'm done."

"I believe you."

Trent was quiet for a few seconds and then flashed her that Denzel Washington grin. "Enough said. I've got work to do." He started to go and then stopped. "Well, there is one more thing. I'm pleased that you and the sheriff have called a truce. To tell you the truth, I'd never seen the side of him we saw yesterday. My respect level went way up."

"Mine, too, Trent. I think things are going to be different from now on."

A loud boom shook the building and the clouds finally broke loose, rain blowing against her window and falling in sheets.

"I'm going to Nick's and get some takeout," Trent said. "Want me to pick up something for you?"

"I'd appreciate that. I'll have a veggie burger with everything and a bottle of water."

"Sweet potato fries?" His voice was coaxing. "Nobody does sweet potato fries like Nick's."

Brill smiled. "Now you're tempting *my* addiction. All right. But a *small* order."

"Done. I'll be back within the hour. I think I'll stop and get another bag of Tootsie Pops. I must be nuts to go out in this."

Trent turned and left.

Brill got up and stood at the window, watching the rain pour from the heavens, blowing in sheets across Main Street and forming swift-moving tributaries that rose higher than the curbs.

How appropriate it seemed that her beloved Sophie Trace should be cleansed after the insidious evil that had taken up residence and trapped both the weak and willing in its scheme. Win Davison was no longer a threat, and the blood he paid to have spilled here had been washed away. But the stain would take time.

Stedman stood at the window in his hospital room, his arm in a sling, and looked out at the gray clouds that had hidden the Great

Smoky Mountains and dumped a couple of inches of rain. The dreary weather seemed appropriate.

He heard a knock on the door and turned just as Ethan hobbled into his room on a walker.

"I came to say good-bye," Ethan said. "I heard you'd been discharged and were waiting for your parents."

Stedman nodded. "I can't believe they called. They want me to come home. They're going to court with me too. My attorney thinks the judge will let me off with probation if I get into a program. I really want to kick this gambling habit."

"That's great, man. This could be a new beginning on a number of levels."

Stedman studied Ethan's face. Even now he seemed to have a peace that made no sense. "I still can't believe you risked your neck to help me."

"I'd do it again. You didn't deserve to be hung out to dry."

Stedman sighed. "Come on. What I almost did was despicable."

"People do terrible things when they have to feed a habit. I have a feeling that, apart from that, you're a pretty decent guy."

Stedman blinked the moisture from his eyes. "Saying thank you doesn't seem like enough. But I'm grateful. I think now I'll get my life straightened out."

"I'll be praying that you do." Ethan held out his hand, and Stedman shook it.

There was a long pause.

Finally Ethan said, "When you get into the program and need to call on a higher power … I'd love to introduce you to the real deal.

I promise you Jesus Christ can turn your life around like you never imagined. He'll set you free."

Stedman looked into Ethan's eyes. "From the gambling, maybe. I doubt there's a cure for the shame."

"Of course there is. That's what salvation is all about. The truth is, we all need the cure. We're all sinners."

"I don't know about that," Stedman said. "But I know *I* am."

"Why don't you come to church with me sometime?"

"I'd like that. I stopped going when Father David got on my case about my gambling. Too bad I didn't listen. I guess I should give you my parents' phone number." Stedman went over to the rolling table, wrote the number on a napkin, and gave it to Ethan.

"Great. I'll be in touch." Ethan patted his good shoulder. "Whether you know it or not, Stedman, you just came through a spiritual battle on the winning side. God wants your heart."

"Can't imagine why."

"Hang around with me long enough, and you will."

Stedman smiled. "Actually, I wouldn't mind if you rubbed off on me."

❊   ❊   ❊

Ethan ventured out into the hospital corridor, using a walker to steady himself.

"How's it feel?" his uncle Ralph asked.

"It's stiff and sore"—Ethan tried not to wince—"but the pain doesn't come close to what I experienced when the bullet was in there. I'm getting better at this. This is the third time I've walked today."

Everyone at the nurse's station clapped when Ethan hobbled past, and he felt the heat scald his face.

Ralph laughed. "Looks like you've got quite a fan club."

"Everyone's trying to make me out to be a hero or something. I'm not. I just wanted to do the right thing. I mean, if right is right, it's right all the time, not just when it's convenient. I couldn't let the police think Stedman killed all those people. He'd have gotten life in prison—or the death penalty."

Ralph was suddenly steely quiet.

Ethan glanced over at him, surprised to see his eyes glistening and his nose red. "What's wrong?"

"Nothing's wrong. I just know where you heard the *right is right* thing. You don't remember, do you?"

Ethan shook his head.

"You came to stay with Gwen and me for a couple weeks in the summer. I think you were about ten. I took you with me on a big job, and you got a kick out of riding in the cement truck and watching us pour the foundation for a strip shopping mall. When it was all done, I discovered my guys had taken some shortcuts that were totally unacceptable. I sweat blood over it. Doing the job over would cost me a whole summer's profit."

"Oh, yeah. Now I remember," Ethan said. "I thought you were mad at me, and you sat me down and told me why you were upset and that you were going to do the job over."

Ralph nodded. "I remember telling you that if right is right, it's right all the time and not just when it's convenient. I can't believe it stuck with you."

"Well, you must have made an impression." Ethan arrived back at his room and went inside and sat on the side of the bed. "Whew! That wore me out."

"You'll get your strength back quickly," Ralph said. "But you're not coming back to work for a month."

Ethan's heart sank. "I have to. Or I won't be able to pay my expenses—"

"Hey"—Ralph held out his palm—"I said you weren't coming back. I've put you on paid sick leave."

"*Paid* sick leave? Since when does the summer help get benefits?"

"Since now." Ralph laughed. "I'm the boss. I can do whatever I want. And I want you back on July one—strong and ready to go."

"What about Stedman?"

"If the judge lets him off with probation—which I think he will—he's going right into a program. If he gets himself straightened out, he can come back to work for me in the fall."

"He's got to feel good about that—*and* the fact that his parents came and got him. He needs their love and support, especially now when he's so down on himself."

Ethan's phone rang and he reached over and grabbed it. "Hello."

"It's Uncle Richard. How're you feeling today?"

"A little beat up. But I've been out in the hall walking three times."

"That's great. Listen, Becca's got a doctor's appointment across the street from the hospital, so I came over to see a friend of mine who had surgery this morning. As long as I'm just down the hall, you want some company? If you're not up to it, I'll totally understand. I should've called first."

"I'm up to it. Come on down."

Ethan hung up the phone. What now? Was he out of his mind?

"Somebody here to see you?"

"Yes, Uncle Richard."

Ralph's eyes grew wide. "I need to get back to the site anyway. Gwen and I will come by later. We're going to have dinner at Nick's, and then she's got choir practice."

"You don't have to rush off."

Ralph's eyebrows formed a bushy line. "You know, after you got on my case about my attitude, I've been thinking a lot about the situation between Richard and me."

"Really?"

"Yeah, thanks to you, I can't say the Lord's Prayer without feeling guilty, and I—"

There was a knock on the door.

Uncle Richard breezed into the room and froze midway to the bed. "You didn't tell me you … had company."

"You didn't ask."

"I shouldn't have invited myself," Richard said. "I'll come back another time."

Richard, face crimson, made an about-face and headed for the door.

"Wait!" Ralph said. "Please don't go."

Richard stopped and slowly turned around. Before Ethan realized what was happening, his twin uncles were locked in a bear hug, both of them overcome with emotion.

"I'm so sorry about Drew." Ralph began to sob. "I wanted to be there, Rich. I just didn't know how to get past *this*—how to say I've been a real jerk. I should've accepted your apology. I'm sorry. I'm so sorry."

"It's okay. It's okay." Richard patted Ralph's back. "You're here now … that's what matters … maybe it's time we started living in the *present.*"

Ethan blinked the stinging from his eyes and hobbled over to the window, his back a curtain of privacy, his heart a fountain of pure joy.

Thank You, Lord. If only Drew could see this.

He looked out at the dark, ominous storm clouds that shrouded the afternoon sky and watched with curiosity as a perfectly round blue hole, almost like a portal, opened in the midst of them.

He started to laugh and cry at the same time.

Knowing You, Lord, it wouldn't surprise me if You arranged it so Drew could see exactly what's going on.

CHAPTER 41

On the weekend before Ethan was to drive back to the University of Memphis, his aunts had planned a huge party in honor of his uncle Ralph and uncle Richard's fiftieth birthday. Over a hundred guests had been invited, including Vanessa's family.

Ethan helped his aunt Gwen and uncle Ralph get the backyard ready for the big event, then went and picked up Vanessa and drove her to the party.

"Your dad must've found the last parking place," Ethan said. "I've never had to park around the block in my life."

"There!" Vanessa said. "That SUV is pulling out. See his taillights?"

Ethan put on his blinker and waited until the SUV pulled out, then slipped in the parking space and turned off the motor.

He got out and went around to Vanessa's door and pulled her to her feet.

"Are you going to be able to walk that far in heels?"

"Heavens, yes. I could walk a mile. These are extremely comfortable."

"You're absolutely stunning in that blue sundress. It matches your eyes." He linked her arm in his. "You ready?"

"I *am*. I can hardly wait to see your uncles together. This has to be so exciting for your family."

He strolled with Vanessa along the sidewalk, trees shading them from the relentless August sun. Between the old character houses with big front porches, he caught glimpses of the green foothills draped in afternoon haze. He felt a twinge of sadness that, by this time next weekend, he and Vanessa would be at opposite ends of the state until Thanksgiving break. Three whole months! A quarter of a year! How would he stay focused on his studies with his heart longing to be with her?

As he got closer to Uncle Ralph and Aunt Gwen's, music and laughter were the predominant sounds. Childhood memories came flooding back to him.

"I wonder how many times Drew and I sat on those old pickle barrels at my grandparents' house and listened to my Grandpa Langley's band play music just like that."

"What kind of music is it?" Vanessa said.

"Cajun. Hear the accordion? The mandolin? The banjo?"

Vanessa shot him a curious smile. "Langley is *Cajun?*"

"No, it's English. My dad's ancestors came over from Britain and settled in the bayou country of Louisiana. My grandfather's great-grandfather had a sugar plantation. It's still a working plantation, but the house is empty. It's called Langley Manor. Talk about a beautiful place."

"So you've been there?"

Ethan nodded. "A few times when I was little. What I remember most is Drew and me getting in trouble for playing hide-and-seek in the cane fields. I guess our parents were afraid we'd get lost in there. Actually, my dad and uncles were all born in Lafayette, Louisiana. The family lived in the area until Grandpa Langley moved to Tennessee and went to work for the railroad. My great-grandparents lived in the manor house back then. It's been empty since they died."

Ethan took Vanessa's hand and went up the front steps, through the house, and out to the back deck. A Cajun band was set up on the deck, playing live music.

In the center of the yard, a white canvas pavilion had been erected and furnished with wood tables and chairs. Brightly colored tablecloths added to the festive look. Over to one side, two men wearing white uniforms and chef's hats stood behind a long buffet table, carving what appeared to be turkey, ham, and beef and serving the guests after they had filled their plates with other selections.

"Let's go see the cake," he said. "Aunt Gwen made it herself."

Ethan led her over to a three-tiered birthday cake, iced in chocolate and pieces of shaved chocolate. White candles covered the top layer, yet to be lit. The cake sat on a giant white ceramic platter, and around the edge of the platter, the words *Laissez les bons temps rouler, Ralph and Richard* were written in chocolate.

"What is that written on the plate?" Vanessa asked.

"It's Cajun French for 'let the good times roll.'"

"Hey, you two."

Uncle Ralph came up to them, looking sharp in a pair of navy trousers and a white Polo shirt. "Did you just get here?"

"We did," Ethan said. "What a great party. I knew you were having a live band, but you didn't tell me it was Cajun."

"Don't you remember when your granddad used to play with the Bayou Boys?"

"Yes, I was telling Vanessa about it just a few minutes ago."

"Those were *good* times. Rich and I wanted today to be a

celebration of the good times past—and yet to come. You two just kick back and relax. Have something to eat. Enjoy yourselves. Vanessa, your family's at that table in the corner. It was nice finally meeting your brother."

"Let's go say hello," Ethan said.

Brill waved to get his attention, and Emily was already headed in their direction.

"Did you get lost?" Emily said. "We beat you by a half hour."

"We had to park clear around the block," Vanessa said, "and we stayed a few minutes and talked with Tessa and Antonio, just to be sure Carter wasn't going to be fussy."

"Well, you'd better have some gumbo." Emily rubbed her tummy. "It's dee-lish."

Ethan went to the table where the Jessups were eating. He pulled out a chair and seated Vanessa, then sat next to her.

"What a great birthday party," Kurt said. "It must feel so good having your uncles at peace again."

"You have no idea. I think the last time I saw them together like this was when I was about six."

Ethan thought he heard someone calling his name and turned, pleased to see his dad making his way toward them.

Ethan stood and embraced his father. "Dad, have you met Vanessa's brother?"

Tom Langley flashed a warm smile. "Yes, Ryan was telling me he just got back from Costa Rica and is starting law school in a couple weeks. I'm so glad you're all here. This is a huge day for the Langleys."

Ethan nodded toward the buffet line. "And it looks like you're serving more than just the fatted calf."

"Help yourselves. This is a momentous occasion." Tom's eyes suddenly glistened. "I don't remember the last time I saw my brothers have fun together."

"We're so pleased to have been invited," Brill said. "We rejoice with you."

Ethan listened to the music, watching the people and eating his fill of delicious food, all the while feeling that same twinge of sadness that reminded him that he and Vanessa would soon be apart.

"I'll be back in a few minutes." He kissed Vanessa on the cheek.

He excused himself from the table and went around to the front yard. He walked slowly down the sidewalk, letting the knot in his throat relax. How was he going to come to grips with the fact that he would be leaving soon?

He sensed someone come up behind him.

"Mind if I walk with you?" his father said.

"Not at all."

"Your mother went down to the Pates' house to watch their little boy so they can come say hello. None of Ralph's neighbors have ever met Richard, and it's kind of a big deal."

Ethan smiled. "Yeah, it is. It's so exciting to see my uncles together. They're like two overgrown kids. It's fun watching them rediscover one another."

"You seem a little blue. Is anything wrong?"

"No, everything's incredibly right."

"Which makes you dread all the more saying good-bye to Vanessa and Carter and heading back to school?"

Ethan nodded. "I guess I'd better get over that real quick, huh?"

"I don't know that it's something you need to get *over*, Ethan.

But you do have to get through it. One more year, and you'll have your BA. That has to feel good."

"It does." Ethan sighed. "But add two years of grad school on to that. It'll seem like forever if it means being away from Vanessa."

"You really love her, don't you?"

"I do. More than I thought possible. I just hope …" Ethan paused. Did he really want to get into this conversation with his dad?

"That she'll wait for you?"

Ethan felt the blood rush to his face. "How'd you know?"

"Oh, Vanessa's a real beauty. I'm sure you're not the only young man who's noticed. But she's crazy about *you.*"

"I know, Dad. But is three years too long to expect her to wait for me? I can't even give her an engagement ring as long as I'm paying tuition."

"Have you asked her to marry you?"

"Not down on one knee." Ethan smiled. "But we both know that's where we're headed. We've talked about it."

A long moment of silence passed, then his dad said, "When your mom and I fell in love, I was in the army, stationed at Fort Bragg. It was torture being apart, and I didn't have money for a ring."

"Did that bother you?"

"Sure it did. I wanted to give her a symbol of my love and my intentions for the future—*and* I wanted the other guys to see she was taken. That's when my grandmother Langley gave me this." He stopped walking, reached in his pocket, and laid a gold ring set with red stones in Ethan's open palm.

"That's Mom's," Ethan said.

"Yes, but it was my grandmother's engagement ring. She wanted me to give it to your mother—until we could afford to buy her a ring."

"That's cool."

"Thing is, your mom loved it and never wanted another engagement ring. She wore it until I bought her that diamond band for our twenty-fifth anniversary. She wanted it to stay in the family." His dad lifted his hand higher. "Take it. It's yours. Don't feel like you have to give it to Vanessa if you don't think it'll appeal to her. She might not be that kind of sentimental. But you might have a daughter someday who would be."

"Are you kidding? Vanessa would love this." Ethan took the ring and brought it closer to his eyes. "I love the way the stones are cut. When I was little, I used to sit in Mom's lap and twist this round and round on her finger and look at each one. I never knew it belonged to your grandmother. This is so generous of you."

"It'd tickle your mother and me to death if you gave it to Vanessa. But it's not going to hurt our feelings if it just isn't your thing."

"Believe me, Dad—it *is* my thing. It's perfect. I just hadn't thought of popping the question so soon—and with so much school ahead."

Tom draped his arm over Ethan's shoulder. "Son, true love will wait for the right time to get married. But if you love her and know she's the one, it's never too soon to tell her so."

❋   ❋   ❋

On Sunday evening, Ethan and Vanessa sat together in the glider on the Jessups' screened-in porch, listening to the crickets.

"You're quiet tonight," Vanessa said.

"I'm just glad for some time alone with you. I can't believe how fast the weekend flew by."

"Or that next weekend you won't be here." Vanessa squeezed his hand. "Sorry. I don't mean to sound so forlorn. I'll be starting a new semester of online classes and will have plenty to do. But it's hard to think of you not being here. I'm so spoiled with us being together."

"I know what you mean. But we're still together for a few more days, so let's enjoy every minute. This has been an *amazing* weekend. My uncles' birthday party was a blast. And I'm glad you got to meet some of my out-of-town relatives."

"I just love your parents," she said. "They're easy to be with. Well, actually your whole family is. The Cajun element was a real surprise, though. And I had no idea your grandfather's great-grandfather settled in Louisiana."

"I never thought to say anything. My family has lived in Tennessee a very long time. But our Cajun ties are strong, as you could tell when my dad and my uncles started playing the accordion, the banjo, and the mandolin. I'd forgotten how much fun it was having music in the house."

Vanessa smiled. "They were the life of their own party. It's astounding what a dramatic difference communication has made in those two—which just proves once again that communication is key in any open, honest relationship."

"I couldn't agree more," he said. *Okay, Lord. Here goes.*

Ethan got up and knelt on the porch on one knee, taking her hand.

"What are you doing?"

"Getting ready to openly and honestly communicate the most important thing on my heart." Ethan held her hand to his cheek. "Vanessa, it's no secret that I love you. Or that you and Carter are the most important people in my life. You're in my thoughts, on my heart, and in my prayers every hour of every day. I can't imagine living my life without you. Our paths were meant to intersect—and I believe you and I were meant to become one."

Ethan reached in his pocket, took out the ruby ring, and held it between his thumb and forefinger.

"This was my great-grandmother Langley's engagement ring. My dad gave it to my mother when they got engaged, and she wore it until their twenty-fifth wedding anniversary. Someday, I want to buy you a diamond ring that we pick out together. But for now, while my money is going to pay for tuition and to keep the old Camry running, would you wear this and let it signify that one day, when the time is right, you'll be my wife?"

A tear trickled down Vanessa's cheek, and she seemed dumbfounded. "Yes! I can hardly wait for that day," she finally said. "The ring is beautiful. And it's so special that both your great-grandmother and your mother wore it."

Ethan slipped the ring on her finger, elated that it wasn't too small, and pressed his lips to her hand. "I love you, Vanessa. I can't imagine my future without you and Carter. We were meant to be together. We'll know when the time is right."

"If we have to wait a hundred years, I'll marry you. I can't believe I'm blubbering all over you. This is just so unexpected."

"Not to your parents. I went to them and asked for your hand, and they gave us their blessing."

Vanessa laughed and cried at the same time. "When did all this happen?"

"After church this morning—when you and Emily went to the nursery to get Carter."

Ethan stood and pulled her into his arms. He held her face in his hands and tenderly pressed his lips to hers, then wiped the tears off her face with his thumbs.

"It's so strange," he said. "When I was little, I used to sit in my mother's lap, twisting the ring around her finger, totally enthralled with the red stones. Who would have ever thought one day I would be giving this ring to the woman I want to spend the rest of my life with?"

CHAPTER 42

On the following Friday morning, just before the first rays of sun peeked over the foothills, Ethan stood at the curb in front of the Jessups' house, his car packed, his gas tank full, and his emotions fragile. His good-byes said, all he had to do now was force himself to drive away—but not until he had a few minutes alone with Vanessa to tell her his surprise.

"Are you going to let your hair get longer again?" Emily said.

"Probably. Mostly because I stay so busy studying that I don't take the time to get a haircut." He tugged the hem of her pajama top. "Don't forget to text me and tell me how you like middle school."

"Okay."

Ryan Jessup caught a yawn, then made a fist and tapped Ethan's bicep. "See you at Thanksgiving."

I doubt I can stay away that long, Ethan thought.

Brill put her arms around Ethan and kissed his cheek. "I'm going to talk to your mother about the Langleys and the Jessups all having Thanksgiving together. The time will pass quickly, and you'll be back here before you know it."

Kurt patted Ethan on the back and shook his hand. "Drive carefully. I know you have a lot on your mind."

"Thanks, I will."

Vanessa's eyes glistened, and her lips trembled. She put Carter in Ethan's arms, and he lifted the baby into the air, then gave him a longer-than-usual hug and handed him to Emily.

Finally Ethan and Vanessa were the only two left standing at the car.

Ethan pulled her into his arms and inhaled the sweet fragrance that he would intentionally recall every time he felt lonely.

"I'll call you from the road," he said. "I'll never be more than a phone call away. And we can text each other a thousand times a day if we want."

Vanessa nodded and sniffled.

"You do know that, once I'm out of here, you're going to be fine? The good-bye is the hard part."

"I know. I'm such a drama queen."

Ethan gently rubbed her back. "Before I leave, I want to share something my dad and uncles told me last night. It was all I could do not to call you right then, but I didn't want to wake you. I could hardly sleep, thinking about it."

Vanessa pushed back and looked into his eyes. "What is it?"

"The three of them got their heads together: They want to give us the deed to Langley Manor for a wedding gift. Can you believe it?"

Vanessa stared at him like he'd told a joke that she didn't get. Finally she said, "That's generous of them. But what would we do with an old manor house?"

"That's what I said, though I have to admit it's exciting to think of owning a piece of my family's history. There's a second part to the gift. If we decide we want to restore the place, Uncle Richard and Aunt Becca will give us Drew's trust fund to use toward the renovation. It won't be enough, but it would make a respectable dent in the costs. And once we're both out of college and working, we could get a loan for the rest. It's something we could do little by little. It would take us years to finish, but it might be fun to resurrect something of my family's past."

"It sounds wonderful," Vanessa said, "but then what? It can't just sit there and fall into disrepair again. It's not like we could afford to live in it."

"Maybe it could be one of those historic old places that people pay to see."

"Ethan, I'm not sure charging admission would bring in enough to pay for the upkeep. Sounds like the kind of place that should be made into a bed-and-breakfast. At least then it would generate enough income to pay for itself."

"Now that's a *great* idea." He felt his cheeks stretch into a grin and then go limp again. "Not that either of us knows the first thing about how to do that. Once we got it renovated, we'd have to furnish it to fit the era, and we'd have to pay a decorator for that. And pay a caretaker to live there and manage the B and B. And we'd need a live-in maid. And groundskeeper. And someone to maintain the integrity of the historic structure. Maybe it's too much work. It's probably a bad idea. That's why my dad and uncles haven't wanted to fool with it." Ethan sighed. "Oh, well. It was fun to think about being entrusted with a plantation house that's been in my family for six generations."

Vanessa tilted his chin. "Since when do you talk yourself out of something you want so easily? People do things like this all the time—just not long-distance. We'd almost have to live nearby to oversee the renovation."

Ethan locked gazes with her. "We really haven't talked about where we want to live after we're married. Can you picture us living in bayou country?"

"I wouldn't rule it out." Vanessa seemed almost giddy. "Tell me again where this place is."

"In the south central part of the state, not far from Lafayette. The manor house and a few acres of property still belong to the Langley family, but the cane fields were sold off decades ago. Maybe we could all drive over there on Christmas break and take a look."

"I definitely think we should. What about *you?*" Vanessa asked, her blue eyes twinkling. "Would you ever consider living in Louisiana?"

"I wouldn't rule it out either. Any place would be home as long as you're with me. Once I'm out of grad school, I could take my counseling degree just about anywhere. Same with your teaching degree."

Vanessa's smile could've melted an iceberg. "Well, I do like adventure. And I *love* Cajun food."

"And I love *you.*" Ethan kissed her forehead and took a step back. "I should get going before I get any more caught up in this conversation. This is so exciting to think about. If I don't get out of here fast, I'm liable to change my mind about leaving."

"And I'm liable to let you. Go!"

Ethan ran around to the driver's side and looked over the top of the car. "I'll call you as soon as I get on the interstate. Don't look so stunned. You're not on candid camera." He laughed. "And as long as we're dreaming, why not think about us getting married next summer, *before* I start grad school? I can't imagine three years of doing this. Think you could handle living in student housing, knowing we're going to own a manor house someday?"

Vanessa put her hand over her heart, and the look on her face was all the answer he needed: She'd follow him to the moon, if it meant they would be together.

He took a mental snapshot of her expression and attached it to the wall of memories he hoped would sustain him in the months ahead. "I really have to go, honey. I love you with all my heart and soul. Tell Carter Daddy loves him and will see him on the webcam."

Vanessa nodded and waved him on, her eyes brimming with tears.

Ethan got in the old Camry, hoping it would get him as far as Nashville before it needed water again. He started the engine and looked over at Vanessa one last time, blowing her a kiss, then pulled away from the curb and into the future—bursting with confidence that, whether they were living in student housing or in the shadow of Langley Manor, he and Vanessa would have the rest of their lives to thrive in the shelter of each other's company.

... a little more ...

When a delightful concert comes to an end,

the orchestra might offer an encore.

When a fine meal comes to an end,

it's always nice to savor a bit of dessert.

When a great story comes to an end,

we think you may want to linger.

And so, we offer ...

AfterWords—just a little something more after you

have finished a David C. Cook novel.

We invite you to stay awhile in the story.

Thanks for reading!

Turn the page for ...

- **A Note from the Author**
- **Discussion Guide**

A NOTE FROM THE AUTHOR

I KNOW THAT NOTHING GOOD LIVES IN ME,
THAT IS, IN MY SINFUL NATURE. FOR I HAVE
THE DESIRE TO DO WHAT IS GOOD, BUT I
CANNOT CARRY IT OUT.
(ROM. 7:18)

Dear friends,

All human beings are born with a propensity to sin, and until we lay claim to the power of Jesus' sacrifice on the cross, we will never begin to experience the emancipation of our fleshly nature.

As long as we're confined to these mortal bodies, the Enemy will fight to control us—body, mind, and spirit. And though many of us will never experience the devastating effects of a drug, alcohol, sex, or gambling addiction, how often do we fall victim to the more acceptable vices, such as overeating, overspending, overworking, overindulging? Denial tends to be the first form of defense, and we ignore the problem until it gets a foothold. Then, rather than letting God's Holy Spirit have the reins, we struggle to tame it in our own strength and realize we can't—that we've become slaves rather than masters, overdoers rather than overcomers.

I admit I have a ways to go before I relinquish control of every area of my life and let the Master rule. But that's the desire of my heart. Those of us who are called by His name do not have to be enslaved by the flesh but can live by the Spirit. It takes faith, discipline, and a burning desire to let go and let God. As odd as it seems, it's only by letting Him take control that we're set free—and able to find true joy and peace.

I love a happy ending! It was fun leaving Ethan and Vanessa filled with excitement and promise, especially after putting them through so many trials in Sophie Trace. But this isn't the ending of their story. Join me for the Langley Manor Trilogy, set in the bayou country of Louisiana, where we'll catch up with the Langleys and find out just what they decided to do with that deed to the manor house. But don't let the chiming of wedding bells fool you—mystery and suspense abound!

I would love to hear from you. You're welcome to join me on Facebook at www.facebook.com/kathy.herman, or feel free to drop by my Web site at www.kathyherman.com and leave your comments on my guest book. I read and respond to every email and greatly value your input.

In Him,

Kathy Herman

Kathy

DISCUSSION GUIDE

1. In your own words, explain what you think 2 Peter 2:19b means: "A man is a slave to whatever has mastered him." Stedman's gambling and Trent's smoking were strongholds that were easy to spot, but would you have thought of Richard's and Ralph's stubborn pride as something that they had become slaves to? Have you ever been involved in or been the victim of an ongoing feud that greatly affected your life? Was it satisfactorily resolved or is it still in progress? Were there deep wounds to be dealt with? Did you feel led to intervene? If so, was that a difficult position to be in?

2. As Christians, we are called to be peacemakers. What is the difference between a peacekeeper and a peacemaker? Which role do you think is easier? Which of the two best describes Ethan's role in his uncles' feud? Had you been in Ethan's place, what would you have done differently?

3. Do you think addictions are sins or sicknesses—or is it possible to make a distinction between the two? If a person is trapped in the cycle of addiction, should that person be absolved from taking responsibility for his or her actions? Did Stedman know right from wrong? Was he capable of choosing better? Why do you think he didn't? If a person came to you with an addiction problem, what advice would you give him or her?

4. Do you think Stedman became addicted to gambling merely because he had a weakness for gambling, or were

there other factors that might have contributed to his gambling obsession? How do you think a person becomes addicted to something? Do you think there might be fewer addiction problems if more people turned to God and allowed Him to fill their emptiness instead of depending on something else? If emptiness is the culprit that leads us down the path to addiction, how can we fill up with the right things? What are the right things?

5. Are you now or have you ever been guilty of any other excesses, such as overeating, overworking, overspending—overindulgence of any kind? Do you find that the longer you allow the bad habit to go unchecked, the harder it is to get back on track? Do you think this is true merely because it's hard to break a bad habit—or is there something about trying to stop by sheer willpower that intensifies the battle? In your experience, how effective has it been for *you* to try to control the excesses in your life in your own strength?

6. Can you name some activities in our modern world that have become addictive for many people (for example, surfing the web, shopping online, texting)? Do you think that many loving and charitable actions are pushed aside because of such "web" addictions? If everyone cut one hour a week from these self-absorbing activities and did something nice for someone else, do you think it would dramatically affect our world?

7. Why do you think humans tend to do things in excess? It is said that self-control is a virtue, but true self-control is

part of the fruit of the Holy Spirit. How capable do you think we are of controlling our carnal nature? Does that ability seem affected by how much we want something? For example, some of us can stay away from potato chips but can't stop eating chocolate until it's all gone. Others can say no to chocolate but can't stop eating potato chips until the entire bag has been devoured. When we say we "can't stop," what do you think we're really saying? Why is it so hard to say no to our appetites? What do you have a weakness for? At what point should a weakness be considered sinful? Is there anything we truly "can't stop" doing?

8. Are children slaves to the flesh or is the behavior learned? Is it ever too early to teach our children to practice self-control? Why do you think self-control is something we must *practice?* Did you like Ethan's advice to Emily on how to quit eavesdropping (chapter 39), or would you have given her different advice? Would Ethan's advice apply to any number of bad habits?

9. Do you think living in a culture of instant gratification has made us almost oblivious to what we are or aren't dependent on? Is it possible that we think we're totally dependent on God, when the truth is we're not being denied anything, so our dependence isn't being tested? Is there any food, object, or activity that if it were taken from you would leave you feeling empty? Be honest.

10. How inclined do you think we would be to engage in excess if we took seriously 1 Corinthians 6:20, which says, "You were bought at a price. Therefore honor God with your

body"? Are there areas of your life that don't measure up to
this admonition?

11. If you could meet one of the characters, who would it be?
What would you say to him or her? Was there an idea,
thought, or principle you took away from this story?